ARE YOU READY... OR WILL YOU FALL?

T H E   L I E

I0586107

KYM STREAT

Clover Life Publishing

© 2017, 2022 Kym Streat

Cataloguing in Publication Data:
First published in 2017 as ISBN: 978-0-6480508-7-2 (pbk.)

Title: The Lie
ISBN: 978-0-6453179-2-3 (pbk.)
Second Edition
Subjects: Fiction

To Andrew, my biggest fan, husband and friend. Thank you for continually encouraging me.

To my Lord Jesus… whom I owe everything!

To all those who are seeking for God's truth…

Dear Reader,

This has taken years, so long in fact that I nearly gave up. If it weren't for God and my husband's promptings, then this would have stayed dormant on my hard drive forever. However, the niggling and nagging to finish this kept gnawing at my heart; maybe because it's truth or maybe it's simply hoping that someone will gain inspiration to pick up the Bible and research the subject for themselves.

Ultimately… you'll be the judge, but whatever you decide, decide to be strong in God for the times ahead.

Kym

CHAPTER ONE

Year 1831

Tommy awoke from his deep sleep. Startled by the bell ringing, his faced grimaced as he squinted at his watch. It was 1:15 am.

What does Father Harvey want at this hour? he wondered.

He quickly got to his feet, put on his trousers and boots and rushed next door to Father Harvey's room, and softly knocked on his door.

Father Harvey opened the door abruptly and said, "Tommy my boy, I'm sorry to wake you at this hour, but I need you to prepare the horses."

"Is everything all right, Father?"

"No, I must get back to Evensmore tonight!"

"But Father, that's over five hours in travel. We've just arrived today and the horses are already spent... and what about your brother's funeral tomorrow?"

"Tommy, please just do as I say!" Father Harvey said flustered, as he turned and closed the door behind him.

CHARGER STOOD a menacing 19 hands high, and Dom was just a tad under. Their massive heads hung over their stall doors while they rested, the breath from their nostrils condensed and furled upward in the autumn chill.

Charger, the bigger and eldest of the two horses, was the first to notice the lantern coming toward the stables. He let out a soft whinny at seeing his friend entering.

Tommy rushed towards their stalls, grabbing their lead ropes

1

on the way. He took Charger's head with both hands and looked him square in the eyes.

"Now, Charger, I need all you've got. Father needs us tonight." He moved over to Dom, who was now wide awake and vying for Tommy's attention. "Dom, you do everything Charger does, okay boy, no folly tonight, my friend. We have important business to attend to."

FATHER HARVEY WAS BUSILY WRITING down the dream he'd been given. Carefully noting every detail, it was so clear in his head, but his shaking hand was making it near impossible for his words to be legible. His emotions overtook him.

"Oh Lord, forgive me... I must stop Father Daniel before he delivers this message." he cried out.

EMILY TUCKER WAS FAST ASLEEP.

"Emmmiilyyy... Emmmiiilyyy my darling... wake up my child." The soothing, melting voice slowly drew sixteen-year-old Emily out of her deep, dreamy sleep.

She looked, and hovering above her was Crystalyn, her spirit friend, with his glow radiating the room and his rather sickly sweet smile warming her face.

He was so handsome, she thought, his golden locks falling gently across his boyish features. She admired his little pixie like face and his tiny transparent wings that seemed to drum a 100 beats a second. She loved Crystalyn. He had become her best friend, someone who she could confide in and trust with her life.

"Crystalyn my friend," she called and happily grinned as she stretched, "what are you doing at this hour—why did you have to wake me? Is something wrong?"

"Emily, dear Emily, I must get you to deliver a message to the Chief, sweet girl," his liquid honey voice crooned, making her heart melt.

"At this hour?" She smiled and giggled. "I can't Crystalyn. It'll have to wait until the morning!" she said wearily. "I'm tired and it's too cold to go out. Besides, what's the urgency?"

"Emily, it is very, very important. You must get up and go now," he insisted, trying to sound soft and gentle but with a coldness coming through.

Emily yawned and stretched again as she rolled over, burying her face back into her pillow and mumbled, "No Crystalyn, I can't, it's quarter after two… I'll do it later this morning."

"Emily, please," he crooned, and stroked her cheek.

"No, I'm too tired. I'll do it in the morning."

"Emily!" Crystalyn raised his voice sternly. "You'll Go Now. Now I say!"

Crystalyn watched as Emily crept quietly out the door, so not to wake her siblings, and headed off down the foggy lane way.

"You're getting less tactful you know Crystalyn. She'll start to see through your charm."

Crystalyn whipped around to face the voice in the darkness. "What would you know, Crechus?" he spat and hissed. The glow emanating around his handsome pixie like figure quickly vanishing, revealing a black hideous being with mottled sinewy skin, red eyes, and dark vascular bat wings. "She's just an expendable pawn in the grand plan—there's plenty more where she came from," he sneered.

"Maybe… but you'd better hope you're right, else Master will have you fried," Crechus said as he burst out laughing. His bulging eyes closed as his sharp taloned hands covered his grotesque facial features in amusement, his black wings and body shook with his rumbling chuckles.

"Shut up, you idiot," Crystalyn snapped.

EMILY TRUDGED THROUGH THE STREETS, holding her coat tight around her to keep the biting cold out.

What is it with Crystalyn lately? she mused. *He used to be fun but now, he's getting too serious and pushy. I must tell him I do not like his attitude lately.*

. . .

JOHN BARNES, Chief of Evensmore Police, heard a soft knock at his door downstairs.

His wife awoke. "What is it?" she whispered.

"Go back to sleep. It's nothing," said John.

He lit the lantern and quickly descended the stairs and opened the door to find Emily shaking with cold. "What are you doing here?" he snapped angrily.

"Crystalyn told me to come and give you a message."

He leaned out the door. "Did anyone see you?" his eyes scanned the surrounds.

"No, well I don't think so, surely not at this hour, anyway."

CHARGER AND DOM were at full speed, their massive hooves were pounding and shaking the stony ground beneath them. The carriage was loudly rattling and shaking as it careered through the forest road.

Father Harvey was busily trying to piece together everything he'd seen and heard in his dream. He was fervently praying that Father Daniel would receive his message with an open heart and he could stop what they had both started.

Angelic Captains Chale and Jophiel were gripping the sides of the carriage towards the front. Lieutenants Seth and Gabe were toward the back, their large majestic angelic wings flat on their backs so not to create any wind drag for the horses, their glory dulled to keep them unnoticed by the enemy. Their focus was ahead, watching intently for any signs that the enemy had gotten word of their mission. It was imperative that their Lord's message got to its destination without fail.

DAVID CARTER'S house was in silence. In the still of the night, everyone was peacefully sleeping in his household. He stirred as he heard a faint tapping at his bedroom window. He looked out toward the noise, and his heart sank. He quietly got up, went down the hallway, and opened his front door.

"I've come to call in that favor," John Barnes demanded.

David let out a deep sigh and hung his head low.

"Remember... you've taken the oath," John smirked.

David closed the door, went to the cloakroom, put on his overcoat, and stepped out into the frigid night air.

Tommy was focused, Charger and Dom were sound horses, and he had faith that they would get them back home safely, but still he diligently watched the road like a hawk.

The moon was bright, lighting the way clearly, but the shadows were eerie tonight. Tommy thought. He wished he was back in his bunk asleep and this was all just a bad dream.

The horses' hooves made the loud rumbling, pounding sound and the carriage rattled and creaked, waxing and waning at every corner and bump along the road. The thin wooden wheels were biting into the gravel, grappling the road for grip.

"Are you all right, Father?" Tommy yelled back, worried that the old carriage wouldn't hold up to the careering speed.

"Yes Tommy, keep going." Father Harvey hung his head out the window and urged Tommy onward.

Tommy hung tightly onto the leather reins; they were straining and stretching under the force of the horses against them. His hands started blistering and bleeding from steering the massive team at such a speed.

Then suddenly, there was a deafening crack echoing throughout the moist night air... and then... there was nothing.

A dark ominous being stood waiting in the bushes. "We've got them." he shouted. "They won't get through with this message. Are you ready to fight?" he asked the other demons gathered with him.

5

"Always," they shouted in unison before they pushed forward in their rage for battle.

SILENCE HIT TOMMY LIKE A THICK, heavy blanket. It filled the night as blackness crept over him. The moonlight glistened on the sweat of the horses' coats. The smell of dirt, sweat, and death lingered in the air.

Hours slipped by.

DAVID CARTER REMOVED his heavy damp overcoat and mud-caked boots. He quietly slipped back into his bed.

IT'S SO QUIET! Tommy thought, *what's going on?*

Tommy awoke with the gritty taste of gravel mixed with blood and saliva in his mouth.

"What's happened?" he whispered, confused and dazed. "How long have I been here? Aaaaaaaagggghh." His cry ripped and echoed through the silent night. He looked down at the gash in his right side and the obscure lump jutting out. *A broken rib*, he thought. "Aaaaahhhhh... Noooo." He buckled under the excruciating pain emanating from his right leg. He looked down and gazed upon its crookedness. He felt blood slowly seeping down his forehead.

Where am I? What am I doing on the road? He thought franticly, his mind reeling, trying to piece together the recent events, but only returning blank.

He slowly maneuvered his body into a position where he could look around. The road ahead to Evensmore was clear.

"Where is everyone?" he whispered.

He slowly turned, carefully to not cause himself more pain, and checked the road behind him. His face recoiled in agony, with images that burned into his conscience forever.

He gently rolled onto his left side and slowly dragged himself back towards the horses—sobs rose into his throat like knots, like lumps fighting to get out all at once.

He reached Dom first. Tommy's body convulsed and the heavy sobs poured out as he looked upon Dom's twisted neck and crumpled frame lying entangled in the leather harness. Tommy reached out his hand to touch his friend—his body was motionless and cold from the night, his coat still sticky from the sweat mixed with heavy dew, his eyes were pale, dull, and lifeless.

He looked up ahead and saw Charger lying behind and off to one side of Dom's body. He slid towards him and then laid his hand upon the big horse's neck. "Oh Charger," he cried. Hot tears started to flow down his face, stinging the grazes and graveled gouges etched into his raw cheeks.

He lifted his hand and saw Charger's thick sticky blood caked to it, glistening black under the moonlight. *Maybe one of the horses stumbled. Or... or there was a hole we didn't see... why can't I remember?* he wondered as he continued to sob and try to work out what had happened, but unable to recall anything.

Confused, he reached out to run his hand down Charger's forehead and felt the syrupy congealing liquid slowly leaching out. "What happened?" Tommy whispered, as he quickly slid himself around to get a better look at Charger's face.

He looked closely and wiped away the blood from Charger's forehead to reveal a large, jagged, cavernous hole with bone fragments clinging to the clotted blood.

He recognized it instantly. "A gunshot wound!" He reeled back, frantically looking around for a stranger in the night. "Who would do such a thing? Oh no, Father," he whispered in bewilderment and horror. "Father," he shouted frantically, "Father Harvey, can you hear me? Are you all right?"

Tommy desperately dragged himself to the carriage that lay broken on its side, wincing at every move—he looked inside, and it was empty. Distressed, he called out again, "Father Harvey."

Nothing!

He slid himself toward the back of the carriage and saw a still figure lying twisted and bloodied on the road. There was no life here.

Tommy started to weep. The pain was too much—confusion and silence overcame him. The night closed in and the darkness swept him away.

CHALE, Jophiel, Seth, and Gabe stood before Darius, the Major General of the Lord's angelic regiment.

Darius looked upon their battered and bruised bodies, torn wings and defeated, despondent faces. "What happened, Chale?" Darius asked sympathetically.

"We were ambushed, sir. Attacked from behind, they were everywhere. They knew! Five attacked me when I looked up and saw the lone figure standing in the middle of the roadway. But it was too late, the big horse went down."

"What of the Saint?"

"I'm sorry, sir!" Chale looked down with tears in his eyes.

"And the boy?"

"He survives," Chale replied.

"Then it has begun."

CHAPTER TWO

Present Day

"**D**addy, can I get a pony?"

Jack Daley looked down into his 10-year-old daughter's clear, innocent blue eyes and his heart melted. He looked back at Jenny his wife; she smiled and gave him that knowing look of—*you knew this was coming, eventually*.

"Well, if Sarah gets a pony, I'm getting a motorcycle, dad," his 12-year-old son Matthew stated.

"Well, let's talk about this later. Right now, we're here to listen to God's word." He smiled down at both of them as they climbed the stairs to the old church building.

"Good morning Jack, great to see you here today." Pastor Peter McKinley grabbed Jack's hand, shaking it fervently. "Jenny, Matthew, oh, and little Sarah... welcome!"

"How are you, Pastor McKinley?" Jack replied.

"Very well, very well indeed. It's such a beautiful day, isn't it? And please Jack, thank you for the respect, but just call me Peter."

"Yes, certainly Peter," Jack said as they shuffled through the door to find their seats.

It was a small church of about one hundred people. This was a vast difference from the city church of 7000 members from where Jack and his family had previously attended. With church interest groups, over forties, fifties and sixties, you name it they had it.

Yep, he thought, *this is the place to be, one service that finished whenever God said it could*. It was nothing for the worship to continue for hours, sometimes until 2 pm. *The Spirit of God really moves here*, Jack thought to himself. *I didn't realize how much I needed this place*.

9

He looked over at Jenny sitting beside him. *How beautiful she was*, he thought. "Thank you, God, for my gorgeous wife," he whispered.

She heard him, smiled, and squeezed his arm. The service was about to start.

On the roof sat Chale and Jophiel, along with a hundred of the Lord's angels scattered around the old church grounds. Chale looked at Jophiel and smiled, his features chiseled, his blonde hair gently shifted in the breeze. They had been friends for eons and had proudly fought many battles together.

Jophiel was the opposite of Chale in many ways, dark hair, olive completion, but both were strong and mighty in their stature. No demon could out maneuver these two Captains.

"I know Chale," Jophiel said, grinning at him, "this is your favorite day!" he laughed, but still kept vigilant.

Chale laid down, relaxing his back on the warmth of the iron roof, his mighty sword by his side; he closed his eyes and took in the music and singing that was emanating from the building beneath. "I love you my Lord Jesus," he whispered, listening as other angels joined in the praises. Like ribbons of colorful hues, the songs flowed upward into the heavens, praising their King.

"They don't realize how important their praises are for us," Jophiel commented. "Battles have been won and lost on the account of worshipping and praying saints."

"But today ALL is well," Chale replied as he smiled and stretched out his wings, basking in the morning sunrays.

Jophiel laughed at his friend as he stood to survey the surrounding grounds, "Yes, all is well today."

"Do I have to go to school today?" Matthew whined to his mother.

"Yes, you do!" shouted his sister Sarah at the top of her lungs from her bedroom.

Matthew rolled his eyes towards his sister's room.

Jenny smiled and gave him a hug. "Come on, otherwise you'll be late," she said.

The three of them walked down the driveway to the front gate and waited for the school bus to arrive.

"I'm glad we moved here, mummy," Sarah said.

"Me too," Jenny smiled.

"I really thought I wouldn't like it because I'd miss my friends, but now I have lots of new friends." Sarah grinned.

"What about you, Matthew? Do you like our new home?" Jenny asked.

"Yeah, it's okay, I guess, but I still miss home," he replied.

Matthew had found it harder to adapt to the new school, and making new friends seemed more difficult for him. Sarah, however, took to it like a duck to water. They all looked up to see the old yellow school bus rattling down the gravel road.

"You have fun today," Jenny said.

"Bye mum," Matthew and Sarah both chorused as they boarded the bus.

Jenny meandered back down the driveway towards the house —she was content here. However, having her parents so far away was hard. She missed them but knew that this was the best decision they had made for a long time. They had to get out of the city, Jack was stressed, and there wasn't any family time any more.

I'm so thankful that Jack gave it up, she thought and smiled briefly pondering over how Jack had always stood out; he was handsome, strong, and stylish. He'd had so much success in his career, but was willing to move for them and escape the rat race. Their life had become just too fast, b*ut not here in Evensmore,* she thought, *this place is like a time unto itself.*

JACK WAS SITTING in his office downstairs typing an email and attaching the software requirements document to send to head office. The software company Jack worked for had begged him not to leave. He was a highly skilled, first-rate engineer, and they didn't want to lose him. However, Jack knew he had to put his family first, not his career that had taken precedent for so long. Therefore, they compromised, as long as they could keep him, Jack could work from anywhere he chose.

There were still the occasional meetings that he physically needed to attend, but they would pay all his travel expenses and he actually seemed to get more done now. There were no office politics or people sticking their heads in for a chat. *I now have the perfect world*, he thought.

Jack thoroughly loved his work and was excited about the project he was working on. He was so proud that he had created the new technology and couldn't wait to get it into the world. He hit 'Send' on the email.

"You want a coffee?" Jenny called out.

"Sure do!" Jack replied as he slowly got up out of his chair, stretched, and walked up the stairs into the kitchen. "And a cookie?" he questioned hopefully.

Jenny smiled at him. "How are you going with the project?" Jenny asked, as she handed him the coffee and biscuit.

"Good so far, no hitches that I can see."

"Great, more time for us." She sidled up to him and gave him a hug. "I love you so much and I'm very proud of you."

"And why would that be?" he smiled down at her.

"Well, you know, this was a big change for you, leaving your fancy office, and moving out here to the country."

"Well, it's worked out okay. I'm pretty much my own boss now, and this place is great—I get to have coffee with my stunning wife whenever I want to. Who could ask for more!" He squeezed Jenny tightly.

"So, what are your thoughts on the pony?" Jenny asked.

"Well, she has wanted one for so long, and I guess there is no real reason why she can't have one now that we have a few acres."

Jenny beamed as she said so excitedly, "Oh, she will be so thrilled I can't wait to see her face when we tell her."

"Me too and Matthew when we tell him he can finally have that motorcycle."

. . .

Lora March ran upstairs in tears to her bedroom.

"Come here, young lady," the voice of Reverend Jim March bellowed. "I will not tolerate your attitude in my house."

"Leave me alone," the 14-year-old cried out, "You don't understand, you NEVER understand!"

"Lora, you will not go to that party. It is not the image that we Marchs' want to portray, do you hear me?"

Lora buried her face in her pillow and screamed, her hot tears soaking into the soft down, her face red and angry. "I hate him, I hate him, I hate him!" she exploded, concealing her cries into the soft feathers.

The demon named Rebellion stood over her, busily whispering, "He thinks he is so righteous, and who does he think he is? He can't rule your life. You're an adult now, you can do what you want and you don't have to do what he says anymore." Lora was taking in all that Rebellion was saying to her.

Reverend Jim March was furious. *How dare she disrespect my authority! Doesn't she understand their position in the community, the image that they need to uphold? I am a man of God; a member of the clergy and my family must remain in good standing with the community. I can't have my daughter showing disobedience—she must submit to my authority.* His thoughts ran wild.

Once again, Rebellion rubbed his hands with delight. He certainly was stirring up trouble in this household, and he loved it.

Two little hideous, scaly demonic imps named Pride and Control were also jumping up and down with glee, shouting thoughts into Jim's mind, coaxing him into an angry stupor. "Yeah, yeah, keep going Pride, that's a good one," said Control grinning with excitement at the discord that they had just created this afternoon in the family.

"Well, you need to see ol' man Jackson!" Ned Tucker, the local grocer, exclaimed. "He deals in horses around here. I'm sure he'll have just the one for yer little girl."

"So where is exactly Mr. Jackson's place?" Jack asked as he handed over his card to pay for the groceries he just purchased.

"He's just up the road a bit from ya's, not far at all. He's got the big old sign over the gate that says, 'Jackson's Farm', can't miss it even if ya tried!"

"Okay great, thanks Mr. Tucker."

"Oh, just call me Ned, you city folk are just too formal," he chuckled and smiled.

"Okay, thanks Ned, I'll see you later," Jack replied as he walked out onto the front porch of the store smack into Bill Johnson.

"Hey Jack, are you coming to the men's group tonight?" Bill asked.

"Hi Bill, sorry, I didn't mean to bump into you. Yes, I'll be there, looking forward to it actually."

"Great to have you folks in town. I'll see you tonight!"

"Yep see you then," Jack said as he walked over to his car, sat down and took a moment and prayed, "Lord, thank you so much for this wonderful town, bless the people of Evensmore for their kindness and acceptance of my family."

Sixty feet away stood two scaly black demons, one much larger than the other, listening to Jack's prayers. "Here's another saint praying," the smaller exclaimed in a whiny voice, his fangs like fine needles showing as he sneered.

"Hmm... We'll have to fix that. We don't need any more of them here," said the larger demon.

Jack drove off, unbeknownst to him with his two guardian angels, Lieutenants Gabe and Seth had been assigned to him and were sitting on top of his vehicle. They made eye contact with the two demons as the vehicle sped away.

"They think they're soooooo good," the smaller demon wiggled his sinewy body in mockery.

"Not for long," the larger one replied sinisterly. "Soon they will be feeling the blades of our swords and face their defeat."

"Yeah, yeah, yeah, take that, you fools." The smaller one

jumped around, waving his sword in the air, acting out a mock battle.

Suddenly, the larger demon grabbed the smaller one by his spindly arm and jerked him around. His piercing red eyes boring into him, his large talons digging into his slimy, pungent flesh. Bearing his large canine fangs, he growled in contempt of the little imp in his grasp whilst he spat, "Don't take this lightly, you idiot— we must keep the saints' prayers to a minimum. Stop acting like an imbecile and get to work." And with a hard smack, the small demon landed 30 feet down the road.

J ack pulled up at the entry of Jackson's farm. He turned and entered the long dirt driveway up to the old farmhouse. It was a neat, white wooden house with the veranda all the way around the front and a quaint little flower garden running along the bottom. *Someone has a green thumb,* Jack thought.

Jack got out of his car, walked up the stairs and knocked on the door. He stood waiting as he heard some clattering of dishes, then footsteps coming towards the doorway.

The door opened and an elderly man dressed in dark blue overalls stood there smiling. "Good afternoon, what can I do for ya?" he welcomed smiling.

"Ah… Hello Mr. Jackson? My name is Jack Daley," Jack said as he held out his hand and shook the man's hand. "Ned Tucker, from the grocery store, said that you sell horses and I'm looking for a quiet pony for my daughter Sarah."

"Oh well, you've come to the right place. Come in, would ya like a coffee?"

"Yes, that would be great!"

Over the cup of coffee, Jack told Ben Jackson about his family, why they moved, how much they loved their new life and the people here at Evensmore, and Mr. Jackson happily listened, enjoying the company.

"So, how long have you been selling horses?" asked Jack.

"All my life, it's in my blood. My daddy, granddaddy, and great granddaddy bought, sold, and trained horses. Back then, it was mainly work horses for pull'en carts and ploughs, nowadays folks just buy them for pleasure or fancy riding." Mr. Jackson pointed to a photo on the wall. "That's my great granddad there when he was just sixteen."

Jack got up, walked over to the wall and looked at the old

faded black-and-white photo sitting in the frame. "Wow, they are big horses," he exclaimed.

"Yep, one of the biggest, 19 hands one of them stood. My granddad told me that his father drove the carriage for the local preacher and these were his horses. He used to talk about them all the time. Pretty fine animals, eh!"

"Yeah, they certainly are." Jack stared intently at the old photo of the boy standing in front of the carriage and horses. "Well, I don't need one *that* big for Sarah," Jack proclaimed as he smiled.

Mr. Jackson laughed. "No siree, I've got just the one for your Sarah."

Jack beamed back a smile. "Great! I'll bring my family over on Saturday if that's okay with you."

"That'll be fine."

Saturday came around very quickly, and Jack and Jenny planned to surprise their children first thing.

"No WAY! Are you kidding me?" Matthew beamed. "I get the bike this afternoon?"

"Oh, WOW! A pony!" Sarah squealed in delight.

Jack and Jenny stood watching their children as both of them were jumping up and down and dancing around, repeatedly singing tunes about ponies and motorcycles.

"Yes, well, this means that you both have to do your chores, homework and clean up after yourselves. No more slacking off," Jenny said loudly over their singing.

Matthew and Sarah both nodded enthusiastically and ran out to the car yelling back, "Come on let's go."

No sooner had Jack stopped the car out the front of the Jackson farmhouse, Sarah burst out running up to the front door and knocked on it.

The door opened, and a short, attractive, bright-eyed elderly woman looked down at her. "You must be Sarah?" she said, smiling.

"You must be Mrs. Jackson," Sarah replied, with a beaming grin.

Jack, Jenny and Matthew got out of the car as May Jackson descended the porch stairs with Sarah. She greeted them with a wave. "Hello, welcome!" she said. "I'm May," smiling warmly as she walked over towards them.

"Hello, pleased to meet you," Jack replied. "This is Jenny, my wife, Matthew, my son and I see that you've already met Sarah."

"Yes," she giggled, "she's a sweetie, isn't she?"

"Ah, Jack!" Ben Jackson called out as he walked out from the barn, "I thought I could hear May chatting." He smiled.

"Hi Mr. Jackson." Jack went through the introductions once again.

"Oh please, call me Ben," he replied. "Well, hello Sarah," he said, looking down at her. "You ready to meet your new friend?"

"Yes!" she beamed, unable to stand still.

"All right then, walk over this way."

They all followed Ben past the barn toward a wooden fence and looked across a lush, grassy field. Ben walked through the paddock gate and let out a loud whistle and they watched as fifteen horses of all colors, shapes and sizes came enthusiastically galloping across the flat toward them and then stopping just before the fence in front of them. The last to arrive was a little 12-hand buckskin pony with a white star on his forehead.

Ben pointed to the buckskin pony. "That's him there, that's Mustard."

Mustard pushed through between the other horses that were jostling for attention and stuck his nose through the railing at Sarah.

Sarah put her hand on his muzzle and rubbed it. "Oh, he is so cute," she said with a giggle.

"Yep, he's a little beauty." Ben slipped the rope halter over Mustard's head. "Come on, little fella." He walked him back through the gate and tied him to the hitching rail in front of the barn. "I've had him for about a year now. His owner out grew him, so I traded him for a bigger horse for her. He's extremely quiet, just right for a beginner, wouldn't hurt a fly."

"He sounds perfect," Jenny said, smiling at Jack.

"You folks want a morning snack?" Ben asked. "May makes the finest cakes around."

"Sounds good to me," replied Jack.

"Well, that's settled then," Ben said. "Sarah, if you want, you can stay out here and get to know your new friend. There's a brush and comb over there if you want to groom him."

"Okay," she replied.

"Me too," said Matthew.

Jack, Jenny, and Ben walked back into the farmhouse. May had already set the table. They sat down and May poured the tea and handed each of them a slice of her freshly baked orange and poppy seed cake.

"Oh May, this is delicious," Jenny exclaimed.

"She's the best cook in Evensmore," Ben replied as he looked at May and rubbed her on the back. "She's won many prizes at the local fair."

"Oh, Ben's just biased." May smiled, slightly embarrassed at the praise. "So, how do you like it here? You bought the Douglas property, didn't you?"

"Yes," Jenny replied, "We love it here—it's like a world of its own."

"It sure is," laughed Ben. "More than you think, I swear time stands still some days."

They all laughed.

"Ben, I'll need your account number so I can transfer the money for Mustard," said Jack.

"Sure, sure," replied Ben. "Ah, I don't know. I'm not big on this cashless business. I miss the old-fashioned greenbacks. I mean, there was nothing like having a wad of them in your pocket. It made you feel like a rich man. Soon they'll be stamping a bar code on your hand like a can of baked beans and scanning yer as you walk through the store door," he chuckled.

They all laughed, but Jack thought it seemed a very familiar scenario, but put it aside for now.

Ben continued, "And what about this economic downturn that's got folks in a spin? I mean, it's not as bad as the great depression but folks are hurtin just the same. The Jepson's place foreclosed last week and the Simmonds are scraping to pay their bank mortgage. I'm seeing more and more people going to the church for handouts. Did you know that we now have a deficit into the trillions? What are we doing to the next generation? Heck, I'm just grateful that we don't have a mortgage anymore, but it doesn't make it any easier for us, either. Sales are down on both horses and our produce. It just ain't right what's happening to good folk all over the place."

"Oh come now, Ben," May said, gently patting Ben's arm and a little embarrassed at his opinionated outburst. "Jack and Jenny don't want to hear you ranting about the economy. Don't mind, Ben, he's got his nose into this stuff all the time. Now what have you got in the way of horse-riding gear?" May asked, quickly changing the subject.

"Um, well we were so caught up in the excitement that we haven't had a chance to get Sarah a saddle or anything yet, as she was so keen to get here," Jack replied.

"Oh, May probably has something stored out in the shed from her riding instructing days you can have until you get one specifically for her," Ben said.

"It might be a little dusty but nothing a good coat of leather conditioner wouldn't fix. Come on, we'll go take a look," said May.

Jack and May walked out to the barn and left Ben and Jenny still talking at the table. May opened the old wooden barn door and walked towards the back.

Jack stood just inside the door, his eyes adjusting to the darkness to see hay bales and various farm equipment stored throughout the large old barn. His eyes settled on what looked like an old horse carriage covered in dust and cobwebs. He recognized it from the old photo inside Ben's house.

"Well, this ought to do," May said as she came out from the back of the barn carrying a saddle and noticed Jack staring at the old carriage. "I've told Ben that he should get rid of that old thing, just taking up space—but he won't, sentimental value he keeps telling me, it was his great grandfather's," she explained with a big smile on her face. "It's broken beyond repair, but he still wants to keep it... Men!" she shook her head.

Seth looked at Gabe and raised an eyebrow.

"Not yet, it's not time," said Gabe.

"... A nd so, 'The Lord gave and the Lord has taken away; may the name of the Lord be praised'..." The Reverend Jim March was in the middle of his Sunday morning sermon, preaching to a congregation of about two hundred and fifty people.

Lora was quietly sitting down the front with her mother, Bethany, trying not to fall asleep. *I can't wait until this is over*, she thought. *I wonder what Meg's up to. Maybe I can catch up with her this afternoon.*

Reverend Jim March, Bethany, and Lora stood by the door, shook hands, and made small talk with the congregation as each one walked outside into a beautiful, sunny morning. Lora was busting to go home, change out of her dress, and find out what Meg was doing.

"Did you enjoy the message?" Jim asked Bethany as they were driving in the car back home.

"Yes, it was wonderful, very well thought out and spoken," she replied with a smile.

Lora took this cue to put on her headphones and pretend she was listening to her music before her father asked her the same question. Jim looked into the rear-view mirror at his daughter but didn't bother to ask for her response.

Lora got out of the car and ran through the front door up to her room and changed into her jeans and t-shirt and rang her friend Meg.

"How was church today?" Meg mocked with a giggle.

Lora rolled her eyes. "Boring, as usual, what are you doing?"

"Well, the fair is in town so, I thought I might go down there and check it out. I think Scotty and Ken are going to be there too."

"Okay, I'll be over at your house in five." Lora hung up. "I'm going to Meg's place," she called out to her parents. "Be back later this afternoon," she said as she ran out the door.

JENNY WAS SITTING down on the front porch, contently watching Sarah groom Mustard. She was talking to him whilst putting plaits in his mane and finishing them off with her own colorful hair baubles. Mustard was enjoying the pampering. His eyelids were low, and he was gradually falling asleep. Jack was down in the paddock, helping Matthew learn how to ride his motorcycle.

"Now this time, go easy on the throttle," she could hear him say after watching Matthew have a near miss with a tree previously.

It was a lovely day, something that they could not have imagined a few months ago. They'd had a good morning, church was great, they'd seen new friends and now were just relaxing and enjoying the afternoon. Evensmore had certainly changed their lives, and Jenny loved it.

Beside her stood her two guardian angels God had assigned, also contently watching the action in the paddock.

"Looks like they are going to have their hands full," commented one guardian.

They both burst out laughing at the sight of Matthew, once again full throttle and out of control, with Jack running in hot pursuit after him.

At this instant, there was a brilliant flash of light and the Angelic Captain, Jophiel, was standing in front of them. One guardian stiffened to attention, prodding the other in the side and motioning to Seth and Gabe to come over and join them.

"Good afternoon, sir," they addressed the Captain.

"How is everything here?" Jophiel replied, smiling at all four Guardians standing at attention.

"All is well," they replied.

"Did he see it?" asked Jophiel.

"Yes," replied Seth.

"Well done," said Jophiel. "As you are aware, the plan is twofold. Jack must find the truth and then use his position to save many others. It is imperative that the enemy does not become aware of our mission. Do you all understand how important this is to the cause?" They all nodded.

"Good. As you were." And with that, he was gone.

THE SMELL of hot dogs and fries, mixed with the sound of cheers and screams from the rides, had the town fair in full swing. Lora and Meg were taking small bites of their pink cotton candy when two teenage boys, Scotty and Ken, came running up behind grabbing them.

"Aaaah, you scared me." Lora laughed at Scotty as he swung her around.

"Hey, I'm glad you're here," he said.

"Me too," she said shyly, admiring his handsome features and tousled blonde hair.

The four of them spent an hour laughing and meandering around the fair, taking rides and filling up on hot dogs and candy.

"Hey," said Meg, "I've got an idea." They all looked curiously at her. "Let's get our fortunes told. There's a lady here that does them."

"Mm… I don't know Meg," said Lora. "I mean, it sounds kind of scary to me."

"Yeah, I don't know if I'm into that sort of thing," said Scotty warily.

"What can it hurt? Come on, who doesn't want to know their future? Besides, it's not real, it's just a bit of harmless fun," said Meg.

"Yeah, but I don't know. I've got a bad feeling about that stuff," Lora replied.

"Come on Lora, stop being a goody two shoes, there's nothing wrong with it," said Meg as she grabbed Lora's arm and dragged her over into the medium's tent with Scotty and Ken following closely behind.

Inside the tent sat an attractive, middle-aged woman, with her hair pulled back in a hair clip, revealing large hoop earrings and a butterfly tattoo on the nape of her neck. She was busily filing her long crimson nails when she looked up at them.

"Hello darlings," she crooned with a smooth European accent, "are you here for your future telling?"

They nervously looked around at each other when Meg piped up saying, "Yes, we would like our fortunes told, please."

"Well, you've come to the right place." She smiled, "I am Carla. Who wants to go first?" she asked as she waved her hand. Meg keenly stepped forward. "Follow me then." She motioned, and Meg followed her into the back room of the tent. The others sat down in the chairs and waited.

After 20 minutes, Meg burst out into the waiting area, beaming with excitement. "Wow, that was awesome! I'm going to marry a handsome, rich, dark-haired man and travel the world, have three kids AND I'm going to live a long, long life."

Lora, Scotty, and Ken sat nervously smiling at her. "Come on Lora, you've got to go next. There's really nothing to worry about. It's so much fun, you'll love it," Meg said.

Lora got up, took a deep breath and boldly marched into the back room and sat down across the table from Carla. She was trying her best to hide her nerves.

"And what is your name, young lady?" Carla asked.

"Um, it's Lora," she replied shyly.

"Aaaaaah... Lora, such a pretty name. Let's see what the future holds for young Lora, eh!"

Carla laid out the Tarot cards one by one in front of her on the table. Raising her eyebrows and making interesting *ooh* and *aah* sounds at each one she placed down.

In the darkened tent, Lora could not make out the big black hand upon Carla's head with long talons tightly gripping her skull, nor could she hear the deep raspy voice speaking deeply into Carla's mind. The monstrous demon with coarse hair and hunch-backed features was looking at a smaller, rough, lizard like demon standing beside Lora.

"Omart, what do you know of this girl?" the big demon rasped to the smaller.

"Well," Omart replied in a high pitch, winy shrill. His spindly arms flailing about animatedly as he spoke. "She's a preacher's daughter, 14-years-old, and she goes to Evensmore High. Oh, yeah, she had an aunt who died about six months ago who she was close to. She has a small white dog called Lilly and had a gray cat that passed away two years ago called Toby..." The small demon continued to give the larger one all that he knew about Lora's past and present.

"Tell me more about the aunt... how she died?" the large demon asked.

"It was in a car accident—her name was Mary Jean Baker. Lora gave her a silver heart-shaped pendant a few days before the accident. Oh yeah, can you also give her a previous life, you know, like an Egyptian princess or something? I love it when you do that," he nervously chuckled.

The large demon resumed his focus, sank his talons deeper into Carla's skull, and began to speak into her psyche.

Carla suddenly stiffened—her eyes became wide, boring deep into Lora's. "Yes, yes, I have something for you, my child. Your aunt is here with us, ummmm, hang on, M, M, Mmm, Maria, No, No, Mary, Mary is the name that I'm receiving."

Lora stiffened in her chair, and her hands wrung nervously. Finally, she said, "Is... is she all right?" her eyes filling with tears.

"Yes, she says that she is fine, that she has passed over to the other side and is enjoying another life peacefully in the universe. She's saying also that it was a quick death, and that she did not feel a thing in the car accident. Yes, Yesss, ummmm, she said to tell you she is still wearing the heart pendant that you gave her for her birthday."

Lora sat astonished and wide-eyed at what she was hearing.

"Also, I am sensing an animal here. A gray cat. He is here with you. The name I'm receiving is T. O. B. Y." She spelt out the letters "Yes, that's it, Toby."

"You mean... Toby has been with me all this time?"

"Yes, my darling, he has!" She continued, "Mmmm, you are also the daughter of a local preacher, but you are unhappy and your soul is searching for the truth. If you keep searching, you will find it, my child. Oooooh, hang on one moment… I'm getting that you, my darling, were of high importance in a previous life. Aaahh yesss… a princess… an Egyptian princess, I believe." Carla smiled and raised her eyebrows to show how impressed she was.

"Wow, how do you know all this about me?"

"I have a gift from the Lord above darling!"

Both demons looked at each other and grinned, bearing their fangs.

"More like from OUR Lord below," Omart crackled.

The larger demon maliciously grinned at the other, drool cascading down his jowls. "The fools are easily deceived, aren't they?" he replied.

CHAPTER FIVE

N *ow, where was that?* Jack thought as he sifted through the papers and documents scattered over his desk. Jack had the house to himself, the children had left for school, and Jenny had gone into town to get some groceries. "Ah, there it is," he said as he picked up the software requirements documentation. *It'll be in here*, he thought.

Jack skimmed through the pages until his eyes stopped upon a requirement. He slowly read it aloud. "The 'I-Chip' shall be implanted into the subject's right hand." *How did Ben know about this?* he thought. *Must have been a lucky guess, because all this is classified.* "Mm… interesting!" The phone rang suddenly and interrupted Jack's thought process.

"Hello," Jack answered.

"Hi Jack, it's Simon. How are things in the country?"

"Great Simon, it's really quiet out here. I'm not missing the stress of city life at all."

"That's great. I'm glad it's working out for you. Listen, how's the documentation tracking for the I-Chip project? We have that review next week and I was hoping you were close to finishing it so I can look at it before it goes before the board."

"No problem, I'm actually sending you the last document today for you to look at."

"That's great. Love your work, Jack! Okay, well I'll let you get back to it then, talk to you in the review next week."

"Thanks Simon, talk to you then."

Jack hung up the phone and busily got back to tweaking the final draft of the Software Design Document. He had felt a greater degree of pressure on this project than normal because, for some reason, there was a rush to push this product out. He really wanted to talk to Jenny about how he was feeling but couldn't because of its Top-Secret classification. *I'm on my own on this one*, he thought to himself.

"Hello Jacky, I'm back!" Jenny called as she strove through the door with the groceries in her arms.

Relieved for the distraction, "Hey, you want a hand?"

"Love one!"

Jack marched up the stairs and out the front door to help collect the bags from the car. "You want me to make you a coffee?" he asked.

"Wow, you have become the real house husband, haven't you?"

"Yeah, well, I'm just due for one and I really need to take a break." He smiled as he followed her and grabbed two grocery bags.

"Is everything all right?"

"Just work," he said as he walked back inside and turned on the kettle.

"OKAY, did everyone print off the first lesson on our study, renewing the mind?" Peter asked. Everyone in the men's Bible study nodded their heads in agreement. "Good then, so let's get started. Ted, do you want to read out the first paragraph for us, please?"

"Do not conform to the pattern of this world, but be transformed by the renewing of your mind. Then you will be able to test and approve what God's will is—his good, pleasing and perfect will. Romans 12:2." Ted read the scripture aloud.

"So, what do you think this scripture means?" Peter asked as he looked around at the nine men sitting in the room.

Ted spoke first. "I guess for me it means that I should think on what God would want me to think upon. For instance, instead of dwelling on something negative, like maybe my anger, I should try to focus on self-control and get some scriptures to back it up."

"Excellent, that's a really good example," Peter said. "Jack, have you got something?"

"Well, I know I really don't do this enough, but I think if we want to renew our mind, then the best way to do it is by reading the Word. Because if we focus on the Word, then we have the mind of Christ and then we can, like Paul said, 'be able to test and approve what God's will is'."

"Yeah, that's good Jack," said Shaun Barnard. "I know I don't read the Word enough, but every time I do it feels like my mind and spirit is being fed, refreshed or something and I'll tend to remember the scriptures later."

The group continued to discuss their thoughts and then broke for supper.

"So, Jack, what projects are you working on?" asked Shaun whilst sipping his coffee.

"Nothing exceptional!" Jack tried to tone it down, but seeing Shaun's face made him feel the need to explain his elusiveness further. "Sorry Shaun, I can't say because of the classification!"

"Ah, so it's some conspiracy, like world domination, or the mark of the beast on our right hand or something?" Ted jested.

Jack looked inquisitively at Ted. "Mark on the hand? You know that's really weird because that's the second time I've heard that in the last month," he exclaimed.

Peter piped up. "The mark of the Beast Jack, in the book of Revelation?"

"Umm sorry, I've been a Christian for two years but I haven't heard of that one," replied Jack. "What am I missing here?"

"Well, Jack, many people don't read the book of Revelation," Peter said.

"Yeah, because most people can't understand it!" laughed Shaun whilst munching on his biscuit.

"Well, yes, it's a bit of a challenge to understand the real meanings behind it and that is primarily why people tend to read the other books instead," Peter added.

"So, what's this mark on the hand thing?" Jack asked.

"It's where people are forced to take a mark that represents allegiance with the Antichrist. Anyone who does not have this mark cannot buy or sell and will face persecution and even be put to death. However, God says that anyone who accepts the mark will go to Hell. It's sort of a lose-lose situation," Ted said with a grin.

"Wow, is that really what it says?" asked Jack, stunned.

"Yeah, it's in Revelation. The Antichrist will be the head of a one-world government and will take total control over everything, including religion, to the extent that everyone's forced to worship him and not God. But thankfully we will not be around to see it, because we are going up," replied Shaun as he pointed heavenward.

"How do you mean?" asked Jack.

"Well, the scriptures say that the church will be taken out before any of this occurs, so we won't go through this persecution. God will remove us before this happens, so we won't be harmed," said Peter.

"Really? Well, that's a relief. It doesn't sound very good," said Jack.

"God revealed this to our two Evensmore preachers, Father Harvey and Father Daniel, way back. It's called the Secret Rapture. So don't worry, we have nothing to be concerned about —Jesus will return for us before anything like that happens. He's definitely going to save His people. Some even say that you can be saved after the secret rapture too and that we get a second chance if we miss out the first time. So, we really have nothing to worry about—God's not going to let his people suffer through the tribulation," said Shaun confidently.

Jack's Guardians, Seth and Gabe, looked at each other.

"We wait." Gabe stated.

Seth nodded in agreement.

JACK CAME HOME from the Bible study and slipped quietly inside the house so he wouldn't disturb his sleeping family. He made himself a hot chocolate, got comfortable in the couch, opened his Bible to the book of Revelation, and read. *Well, the first bit is straightforward*, he thought, *it shouldn't be too hard if this is the genre.*

P eter and Jack sat in the corner table at Betty's Cafe.

    "You know, I started to read the book of Revelation the other night after Bible study and you were right—it's hard to understand. I mean… I'm not a big fan of fiction writing or Sci-Fi but this is really way out stuff, all these visions, et cetera," Jack exclaimed.

    "Sure, I know how you feel. That book of the Bible is not an easy read, but if you keep persisting and re-reading it, it actually starts to become clearer," he replied. "Now, before you start, ask the Holy Spirit to help you understand and reveal the things that He wants you to learn right now. He will do it, but be persistent." Peter paused for a moment. "I guess you could liken it to cleaning a dirty window. At first, all you seem to do is smudge it and make it worse, but with more paper towel, cleaner, and elbow grease, the clearer it becomes. Also, don't just look at Revelation, look at the other books as well, a lot of them have references to the end times too."

    "Mm, well all right… I'll just stick at it then," he smiled.

    "So, how do you like it here?" asked Peter.

    "We have really settled into this place. It feels like we've always belonged here. The church is fantastic. I actually want to commend you, we really are getting a lot out of your services."

    "It's not me, but the Lord—He's the one who has built it. When I first took over, there were only seven of the congregation left in the church. It was bound to be closed; I know one hundred and twenty isn't very big compared to what you're used to, but it's a steady growth."

    "Well, what I'm used to wasn't exactly cosy; it was big and lacked connection and relationships. But I didn't realize that this little church was on the brink of closure. So how did you turn it around?"

"Well, I believe in stating the truth, straight from the Bible. Some preachers like to count their congregation numbers and teach so as not to offend. They live in fear of losing their people, and so do everything they can to keep them. Unfortunately, it's become more like a business to them. They want the numbers so they can pay the mortgage and bills so they are careful not to upset anyone—it becomes a vicious circle. However, with this church, I knew God put on my heart to preach the truth, speak out His Words, seek Him for what He wants to say to His people and that's exactly what I did. I really had nothing to lose because we only had a small group of people and I just knew God wanted this church to flourish. Slowly but surely, it grew. People got excited and returned and brought others with them. It was all God, not me."

"Well, you certainly give some profound messages. I mean… it is totally different from where we have come from. I've never really heard the message as strong as you teach, it was more… oh I don't know, I guess, encouragement you know, 'You can do it' mantra style, or drawing from their own experiences and not much of the Word coming through and how to overcome and so forth."

Peter chuckled and replied, "Yes, I know what you mean. I've heard *a lot* of those messages myself. No…" Peter paused, "I'm not afraid to lay it on the line and speak about the uncomfortable things people want to ignore or brush over like Hell and the unseen spiritual battle that goes on around us. I ensure I make it clear in telling the congregation that they need to be fervent in following Christ and not to be slack followers. I guess, at least I will have a clear conscience in knowing that I stood firm in preaching the truth."

"Well, you certainly do! It's like breathing fresh air after so long. I think I was spiritually starving and didn't realize it. I was saved at my previous church. I read the Bible at first but have since let the business of life encroach on my time with God." Jack paused and then continued, "I'd hate to admit it but I hardly even pick up my Bible now and that's my own doing. I can't blame the church for its lack of teaching—I should look after my own spirituality and read the Word myself."

"I'm glad you see it that way." Peter smiled. "But unfortunately, your story is a common one. You see, God really convicted me at my last church. At every service, there was an altar call given. They simply said, put up your hand if you want to know Christ as your Savior and then pray this prayer and you're going to Heaven. Well, that was fine, but it just never sat right with me and God kept leading me back to the Word to look at scriptures like Matthew 7:21. 'Not everyone who says to me, 'Lord, Lord,' will enter the kingdom of heaven, but only the one who does the will of my Father who is in heaven,' and Matthew 16:24 'Whoever wants to be my disciple must deny themselves and take up their cross and follow me'."

Peter paused before he continued. "So, I started to question our methods of saving people. Were we just packaging it up to make it sound so easy that you could still live your life as you always have been—there was no real change needed and that it was a sure ticket if you said, *Yes*. Because the sad thing was that I would see so many people put up their hand and not have a real *heart change*. I mean, their character just *wasn't* changing. They were still battling the same demons' years later. For instance, they were still eagerly drinking or doing drugs, or actively watching pornography, stealing, or happily still living with their girlfriend or boyfriend, et cetera. I was not seeing any overcomers because they weren't being taught to strengthen their relationship with Christ. They weren't told to leave behind their sin or get into God's Word... or fervently pray for God to help them change and be dedicated and follow through." Peter looked up to see Jack looking a little perplexed.

"Sorry Jack, let me explain further... you see, when you accept Christ, your spirit is made new and you become a *new* creation, but your soul and body will still try to conduct the same behaviors as before. Your existing behavior is who you *used* to be, but not who you are *now* with Christ as your Savior. However, to change your soul and body you have to seek God, read his Word to transform your *nature*, but also actively try to stop doing the sin. God will always put the desire in your heart to do this... but it can be deliberately ignored. So that's what I was seeing—a continual pattern of wilful sin."

Peter took a long breath before continuing. "When these people did sin, there was simply no remorse or repentance. They just continued as they were before, and that's what really disturbed me. If people are seeking God, they will see a change and when they do make a mistake, *which we all do*, they will earnestly repent, and try harder. That's a heart change."

Gabe and Seth were listening intently. "This is good. This kind of discussion will help strengthen them both." Gabe stated.

"Yes, we need to be watchful, the enemy won't like to hear this." Seth concluded. They both looked at each other and nodded in agreement.

Peter sighed. "Anyway, there seemed to be more backsliders than overcomers, and I saw many of these people eventually turn away from God... and it broke my heart. So when I came to Evensmore, twelve months ago, I decided I would be straight about becoming a follower of Christ, so people knew what they had to do, how they had to change, and what they had to look forward to. That's why when someone accepts Christ we talk to them straight away and also encourage them to do our new Christians' course, get water baptized and receive the Holy Spirit, like Peter says in Acts 2:38."

"Well, I can honestly say that I have never heard an altar call quite like yours," Jack said, smiling. "You certainly make it clear."

"It's truth!" Peter exclaimed. "People need to have that revelation on what it means to follow Christ, and what they will face in their eternity without Him—that we must deny ourselves and put away the old nature. But also understand that when you seek first the Kingdom of God and be obedient to Him, you will have the God aligned desires of your heart. Therefore, you are not really losing anything but gaining everything, plus eternity. That's why I preach it hard. I mean, if you were to buy a car, wouldn't you rather the sales person was up front and told you everything about it so you could make an informed and committed decision before purchasing it?"

Jack nodded in agreement.

"Well, it's the same thing—we need to let people know the cost of following Christ, letting the *old* self go, but show them that the benefits far outweigh the things we have to leave behind."

Gabe noticed the slight shadowy movement first. Peering through the café window was a small black messenger spirit intently spying on Jack and Peter's conversation. Gabe subtly signaled Seth and drew his attention to the small demon fixated, gazing through the glass.

Seth coolly moved over towards the café door behind a large pot plant so as not to draw any attention, and then, with lightning speed, he dashed outside, clasped the tiny demon behind the neck, and picked it up.

"W-w-what are you doing?" It squealed in fear.

Seth placed the demon down and spun it around to face him. It flapped its small black wings to regain its balance as Seth drew his regal sword, holding the radiant blade against its slender throat. "No... what are you doing?" Seth demanded.

"N-nothing, I was just passing by and was simply curious."

"About what?"

"Just curious." It smiled a set of misshapen rodent teeth. Seth pushed his blade a little harder. "W-w-wait... I was just listening, that's all, nothing bad... just listening."

"Why?" Gabe spoke sternly, now joining the conversation.

"I have no real reason... I-I-I'm just doing my job, you know... I just watch and listen for things."

"What have you heard?"

"Nothing... I heard nothing—they're just talking. Nothing unusual." It smiled meekly.

"You have no business here then," Seth responded as he dropped his grasp, withdrew his sword and stepped back, letting the spirit go.

The demon immediately took flight, its wings flapping and beating as fast as it could to put as much distance between him and the angels.

Gabe and Seth returned to Jack's side.

"I mean... you are a relatively new Christian—tell me how it felt when you accepted Christ." Peter asked.

"It was amazing," Jack exclaimed. "I went from a person who worried and stressed over every little thing. I would strive to get ahead in life, in my career, and try to control *all* of my circumstances. It was tiring! But then, when I accepted Jesus... well, I can't describe it. It was as... a *weight* was lifted off. I slowly felt peace and learned that God was in control, not me. However, letting go didn't come overnight... it was a gradual change, but little by little, I felt I could trust Him with my circumstances and give my worries over to Him to sort out... and He did. I would never go back, Peter. I'm completely a different person now."

"That's the key," Peter said enthusiastically. "Giving over your life to Him so He *can* direct your path, but not all people do this. I mean, in Matthew 7:22-23, Jesus states, 'Many will say to me on that day, 'Lord, Lord, did we not prophesy in your name and in your name drive out demons and in your name perform many miracles?' Then I will tell them plainly, 'I never knew you. Away from me, you evildoers'."

Peter hesitated before he continued. "Now that really got me thinking... I thought, well, they obviously made a decision for Christ at some stage, because they had that authority by His name to cast out demons and perform miracles, but they never continued in a relationship with Him. It made me realize that many people who think they are going to Heaven may not be. John 15:6 states, 'If you do not remain in me, you are like a branch that is thrown away and withers; such branches are picked up, thrown into the fire and burned'. I think this statement makes it very obvious if you do not remain in him what will happen. But... understand that you don't lose your salvation just because you accidentally sinned, or made a mistake, but if gone unrepentant... then it may lead you to drift away to where you no longer remain in Christ."

Peter picked up his coffee and took another sip. "Further to this, 2 Peter 2:20-21 tells us 'If they have escaped the corruption of the world by knowing our Lord and Savior Jesus Christ and are again entangled in it and are overcome, they are worse off at the end than they were at the beginning. It would have been better for them not to have known the way of righteousness, than to have known it and then to turn their backs on the sacred command that was passed on to them.'"

Peter took a breath, "Now that scripture is talking about Christians who turn away from God and return to their sinful nature. Therefore, it's not a *onetime* prayer thing, it's a life walk. I realized people were not aware of this—you *can* lose your salvation by not abiding in Christ. So, I decided then that I would teach the congregation the truth, I also stopped doing a traditional version of the 'sinners prayer' as I felt it could be misleading, leaving people thinking that's all they have to do... unfortunately, it didn't go down well with the senior pastors in my previous church and many of the congregation complained and said that it was too confronting and I should soften my messages. Now what's that telling you?"

"So, what you're saying is that you can pray the sinner's prayer, but you still might not make it to Heaven? Wow, I mean, I thought that once you accepted Christ, then you are assured to go to Heaven no matter what!"

"Well, no... but I'll explain further." Peter smiled. "It's not 'no matter what', but that's what a lot of preachers are saying and honestly believe. They say, 'once saved, always saved', but it's completely false. If you read the scriptures, Jesus makes it quite clear. Take the example of the letter to the Laodiceans in Revelation 3:15-16, 'I know your deeds, that you are neither cold nor hot. I wish you were either one or the other! So, because you are lukewarm—neither hot nor cold—I am about to spit you out of my mouth. Also look at Revelation 3:1-5." Peter opened his Bible and read the passage.

'... I know your deeds; you have a reputation of being alive, but you are dead. Wake up! Strengthen what remains and is about to die, for I have found your deeds unfinished in the sight of my God. Remember, therefore, what you have received and heard; hold it fast, and repent. But if you do not wake up, I will come like a thief, and you will not know at what time I will come to you.

Yet you have a few people in Sardis who have not soiled their clothes. They will walk with me, dressed in white, for they are worthy. The one who is victorious will, like them, be dressed in white. I will never blot out the name of that person from the book of life, but will acknowledge that name before my Father and his angels.'

Jack suddenly interrupted Peter. "I will never blot out the name of that person from the book of life?" he leaned forward with a concerned look upon his face. "So, if Jesus is saying here that He won't remove your name, then there's an implication that your name *can* be removed? This is scary!" Jack shook his head.

"Yes, I can see you are realizing the enormity of this. Many people are unaware of this possibility. It's a fact, and it's stated clearly. Think on where it says, 'Strengthen what remains and is about to die' and also, 'But if you do not wake up, I will come like a thief...' Jesus is warning them to wake up, repent and get back to following him wholeheartedly."

"So, these churches Jesus is writing to, they are Christ followers?"

"Yes definitely, they once were fervent for Christ but then became lukewarm. They became spiritually dead, not seeking God's presence. In 1 John 2:4, Jesus said 'whoever says, 'I know him,' but does not do what He commands is a liar, and the truth is not in that person.' Now where do liars go?... So I'm telling you that lukewarm is just not acceptable. Yet many people go through their Christian lives being lukewarm for Christ. You can't be half a disciple, and God makes that clear in His Word. Like I said... I'm afraid that many people who say their Christians may not be going to Heaven."

"Really? You've got me quite concerned"

"Please, don't get me wrong, Jack. There is God's grace and He will cover our sins and mistakes if we earnestly repent, but if you are not trying to follow Christ, like trusting Him with your life and decisions, reading His Word and trying to be obedient to it, seeking His presence and asking for forgiveness if you do sin. But just simply going to church on Sunday, singing a few praise songs and then living your life like you used to before you were saved, then I have to question your salvation. This really concerns me because there are many Christians who are living their lives thinking that God's grace will cover them always and that they have a one-way ticket to Heaven. I think people feel that they can't lose their salvation no matter what. It's definitely not so! Each one of us must actively be seeking and pursuing God's Will. The church desperately needs to return to the first love like it states in Revelation 2:4."

Jack was pondering everything that Peter explained before he admitted, "It makes me realize that I've been so slack in reading the Word and spending time with God. I really need to wake up to myself and take this seriously."

"Good," Gabe exclaimed. He and Seth were still listening attentively to what Jack was saying and were excited that he was now understanding what it really meant to follow the King.

"This is the start—we must continue to encourage him to seek the truth," Seth stated. "However, we must watch out for him—the enemy will not like where he is heading."

"You must take this seriously." Peter paused. "No one can afford to be lukewarm! I guess, Jack, it's like this… you have met me, but don't really know me yet. The only way to know someone is to spend time with them and to form a relationship. It's the same with God, you can ask Him into your life, but if that's all you ever do, and not seek to fellowship with Him and know His ways and change *your* ways, then you do not have a relationship with Him, just an introduction to Him. We cannot go through our whole lives thinking that everything will be fine and God will just allow us into Heaven because of one prayer that we've long since forgotten. There needs to be that heart change and a pursuit of God."

Peter took a breath before he continued on another train of thought. "I think many Christians don't realize what can hold you back in your God walk—I mean, a good example is harboring unforgiveness. Now this is something that will stop you from entering the Kingdom. It states it clearly in Matthew 18:21-35 where He tells a parable about the king rescinding his servant's debt because the servant didn't forgive another. I have actually seen countless people come to church who have been hurt by others, and are still hanging on to this resentment. This will stop them from going to Heaven if they don't deal with it and repent." Peter paused, sensing the concern in Jack; he thought it best to shift the subject to a much lighter tone. "So… How is your family?" he smiled.

"They're great." Jack lit up again. "Sarah just loves her new pony, Mustard, and Matthew is mastering his motor bike. Every Saturday, we lead Mustard and Sarah over to Ben and May's to have riding lessons. Matthew follows on his bike and Ben gets on his quad bike and they ride all over the property, it's good to see them enjoying the country life. I'm going to get a motorcycle myself so I can ride with Matthew."

"The Jacksons are lovely people," Peter stated.

"Do they go to church?"

"They go to Reverend March's church down on South Street."

"Oh, I wasn't sure, and I didn't feel comfortable enough to ask Ben what they believed."

"Yeah, Ben's a stickler for tradition. Most of his generation went to that church, but I don't know where he is at with his faith. I have sat in one of Reverend March's sermons and it is quite different to mine." Peter left it at that.

"Ben really knows his stuff about what's happening to the world economy," Jack said.

"He sure does." Peter chuckled and continued explaining, "And rightly so, as many people prefer to stick their head in the

41

sand and ignore what's going on around them. A lot of people are in trouble, we have had a tremendous increase in handouts of food and bill vouchers just these past few months. But God is still in control and He knows what's going on, we just have to help those who are in need."

Jack looked at his watch. "Ah, sorry Peter, I have to go—I promised Jenny I would be back for when the children got home. She's playing tennis this afternoon. Thanks so much for the chat and coffee," he said as he rose to leave. "Hey would you like to come over for dinner this Friday night? I'll check with Jenny to see if it's fine, but I'm sure it would be."

"I would love to, thanks."

"Okay great I'll call you to confirm details then." Jack smiled as he turned and left the cafe.

"**D**o another princess one!" the demon Rebellion said to
Crystalyn.

"Shhhhh, I *KNOW* what I am doing, so shut up and let me do
it," he snapped back as he probed Lora's sleeping head with his
long, silvery, thin talons. "She will believe, I just have to go slowly,
it works every time!"

Rebellion grinned, a slimy mouthful of sharp yellowing fangs,
his eagerness nearly getting him slapped. These two were
delighting in twisting Lora's thoughts into believing what they
were telling her. Their malicious minds were intertwining with
hers to control her thinking.

Lora tossed and turned in her fitful sleep, making small
muffled noises, her body occasionally twitching sharply as if she
was running, escaping in her dreams.

The two demons just grinned at each other as they continued
their night's work.

EVERYONE WAS asleep in Jack's house, except for Jack; he too had
been tossing and turning, unable to sleep soundly. Gabe and Seth
stood casually nearby, watching Jack as he fidgeted and shifted
restlessly. They both felt the presence of the Holy Spirit moving
around Jack, urging him to get up and read God's Word. They
both waited patiently until Jack gave in and quietly grabbed his
Bible off the bedside table and crept out into the living room.

"Finally!" Seth said to Gabe as they followed him out of the
bedroom.

Jack sat for a while, contemplating his conversation with Peter.
He prayed,

"Father, please forgive me for my lack of conviction for your cause. I desperately want to be fervent in seeking your will for my life. I'm so sorry for not reading your Word, praising, and praying regularly. I ask for your forgiveness for any sins that I have committed. I also willingly forgive anyone who wronged me. Thank you for saving me and choosing me to be your own—please help me to love people and be passionate about sharing your message of salvation. Amen."

Jack flipped open his Bible. "Okay, here we go again… Revelation," Jack mumbled to himself and prayed again, "Lord, please reveal what you want me to see in your Word tonight. Please give me wisdom and knowledge to be able to understand your teachings. I ask that your Holy Spirit guides me. Thank you in the name of Jesus, Amen."

Jack opened his Bible, found the book of Revelation, and read. He came to Revelation 3:5. "Ah, that's what Peter was talking about… mmm, it does seem that your name could be removed." He pondered this and continued on reading, trying to take in the words on each page.

Seth stood nearby. His countenance glowed as the Holy Spirit prompted him. He waited until Jack was near a certain passage and he reached out and touched Revelation 13:16 with his sword and made the words literally glow and jump out off the page at Jack.

"He also forced everyone, small and great, rich and poor, free and slave, to receive a mark on his right hand or on his forehead." Jack read the words aloud slowly, taking each one in.

"WOAH! What? Hang on, right hand or forehead?" he said as he reread the passage again. "This can't be right, is this it? Is this the mark?" He jumped up off the couch and started pacing, his thoughts reeling with realization; *Oh No, this can't be right.* He sat back down and re-read the passage over again, as well as the next verse, slowly regaining his thoughts. "This must be a mistake," he said, re-reading the passage once again. *It can't be coincidental, surely. Does this mean I'm involved in creating the mark of the beast? Is this what I've been working on? No, surely not!* He continued, trying to make sense of his thoughts.

Seth and Gabe looked on and waited.

"This is the beginning of Jack's journey," Gabe stated. "He *must* fulfill what God has called him to do."

Jack got up and started pacing again, rubbing his head with his hands, moving around the living room. A twisting knot was forming in his stomach as he was trying to take in this revelation. *This can't be true, surely. Maybe it's something else—maybe I'm not really working on this stuff, I mean, this is too soon and this Revelation passage is way off into the future; I mean, we are not supposed to be here when this happens.* He paced the floor, mumbling aloud to himself, "it's got to be just coincidental."

Jack went into the kitchen and made himself a hot chocolate, but could not shake this feeling of trepidation that lingered over him. *Oh, God, what if it's true? What if I am creating the very thing that will make millions suffer… the creation of the enemy's mark? Lord, help me, give me wisdom. What do I do?* Jack felt sick—his stomach felt like it had twisted around like a wet wringing towel, and he felt the pain of the acid and bile rise in his throat with each worrisome thought.

Seth and Gabe stood by and watched Jack in his emotional turmoil.

"Let him be for now," Seth said. "The Lord will reveal to him what needs to be done."

Gabe responded with a nod of agreement.

DAYLIGHT BROKE to reveal a beautiful Friday morning. The sun was rising with its light rays streaking orange and red hued ribbons across the morning sky, and the birds were twittering and singing choruses to bring in the new day. However, Jack was still sitting in the couch, his tired listless eyes fixed on the passage in the Bible. His thoughts dulled to a feeling of overwhelming guilt and hopelessness.

"HEY MEG." Lora waved as she ran towards her best friend.

"Hey, did you finally do your math?" Meg asked.

"Yeah, it was boring, but I finished it late last night," Lora replied as they both walked into class.

"I didn't finish mine," Meg cringed.

"Ah no Meg, not again. Mrs. Pempie is really going to get mad at you, this is the third time now."

"I know, I know, I got watching TV. I'll just have to come up with another excuse. Maybe you could distract her or something." She looked pleadingly at her friend.

"I'll think of something." Lora shook her head in empathy.

"Okay, settle down." The high school teacher, Mrs. Pempie, raised her voice over the noise of the students' babble. "I want you to open your textbooks, and I'll walk around and look at the exercises I gave you to complete."

"Excuse me, Mrs. Pempie," Lora piped up in amongst the frenzy of students opening their texts. "I was wondering if we could go over exercise 16, 17, and 18 in the text as I really struggled with that."

"Yes, that will be fine Lora… who else wants to go over these?" There was a show of hands.

Meg mouthed the words, "Thank you."

Lora grinned.

"That was a lovely meal, Jenny," said Peter. "Thank you so much. It's been a long time since I've had such a pleasant home cooked dinner. Jude used to be a superb cook. I suspect the Lord has her in the kitchen whipping up something as we speak," he chuckled as he and Jenny walked into the living room to sit down with their coffees.

"How long has it been?" Jenny asked.

"Jude passed away just over 11 years ago now. I miss her greatly—we were best friends. She was only 48 when her heart gave out."

"Wow, so young," Jenny replied.

"Yes, it was young, and I went through a stage of being angry with God, but I know God doesn't bring death. We live in the enemy's world. I look back now and know that we didn't have a healthy lifestyle. We were both very overweight—we ate the wrong things like takeout, lots of fried food, and enjoyed our sugary drinks and cakes and we didn't exercise. The Bible clearly states to look after your temple and we weren't. Eventually the body gives in to disease. It's not God's fault, but our very own doing. It's our responsibility to look after ourselves and live healthy. I see so many people come crying to God to heal them from diseases that could have been preventable if they had just looked after themselves. So now I try to eat a healthy diet of fresh fruit, vegetables, juices, meat and fish. I try to stay away from sugar and have a small amount of carbs, and I exercise for at least half hour each day. I try to incorporate many raw foods into my meals and I feel like I'm 20 years old again. It's just a pity that Jude wasn't with me to enjoy it fully."

"You didn't want to remarry?" Jenny asked.

"No... no one could replace my Judy. I didn't have the desire to. I have my son and daughter and now I have two grandchildren, so I'm content."

"They're asleep!" Jack said as he came downstairs and joined Peter and Jenny.

"What's wrong, Jack? You're not yourself tonight," Peter inquired.

Jenny looked up at Jack and raised one eyebrow. Jack sat down next to Jenny on the sofa, picked up his coffee and took a few sips, then gathered his thoughts. "Well, you know that I'm currently working on a major project at the moment that is highly classified."

"Yes, you've mentioned that previously."

"Okay, well, I really need to talk to you but I'm torn between confidentiality and honesty."

"How do you mean?"

"Meaning I could get fired, lose all credibility, get the pants sued off of me and go to jail if I tell anyone about this information."

"Mmm, well, I see your dilemma then. Have you sought the Lord about telling me?"

"Yes, and I feel that He is directing me to talk to you."

"Well, you know it would be strictly between you and me Jack, I will not talk to anyone else about what you're going to discuss, and besides I have obligations to privacy as well."

"I've told Jenny," Jack said, as he looked over to her sitting beside him on the couch. "I couldn't keep quiet any longer, it's just consuming me." Jack sat anxiously wringing his hands, looking towards the floor.

"I've been working on this project since conception," he continued. "I mean, I was the one who came up with the initial concept. We all thought it was a brilliant idea. The customer was over the moon at its simplicity, technology and the problems that it could solve. I was the shining star on this one, so they let me run with it. I spent countless hours fleshing out requirements and researching new technological advances. I was being paid a bomb as the Engineering Lead and they kept bumping up my salary, as the customer was so happy with my work. I had some of the top R&D professionals assigned to me to gather any information that I required. I didn't realize how immense the customer's corporation was, but they were paying us big money to pursue this and bring it to fruition quickly. But I didn't know Peter, I just didn't realize, how could I? But I should have known—I mean, I started looking at this concept two-and-a-half years ago, just before I became a Christian. So why didn't God tell me not to do it, or to stop? Why didn't someone let me know?" Jack held his head in his hands and then looked up helplessly at Peter.

Jenny had her arm around him with tears in her eyes, never seeing her husband this distraught before.

"What do you mean Jack, you're losing me?" Peter looked confused.

"Peter, it's the mark... the mark of the beast, the one mentioned in Revelation."

"How do you know?"

Jack knowingly chuckled to himself and shook his head. "Oh, I know because I know this project like the back of my hand... no pun intended. I wrote it and created it, and it is already in testing as we speak. They rushed this one through, as I've never seen before. I was so excited about it because it was like my very own baby being birthed into the world. It's a brand-new advancement, which meant also for me that I too would become a sort after prize possession, so it was a real win-win for both parties."

"Sooo... what you're saying is that you have created the mark of the beast?" Peter said slowly, thinking about his question.

"Yes, the one mentioned in Revelation."

"Okay... so what exactly makes you think that this thing... this concept you're working on is the mark?"

"Well, firstly it looks so simple, innocent even, and to me it was a way to solve the problems in the world. It's a brilliant idea that would mean that our world is a safer place. Besides, the concept isn't entirely new—we've been using this technology on our pets and livestock to keep track of them. So I took a step further and applied the concept to human life."

49

"Right... go on."

"Well, we have so many problems in the world... like identity theft, monetary funds being stolen, credit cards, bank cards, licenses, or passports being lost or taken. This was the initial concern for our customer, but I took it further and suggested it's used to find people who have gone missing—children, the elderly, our armed forces, criminal tracking, identification, keyless entries. Also, for information storage, such as medications and health, which is brilliant for those who are unable to talk for themselves. There are numerous things that it is useful for, and I was completely thinking of helping our nation with safety, law enforcement, security, and justice. With the technology we have now, our satellite could track anyone. I mean, if I had this implant, I could be doing 140 miles per hour in a 40 zone and get pinned for it via the satellite. I could even start my own car or unlock my house door with my hand."

"You said implant—I thought you meant a mark?"

"No, sorry it's an implant, a very tiny microchip."

"But the Bible definitely says a mark."

"Well then, so would John have known what a microchip was back then?" Jack looked questioningly at Peter.

"Yes, I see your point."

Two black messenger demons were in hiding, crouching low in silence behind the TV cabinet, intently listening to the conversation. They weren't happy, "Not good, we must get word to the Master." one said to the other.

Jack continued. "Revelation says that no one can buy or sell unless they have this mark. They're not going to tattoo a number on your hand or forehead—that's way too primitive, and there's no need with the technology that we have now. It's designed for convenience and speed. For instance, when you go to a grocery store cash register, you will get your hand scanned and the amount will come straight out of your bank account, as it does now with your card. This replaces all cards. Its genius! However, it also means that if the implant is enforced and people refuse to have it, then they cannot buy and sell without it. Just like cash is now—

useless. Do you see where my concern is, Peter? Do you understand the parallel with the passage in Revelation? It is way too close for my comfort, it's got to be it."

"Yes, I see," Peter said as he pondered his next question and silently prayed for God's wisdom. The Holy Spirit was ministering to him and he could feel it.

Jack and Jenny sat in silence, with Jack occasionally looking downward and wringing his hands in turmoil.

"I have this on my shoulders," Jack said as he looked up with tears in his eyes and his brow deeply furrowed. His emotions overcame him. "What have I done? I have aided the enemy of God— I have been his tool to bring this into realization. I never thought of it being enforced upon people. I have created the very thing that could destroy millions of lives." Jack started to sob, placing his head in his hands, his body shaking and letting out deep cries of anguish. "I have to quit, I have to tell them I'm off the project."

Jenny cried also, seeing him in this state, holding Jack as wet tears flowed down both their faces.

Peter sat in silence, waiting until he felt a prompting from the Holy Spirit. He leaned in closer towards them. "Jack," he said, "don't you think God knew this?"

Jack looked at Peter questioningly, but said nothing.

"Don't you think that this was a part of God's plan? It is written, it's in front of you in the book of Revelation, and God himself wrote it. So why not you Jack? Why wouldn't God use one of his very own children to create this? If it was not you, it would have been someone else. If God hadn't wanted you to do this, he would have got you out of it whether you liked it or not."

Jack looked at Peter. "Do you think so?"

"Yes Jack, I *KNOW* so! Have you read the book of Esther?"

"No."

"Well, this is reminding me of that story, you might want to read it sometime. I won't go into detail but I think, who knows, maybe it was for a time such as this that you were placed into that project."

"I don't understand," Jack replied.

"You will when you read Esther. Don't do anything rash, do not quit your job. I will seek God on this and I want you both to do the same, okay. But don't go letting the guilt of the world fall upon your shoulders—there is no need. This is God's story and His plan. He knew all along what your destiny was. You have a calling on your life, Jack, a big one. I knew that the day I met you. I'm not sure yet what it is, but God is going to reveal it to you soon. Get into the word, pray, wait upon God and trust that He has everything in control, okay?"

"Okay," Jack replied hesitantly and clearly unconvinced.

"Jenny?" Peter looked at her and asked.

"Yes, we will," she said.

"Okay, let's pray!"

"Let's go," one demon hurriedly whispered in a faint, raspy voice. "We *must* warn the Master." The two messenger demons quietly started to creep out from behind the cabinet.

Seth and Gabe suddenly both heard the scraping sounds of long talons on the floorboards, along with the rustling of leathery wings. They knew instantly what the sound was as they spun around and dived, catching the two demons by surprise. They both pinned them tightly with their swords against their chests.

"These two *must* be vanquished—they have heard the conversation and will warn the others. We cannot afford *this* plan to be discovered." Gabe stated.

Seth agreed as they quickly plunged their swords into the two screaming black demons, finishing them.

CHAPTER NINE

L ora and Meg sat quietly in the schoolyard under a tree, eating their lunch.

"Hey, Meg, I'm having some really weird dreams lately, ever since we went and saw that fortune lady at the fair," Lora said.

"Yeah? Like what?" Meg replied inquisitively.

"Well, you know how she said that I used to be this princess in another life?"

"Yeah."

"It's all about that, like I'm there, living and doing what the Egyptians do. It's just really weird and I'm not sure if I like it."

"I think it would be cool. I wish I had a past life. I mean, you're learning how they live, what they did, I guess. I'm not sure if it's real though, it's probably just dreams. I wouldn't worry about it."

"Yeah, I guess, but the thing is that the other night there was this girl in my dreams and she was telling me she was my best friend. She too was dressed as a princess."

"WOW! What did she say?"

"Well, she said that I died when I was 17 years old and that she is so happy to see me again. It's weird. Oh yeah, and she said she wanted to meet with me again. It's sort of freaking me out."

"Hey go with it, it sounds like fun. What can it hurt? Besides, it's not real, they're just dreams. Just say that you want to meet with her and see where it goes. My mum knows a bit about this stuff. She said that her grandmother used to be into it. I'll ask her if you like. Just don't tell your dad though," she laughed.

"Yeah, that would freak him right out." Lora smiled.

Crystalyn and Rebellion sat attentively, listening to every word the girls were saying.

"Nice work," said Rebellion.

"I told you slow and steady reels them in. They are so predictable!" Crystalyn replied.

They both looked at each other and snickered, bearing sharp yellow fangs, their red eyes squinting as their black wings were unfurling and shaking with each rumble.

JACK WAS STILL NOT right in his emotions. He hadn't slept properly for weeks. He had headaches, his eyes were bloodshot, and he looked like an unshaven wreck.

He sat quietly at his desk but couldn't work as his heart just wasn't in it anymore. There was no drive, no more excitement, just pure dread. "What am I going to do?" he said aloud with his head in his hands.

Gabe and Seth stood nearby, their hearts going out to Jack, seeing him in his turmoil. As Jack sat silently in his chair, Gabe leaned over to him and whispered, "Just pray, Jack, pray." Jack breathed out a sigh and then started to whisper a very soft, faint prayer, but then stopped in silence.

"Pray Jack, come on," Seth whispered.

But Jack said nothing.

"HOW WAS SCHOOL TODAY, LORA?" Jim asked as they sat at the dinner table.

"Fine," she replied.

"Are you keeping up with your schoolwork?"

"Yes," Lora said as she secretly rolled her eyes and shoveled more potato mash into her mouth.

"That's good, because your studies are very important if you aim to get anywhere in this world."

Whilst her parents talked, Lora continued to eat her dinner quickly so she could leave the table and get up to her room and away from her boring father.

"May I be excused, please?" she asked politely.

"Sure," Bethany replied, "just leave your plate on the sink darling; I'll clean it up for you."

With that, she was bounding up the stairs into her room. *Finally*, she thought, *a bit of peace and quiet. Man, why do I have to have such a stiff, old-fashioned, boring family? It drives me crazy sometimes. Maybe I'll just go to bed early and try to meet Crystalyn tonight.* Lora read a book, then switched off the light. As soon as her head hit the pillow, she was asleep, dreaming.

In her dream, she was standing inside an enormous palace. She looked at her clothes and was wearing a tight-fitting light blue dress like an under slip with thin straps over the shoulders. It reached down to her ankles, and it felt very soft and flowing. She felt the weight of the chunky jewelry around her neck and her dark hair softly falling down around her shoulders. *This feels so real*, she thought.

"Ana!" she heard someone shout, "Ana, you came back." She looked around to where the voice was coming from and it was Crystalyn, the princess girl she had met previously in her dreams. Crystalyn wore a soft white flowing dress with a large yellow sash around her waist. Her hair was jet black and straight, with a gold band around her forehead. Her eyes were the deepest green with thick black kohl eyeliner, her lips were bright red, and she wore a magnificent golden and red gemstone collar around her neck. She was beautiful.

"Ana, I thought you would not return. I have waited for you," she said.

"I don't understand. My name is Lora… not Ana," Lora replied.

"In your world you may be Lora, but to me you will always be my best friend Ana… I can call you Lora if you wish?"

"Yes, please, it's too confusing," Lora responded meekly.

"We have much to catch up on. Come on, let's go out to the garden." On saying that, Crystalyn grabbed Lora's hand and lead her outside into the beautiful sunlit garden. They sat near a clear blue pool.

"You said I died when I was 17?" Lora asked.

"Yes, you drowned, just here in this pool," Crystalyn said.

"How? Couldn't I swim?"

Crystalyn laughed and replied, "Yes, silly, you could swim very well. I'm not sure how, but your father found you here lying face down, afloat. Your father was heartbroken. Oh, how I've missed you. It hasn't been the same since. I'm so glad you're back—we can now live together free in the universal conscience."

CHAPTER TEN

TUESDAY

"Hey Peter," Jack said, "thanks for coming over."

"No problem. How are you feeling?" Peter looked at him, shocked at his disheveled appearance.

"I have written my resignation."

"No... Jack?" Peter said in shock.

"I just can't do this any longer. I mean every phone call and meeting, I can't shake the feeling that I want out. Some days I feel physically sick just thinking about it. I really don't think I can do this, Pete! What if this is God's way of telling me to leave it," Jack responded, worried.

"Is that what you're really sensing or is this your head talking?"

"Maybe it's my head," Jack paused. "But I don't know what I'm thinking—I feel so torn. I can't tell if it's God or me. One minute I feel I *can* do this and the next I'm doubled over with anxiousness. I mean, what is that telling you? It can't be right... Right?"

"Listen, God will not give you something that He hasn't equipped you for. He is always with you to guide and help you fulfill His will for your life."

"How do I know it's His will and not just a massive mistake? That I've gone off track on my own tangent and created something I thought would be awesome, but is actually devastating... how do I know?"

"You know, deep down. Listen to your heart, not to what your head is telling you. Get your emotions out of it. I know you want to run and leave this behind you, but how can you? I know you Jack, if you left now you would always wonder."

"Would I... really? I think I would feel relieved! Anyway... why me? Why would God have me invent this, thinking that I was

57

changing the world for good and it turns out that it's the opposite?"

"No, you wouldn't feel relieved—you're not made like that. God created you for this—you may not see it, but I *know* in my heart that it's right. I've said it before, why *not* you? It was going to happen anyway, whether it was you or someone else. Think about that. Do you really know why God has placed you in this situation? I mean, come on Jack, who better placed than someone who knows the system intimately, who designed and built it, who knows its capabilities… along with its flaws?"

"I don't know. I just don't see how it can be what I'm supposed to be doing. I really think I should resign and leave this all behind me."

Gabe looked at Seth concerned and said, "He must not quit."

Seth paused for a moment before walking over to Peter and touched him gently on the shoulder, speaking into his spirit, coaxing him to continue to help encourage Jack to stay.

"Okay," Peter continued, "I fully understand what you're saying, but let me tell you this. We have such a short time here on earth—this time is like an interview for our eternity, so what we do here on earth counts. Sure, we can become a Christian and go to Heaven, but I want a 'well done, good and faithful servant' statement when I greet Jesus." Peter paused momentarily and changed his tact. "Jack, did you know that there are rewards and a hierarchy in Heaven?"

"No."

"Well, there is, and these high positions are not reserved for only people who are preachers or… volunteer aid workers. It's for those who fulfill their calling in their lives. Paul says in 1 Corinthians 9:24, 'Do you not know that in a race all the runners run, but only one gets the prize? Run in such a way as to get the prize'. So run your race to win.' And the last part of 1 Corinthians 9:25 says '… but we do it to get a crown that will last forever'."

Peter continued, "So this means that we all have our *own* race to run. Jesus didn't call us to *all* be preachers or like Mother

Teresa. Each of us has an individual purpose. God places this on our lives. For instance, for one person, it may be to be a great wife to her husband, mother to her children and to raise them in a godly way. For another, it may be to become a businessperson and help fund the Kingdom of God, or to adopt orphans, or become a teacher or a movie star and affect the film industry. It's individual, and God will show each one of us what He wants for our lives. However, we can hinder this with our own will, our own wants, or fears. We may not get the rewards in Heaven that we would have received if we had followed our calling. I think people get confused and assume that the pastors or missionaries will get the greatest rewards, but it's not so. Those who achieve their individual calling will get the rewards."

Peter took a deep breath before he made his next point. "Jack, God is making it very clear to you that *this* is where He wants you right now, so please do not listen to doubt or fear, because it could affect your calling. It is crucial at this point in time that you stay the course and complete what God has asked you to do. Because you actually don't know why He has you in this position, what if it's to do something great for His people?" He paused, looking solemn. "For I believe that if you intentionally refuse what God has called you to do, then it is the sin of disobedience... Jack please don't reject what God has asked of you."

"I see what you're saying," Jack said with emotion, "but how do I know that *this* is where I'm supposed to be? I have so much doubt, and I'm afraid that you are right... fear."

"You need to press into God and get the answer for yourself. I can't convince you, no one can... you have to get this from God. Promise me you will stop the turmoil and indecisiveness and simply go to God for the answer. Your future is riding on it."

"I will."

THAT NIGHT, Peter sat quietly in his couch and prayed for his friend, hoping that he had taken his advice.

· · ·

THE ANGELS also hoped that Jack had listened. They looked at each other, "He cannot falter... for this is hinging upon him," said Seth firmly.

"SO YOU'RE TELLING me that this stuff could be real?" Meg asked.

"Yes Meg, I mean, really real," Lora replied.

"Mm, well, I did ask my mum, and she said that she used to play around with it but didn't take it seriously. She told me that it wasn't real, just pretend and it's really only your imagination."

"Well, I think it's real. It feels real, and it's getting *more real* to me. I go there every night now and Crystalyn and I, we are such good friends, like you and me Meg. I can tell her everything."

"So you now have two best friends, one real one and one imaginary," Meg chided, but a little jealous.

"Meg you're my number one friend and Crystalyn... well, I don't think it's just in my head. Why don't you try it and see for yourself?"

"How am I going to do that? I can't just make up someone. I don't have a vivid imagination like you do, Lora."

"Well, I don't know then. I guess... maybe just ask for a friend before you go to bed or something, maybe it will just happen."

"Maybe," Meg replied, but she was not keen about the idea.

WEDNESDAY

Jack had pondered what Peter had said. He had looked up the scriptures and spent time alone in his office, not doing work but simply sitting quietly and reassessing everything. However, he struggled to shake the ominous feeling of guilt that hovered over him like a persistent vulture. He decided to re-read his resignation letter.

Gabe and Seth stood beside him, looking concerned at what Jack was contemplating.

They stood by and watched as he tweaked some wording, then

moved the mouse curser over the 'Send' button on his email. Jack hesitated.

Gabe quickly glanced at Seth and slowly shook his head, as he said, "No… don't do this, Jack."

Seth moved swiftly, his sword lighted with fire as he plunged the blade into the wireless router at the very moment Jack went to hit 'Send.'

Jack suddenly saw the words 'Internet connection is down' appear on his computer screen. "Oh great, my day just gets better." He said despondently as he got up to check the router. He sat there for a further 10 minutes trouble shooting the error before giving up and going downstairs into the living room.

Seth removed his sword from the router and they both followed Jack. They watched as Jack picked up his Bible. Seth prodded. "Pray Jack, you will get the answer you need, just pray."

Jack felt the prompting and his lips began to move, "Father, I feel so terrible and so guilty for what I have done. I feel helpless and stuck. I need you to guide my steps, to give me strength and help me continue. I can't do this without you. I need you more now than I ever have. I have unknowingly created something that will adversely change the world, I feel like I'm sending people to their death. Please help me God, please come to me and give me direction. Show me your will because I'm so, so lost and don't understand. I need you to tell me if I'm to *stay* or to *leave*, please help me… just help me God."

As Jack sat there, he couldn't physically see the results of his prayer at work and the many iridescent angels who were dropping down into his room, ministering to him, giving him comfort, peace, and imparting wisdom and strength. Their massive wings were enveloping him, their glory radiating and emanating through Jack's body.

Jack just sat quietly in silence, waiting. Slowly he could feel a sensation flowing through him, a shift in his emotions, a strengthening but also a calmness and peace that he had never experienced. Then suddenly, clear strong words broke through, a stirring deep within his heart, as he had never felt before. He listened, and he heard.

"I love you, Jack. My ways are not your ways. Just trust in me and *stay*. Proverbs 3:5."

"Proverbs 3:5, Proverbs 3:5," he repeated as he picked up his Bible and quickly opened it to the passage. "Trust in the Lord with all your heart and lean not on your own understanding," he read. "Wow, I think I just heard from God." His excitement and joy rising as he kept re-reading the passage. "Okay Lord, I've heard you… I'll stay! Thank you, Father. Hey, Jenny," he called.

Jenny came racing in from the kitchen calling, "What's wrong?"

"Not wrong, but right. I just heard God speak to me," Jack said in his excitement.

"What? How?"

"I know, it's amazing, I've never had this happen before, maybe because I have never given Him the chance and listened. But I did, and it was so clear, like someone just spoke right into me… right through me even." Jack was speaking a million miles an hour, expressing his excitement.

"Well, what did He say?" she said excitedly.

"He told me that He loved me, to trust Him and to stay, and then I got this scripture. Look, here it is," talking elatedly as he pointed to the passage in the Bible.

"Wow, that's awesome, and Jack you look different, lighter or something." Jenny looked at his face.

"I am Jen, I feel it, I know now that God is in control of this situation, there are no coincidences, and I *am* in His will. It's such a relief, I feel like a weight has been lifted off me, and you know what the exciting part is?"

"What?" She smiled.

"Finding out what He has in store for us."

CHAPTER ELEVEN

FRIDAY

"Thank you," Jack said with a smile as the waitress at Betty's Cafe put the two coffees in front of Jack and Peter.

"Well, you're looking better. I have to admit, I was very worried about you. You looked terrible." Peter smiled.

"Thanks Pete," Jack chuckled, "I feel much better... but I still have my occasional moments where doubt creeps in."

"I've been praying that God would give you some direction."

"Well, it worked. He has." Jack beamed.

"And?"

"I took your advice and prayed about it and had an amazing experience. I heard God tell me to stay." Jack grinned. "But that still doesn't make me feel comfortable about the whole idea. My head is still telling me to leave."

"That just sounds like fear. I've learned to always go with the last thing God told me. If He said stay... then stay." He smiled reassuringly.

"Thanks for your advice." Jack continued, feeling a renewed sense of clarity. "I guess now I'm looking at it this way. It may not be the actual I-Chip itself, but what it represents. I mean, once everyone has the implant, then how much easier is it to enforce a one world government regime and religion. All money will be electronic and if you don't have the I-Chip, then you can't buy or sell, no one will accept any other form of currency. They could easily just wipe your bank funds to zero and you couldn't do anything about it."

"So you think it's still the mark?"

"Maybe not the I-Chip itself... I mean... what may happen is that the Antichrist will request everyone to add another number to their personal identification on the chip to verify that they are in allegiance to him. For instance... I don't know... your I-Chip ID may be 12345, then if you accept the mark, they add the 666 on the end of your ID or something. I'm really not sure, but I do feel the I-Chip will be the vessel in which it is enforced."

"Yes, you could be right, but our hope is that we, the saints, will not have to endure."

"Mm, I hope so because this thing is going full steam ahead, Peter. We already have families volunteering to be the first to receive it. I mean they can't wait."

"Really?"

"Yes!" Jack paused and quickly changed the subject, as he didn't want to think any further about it. "But, on a lighter note, well, I've really been studying, I mean like never before. God has given me this, um, I don't know, an unquenchable thirst to get into His Word. I keep having this urge to read about the end times, the book of Revelation and other scriptures related to the return of Jesus."

"That's great!"

"Well, I have a question for you—I can't actually find where in the Bible it says that the church will be removed before the Antichrist takes control. I've looked repeatedly and maybe I'm just missing it completely. I mean, it must be in there for people to believe it, right?"

"Well, actually there is no scripture that specifically states that the church will be taken out *beforehand*, however they do allude to it. Many Theologians have studied the scriptures to back up this theory. Namely, in 2 Thessalonians chapter 2 verse 6-7, Paul says that there is a restrainer who is stopping the Antichrist from being revealed and once he is removed, then the Antichrist will become the world ruler. The belief is that this restrainer is the Holy Spirit and therefore the removal of the Holy Spirit will also mean the removal... or rapture of the church." He paused briefly. "It is in the character of God to deliver His own from the greatest times of trial. You take, for example, Lot, Rahab, Noah. Romans 5:9 says, 'Since we have now been justified by His blood, how much more shall we be saved from God's wrath through Him' and 1 Thessalonians 1: 10 'and to wait for His Son from heaven, whom

He raised from the dead—Jesus, who rescues us from the coming wrath'."

"Well, sounds like there's evidence to back it up—it just doesn't stand out. I'll have to study these further," Jack said as he busily scribbled the scriptures down on his notepad.

"I'll drop over some books you might like to read. It's a fiction series about the rapture occurring and what happens to the people left here on earth. They are pretty much aligned with what we have been taught."

"They sound great, thanks."

"This should get Jack researching things," said Gabe.

"Yes." Seth replied. "We need to speak into Jack's heart and mind and let him know what the reality of all of this is. Let's keep our eyes open to counteract the enemy. They won't be happy when Jack finds out what really is going on."

"Yes, lives are at stake here so we have to be vigilant."

"YOU CALLED TO SEE ME, MASTER?" Crystalyn said, bowing low and squirming uncomfortably amongst the hordes of other demons gathered in front of a colossal beast sitting on a large ornate throne.

The creature's eyes emanated pure evil and hatred. His wolf like muzzle sneered at the demons standing before him—his teeth were like long thin spikes ready to impale their prey. The gnarled horns were thick, sweeping backward across his skull. Scars covered his body, stemming from great battles, both with angelic hosts but also with his own kind. He was a force to be reckoned with, a malicious being that every demon in the region feared. He was Major General Lothar, the commander of the region's army.

"What is your progress?" Lothar asked.

"I have the girl and it is only a matter of time Master, everything is going to plan," Crystalyn responded meekly.

"What form have you become this time?"

"I have befriended her as an Egyptian princess, my Lord." He smiled and bowed low again.

"Good," Lothar grinned, very pleased with Crystalyn's response. "Now what is this I hear of Jack Daley?"

"I know nothing of Jack Daley, sir!" Crystalyn replied, looking around nervously in case it was something he was actually supposed to know.

OOOOMPH! A tiny demon with rodent teeth landed in a crumpled heap, wincing before Lothar. Snickers were heard from the hordes of where he was pushed. Shaking with fear, he stood up to address the General. "Jack Daley will not be a problem," the small ugly frame wheezed out, "he is just curious and will not interfere with our plans."

"LIES!" Lothar roared, his voice vibrating and shaking the cold stone walls, sending the dark crowded room shuffling backward in fear. "You know nothing of the saints, you imbecile," he bellowed. "Curiosity is never peaked without a reason—the enemy has been working. Don't be so lax and get out there and do your job." He grabbed the small gangly demon tightly around the neck, slowly squeezing him until his red bulging eyes were frantic, and threw him back into the horde with a thud. Demons went tumbling, screaming, and fluttering around in a panic. Chaos and fear had erupted in the rooms of the abandoned pump station.

THAT NIGHT, Jack was sleeping so peacefully, until it stealthily entered the room. It slowly crept up and started baring its full weight down upon Jack's body, willing him to die, crushing the air out of him slowly but intentionally.

Jack gasped and started trying to fight back in confusion, half-dreaming and half-conscious as he struggled to understand what was going on. *Was this a nightmare?* he thought. He could feel his assailant smothering him, but couldn't move. His eyes were shut but dancing rapidly—he felt paralyzed. His limbs would not respond. He tried calling out, but couldn't speak—its weight was intense and meaningful. He felt the fear, but he could not wake up. He knew he was in the realm of lucid dreaming, but could not break out of it. The fear was intense—he could feel it, but had no power to overcome it.

It continued to crush and smother its victim mercilessly. It grinned with pleasure, seeing the desperation and terror etched all over Jack's face. Its talons sank in deep and curled around Jack's larynx, its other slimy six arms wrapped tightly around his body like a boa constrictor's vice like grip.

J-J-Jesus, Jack tried hard to whisper, but nothing came of it. He couldn't speak, he couldn't move, but he felt every ounce of the evil force bearing down on his chest.

Wake up, wake up. Jack willed himself to consciousness but failed. *Wake up!* He felt powerless, caught in the twilight zone. He was trapped in this hallucinogenic state of terror that was colliding with the natural dimension. The entity pushed down, squeezing tight, gripping harder and harder.

"What are you up to, Jack?" Its deathly voice rasped with hate and curiosity.

Jack's heart raced in terror as he heard those words project directly into his mind—he couldn't speak, he was mute, and it was all over him, upon him and in him. Its black limbs clasping, locked through his torso, he could see it all in his dreamlike state with his eyes closed... his fear escalated. He squeaked out a sound, but it gripped harder.

Help me, help me... Jesus, Jack thought, but the words could not pass through his lips. He started gasping and choking—he could feel his heart racing and hear its loud echoing, the blood pounding in his ears.

"What are you looking for, Jack?" it asked again, releasing its grip around his throat just enough for an answer.

His fear intensified. He still couldn't speak, he couldn't move, he couldn't breathe, he tried, and tried and tried... until he finally broke through, "JESUS!" he yelled.

"Stop pursuing this," it screamed into his conscience, as it dropped its grasp and quickly glided back through the wall into the black night.

Jack instantly became wide awake. He saw the dark shadow silently leaving.

Seth and Gabe urgently entered the room with their swords drawn to find Jack gasping and holding his throat.

"What's wrong?" Jenny stirred sleepily, "I thought I heard you yell something."

"Sorry, I didn't mean to wake you. It's nothing sweetie… just a bad dream," Jack responded, but he knew it wasn't. He lay awake for hours, thinking about what had just happened.

CHAPTER TWELVE

I t was 2 am. Crystalyn spoke deep into Lora's mind, whilst Rebellion looked on in awe at the mastery at hand.

"I like how you do this," Rebellion stated with eagerness. "So, what are we doing with her tonight?" he asked.

"As always," Crystalyn spoke confidently and authoritative as if speaking to his protégé, "we go very slowly so not to spark any skepticism or confusion. We don't want to frighten her away but reel her in so she trusts completely—it's all about timing." He grinned, showing his row of thin sharp teeth.

Lora was dreaming deeply. She and her princess friend Crystalyn were sitting beside the shimmering clear pool talking.

"So, is Jesus real then?" Lora asked.

"Yes, he is a highly ascended master who came to show us the path to a higher consciousness. He came to teach us how to redeem ourselves by discovering the Kingdom of God within us."

"But he's God's Son right, like my dad tells the congregation?"

"Well, yes and no, you see, that's a fabrication that the world has been led to believe. We are actually all gods ourselves. There is not one God, but many, many gods. We all aspire to gain elevation into a higher natural state. Besides, don't believe that nonsense. How can there be just *one* when we are *all* gods?" Crystalyn emphasized.

"I thought that's how it was—I mean, that's all I've grown up knowing. That's all I've been taught," Lora responded, confused.

"Well, you've been misled Lora, you need to think for yourself now." Crystalyn sighed sympathetically, "I really feel for the poor souls who have been indoctrinated with these kinds of lies. They are chained and bound and cannot be free until they know the real truth," Crystalyn said passionately and convincingly.

"Wow! I would never have known," Lora said, stunned but admiring her friend's deep knowledge.

Rebellion smiled at Crystalyn in wonder. "You're so smooth," he praised.

"I know, but they make it so easy. They will believe *absolutely anything*," he snickered.

"HI PETE, it's Jack. When you get this message, well that's if you have some time, can you please call me? I have some questions. Oh, and I hope you're having a great time at your son's place, too. Enjoy your new grandkid. See you later."

Jack hung up the phone and went about his day, still disturbed by what happened the other night. He desperately wanted to talk to Peter about it, but didn't want to spoil his family holiday.

"YOU SHOULD SEE him work Master, it's amazing at what can be achieved in one night," Rebellion praised as he and Crystalyn both stood in front of Lothar.

"So Crystalyn, obviously you're making progress with the girl?"

"Yes, my sire, she is coming along nicely. I have now seeded doubt in her mind regarding her beliefs and will now attempt to distance her from her friends and family. She will trust only me for advice, my Lord."

"Good, good." Lothar grinned, liking what he was hearing. "The plan seems to be coming along nicely then." He stated as his immense gaze looked over his gaggling hoard. "Has Jack Daley's enthusiasm been quashed?"

A small messenger meekly stepped forward. "Sir," it bowed low, "we are making every attempt to dissuade him from doing any further research on the subject. We have now made two attempts, but have to time it when the Guardians are not watching."

"Well… try harder. I'm hearing that he still has his nose in *that* book," he spat with venom. "And that the hosts are eagerly encouraging him to do so."

"We have everything under control sir, it will be fine."

"IT WON'T *BE* FINE," Lothar yelled as he smashed his fist down and picked up his sword and swung it furiously, cracking it hard on the stone floor. The hoard scampered and scrambled backwards in fear of retribution. "You obviously do not understand, you imbecile. Something is up and I want to know what it is and why. Do you HEAR ME?" Lothar's voice vibrated, shaking the cold stone walls, his rank breath rushing out like a gale-force wind, making the messenger teeter backwards. "It's important to us because it's IMPORTANT TO THEM… GET IT?"

"Y-Y-Yes S-sir," the timid messenger stuttered in fear.

"GO NOW!"

The messenger didn't waste any time getting out of his presence. He flew out and landed in a distant tree, trembling before he could compose himself and fly further onward to Evensmore to deliver his dispatch.

It was 2.30 am. Again, Lora was deeply dreaming, sitting with Crystalyn under a tree on a hill in a lush, grass-filled field. She could feel the wind gently caressing her cheeks.

"The fortune teller at the fair, you know… Carla. How did she know so much about me?" Lora asked.

"We all know everything about everyone—it's the universal mind. It's all knowing and all powerful. Carla has the special gift of being able to tap into it and gain the information that she needs."

"Wow, I wish I could do that."

"You can learn—I can teach you. You can also command the universe too—its power can give you the desires of your heart," Crystalyn responded happily with beautiful translucent green eyes glistening.

"I'd love that," Lora stated excitedly.

Rebellion sat and listened intently, learning the ways of Crystalyn, the familiar spirit, demon of disguise. He waited until Crystalyn had finished his night's work before he spoke.

"I think I could start doing that."

"Just like I showed you, it's easy. Just do it slowly and build trust."

"The spiel about the fortune teller, that was gold," Rebellion sniggered with excitement.

"I know. I love telling them it's a *special gift*. Stupid fools," Crystalyn scoffed, extremely happy with his night's efforts.

JACK LEFT the house and went for a walk out onto his property. He hadn't spoken to Jenny about what had been happening, as he didn't want to scare her, but he desperately needed to speak with Peter. He tried Peter's mobile phone again and sighed in dismay when it went straight to the message service.

"Hi Pete, it's Jack again, listen I *really* need to talk with you. I can't explain over the phone, but some weird stuff has been happening... and well... I don't know what to do. Please call me when you get a chance. I'll talk to you soon." He sighed. "Hopefully!" Jack said after he ended the call.

"Jack, I'm worried about you," Jenny said, as he entered the house. "You look terrible!"

"I've just been having trouble sleeping—it's nothing to worry about."

"What is it? Work?"

"It's a combination of things. I'll be okay. I just need to get back into my sleeping pattern again. Don't worry," he said as he hugged her and kissed her forehead. "Now, how about a coffee?"

IT WAS SATURDAY NIGHT, and Meg was sleeping over at Lora's house. They did this once a month and alternated between each other's houses. As usual, they had stayed up very late into the early hours of the morning and had both fallen asleep exhausted after watching a movie marathon.

Lora was fitfully dreaming and making funny noises. It woke Meg up. She looked over at her friend and her skin prickled as she felt her hair stand on end. She was being watched. Something malevolent was staring back at her. She couldn't make it out, but she felt its eyes boring into her soul and it was not welcoming. It gave her deep shivers, so she quickly snuggled back under the covers in fear and pulled the blanket over her head, hoping that it would provide protection. She was terrified—the feeling was so strong it freaked her out and she lay awake for the rest of the night, not game to move an inch.

JACK ALSO WAS LAYING in fear, unable to sleep, waiting again for the assailant, but to his relief, it didn't come this night.

Morning came around quickly and Jack threw himself into his work. He hadn't picked up the Bible since the first night of the encounter and was in trepidation about the warning that he received.

Seth spoke. "He needs to learn how to handle this."

"He is still new, and he doesn't understand yet. He hasn't been taught, however, this *will* strengthen him." Gabe responded.

"Agree… Peter will be home soon and will help him understand. In the meantime, we will be on the lookout."

"DID YOU FIND OUT ANYTHING?" Lothar's deep, menacing voice rasped.

The meagre messenger again stood timidly, shaking before the grand beast. "The nocturnal spirit hasn't yet succeeded in its mission," it said meekly, "but I'm sure it will very, very soon," the messenger exclaimed.

"It better, else you both will no longer be living in this realm," Lothar sneered, growing impatient. "I have also been notified that Jophiel is in the region."

"It still should be fine Master, don't worry we have it under control." It squeaked timidly.

"Do you even understand who I speak of, small spirit?" Lothar challenged, his fists clenched tightly with anger. "Jophiel is only sent when there is a vital mission to accomplish. SO, DON'T YOU DARE tell me that it's under control when I know what *this* host of Heaven can do to us. DO YOU UNDERSTAND?" He roared with tornado like breath rushing through his fierce jowls. "FIND OUT NOW." He screamed as he smashed his giant curved sword down, sending sparks across the room.

The messenger quickly left the building and flew straight away to deliver its report.

"You must make progress," it squeaked at the nocturnal spirit that was hiding in the blackness of a dark cavern in the daylight hours. "Lothar is very, *very* angry with us, you need to find out what's going on."

"Hey Lora, were you having a bad dream the other night when I stayed over?" Meg asked.

"Um, I can't remember. No, I don't think so. I was just meeting up with Crystalyn again like I do every night."

"Oh, okay."

"Why do you ask?"

"No reason, you were just making funny noises. I thought you were having a nightmare, that's all."

"No, I sleep really well every night and dream so clearly." She beamed.

"Really?"

"Yeah, why do you sound so surprised?"

"Well, do you feel something watching you at night?" Meg shifted uncomfortably.

"No, do you?"

"Umm, maybe it was just my imagination then. I thought I felt something else in the room the other night, that's all."

"I've never felt it and I'm sure if there was something weird Crystalyn would tell me."

"Okay sure. Let's go get a milkshake," Meg responded quickly to change the subject and headed towards Betty's Café.

"We must rid ourselves of her, she could jeopardize everything." Crystalyn looked over at Rebellion, very concerned.

"How can she jeopardize anything? She's just a stupid girl."

"Don't ever underestimate the humans' bond, numskull," he spat venomously. "I've had many failures because of a nosey friendship getting in the way. She sensed me the other night, she was looking right at me... so just shut up and do as I say if you want to continue to learn this craft," he said with hatred. "Besides, if we stuff this up, we will be no longer if Lothar gets a hold of us. Now get to work," he ordered.

J ack had lain awake in the night hours until his eyes finally succumbed to the drowsiness.

Gabe saw him first and chased the scrawny black demon down the stairs into Jack's office. Seth was close behind in hot pursuit.

It was 2.37 am when it attacked. This time, it wanted an answer and Jack could feel in his dreaming state the hatred and determination emanating from it. The entity wound its several limbs around Jack's body and again squeezed his larynx tight. This time he could feel its long talons biting into him, boring into his very soul. The pressure was intense, stronger than the other times, but again he felt paralyzed, unable to move a muscle—his voice constricted. He felt as though he was again choking, trying to scream out.

"What are you after Jack, what are you looking for in the book?" it probed, projecting its voice into Jack's mind.

SETH AND GABE danced around the desk, the tiny demon just keeping out of harm's way, dodging, flitting and fluttering around the room, its small wings beating rapidly to avoid contact. They were trying to swat it with their mighty swords.

JACK AGAIN WAS STRUCK with fear, but also confused about the question. He started to panic. The massive entity squeezed him harder. He felt as though he was going to explode under the sheer pressure.

Wake up, wake up Jack, c'mon, wake up. Again, he willed himself to regain a conscious state. He saw the spirit, its blackness enveloped him, hovered over him and thoroughly encased him. He was smothering under the heaviness of it resting on his chest.

The fear in him rose to new heights. He tried again to scream, but there was nothing. It had a grip on his larynx, and he could do nothing. *Please, Jesus, Jesus, Jesus.* He repeated over and over loudly in his mind, willing the words to come out of his mouth. Caught between the two realms, he couldn't escape.

IT DANCED, it flitted and leered at them. But Seth and Gabe just couldn't grasp a hold of it. It was always just out of their reach.

THE LARGE ENTITY GREW IMPATIENT. "I need to know what you're looking for. Why are you so consumed with Revelation?" Its rasping voice reverberated loudly throughout Jack's thoughts.

Jack squirmed, he tried to open his eyes. He yearned, pushed, and tried to make himself wide-awake—he had to fight this thing, and this had to stop. His life and his sanity depended on it. Suddenly, he broke through just enough to make a loud muffled cry.

GABE HEARD it first and flew with all his force upwards towards Jack's room. Seth followed and both of them ploughed through the floorboards and slammed hard into the dark being, knocking it off Jack and tumbling onto the floor. Its several arms grappled, scratching and clawing as Seth held it down, his sword to its throat, ready to slice.

Jack gasped and came out of his hallucinogenic state. He got straight up, ran down the stairs, and fell on his knees and wept, shaking with fear. The sweat was pouring off him.

Jenny was still upstairs, peacefully sleeping.

"What are you doing here?" Gabe demanded of the captive entity. "Why have you come?"

"I should be the one asking *you* that," it spat. "Why are such high-ranking angels guarding this mortal? Why is *he* so impor-

77

tant?" it hissed. "One might think there is more to his destiny than we know?" It smirked.

Gabe and Seth both looked at each other. Seth spoke as he pushed his sword deeper into its skin, slowly cutting its putrid epidermis. "Tell us what you are after?"

"My Master is simply curious why Jack is so consumed in reading the book."

"He's simply curious, just like any *other* saint who wants to read our Lord's Word," Gabe responded sternly.

The demon squirmed uncomfortably at that thought. "But it's *not* just like anyone else, is it? Why would two lieutenants from *Jophiel's* regiment be guarding this man, unusual don't you think?" It leered knowingly. "Obviously it *is* something, isn't it?" It grinned maliciously. "You *are* up to something... I wouldn't be messing with *my* Master's plans if I were you. I've seen many members of your pathetic army slain by him."

"Shut it," Gabe said impatiently. "If you have nothing more to say, then we will finish you and your silly little messenger spirit."

"He'd be long gone by now," it sneered. "You will never win this. You should quit now and simply give up—you are all doomed," it ranted in a frenzy of hatred whilst Seth held it down tight. "We will win, we will get far more souls than you, you just wait and see, you just *wait* and se—"

Seth cut it off as he plunged the shining sword through the assailant. He was finished.

"Jack, I got home late last night. Are you alright?" Peter said over the phone.

"Pete, I need to talk to you straight away."

"Okay, I'll see you at Betty's in 20 minutes."

Meg's mother Patty was serving up scrambled eggs on toast for breakfast. "What's happening at school today?"

"We've got the sporting event on. I'm aiming to beat Lora this time." She grinned.

"Good for you… you are a fast runner."

"Yeah, but Lora is faster though." She giggled.

"How is she anyway?"

"It is weird mum, she's dreaming of this friend all the time, and it's making me feel uneasy."

"They are just dreams honey, it's all harmless."

"I guess you're right, they're just dreams," she sighed. "Anyway, I had better go—we are going to jog to school together to warm up. Wish me luck." She beamed.

JACK TOLD PETER EVERYTHING. His emotions flooded his sentences, and he could hardly contain himself.

"I'm so sorry, Jack. I wish I got your messages sooner. Tyler, the little rascal," he giggled, "threw my phone into the pool. I simply didn't bother getting a new one or even thought to check my message service."

"Well, it's been terrible. I don't know what to do, I can't sleep, and I don't know when it's going to happen again."

"Mmm it's strange. I have heard of this but never experienced it myself. It's obviously wanting something, or trying to stop you doing something." He pondered on this. "You said it spoke?"

"Yes, it asked me why I was consumed with reading Revelation."

"That's interesting, keep digging Jack, it's trying to stop you from finding something."

"But what? What do I have, or what am I doing? I'm really frightened Pete, I'm frightened to go to sleep, for my family… for me. I mean, I thought I was going to die the other night. It's so crazy, I don't even believe in this stuff."

"Do you believe the Bible is God's Word?"

"Yes," he sighed, frustrated.

"Well, you can't believe in some of the Bible and not the other —it doesn't work like that! How can you *not* believe in the demonic? Jesus cast demons out of people. He also commanded

His disciples to do the same. The Bible says that we do not war against flesh and blood but the spiritual realm."

"I guess… I've just not really thought about it. It certainly wasn't taught in our church back in the city. I'm not big on fiction and that's what it seems like, just fairy tales about ghosts and goblins. Besides… I'm so exhausted and feel really angry that this is all happening," Jack sighed and continued, "and I don't know what to think. I just know what I'm experiencing feels so real."

"Well, Jack, I'm telling you now, it's real. There are angels and demons, and there is a battle waging. Don't be so blind to go through life as a Christian thinking that this isn't true. Jack, *WE* live in the fantasy world, we are blinded to the spiritual realm, but it is there. It's the real world and you're getting a glimpse." He paused. "We need to pray for your protection and bind up the enemy—they do not want you to find something. I just don't know what it is yet."

"Me neither, I'm simply reading the Bible for goodness' sakes."

LOTHAR WAS ANGRY… very angry. "Banished, BANISHED? Another one of *mine* gone!" he ranted. The small messenger standing in front of him quivered at his response. "Keep trying to dissuade him, use what you can," Lothar spat, defeated in disgust as he walked out of the dark, cold room.

JACK WAS ALONE in the house, and he opened his Bible for the first time in weeks.

"Good." Seth said, "we need to keep encouraging him to seek the truth. The plan depends on it."

Gabe watched over Jack's shoulder as he skimmed through the Bible pages listlessly, a little despondent and lost. Gabe reached forward and, with a quick flick of his finger, flipped the pages open to Revelation.

Jack started to read.

C rystalyn hovered over Lora in her dreams, beckoning her to go into a deeper, subconscious state. His princess form took her to the blue pond again, and they sat peacefully dipping their feet at the cool water's edge.

"What is my purpose?" Lora asked earnestly.

"Your purpose is to help others and to assist me in creating peace and unity in this township."

Crystalyn continued to speak into Lora's mind and she believed every word.

THERE WAS NO VISIBLE MOON; the clouds were thick and blanked out any speck of light that attempted to peek through from the night sky. The demons loved it, and this atmosphere was exactly what they savored.

JACK WAS RESTLESS. He tossed, turned, and tried to ignore the slight lump in the mattress. He laid wide-awake, waiting for sleep to overtake him and when it finally did, it had only felt like moments. He awoke with a start, jerking upright as he heard something downstairs.

He checked Jenny; she was still sleeping peacefully, as he gently pulled back the bedcovers and stood quietly, unmoving, not breathing, but intently listening.

He heard it again.

Someone was in the house, he knew it—he felt his skin prickle and the sudden rush of adrenaline pulse through his system. He could hear his heart rate thumping inside his head as he slowly crept out the bedroom door. He walked cautiously towards the kid's rooms and peered through each of their doors to ensure they were safely sleeping. Before leaving Matthew's room, he quietly reached around and grabbed the baseball bat that sat just behind the door. He slowly descended the stairs, armed and ready.

Suddenly, he heard the noise again, but this time something fell onto the floor with a loud clattering. He waited with the sensation of complete fear clasping his chest—he raised his bat, ready for the swing. He would do anything to protect and defend his family.

PETER WOKE WITH A JOLT. He felt a sudden pressure to pray for Jack. Quickly, he scrambled out of bed in obedience and fell desperately onto his knees. He interceded for something he didn't understand.

JACK'S FOOT stepped off the last stair and landed on the floorboards below—it loudly creaked. He suddenly froze and took a scant breath, listening and waiting, hoping that it hadn't given his position away to the intruder.

He heard the noise again.

He reached around and fumbled for the light, but as his fingers flicked the switch, the bulb brightly sparked, popped, and blew out, leaving him in complete darkness. His hair bristled… he could feel them coming towards him with a rush.

PETER CONTINUED to kneel at his bedside and pray. He didn't understand what it was about, however, he could feel the sheer urgency.

JACK WAS HIT in the chest with full force. As he staggered backwards, he swung his bat hard, but connected with nothing. Swiftly, he was hit from the back and shoved forcefully forward, smashing into a cupboard, rocking the contents inside. He fell onto his knees and fumbled in the darkness for his bat. He grasped it and started again to swing wildly at the blackness that surrounded him. He felt fear like never before—the atmosphere was thick and heavy with an invisible evil force. This time he could hear them… but it wasn't anything human.

PETER CRIED OUT TO GOD, desperately interceding for whatever was happening to Jack. He prayed and prayed… and prayed.

THE ROOM WAS full of black demons, swooping upon Jack, taunting him, and pushing him onto the floor. One grabbed a Bible off the couch and ripped its pages out, scattering them across the room.

Another threw a lamp at Jack, hitting him hard in the shoulder.

Several jumped upon him, weighing him down. He fell hard, hitting his head on the hardwood floorboards. His head was pinned, and his cheek was pressed firm, crushed on the rigid boards beneath. "Leave it alone Jack, we *will* kill you." He felt the hot breath against his ear.

Seth and Gabe were experiencing their own traumas. They had stayed close to Jack, however, had been separated in the fight. Jack was over the other side of the room unprotected, whilst they were staring at three enormous beings.

The largest of the three held his sword ready, its sharp steel blade was curved like a large sickle, and its jeweled handle beautifully glinted in the night, obscuring its bloodied intent.

They all stared at each other, none willing to make the first move.

. . .

Peter continued to pray passionately, "God, I don't know what's happening, but please protect Jack. Keep him and his family from harm."

Jophiel and Chale had heard the cry. They launched into full flight, and their army's best were close behind.

Jack forced himself back onto his feet. He continued to swing violently, and he sent a glass vase smashing to the floor in his aggressive defense. He could hear the laughter from his unseen assailants and felt the demonic whirlwind encircling and pressing into him. The fear rose in his throat—he did not know how to defend himself against the unseen.

Again, he felt the powerful attack from the back, pushing him forcefully forward into the wall. Again, he felt the hot, coarse breath against his ear. "Stop seeking and leave it alone." Its foul breath lingered in the air.

Seth made the first move, like lightening he dove low and hard, sliding across the polished floor underneath the three massive beings' trunk like legs, to arise swiftly behind them, taking them completely off guard. They didn't even have time to take a swing. Two dark beasts lurched around to defend themselves, whilst the other made his attack on Gabe. Their swords clashed and sparked. The battle was on.

Jophiel and Chale could see the small town in the far distance. They both looked at each other with concern.

"We have to make it before he is hurt... or worse." Jophiel yelled with apprehension. Their wings were flat against their backs; they were at full speed, like hot blazing comets piercing through the cold blackness before them.

· · ·

JACK COULD FEEL the weight bearing down on him. He was beyond fear—the paralyzing panic engulfed him like an icy liquid pulsating through his veins. He was drenched in sweat, his jaw was tight, his breathing was rapid, and his heart thudded fiercely in his chest.

"Stop reading the book." It again rasped in his ear.

Gabe was fast and had already maimed his attacker. He left him lying on the floor writhing in agony from his missing leg, arm, and wing.

Seth had only one attacker left. The other was now simply a cloud of thick gray smoke swirling in the tumultuous dark evil swarm.

Gabe ran towards Jack to pick off the black hellish demons holding him down.

"Use your authority, Jack." He cried.

Through his fear-ridden mind, Jack had faintly heard something.

"Do what Peter taught you," Gabe again shouted as he continued to sweep back and forth with his sword, cutting and slashing torsos and wings, smashing through the tornado of blackness.

Jack heard it clearly this time, and he remembered. "In the name of Jesus," he shouted, "I command you to leave my house now."

The sudden rush of the demonic exit was like a vacuum sucking the air out in an atomic blast. As the hordes of demons were leaving the house, Chale, Jophiel and their mighty armies descended with a loud war cry echoing through the darkness. Their thundering wings resounded through the cool night air, their radiating light pierced through the darkness as they sent terror into their enemy. Not all escaped to tell of the tale.

PETER FELT the urgency suddenly dissipate; he hesitated before he picked up the phone.

. . .

"WELL DONE. YOU SAVED HIM." Jophiel commended Gabe and Seth as his army continued scouting the area for more of the enemy. Some were still chasing after demons, streaking through the night sky in hot pursuit to claim victory.

"They took us completely by surprise," Gabe said, still edgy from the battle.

"We were not ready, Captain." Seth commented despondently.

Jophiel reached out and put his hand on Seth's shoulder. "You did well, my friend." He comforted. "Fear not, for this will only strengthen him."

Jack sat in the couch after he had finally calmed his nerves. He was assessing his wounds and the damage to the house when the phone rang.

"Jack, are you all right?" Peter spoke desperately.

"No... well... I am now, but no... Pete, I don't know what just happened." Jack detailed emotionally. He then recounted the entire story.

"We must encourage Jack to continue," said Jophiel, addressing the angels gathered. "I'm hoping that this will spur him on towards the truth and not deter his hunger. Don't let the enemy near him from now on. We must be diligent and ensure that the plan is not hindered."

They all nodded in agreement.

Seth and Gabe made sure to guard Jack closely.

CHAPTER FIFTEEN

The leaves had turned a mixture of rusty red and yellow. Most had curled on the ground, but some still hung desperately to the bare branches. The late autumn chill had set in and winter was edging around the corner.

Mustard had his thick winter rug on and was lazing in his stable while the Daley's fire was gently flickering, comfortably warming the house in the morning frost.

Jack had continued to spend the passing months researching the Bible, his hunger for more evidence unquenched. He had not seen another attack since that night and he was relieved. He felt strong, confident, and safe.

* * *

THIS WAS a cold Thursday morning and Peter and Jack were sitting by a warm, sun-filtered window at Betty's Café.

"It's the Holy Spirit holding the Antichrist back!" Peter stated.

"No, I don't think so, Peter. How do we know He's not referring to a specific angel or something else assigned to hold back the Antichrist, and when he is removed, the lawless one will be revealed? In that scripture, it says '... till he is taken out of the way' the 'he' is a lowercase h, whereby when the Bible refers to God, Jesus or the Holy Spirit, it's always with a capital, so I think the restrainer is someone... or something else. Anyway, I'm not seeing the evidence anywhere in the scripture, so why do you say it *has* to be the Holy Spirit, or the church?"

"Well, I've always believed... and been taught that."

"Taught by whom... by man?" Jack interrupted.

"Yes," he smiled as he said, "by man, that the church will be taken out, then the Antichrist will appear."

"So, where are they getting it from? Where in scripture? Where from *God's* word?"

"Only in 2 Thessalonians 2:7, that I know of."

"Therefore, the 'One' may not necessarily mean the Holy Spirit."

"Maybe. I guess I've never really questioned it because they were prominent scholars and theologians. I simply believed them."

Jack raised his eyebrows. "They are still men, not God," Jack continued. "Okay, if what you say is true, then Jesus will have to appear *two* more times, one secretly when He comes to get the church and another when He condemns the people — that is Armageddon, is that true?"

"Mm," Peter mumbled unconvincingly.

"Look, I don't know if I'm right or wrong, but I know God has put this desire in me to find out the truth about this. I feel He keeps telling me not to listen to man's theory on this, but only to His voice. It seems that every day something else points to us having to endure this whole tribulation thing. But… I also feel like I know nothing. I'm not a scholar, I didn't go to Bible school, so who am I to question this teaching? You know what… I really hope I'm wrong because I don't want my family or myself to have to go through this—I want the easy way out too." Jack paused. "But what if I'm not wrong, Peter? What then, how will it affect the church? You know that scripture that says that many will be offended and fall away?"

"Yes."

"Well, what if Jesus is talking about this very thing?"

"How do you mean?"

"So how will it affect the Christians who think we don't have to endure, who are banking on going up to Heaven beforehand?" he paused, "Like Shaun, for example. Do you think they will be upset that they *have* to endure this and get angry with God for letting us go through this? Maybe become offended and maybe even fall away?"

"Mm, you could be on to something here—go on."

"I guess what I'm saying is this. If you were living your life happily and then found out that tomorrow you would have to fight the heavyweight boxing champion of the world how would you feel… or fare in the fight?"

"I'd be really upset, scared and would probably get pulverized in the first round."

"My thoughts exactly. But what if you knew beforehand, like say two or three years?"

"Well, I'd have more of a chance because I would prepare, train, and get in shape and at least give my best fight… even at my age," Peter chuckled.

"Exactly! If people aren't prepared, they will be susceptible to caving in, to cracking under the pressure, to not stand and fight for what they believe in."

"So what are you getting at, that we are not prepared? I have always said to the people to be prepared for the return of Christ, I've never told them otherwise."

"But what if that *return* is at the very end, not at the beginning? I'm saying that we need to get a strong message across to prepare for the end times and not think we are leaving beforehand. How serious have your messages been?"

"Ah… I guess, I tell them, but I'm not sure that they take it too seriously. I mean, I haven't preached on the end times because I've always believed that we would be taken up before the tribulation occurred."

"Well, I believe the message needs to be stronger, to explain not to hang onto the hope that we are going up before this happens, but to live as though we have to go through this, otherwise we don't stand a chance. From reading into the scriptures, many will suffer under torture, cave in, accept the mark, and worship the beast. Many Christians will end up going to Hell because they were not strong enough in their faith. They fell and lost it in the end."

"Wow, God really has been working on you!" Peter shook his head in amazement at seeing Jack's passion.

Jack became even more passionate. "We have to have an attitude, a mindset as though we will go through this tribulation. We need to be fervent in pursing God *right now*, Peter, to immerse ourselves in knowing and learning His word, get closer to Him and strengthen our faith. If we do this, we will endure it and not be deceived. If I'm wrong and we go out beforehand, then that's *fantastic*. We haven't lost anything but gained a greater relationship with Christ and believe me, I'm all for that scenario."

"Me too."

Gabe and Seth clapped their hands and smiled.

"I DON'T BELIEVE in God anymore," Lora said to Meg as they casually had their lunch, sitting with their backs against an old tree in the school grounds.

"What?" Meg replied in astonishment.

"Well, Crystalyn says that there are many gods, many religions and all of them lead to utopia—one universe, it's really *one* religion, Heaven or whatever you want to call it. It doesn't matter, it's all the same. Crystalyn's been teaching me how to control the energy of my mind and body and once I've done that then I can advance to conquering the energy of the sun, moon, earth, and the greater universe. I then will have a full understanding of truth and creation and myself. So, there isn't *a* God... we are all gods in ourselves, the power is *within* us." She finished with her hand on her chest for emphasis.

"WOW!" Meg looked at Lora in astonishment. "I've never heard you talk like this. What about your father... he's going to absolutely flip."

"Well, that's just it... who would want to follow a God like *HE* believes in, with all these rules and regulations. Do this, don't do that. I'm sick of it and my mum just puts up with being trampled on like a doormat. She does everything, yes sir, no sir, your preaching was wonderful, blah, blah, blah," Lora said mockingly. "It's sickening. I don't want to follow a God who expects you to act like that. I want freedom, Meg, that's what I want, the freedom to be me. Crystalyn seems so happy to have *that* freedom, and with being in another realm, that's how we can meet in the universal conscience."

"Mm, you're really getting into this aren't you? I mean, come on Lora, it's not *real*, it's just make-believe. You can't take this seriously, surely!"

"It's not fantasy!" Lora snapped, her anger showing. "You can't say that. Crystalyn *is* real, and a wonderful friend to me. Haven't you been listening to what I just told you?"

"WHOA! Lora, settle. Don't be so serious," Meg replied, trying to calm her down. "Lora, you've *REALLY* changed. I don't think meeting Crystalyn has been very good for you. In fact… I think it's been the worst thing that's happened to you… you've just changed so much."

"You're *SO* wrong, Meg. Meeting Crystalyn has been the *BEST* thing that ever happened to me. You obviously don't know me well enough to see how I've been so much happier."

"Ah sorry, but all I see is you are more confused, frustrated and angry at the world… not happier," Meg said sarcastically.

"Take me as I am Meg, cause this is the new me. I'm just standing up for myself, like Crystalyn is teaching me. I'm the one in control of my life and I can command the universe to give me what *I* want, not rely on anyone else. You're just jealous and you don't understand me." She paused. "So, if you don't like it then don't hang around me anymore."

Those words hit Meg with a thud; she was stunned and hurt at the same time. Confused at where this simple conversation had led. "Lora, I'd like to stay friends, but you're really starting to worry me. You've changed."

"Well, you decide what you want to do. I don't need you—I've got Crystalyn," she snapped.

"Okay then… looks like you've made your decision. I'll see you around." With that said, Meg got up, brushed off her school dress and walked away with tears streaming down her face, wondering what had happened to her best friend.

Crystalyn sat quietly beside Lora and was extremely pleased.

Rebellion spoke, "Done!" He grinned back at Crystalyn satisfactorily.

THAT NIGHT, Meg cried herself to sleep.

CHAPTER SIXTEEN

I t was a glorious mid-winter's morning, and the sunrays were dappling through the branches of the trees in front of Betty's Café. Betty had just opened her doors and Jack and Peter were the first to order breakfast.

"So what's happening now?" Peter asked Jack, whilst sipping his cappuccino.

"Well, it's moving into production. They are asking for more volunteers to be the first to have it implanted. Everything is ready. We've been tracking the previous people who volunteered for the testing for the last few months and it's working successfully. It's had great reviews and feedback from the users; they love the convenience of it."

"Wow, so soon, who would have thought?" Peter said, astonished.

"I don't know what to think anymore. Here I am working on a technology that can destroy thousands, but I still feel peaceful about staying on this project. Weird!"

"Not weird, God's Plan!"

"Yeah, I know… I trust Him. It's just hard when my brain gets involved and tries to rule over my heart. Jen says I think too much. I can't help it. That's the way I'm wired," he said to Peter with a smile. "Anyway, I've been doing more research and I'm more and more convinced that we will not be raptured before the tribulation period."

"Well, you've put a pretty convincing argument together so far Jack, I've had a lot to chew on since our last catch-up."

Jack laughed. "Well, you know what they say… opinions are like noses, everyone's got one and they all come with holes in them."

Peter laughed. "Ah yes, how true, I like your humility." He smiled.

Jack continued on a serious note. "I just feel like God is just leading me to evidence, pointing to endurance. I've been thinking about the world situation at the moment. You know with the economic crisis, the wars and terrorism, it's really interesting to see that nearly every country is struggling and has gone into enormous debt for survival."

"Yes, I know what you're saying. This scenario reminds me of the Bible story of Joseph."

"What, his multi-colored coat?" Jack grinned.

"No," Peter smiled, "you see, Joseph was commissioned to save Egypt. He took a 5th of all produce from the people in the land for seven years whilst there was plenty. When the famine hit, the people came to him for food and he sold them back the produce. When the people could no longer give him money for the produce, he asked for their livestock. Now, you have to realize that livestock back then meant that they had a way of living, that is, cows bring milk, sheep for clothing and meat, horses for travel, chickens for food. So when the livestock was gone, it produced even more poverty in the land, as the people could no longer be self-sufficient. When the people could no longer give Joseph their livestock, they told him that they would give themselves and their land to the Pharaoh in exchange for food. This was fine because all Joseph wanted was to save the people. So when the famine was close to the end, Joseph told the people to go back to the land, which was now all owned by Pharaoh, and sow the seed that they had been given. However, one fifth of their produce belonged to the Pharaoh. So in essence, the people were working for the government on government land. So, do you see how desperation can lead to government dominion and control?"

"But we are not in famine," Jack replied.

"No, but we are in a similar situation where our country can be brought to its knees. People are desperate now. We are very reliant on the economy and if it gets any worse, people will be looking for a way out. Look at the Great Depression, it started with the fall in stock prices in 1929 and created worldwide fear and devastation. This type of scenario leads to the perfect time for governments to step in and have the people's total reliance on them."

Jack pondered for a second before he spoke. "Well, maybe this is what it's all about. This is how the mark will be implemented. The world will be in a position that its people are so desperate and reliant on the government that they will gladly take the mark."

"Exactly, but I'm still hoping that we will be removed from this world before it gets to that point."

"I know and so do I, but I'm not totally convinced. As I mentioned before, I feel that God's people will have to endure."

"USELESS IDIOTS, how hard is it to stop a mere human?" Lothar fumed.

"He's heavily guarded, they won't leave his side," a tiny meek voice returned. "Besides, he doesn't have any evidence, does he? It's simply his theory, with nothing to back it up. Our scheme is engrained throughout the world. It can't be changed easily without solid proof. The Christians believe it as truth, my Lord." It assured shakily, not knowing how Lothar would respond to his sudden boldness

"Mmm... yes, maybe you're right." He paused and tapped his long black talon on his gargantuan chin. "That preacher will take some convincing, anyway. This town is engrained with the teaching, so maybe it won't matter, he may simply be harmless to our cause." He thought about it further and said, "But still be on guard, I don't like the way he is being protected by such-high ranking hosts, it may come to nothing, but if I know my enemy," he paused in deep thought, "they are up to something. Leave me!" he signaled with his giant clawed hand.

The messenger flew out of the window quickly, relieved to survive another day.

THREE WEEKS LATER.

"That was such a lovely dinner Jenny, thank you so much for inviting me around."

"You're more than welcome, Peter," she smiled as she took away the dishes and packed the dishwasher.

"Oh, I'll help you do those," Peter stated.

"No, just relax. Why don't you and Jack go into the living room. I'll follow later with some coffee and dessert when I'm done here."

Peter wandered into the living room and sat opposite Jack in a large, soft leather chair.

"Okay Jack. I'm prepared for you now." He grinned, eager for the debate to start again. "I too have been thinking about your argument, about us not going out before the tribulation. So I want you to consider this fact. Noah was saved from the flood, Daniel was saved from the lions, and Shadrach, Meshach, and Abednego were saved from the furnace and were untouched by fire. Our God saves His people. He takes them out of harm's way," Peter said with assurance.

"Yes, I agree… you're totally correct, and I too have thought about this. However, the common theme is that they *still* had to go through these situations. Noah had to endure the flood. He wasn't miraculously beamed up into Heaven and saved. He had to prepare and build the ark, load the animals, and ride out the storm. Daniel had to go into the lion's den and those three boys had to make a stand and go into the fire. I never said that God would not be with us, but I believe like Noah, Daniel and the boys that we will have to go through this, for how long I'm not sure, but we will have to endure part… or all of it. Endurance is all through the Bible—I'm not saying that we *won't* be supernaturally helped and protected, but I still believe the enemy will persecute us. I believe that those who have a strong relationship with Christ will have the strength to get through this. But that's the key, *a strong relationship*, because we will be tested. Look here," Jack said as he started reading some Bible passages he'd been studying.

"Matthew 24:12-13 says that, 'Because of the increase of wickedness, the love of most will grow cold, but he who stands firm to the end will be saved.' And Daniel 7:25-26 says, 'He will speak against the Most High and oppress His holy people and try to change the set times and the laws. The holy people will be delivered into his hands for a time, times and half a time.' That's three and a half years," Jack added, "but the court will sit, and his power will be taken away and completely destroyed forever.' And Revelation 14: 10-12 '... There will be no rest day or night for those who worship the beast and its image, or for anyone who receives the mark of its name. This calls for patient endurance on the part of the people of God who keep His commands and remain faithful to Jesus.' There's so much more Peter," Jack exclaimed as he continued to read out the passages that he had book marked in his Bible.

"Also, take the passage in 2 Thessalonians 2: 3 '...Don't let anyone deceive you in any way, for that day will not come until the rebellion occurs and the man of lawlessness is revealed, the man doomed to destruction.' And Matthew 24:24-31 states that, 'Immediately after the distress of those days the sun will be darkened, and the moon will not give its light; the stars will fall from the sky, and the heavenly bodies will be shaken. Then will appear the sign of the Son of Man in heaven. And then all the peoples of the earth will mourn when they see the Son of Man coming on the clouds of Heaven, with power and great glory. And He will send his angels with a loud trumpet call, and they will gather His elect from the four winds, from one end of the heavens to the other'."

Jack paused, checking that Peter was still with him. "This passage specifically says that after these things happen that *all* nations will see Jesus return and they will mourn at the realization that He is King and *then* we will be gathered up. There are many more scriptures, but I won't go on. However, what really got me was this sentence in John '...and I will raise him up at the last day'. It's repeated four times in chapter 6. So it got me thinking, what is the last day? There are many references to the Lord's Day, that it is a day of His return and the destruction of all sinners. So is Matthew 24:24-31 referring to the last day? I think it is, and this will be the time when we go heavenward and not beforehand," Jack concluded.

"WOW!" Peter nodded his head in agreement. "You know, I cannot believe how much you've changed over the last 14 months that we've known each other. God is really stirring your heart on this. Okay, what about Matthew 24:40-42 where it states that, 'Two men will be in the field; one will be taken and the other left. Two women will be grinding with a hand mill; one will be taken and the other left. Therefore keep watch, because you do not know on what day your Lord will come?'" Peter paused before he continued. "This is talking about the day Jesus whisks His believers away in the rapture. This is what the theologians state as proof of this occurrence happening in the future, and I believe it to be so."

"Yes, I definitely can see how it can be derived as such. However, I too have pondered this scripture, and I feel it needs to be taken in the full context of the passage, not just the end sentence. When you read the full passage, Jesus is talking about the days of Noah being like the coming of the Son of Man. He's talking about the evil in the world and these sentences, I feel, are simply referring to one of the righteous being saved, like when they boarded the ark, and the other is the evil person being left behind to perish in the flood. I don't feel that this supports a secret rapture occurring before the tribulation at all. It doesn't mention the timing, it's just simply stating that the righteous will be taken and that could be on the very last day when Jesus returns."

Peter interjected before Jack could continue. "Well, what about the passage in Revelation 3:10-11? 'Since you have kept my command to endure patiently, I will also keep you from the hour of trial that is going to come on the whole world to test the inhabitants of the earth. I am coming soon. Hold on to what you have, so that no one will take your crown.' Now this is solid evidence that Jesus will not let us suffer and will return for us quickly before the hour and this is what we were taught at Bible school by top scholars."

Jack earnestly responded. "Yes, again, I'm not refuting what you're saying, however, do you think that Jesus is actually telling us that He will *always* be with us until the very end and that He will help us through this hour of testing? That He will be with us to help us avoid temptation, just like when He was praying in John 17:15 and said, 'My prayer is not that you take them out of the world but that you protect them from the evil one.'"

Jack paused before continuing, "Pete, I can see your view and how you are reading it this way but I simply see it differently as I don't believe that He's saying that we are departing but simply stating that we will have much help in this hour. Also think about this... what if the hour of trial that He is talking about is actually Armageddon? What if the Last Day is the hour of trial, which is actually the great battle and He will take us out *just* before it starts?"

"Okay," Peter sighed, putting his hands in the air and feeling a little conquered, "you make several good points that I simply cannot argue. I've been praying about this too. Every time we meet you are stirring my spirit and making me see it differently and it's going against all I've been taught... but I think I'm starting to believe that you are right. As much as I don't want to say it and wish you were wrong, my spirit confirms it. I too have been struggling with your concept, as I really don't want to believe that what you're saying is truth. I just don't know how to process it. I've been asking God to break down my own barriers and belief system, because all the teachings I've heard on this subject have been about taking the church out before the tribulation. Not one Bible teacher, lecturer, preacher or theologian that I've come across has said that we weren't leaving before the suffering started. It's been engrained into the system as truth and from what you're saying, it seems as though it's all been false doctrine... a tremendous *lie* to deceive us." Peter paused. "And sadly, and unbeknown to me, I guess I felt a security, a strange safety in thinking that we will be saved. So, I am coming around Jack." Peter smiled. "God has been working on me. It's hard to swallow that I possibly have been teaching God's people incorrectly, that I too have been deceived in thinking that we will be saved in the way that *we* want to be saved." Peter sighed with a slight curl of his mouth.

"So, how do you feel now? I mean, I could be totally wrong," Jack stated.

"No Jack, I think you're right. As I said, I have been praying and slowly coming around. I just wanted to put forward some more arguments before I gave in to you." He winked cheekily as he continued. "But to be honest, I'm feeling very nervous, actually. I'm concerned for God's people and myself. I mean, it puts a different spin on things now, doesn't it? We can't just say, 'Oh well, we won't have to go through it, lucky us, poor them.' It's a bit overwhelming and I have a sense of urgency to get people right with God. Get them prepared by increasing their faith and relationship with God."

Peter paused. "That's the only thing that will get us through. I feel that I now need to set things straight in the church and to reveal what God has shown you and to ask for forgiveness for my own shortcomings in this matter. I should have studied this myself instead of blindly following others before me. It shows that we must put our trust in God's Word, not in man's opinions, views, or claims. We must pray and listen to what God is telling us. Exactly as you have been doing, Jack, I really take my hat off to you, I'm so proud of you. You have come into Christianity with no pre-conceptions, hardly knowing the Bible when I first met you, and God has really used this childlike belief. This is why He states to come to Him like little children, because children don't come into this world with preconceptions and existing beliefs. You can tell them that a bunny lays eggs at Easter and they believe it whole-heartedly. This is the childlike faith that Jesus was talking about. Unfortunately, we take on board people's opinions, or what they deem is a *word* from God."

"Well, it says that people will be deceived," Jack said.

"Yes, and they will if they are not grounded in Christ, knowing the truth. The enemy is extremely cunning, and will use any measures to steal God's people away, even by mimicking Him. Take the verse in Matthew 24:24-25, 'For false messiahs and false prophets will appear and perform great signs and wonders to deceive, if possible, even the elect. See, I have told you ahead of time.' You're right, it's all been a lie, and people who are not strong will fall for it and bow down. Jesus explicitly states how He will return, so we must not be fooled into thinking it has changed."

"I'm glad you're now with me on this. I thought I may have been way, way off." Jack smiled with a sense of relief.

"No, God is using you to get the message across that we cannot be lax in our spirituality. You know, this has greater implications than what we are talking about here. The fact that Christians are being deceived into thinking that they would not have to endure; they are also becoming nonchalant in spreading the word of God too. It's like the security of knowing that they are going up beforehand is leading them to not only be slack in their relationship with Jesus, but also in telling others. As Shaun said, some are even thinking that they will have a second chance if they miss the first coming. What you said before about the restrainer not being the Holy Spirit, I now think you are right. It can't be because 1 Corinthians 12:3 says, 'Therefore I want you to know that no one who is speaking by the Spirit of God says, 'Jesus be cursed,' and no one can say, 'Jesus is Lord,' except by the Holy Spirit.' So really, if people think that they have a second chance to come to God after the rapture, then it's false because a person can only come to Christ through the Holy Spirit—there is no other way. So it's definitely not the Holy Spirit who is removed."

Peter smiled, shaking his head in realization of the years that he was misled. "You're right Jack, there is *no* pre-tribulation secret rapture... it's been a huge lie all along. We have simply been tricked and have become lazy with our own faith. I'm not speaking for all. There are many people out there doing their best to spread the gospel, but it seems that many Christians have lost their fire and are happy to coast to the end. We, as the body of Christ, have lost our desire to know Him intimately. We are just happy to be born again but not grow in our relationship, but we have to, otherwise we won't survive. I don't care if I die because it means to be with Christ, but I don't want to see people tricked and deceived. This is worse than death, to spend an eternity in Hell, a never-ending torture. I can't bear the thought of not having an opportunity to save someone from that suffering."

"You're right," Jack said, "the best way to immobilize your opponent is to lure them into a false sense of security, and that's just what Satan has done. By spreading this belief system throughout the Christian faith, it has caused them to become stagnant and lazy. It's like country *A* telling country *B* that they will no longer attack, so, in good faith, country *B* decreases their military forces, relaxes and then WHAM, country *A* attacks and gets the upper hand. Anyway, if this I-Chip is any indication of how quickly we are moving into the final days, then this is really urgent."

"Yes, you're right... you are right!"

Both Jack and Peter suddenly looked over at the TV screen. A news topic had caught their attention, so Jack quickly unmuted the sound so they could listen.

"The economic downturn, increase of war, terrorist attacks and one world government will be the topic of the global INAT forum held here in Jerusalem." The newsreader stated on the television. "Jason Crane's speech will aim to encourage the world leaders to find a solution to these growing problems that are threatening our very existence."

"What do you think of this Jason Crane guy?" Peter asked Jack.

"Well, I asked God the same thing, and I got, 'A wolf in sheep's clothing.' So if God doesn't trust him, neither do I." Jack continued, "It's exactly what Ben said. Our country and others around the world are in so much debt. I did some research today and, in our country alone, each newborn baby, in effect, already owes the government $70,000. I'm not sure about smaller per capita countries, but what are we doing to our next generation? People are so overwhelmed; they are looking for answers now to get them out of trouble. And they'll probably look to this guy for the answers."

"A bit like the story of Joseph, don't you think?" Peter said.

Jack just smiled.

T he sun was shining, birds were chirping on this glorious Saturday morning. Sarah was already in the arena riding Mustard, and May was instructing her. Matthew and Ben were on their motorcycles checking the cattle and horses, and Jack was aimlessly wandering around the farm. He wandered into the old wooden barn and thought that he should get some hay for Mustard when Sarah had finished. The smell of fresh Lucerne hay and dust lingered, and it took some time for his eyes to adjust to the dimness inside. *They should get some windows in here*, he thought. He wandered over to an old tractor and leant his back against it, facing outward towards the big barn doors, enjoying the view of his daughter happily riding around the arena in the distance.

"It's time," Seth said to Gabe.

Gabe gently lifted his majestic sword, and it started to emanate a bright, penetrating light. He gently laid its piercing tip against the old dusty and broken carriage as he delicately scraped it along its cracked wooden side. *Screeeeeeeeech!* The sound rang out through the barn.

Jack jumped, startled by the unusual noise. *That was weird*, he thought as he walked curiously over towards the old carriage to see where the noise had come from, thinking it may have been a rat. He laid his hand upon the damaged structure, its wood badly gouged, scratched, and splintered in some areas, clearly unrepairable. "You are a mess," he said aloud. "What happened to you, eh? Must have been a pretty nasty accident." He continued to lean over and peer into and around the carriage, surveying its damaged and misshapen frame.

Seth motioned to Gabe. "Now!"

Gabe put his sword into the carriage under the broken and collapsed passenger seat and gave it a quick shove. *POP!*

Jack quickly wheeled around to see where the strange sound had come from. He watched as an old dented canister rolled out from the passenger door, clunked down the smashed stair and landed on the dusty floor with a thud before his feet.

What's this? He thought, as he leant over to pick up the dusty and damaged cylinder. He held it for a while and looked it over before he tried to pry off its lid. *Mmm, this isn't easy*; he thought as he struggled with it. It wasn't going to budge. Gabe decided he couldn't wait and held out his sword, touching the canister with the glowing tip.

THOOP! The lid popped off into Jack's hand. *This is getting weirder,* Jack thought. He looked inside to see yellowed paper rolled up like an old preserved manuscript. He gently pulled it out. *It looks like a letter*, he whispered as he gently rolled out the pages and started to read...

12th day of November 1831

My dear Daniel,

Oh, where do I start? I am in utter turmoil! I will try to make sense of what has happened, therefore I am writing this so not to miss any detail for when I arrive this morning to see you and stop you from presenting our new theory at the ministry conference.

Firstly, my dear friend, please let me explain. Our discovery is nothing but a lie, a deception from the enemy himself. I know this because an angel from our great Lord himself came to me last night. I will try to explain in detail what occurred.

I was asleep, weary from my long travels, when a strong wind came blustering through the window, blowing the curtains and startling me. I was certain that I had closed the window due to the brisk night air, but it was not any ordinary wind, for when I opened my eyes the power and the light that emanated throughout the room was near blinding. When my eyes adjusted, I saw the angel of the Lord standing at the end of my bed. I was instantly fear stricken and could not move nor speak; it was as though I was frozen.

The angel spoke and said, "Do not be afraid, for I have come to deliver a message from Jehovah your God."

I could not utter, but just laid there staring wide-eyed in fear, waiting. He continued to speak.

"Benjamin, servant of the Most High God, look closely at what I have come to show you."

Daniel, it was like a window opening at the end of my bed and a clear vision appeared within it. It was most extraordinary and frightening at the same time.

I looked intently at this window and watched carefully; this is the account of the horror I saw.

People, crowds of people, were gathered together. It must have been hundreds of thousands or maybe even millions, I couldn't tell as the mass went beyond my vision. However, there was something wrong with these people, many were emaciated and impoverished and looked as though they were starving. As they were crying out, I watched as a powerful man stood in a temple and ordered these people to bow down to him. He said that he would give them what they need if they worship him. Some did, but others refused. Therefore, he laughed and said that the God they believed in will not come to save them. He said that he is the true and living God and they must obey his commands and bow down and worship him. I watched as many people started to weep and become angry with our Lord. I heard them cry out in anguish, looking heavenward, saying, "You lied, you said that you would come and save us before this time, what kind of God are you?" They started to blaspheme God. I watched as many turned away from their faith in anger and desperation, offended that they had not been delivered from their distress. I could hear some of them saying that this man must be God because of the signs and started to walk forward with their arms raised in worship. I started to weep as I watched so many willingly bow down to this powerful man and lose their salvation. "Why aren't they being saved?" I cried out, "Why are they angry at God?" I started to sob.

The angel once again spoke and said, "Benjamin, they are deceived. Do not deliver your message tomorrow, for it is a message straight from the evil one to destroy God's people, to distort the truth and to lure them into false-hood about not having to endure to the end. It will weaken them and hinder their faith."

I observed closely, as many people walked forward to receive a mark on their skin and pledge their allegiance to this man. I heard them say that he must be the true God because their God was supposed to deliver them before this troubled time, therefore he must be their redeemer. I also saw that those who did stand firm and refuse were killed. I started to weep; this was far too much to bear.

Then, this vision suddenly disappeared, and another came into view. I watched intently as I saw Jesus returning with a flash of lightning throughout the heavens. All the kings and nations throughout the world could see Him. I saw this amazing sight, too much for mere words to describe. Many of our Christian brothers and sisters rose up and met our Lord in mid-air. I watched in awe as everyone in the world could see His return. All kings fell down on their knees, and mountains trembled. Then Jesus, the Lord himself, looked right into my eyes and spoke directly to me. "Benjamin, very soon I will come. Tell my people to endure, be strong, and resist temptation, and do not be deceived. Blessed are those who endure until the end, they will earn the crown of life."

Then the vision vanished. The angel turned to me and spoke once again.

"Benjamin, you have been given an account of the future. Take heed of what you have seen. There will always be followers who fall away, however, many more will fall away if Daniel delivers his message," he said gravely. "You must stop what has begun as it is not of the Lord."

With that Daniel, I started to cry out with overwhelming anguish for forgiveness and the angel reached out and touched me, and the love was immeasurable. He said, "Do not be upset servant of God for you are very much loved." The peace swept over me and I felt restored. I looked up at him and he said, "Go at once!"

That's when I woke up Tommy. I am writing this while he is preparing the horses as I am hastily making my way back to see you, Daniel. We must not share this theory because it is not truth and will deceive many Christ followers into believing that they will not have to endure until the end. It is clear now to me the deception that the enemy has laid. Cunningly, it will make people think that they do not have to be concerned about the troubles in the end times. If we speak of our theory, many people will believe they will be taken up heavenward and saved beforehand. It is a lie that we have been fed, Daniel, and we must not share it. It must be stopped!

I eagerly wait to meet with you and tell you of this account in person,
but for fear that I may miss any detail, I will have you read this letter first.
Your brother in Christ, Father Benjamin Harvey.

Jack stood there silently in amazement, barely moving as he re-read the fragile letter again in awe. He lent back against the old carriage to steady himself, marveling at how remarkable this old letter was, feeling thankful and overwhelmed from the message he read before him.

"WOW! This is exactly what God is telling me. Thank you, Father!" he exclaimed as tears started to well up in his eyes, his heart full of overpowering relief at the confirmation that God had given him. "Thank you so much God for showing me that this is of you, that I am on the right track, Father you are so awesome." He started to thank and praise God over and over, his heart bursting with appreciation, reverence and excitement all at once.

After several minutes, Jack composed himself, wiped the tears of relief and joy from his face, and placed the letter back into the canister… but ensuring that the lid wasn't on too tight. He heard the motorcycles pull up outside and went over to show Ben what had been hidden inside the old broken carriage for so many years.

Undetected eyes were watching Jack from a dark corner of the barn. Unbeknownst to the Guardians, a scrawny little demon saw everything that had just occurred.

A SCREECH and a ruckus erupted in the old pump station as a flutter of membranous wings from a tiny black creature landed in front of Lothar.

"I bring urgent news, great Master," he panted, trying to catch his breath, a look of concern upon his ugly, misshapen, impish face. "They have found *THE* letter!"

"WHAAAT?" he said, exploding with a roar, his voice vibrating from wall to wall. A mass of demons started fleeing in all directions to avoid any wrath that may come from this disturbing news.

"Why has this been found? It was supposed to be DESTROYED!" he bellowed, his screaming voice echoing through the empty, cold, dark rooms. "It should NOT EXIST!" He screamed, standing and waving his sword at the little imp. "Are you sure?"

"Y-y-yes M-mm- Master," he stammered, "I saw the Guardians show Jack Daley, and he read it out loud, sir."

"How did THEY have it?" he fumed as he wheeled around staring angrily outwards towards his troops.

"It, well, it w-was hidden in the old c-c-carriage all along, sir," the small demon replied, terrified at what may happen next.

"Where is Crechus?" he hissed. "Send me Crechus!" Lothar was fuming, his hair bristling, drool cascading down his jowls, his eyes glowing red with anger. "Bring me Crechus NOW!" he screamed as his giant black sword came down, cutting one demon in half, leaving a swirl of black mist in its place.

With a panic, the scrawny messenger flew terror-stricken out of a broken, jagged window in a desperate search of Crechus.

CHAPTER NINETEEN

It was Monday and Crystalyn took a deep breath and transformed into the beautiful princess Lora had come to know. Crystalyn had become so real to Lora, to the point that Lora did not have to go to sleep any more for them to meet. They could have a conversation at any time, and it was proving to be a distraction.

"Lora March, what did you just say?" Mrs Pempie, her teacher, asked in annoyance.

Lora giggled and looked directly at where Crystalyn was standing, invisible to anyone else. "Nothing, Mrs Pempie," she chided, and tried not to make any more disturbances. "Crystalyn," she whispered, "stop it. You're going to get me into trouble."

Meg sat across the room and just rolled her eyes at the scene that was becoming more and more frequent every day. She was annoyed with Lora, but at the same time, very, very concerned.

PETER, the Jackson's and the Daley's were gathered together in May Jackson's kitchen.

"This is amazing Jack," Peter said, "it's like God has confirmed everything that you have been feeling." He smiled.

"I know," Jack replied, "I can hardly believe it myself. I had to reread it several times before it sunk in. I mean, what an amazing find," he exclaimed with excitement.

"Well, who would have thought?" Ben declared, throwing his arms up with flamboyancy. "After all these years sitting in that old barn. See May," he turned towards her, "there was a reason why we Jacksons couldn't part with that old thing." He smiled. May looked back at him with a loving grin and patted him on the back with a knowing smile.

"I'm not sure what you believe in, Ben, but this letter is pretty controversial," Jack stated.

"Oh Jack, I believe in what the Bible says, always have. We only go to Reverend March's church because of tradition. I know he's a white washed empty old tomb, but I just could never go for the happy, clappy, hands in the air, dancing around services that you folks have." At that comment, May quickly jabbed Ben in the side with her elbow. Ben jumped. "No offense to you, Peter," he said sheepishly, realizing who he was sitting with.

"None taken!" Peter smiled.

"Actually, it was the good Reverend himself," Ben motioned to the letter held in Peter's hand, "Father Harvey, who told my great granddaddy Tommy about Christ. Tommy was a good man who brought up his family to love God and his generations followed, all because of Father Harvey."

"Did your grandfather ever mention Father Harvey's accident?" Peter enquired.

"Well, I can remember my granddaddy telling me that his father, Tommy, didn't talk about it too much. He only talked about it a few times when my granddaddy asked about the old carriage in the barn. But the story did sound strange. He said that Tommy loved driving for the Father and that he was a good man, but he did in fact say that he thought that night wasn't an accident."

"How do you mean? The papers all stated that it was an accident," Peter asked, with a concerned look on his face.

"Well, that's what the folk around these parts were told by the chief of police John Barnes, and lead to believe, but Tommy wasn't so sure."

"Please continue," Peter motioned.

"Apparently the story that ran in the newspaper the next day was that the police investigated the wreckage and determined that one horse had thrown a shoe and because of the reckless speed that they were traveling the horse stumbled and couldn't regain his footing, went down bringing the other horse with him. Tommy was catapulted over the front; Father Harvey was thrown out the side and killed instantly." Ben paused. "But Tommy never believed it."

"Really... Why?" Jack questioned, eager to hear the rest of the story.

"Well, when Tommy was recovering in the hospital, the chief of Evensmore Police, John Barnes, came to see him and Tommy told the chief that he believed that Charger, the lead horse, had been shot. But the chief would have none of it and told Tommy that he's just had a bad accident and he was purely imagining things. But Tommy went on insisting that the horses were sound and had fresh shoes only put on two days before, but the chief wouldn't listen and told Tommy to leave it well alone. Tommy thought it all sounded very strange and asked to see the horse's remains, but the chief said that they had already been disposed of due to the nature of the accident, they had to act quickly as people were extremely disturbed about the incident."

Ben paused for a moment. "My granddaddy said that Tommy never trusted the police after that day and believed that it was a conspiracy and that the Father was deliberately murdered for some unknown reason. He said that he never knew why Father was in such a desperate rush to get back to Evensmore by early morning," Ben concluded.

"Well, I guess we know now," Jack said. "So did Father Daniel actually deliver the message Father Harvey was trying to stop?"

"Yes," Peter interjected, "he delivered it at the Evensmore fellowship gathering that very morning. Apparently, he did not know about the accident until after the conference had finished that afternoon. He was so devastated at the news about his best friend that he had to be hospitalized. The authorities had been determined to keep it quiet until the finish of the conference as there were so many religious officials in attendance, they did not want to cause concern or interfere with the message."

"You certainly know a lot about it," Ben stated with a grin.

"Yes, I do actually." He smiled back. "I made it a point to

study the history of this area when I moved here. I also was secretly a little excited that I came to the town of the founders of the secret rapture theory."

"It's so remarkable that this is the little town from where it all started," Jack stated.

"Yes, what started in Evensmore nearly 200 years ago has gone full circle… the truth is now revealed," Peter replied.

"WOW! I still can't believe it… I mean hidden away *all* this time," Jack said, looking at everyone in amazement.

"We'll, I'm now sure that's the reason Tommy kept the carriage," Ben said. "For some reason, they didn't destroy it and allowed Tommy to take it. I really don't think he honestly thought it could be restored. I think he knew that there was truth hiding somewhere there and was hoping that it would be revealed some-day. He told my granddaddy that he wanted the carriage kept safely in the barn, tucked away so no one knew about it. May always chided me about that old thing taking up space—I nearly did get rid of it once, but something in me just told me to keep it there. Lucky, I guess." Ben smiled.

The others let out a small chuckle and agreed that it was very fortunate indeed.

Jophiel looked over towards the great Warrior angel standing beside the wrecked carriage and raised his hand in salute for a job well done. The angel proudly saluted back and smiled graciously… unfurled his giant, magnificent white wings, and left his post with a blaze of glorious light for the first time in nearly two hundred years.

"You lied to me, Crechus," Lothar said in a low hissing voice. "Explain yourself!"

Crechus stood before Lothar, feeling the hate emanating towards him as he quivered with fear. The hordes of other demons gathered around at a distance and waited silently to see

the show slowly unravel. Teeth bared and grinning as they antici-
pated what was to come.

"I-I-I..." Crechus stammered, "We, well, we umm, I, and..."

"DAMN YOU!" A fist came down on the large ornate throne
arm Lothar was sitting on. "Talk, don't stammer, you imbecile!"
he roared.

Crechus took a deep breath, trying to stifle his quavering voice
and stop his fear-ridden body from shaking. He could hear
chuckles coming from the other demons in the crowd. "We, we
couldn't find the letter," he started, "we went all through the
carriage and looked on the preacher's body for it but we couldn't
find it, we then thought it may have blown out of the carriage
alongside the road so I sent the scouts back to look for it. They
returned with nothing, so we assumed it had been destroyed in the
accident."

"ASSUMED? ASSUMED? You based this entire mission on
an ASSUMPTION!" he roared, spittle flying out of his jowls, his
anger growing intense.

Demons stepped back further in fear, grins had turned into
grimaces of trepidation, as they knew what could happen when
the Master was enraged. A few left, flying out the dusty broken
windows to avoid any fallout from this gathering. However, most
stayed, their curiosity and taste for blood overriding any fear they
felt.

Lothar continued his rage. "Do you realize how long this has
taken?" he hissed venomously. "I spent years sowing this seed into
those two pitiful preachers to see it finally become a common
belief. The plan had worked... we had them... but you... you
idiot have strengthened the enemy's mission because of this blunder. You have potentially sabotaged everything. This was to help
us take as many souls as possible, to weaken them... to trick
them... and now you... YOU!" he pointed angrily, "careless,
stupid fool could have hindered this. You have potentially given
Jack the evidence he needs." He quickly lunged forward and
grabbed Crechus around the throat, picking him up so he was
level with his evil face, his hateful gaze boring into Crechus's

desperate bulging, fear ridden eyes. "I could kill you with one hand, Crechus, and I don't see why I shouldn't."

Crechus's eyes widened, gasping from the tight grip around his throat, his arms and legs flailing, trying to hold on to something to ease the searing pain of hanging from his neck.

"Don't send me away Master... please," he managed to wheeze out through choking breaths.

"Why shouldn't I?" he said as his gray putrid breath furled upward between them, their noses nearly touching from the closeness. Crechus started to gasp frantically, panicking as Lothar held his grip tight. He grinned as he watched his prey's life quickly ebb away.

THUMP! Lothar let go of Crechus and he fell hard into a choking and gasping heap in front of his feet.

"You *will* make amends for what you have done," he said through his clenched jaw. "Your work is not finished." He looked at the hordes of demons in front of him and all around the building and spoke, "I want you *ALL* to make Jack Daley's life a living *HELL*, go and wreak havoc on that family. He will not win this battle. Go NOW!" he screeched.

Suddenly there was a burst of thrashing, panicking wings, screeches and screams as demons flew out of every exit and opening in the old building to carry out Lothar's bidding.

CHAPTER TWENTY

It was early Tuesday morning when the demon of Sickness lurked near Jack Daley's house. With no utterance, the dark shadow was stealthily creeping, peering into the house windows, and moving cautiously so not to be detected by any Guardians. The demon appeared resembling every disease possible, reeking with his pungent stench, covered in cysts, yellow seeping sores and warts. Parts of its grayish colored flesh was hanging in shreds and profusely rotting.

He gradually entered through the outside wall, absorbing the solid brick mass before passing through the other side and eagerly made his way to Matthew's room, pleased that there were no Guardians and that Matthew still lay sound asleep in the early hours. Sickness dug his long silvery hooked talons into Matthew's body, tightening his grip and securing his hold on the boy.

Matthew woke with a jolt, and a flood of nausea and pain rose over him like a tidal wave. His stomach lurched, cramped, and convulsed. Without having time to get to the bathroom, he vomited over his bed cover and cried out in agony.

The Guardians were first on the scene, the pungent stench hitting them in the face like a solid brick wall. They knew instantly before entering the room what was in there. They all stood watching the slimy demon work Matthew's body, slowly infecting him.

"Why weren't you here watching him?" Gabe said with annoyance, looking at Matthew's Guardians. "You were supposed to protect him. Where were you? What were you doing?"

They both hung their heads and apologized at their failure in protection. "We heard a noise in the living room and went to investigate," one of them sheepishly replied. "It clearly was a diversion."

Seth placed his hand on the Guardian's shoulder in reassurance. "You know how the enemy works. We must be vigilant to not let our guard down," Seth said. "They obviously know about the letter and will try to attack this family; we must be alert to everything around us."

"We need reinforcements," Gabe said, and they all nodded in agreement.

Jenny burst through the door upon hearing Matthew's cries. Shocked at the mess all around Matthew, she rushed over to his bedside, with Jack close behind. "Oh honey," she crooned, "what's wrong?" she said with her hand on his forehead, feeling his temperature rising.

"I feel sick, mummy, really sick. I have sharp pains in my tummy." He wrenched forward in agony.

"Where?" Jack asked.

"Everywhere dad, it just hurts all over my tummy, and I feel so sick." With that, his body convulsed, and he started vomiting again.

The demon of Sickness continued to work into Matthew's body, focusing solely on infecting him. His long silvery hooked talons had now fastened tightly to his young victims' body. *Master will be pleased*, he thought.

Jack ran out to the hallway and immediately rang the doctor.

"I'm sorry about the mess, mum," Matthew said, as his eyes filled with tears.

"Don't worry about that, Matthew. It doesn't matter," Jenny replied. "We've just got to get you well."

Within 10 minutes, Jack looked out the window to hear the ambulance siren coming down the road.

"They're here," he said. "Let's go!"

THE SMALL GRAY spirit waited until everyone was gone. Its diversion had been very successful. It floated gently and quietly into Jack's office, looking around for the letter. When it saw the timeworn canister, it made a rapid beeline for it. It clasped the round tin in its tiny claws and then turned to leave.

"Ahem." Chale cleared his throat to draw attention.

The small spirit quickly tried to exit, but Chale lunged forward and pinned one of its wings against the wall with his sword. The tip pierced straight through the leathery membrane into the plaster.

"Eeek!" it screamed in panic, flapping its free wing rapidly, trying to break loose, causing its pinned wing to tear slightly from the impaling of the angelic sword.

"Drop it!" Chale said sternly.

It instantly dropped the canister with a *clang*, and it rolled along the wooden floor.

"Why are you here?"

"M-m-master t-told me t-to steal it." It shook violently with fear, looking up at the great warrior that held him captive.

"Why?"

"C-c-cause its e-evidence. It-it may ruin the plan."

"Good… Tell your master he failed." Chale smiled satisfactorily, pulling out the sword from the wall and releasing his foe.

The spirit dropped to the floor.

"Leave and don't return, else I *will* finish you."

The spirit left in a flurry out the window—he got some distance before he landed, looking in the direction of the old pump station. He decided not to return, as he knew Lothar would execute him. He recommenced his journey but flew in the opposite direction… far away from Evensmore.

THURSDAY LUNCHTIME CAME AROUND VERY SLOWLY and Jack was at Ben's farm for some timeout from the hospital. "How's Matthew?" Ben asked.

"He is still in hospital. They are not sure what's causing his sickness and they're still running tests," Jack replied. "Jenny is with him now."

"He's got a slime drip in his arm," Sarah said to Ben, screwing up her face in disgust at the thought.

"It's a *saline* drip, sweetie," Jack said, amused at his daughter's misinterpretation.

Sarah just shrugged and looked at Ben and said, "Well, it sounds yucky anyway. I'll go get Mustard ready," she said as she led Mustard over to the hitching rail.

"We've been at the hospital since Tuesday, so I thought I'd bring Sarah out for her lesson to try to get her mind off Matthew. She's been very upset and worried about him. We all have," Jack said.

"Well, doctors are pretty good these days. He'll be fine."

"Yeah, I hope so, Ben. Listen, I'm going straight back over there as soon as we leave here. Would you mind if we left Mustard here for the night? I'll take him home tomorrow?"

"Sure, not a problem, we love having the little guy around." Ben smiled.

IT WAS a glorious sun-filled day outside, but Lora was in her darkened bedroom with several candles set out in the pattern of a five-point pentagram, along with thick heavy chalk lines drawn across the worn oak flooring. The dense black curtains were drawn, and the room was dimly lit by the orange flames flickering and dancing, being pushed by a rogue breeze that had snuck under her locked door. She and Crystalyn were spending the afternoon creating incantations and rhymes.

"Ah, that's a funny one!" Lora said, laughing. "Hey I got one," she said as she started a little spell.

As they both sat on the floor in the room, Crystalyn could see the invisible blackness getting thicker and thicker; a dark cloud was drawing in on the town of Evensmore, unseen by human eyes. Crystalyn sat there and grinned at how easy it was to call them in.

. . .

Sarah and Mustard were doing a beautiful extended trot around the arena.

"Oh Sarah, he looks lovely!" May called out. "Now put him into a circle for two laps and canter down the center line, then halt."

Unbeknownst to everyone, something was watching. A dark shadow ever so slightly moved, red eyes were staring, twitching and waiting. A small goblin was hiding behind the midpoint arena post.

As Mustard came cantering down the center, the black stringy demon took his chance. He ran out in front of Mustard and leapt onto his neck, sinking his barbed teeth into the side of him. Mustard suddenly reeled sideways and groaned in agonizing pain. In confusion, he panicked and bent himself back and launched upward, rearing into the sky whilst letting out a deep chilling scream. The demon bit harder, also sinking his claws deep into the pony's flesh. Mustard tilted on his hindquarters as he wrenched sideways and twisted backwards… falling to the ground, landing on top of Sarah.

Work completed, the demon fled.

Mustard writhed on the ground, desperately trying to get up. He quickly scrambled to his feet and started to shake and snort as he looked down at Sarah's still, motionless body.

In a split second, upon hearing the screams, Jack was by Sarah's side, crouching over her. May was already on her mobile calling an ambulance as Ben gently moved the traumatized pony away and checked him over for injuries.

"No, no!" Jack cried in panic, crouched over Sarah, desperately wanting to hold her, but fearing not to touch her. All he could do was sit beside her in the dust and sob, praying aloud, "God please, please no, not my little girl. Please God save her."

"She's still breathing, Jack," May stated as she stayed amazingly calm in the crisis.

They all looked up upon hearing the siren and seeing the ambulance speed into the driveway. Within minutes, she had oxygen, a neck brace and was on the stretcher in the ambulance with Jack in the back crying beside her.

THWACK! "SCREEEEECH... don't hit me, AAAAHHHH, don't hurt me," it cried as it was ducking and weaving, flapping around, avoiding the angelic blade of Seth. "OOOOOOHH, please, OUCH, NO, please, please." Seth had it cornered, his blade hard pressed against the little demon's neck. A gooey green moisture started to glisten on the sword that was slowly cutting into his slimy flesh. "OOOOCH, please, I'll tell, I'll tell, Yesssss, I'll tell you everything, just don't kill me... spare me, please."

"Then TELL!" Seth said sternly.

"I-I'm just following orders," he squeaked, "Master is upset that you have the letter."

"What's the plan?" Seth asked.

"I don't know," he wheezed. "We were just told to make trouble."

Seth pressed the blade harder. The slimy ooze started to flow more freely, and the demon started to scream and squirm.

"I know nothing, nothing more, I swear," he cried out in pain.

"Then go and don't return." Seth stepped back and released him.

The demon whimpered and scampered away, limping and half fluttering, trying to gain some lift, but his torn and tattered wings were too damaged to give flight. He limped back toward the old pump station, hurting and complaining, however very pleased with himself at the trouble he had caused.

JACK AND JENNY were at their little girl's bedside. She was asleep, but the fracture in her leg and her broken arm was causing her to writhe fitfully with pain. Jenny stroked Sarah's forehead as tears fell down her cheeks.

"What's going on, Jack?" she looked at him. "We have two children in hospital within a week? What's happening to us?"

"I don't know," he sighed in defeat. "I *just* don't know."

· · ·

LORA AND CRYSTALYN had finished playing the spell game. The candles were blown out; floor wiped clean, curtains pulled back and the orange glow of the sunset gently filtered through the open window. Crystalyn was very pleased at what they had achieved this day.

"ABOUT TIME you halfwits made some progress," Lothar bellowed, looking down at his horde of gaggling and salivating minions. "I want to see more of what went on today. Do not let up, be relentless!" He paused, scanning the jostling underlings. "Where is Crystalyn?"

Slowly, Crystalyn weaved through the middle of the crowd, edging gradually toward the front.

"Here, sire." He bowed down low, deliberately making a show of it. The others snickered.

"Ah, Crystalyn, once I thought you were just a whiny fool, a thorn in my side, but you have proved today that you do have some worth."

"Why thank you your Majesty!" Again, he bowed low accepting the accolade, Lothar clearly enjoying his reverence.

"Continue working with the girl and create more of what you did today. She is fast becoming an asset. Better than some others you have coached in the past."

"Your wish is my command," he responded, bowing and backing away slowly into the crowd behind him, relieved that he had survived the encounter.

Chortles and jeers were heard. "Moron, crawler, sycophant," the other demons whispered and sneered, baring their teeth with hatred as he walked by.

PETER SAT in his room praying for Jack and his family when his phone rang.

"Peter. It's Jack!"

"Jack, how is everyone?"

"Not good. Jenny fainted momentarily at the hospital and they have her in a ward there as well under observation. They think it's exhaustion, but they are running tests on her too. I've had to come home and get clothes for my *whole* family. Gees Peter… what's happening? What have I done to deserve this? I thought God was here to protect my family and me. I just don't get it," Jack stated, sitting despondent in his living room, rubbing his head in despair.

"You're under attack," Peter said. "We must pray for protection and bind the enemy. They are obviously not happy about what God has been revealing to you. That's what it's been about Jack, can't you see it now? That's why they sent those demons to torment and dissuade you all those months ago, to try to stop you from finding out and exposing the truth."

"You really think so? You really think they would go to such lengths?"

"Of course, c'mon Jack, who are you kidding here? They planted this lie nearly 200 years ago. Do you think they want the truth exposed before they get any benefit from it? This is not a game. Their aim is to get as many souls as possible, by *any* means or trickery. It's exactly like you said, Jack. The enemy set out to deceive us all along with that falsehood and to lure Christians into that belief… it did me."

"So, you think that they are targeting my family in retaliation?"

"Yes, I do, but God is greater than Satan, so there is nothing to be afraid of. We have won, and we have the authority through Jesus Christ. We just have to apply it and speak it out. I have the rest of the church praying for your family. So let's pray!"

"Now Lora," Crystalyn said, "it's a full moon tonight, so let's have some real fun."

"Already… we did the magic this afternoon."

"We just need to do some more… that's all," Crystalyn

responded with excitement, still on a high from the praise received from Lothar.

"Sure, what do you want to do?"

"Well, let's…" Crystalyn suddenly paused and pricked an ear eastward.

"What's wrong?"

"Ah, nothing… it's nothing," and simply continued. However, Crystalyn had felt the shift… and wasn't pleased.

CHAPTER TWENTY-ONE

J ack and Peter continued to pray over the phone, asking God for protection, claiming healing, and health to his family.

Unseen by human eyes, their prayers were being answered as powerful lucent beings started plummeting earthward from the heavens into Jack's house and all around his border. The newly arrived angels formed a guard around Jack's property, strengthening and fortifying the boundary.

The hospital room where the children recovered started filling with a vivid brilliance, as the glory of the heavenly beings filled the space.

"We have the numbers now," Gabe stated.

"You can't touch me," Sickness shrieked at the angels in Matthew's hospital room, his voice full of panic and defiance. "I have a right to be here—this boy is always feigning illness."

"O really, you have no rights at all. We have every right, so leave. The prayers of God's people are more powerful than your 'so called' power," Gabe commanded.

JACK AND PETER FOCUSED, unrelenting in their prayers as Peter started to claim authority over Jack's family. "I command sickness to leave in the name of Jesus. You have no authority over the Daley family—they are sons and daughters of the Most High God. Be Gone in Jesus' name!"

At those very words, like a powerful electric shock wave, the demon was thrown backwards off and out of Matthew's body, slamming hard against the back wall of the room with an unseen force. He lay confused with his gray rotting wings spread and his body hunched and crumpled. The demon started whimpering and cursing as he came to, his sinuous slimy gray arms reaching out, sliding his decaying body forward again to take hold of Matthew. His silvery hooked talons clicking on the hard vinyl flooring as he slid onward towards his prey.

A towering, athletic angel stepped forward with his sword aflame—he swung his mighty blade. *WHACK!* The massive weapon cut cleanly through the demon's torso and a black, gray sludge splashed on the hospital walls and floor. In a puff, he was vaporized, leaving just the dissipating black smoke and a sickly stench aftermath.

OVER THE PHONE, Jack and Peter continued to pray together. The presence of the Lord could be sensed. Like thick heavy dew, it came down, blanketing them both in warmth of peace. Angelic beings all around joined them, whilst more and more angels dropped from Heaven, filling the house and the surrounds. The prayers from the church saints were floating upward and emanating outwards, lifting the skies and breaking through the dense, foul blackness that was trying to encroach upon this family.

"PULL BACK AND RETURN!" a demon shouted back towards the heavy black mass. In a flurry and panic, they retreated and took to the skies, screeching and howling in terror. Some managed to avoid the strong metallic blades of the angelic warriors descending from the heavens. Others were not so lucky, leaving a trail of shadowy smoke in their aftermath.

IN SARAH'S ROOM, many of the Lord's hosts had arrived. The angels felt the Holy Spirit stir within the room and an angel with the gift of healing stepped forward and lay his golden, shimmering hand upon Sarah's little forehead. Instantly she became well.

. . .

JACK AND PETER were still talking on the home phone, thanking and praising God when Jack's mobile phone rang—it was Jenny. "Hang on for a moment, Peter," Jack said as he answered his mobile.

"You're not going to believe this," Jenny said.

"What's happened?" Jack said excitedly.

"Well, it's the kids—it's just crazy over here, the doctors are so confused, Matthew within minutes is back to normal. His color returned—he's sitting up, eating like a horse, and he looks like he never was sick. The doctors can't believe it and Sarah…well," Jenny choked up up, "it's like it never happened. Her broken leg and arm are not broken anymore and all her scratches and bruises have completely disappeared. Everyone's in a frenzy of excitement here—it's… it's a miracle, Jack, and the peace of God… it's like—I can't explain." Jenny laughed. "It's just crazy—the medical staff are just going wild with excitement. And I'm… well, I'm great too!"

Jack started grinning with relief and joy. "WOW! Jen, I'm coming over right now," he said and hung up his mobile and went back to the phone. "Peter," he said, "they're healed!"

"Hallelujah!" Peter raised his arms. "Thank you, Jesus, thank you," he praised, dancing with joy.

IN THE COVER OF DARKNESS, Jophiel and Chale secretly gathered in their armies. Their appearances dulled to near invisible, so the enemy could not detect them.

Jophiel addressed the many combat angels assembled before him. Some stood over twelve feet tall. Their massive solid muscles bore marks of previous battles where they had vanquished countless demons.

"The enemy knows about Jack finding the letter," he spoke clearly, "and they are aware of how it can obstruct their plans. Nevertheless, it is imperative that they do not find out about Jack's *other* mission. We must be extremely vigilant in keeping this from them. Do everything you can to keep them away from Jack, deter them with any means possible."

Chale spoke up, reiterating the assignment's importance. "Jack's mission will bide more time for the saints to prepare. He *must* not be found out or hindered in any way. Souls are depending on it, and our King does not want any soul to perish. Therefore, be forever on guard and prevent the enemy from finding out the real mission."

SUNDAY MORNING ROLLED AROUND SO QUICKLY. The sun was brightly shining, and the sky radiated the most vibrant of blue. It seemed like a thousand angels had gathered in the old church grounds, standing and watching as the saints filed into the worn church building.

Peter took his position in the front and asked his musician team to start the worship. "Let's praise God, let all of creation sing," he said to his congregation.

The angels' voices echoed out throughout the surrounds, joining in with their human counterparts, praising their mighty King and creator. With utmost worship, the saints sang, their spirits lifting. Some angels were watching in awe as they could see each saint glow brightly within their hearts, physically witnessing their love for the King.

When the praise songs had finished, Peter asked Jack to come forward and explain the miracle that had occurred with his family. There were many staff members from the hospital in church for the very first time. When Jack had finished, people started shouting and praising, and in an element of spontaneity, the worship and music started. Peter decided to let his sermon go for today and continued worshipping. Glorious songs filled the sky like rainbows of color as both saints and angels praised their Lord God.

Jophiel stood on the rooftop of the building looking outward across his army, scanning the surrounds to ensure the enemy hadn't come to spoil this day. He suddenly became solemn, remembering the fierce battle he had over a thousand years ago with Lothar. He gently rubbed his chest where the long, faded, calloused scar still tingled slightly when touched. *I'll be ready for you next time,* he thought. He looked over at Chale *If it wasn't for his good friend, he would not be here.* Jophiel turned and spoke to Chale. "This is just the start, you know."

"I know Jophiel… but today is the Lord's Day!" Chale smiled back, unfurling his magnificent white-feathered wings, lifting his arms heavenward and closing his eyes in praise.

Jophiel smiled back at his friend and took his cue. He closed his eyes and did the very same.

"You're nothing but a bunch of imbecilic FAILURES." Lothar was sitting on his throne, glaring down at the throng before him, his teeth bared like a rabid dog in a full rant. "I could have done a better job MYSELF," he yelled. "You're all a bunch of weaklings—what a pathetic and ineffective attempt. You call that an attack? It was useless! All it has done is strengthened the enemy's side. It makes me sick!" He spat with vengeance and hate in his eyes. "You idiots, look what you've done." He pointed in the direction of the church grounds. "More of our enemy is arriving daily, the saints are fervently worshipping, and NOW they have more converts," he shouted. "What have I got to report now to the Great Master? That *everything* is compromised, that the letter has been FOUND, and the enemy is *stronger* than ever—you will *ALL* pay for this. If I go down, you will ALL go down," he shrieked at them, cursing as he launched upward with the force of a torpedo, soaring out of the building with a roar, vaporizing some demons, and leaving others spinning in the air with the power of his exit.

The angels suddenly jolted and stopped mid praise as they heard the loud angry roar across the skies. They looked up and saw the dark figure of Lothar in the distance heading out towards the West, leaving a trail of black furls behind.

"Must be bad news," Chale said to Jophiel, smiling mischievously.

CHAPTER TWENTY-TWO

"Let's do another one," Lora said as she was sitting in her candlelit room with her beautiful princess friend, Crystalyn.

"Mmm, well, we could do one for Meg," Crystalyn giggled. "She hasn't been a good friend to you, has she!"

"Yeah, that would be fun... let's do it!"

"Lora, who are you talking to?" Her Mother Bethany stood outside her bedroom door listening intently.

"Ah, no one, mum, I've got the radio on... it's just a talk show." She looked at Crystalyn, trying to muffle a giggle.

"Okay, well, dinner is almost ready. Come downstairs in about fifteen minutes," she said as she walked away with a perturbed look on her face.

"Good, she's gone," Crystalyn said, "come on, let's do it."

Lora grinned mischievously as they laid out some items that Meg had previously left in her room.

"What about a rash?" Crystalyn asked.

"Yes and do something with her nails because she is always primping and fussing over them." Lora grinned maliciously.

"All right then," Crystalyn said. "Just repeat these words after me..." And Lora enthusiastically repeated Crystalyn's words over Meg.

CHALE ARRIVED out the front of Peter's house and signaled to Peter's many Guardians.

"It is time," was all he said to them and then, with blinding light, shot upward into the air, spinning and turning, heading heavenward.

Peter's Guardians gathered around him, and one of them

131

touched him with his sword. Peter, feeling something stir in his spirit, walked into his kitchen, sat down, took a deep breath, and prayed. The Guardians stood back in awe, watching their favorite sight unfold—like a cool, soft, delicate breeze, the Holy Spirit entered the room and enveloped Peter as he prayed.

"Lord, forgive me for all my preconceptions and misconceptions about the future. I know you have revealed to Jack the truth, and you want me to spread the word about this truth. Please guide my steps and give me strength. You are the only one who knows our future and I ask Lord that you help me deliver your message completely in the way that you want it." Peter continued to pray and sat there for nearly an hour, basking in the peace that surrounded him. His Guardians sang together as well, while the Holy Spirit strengthened Peter and gave him the message.

CRYSTALYN FELT someone watching them from the corner of the room. He knew instantly who it was, but had to wait until Lora had left.

"What are you doing here?" Crystalyn hissed with sheer hate, his princess façade immediately disappearing.

"I just wanted to see you at work." Crechus replied with a wry grin. "Nice disguise by the way... very feminine."

"That's what I do Crechus, that's who I am, the principal of camouflage," he said sarcastically. "Anyway, you shouldn't be here, you are hindering my work."

"I just wanted to see for myself why the Master is so pleased with you." He glared with jealousy.

"You should take my example, Crechus, and just do your job. Leave me now," he spat angrily, "I have work to complete."

THE PHONE RANG, and Jack answered—it was Peter. "Jack, I just wanted to call and thank you for your testimony on Sunday, it was wonderful and it really stirred the congregation," Peter said.

"It was my pleasure. I really enjoyed telling everyone about the miracle that God did for my family," Jack replied. "I too felt really strengthened just by retelling it."

"Listen, I'm going to start a series of sermons on the end times. I want to put forward what has been on your heart. Will you help me?"

"For sure, you've got my full support!"

"Great, can we meet up tomorrow; say 12 noon at Betty's?"

"See you then."

"Excellent! Thanks, Jack," Peter said, then hung up the phone.

CHALE STOOD AGAIN BEFORE DARIUS, the Major General of the Lord's angelic regiment.

"You bring news from Evensmore, my friend?" Darius asked.

"Yes, Major, the signal has been given, and the Lord has been ministering to Peter," Chale replied.

"Good work, Chale. Tell Jophiel and the others that I am well pleased with them. So far, everything is going to our Lord's plan. All towns and cities are at the same stage, except for the township of Stanton. Lothar has placed discourse into the saints and has gained ground there. However, it is all part of God's plan, so go back and keep up your good mission."

"Thank you, sir," Chale said as he saluted, turned, and returned to earth where Jophiel and his comrades were stationed.

"MUM," Meg screamed out. "MUM, can you come here NOW!" she yelled with an element of concern in her voice.

"What's wrong, honey?" Patty asked as she walked through Meg's bedroom door.

"Look, my arms and my hands and, and *my nails*," Meg said with tears of panic in her eyes.

"OH Meggie!" she said in horror, holding and assessing her daughter's arms. "What have you done? Did you touch a poisonous plant or something?" She looked up, concerned at her daughter's condition.

"No, I've done nothing; it wasn't there when I went to sleep." Meg cried as she looked at her arms, red and blistering. Throbbing with the pain, she surveyed her hands, looking at her once beautiful nails that were now different shades of brown, with crumbling and cracking edges.

"I'm taking you to the doctor. You're not going to school, get dressed. I don't know what this is," Patty said as she rushed downstairs and grabbed her bag and car keys.

"THAT SOUNDS GREAT!" Jack said to Peter as they both sat in Betty's Café.

"It was really an experience yesterday. It felt like the Holy Spirit was speaking directly to my spirit, giving me the message that He wants to convey next Sunday."

"Wow, I would really love to experience that."

"You will," Peter smiled. "Come on, let's order. My treat!"

A MESSENGER SPIRIT stood before Lothar, "I bring more news, sire." It bowed before continuing, "The preacher is going to spread the word. He is fully convinced now that he has the letter, the enemy has been working."

Lothar sat in silence for a moment, seething before he finally spoke. "So it is no longer Jack that is our threat, but the spreading of the truth that must be stopped." He stood up and slowly looked around, glaring at the crowd gathered before him. "Where is Crechus?" he demanded.

"N-not here, s-sire," a demon in the horde meekly spoke.

"Then tell him *he* must stop this, for it is his BLASTED MISTAKE!" He suddenly exploded.

"I'M REALLY LOOKING FORWARD to it Jack, I can't wait to deliver this message. I feel like my spirit has been renewed and I have a fresh perspective on things."

"That's really good… I can't wait to hear it." Jack smiled as he bit into his ham, cheese, and tomato toasted sandwich.

"I mean… it feels as though that this message will set everything back to how it should have been…" Peter took a bite of his sandwich, "to reverse what started in Evensmore and make it right. It will be a message of God's people enduring the end times… not escaping it." Peter stated excitedly.

"I agree… it's going to be awesome." Jack smiled as he continued to chew.

JOPHIEL STOOD before Darius in the heavenly realms. "Peter is preparing to deliver the message, however, the enemy knows and is stirring."

"The enemy will retaliate and try to stop him," said Darius. "Peter *must* deliver this message and fulfill this part of the plan. Be wary."

"EEEK, you idiot. What do you think you're doing?" Crystalyn angrily said to Crechus. "Get your stinking hands off of me!"

Crechus released the grip on the scraggy demon. "You have to get to the preacher; he's going to spread the word."

"Why should I? It's not *MY* problem," he spat.

"It's EVERYONE'S problem, stupid. Lothar will kill us all if we fail, so don't think that you're any different. Just do what you've done before."

"Well, it seems, Crechus, that *I* do *MY* job very well, but you don't and that gets us *ALL* into trouble. This is all YOUR FAULT." He returned with a snarly grimace.

Crechus leapt at Crystalyn with sheer anger and hatred, wrapping his hands around his tiny throat, choking and squeezing his black, lizard like slimy frame tighter and tighter.

"You need me," Crystalyn wheezed and rasped out.

Crechus reluctantly dropped his clasp and let Crystalyn

collapse on the ground, gasping and holding his hurting throat. "Just do it," he said as he quickly scuffled away.

"What's wrong Crystalyn, you look pale?" Lora said as she came back into her room to find Crystalyn panting and breathless, but retaining the glorious princess like form.

"Oh, nothing, I just was a little tired, that's all… needed a little rest," Crystalyn replied sweetly. "Listen, we must do something right now, it's very, very important."

"Sure, what is it?"

"Well, remember the fun we had the other day?"

"Yes," Lora replied.

"Well, we must do it for someone else."

"Who?"

"Oh… it's no one you actually know. We're just going to do it for amusement, that's all."

"Great, sounds good," Lora replied with an excited smile. "I'll go get the candles ready and draw the pentagram."

Lora and Crystalyn sat in her room and started to chant, saying disturbing words over Peter. Demons in the old pump station cocked their heads to listen, and upon hearing the mantras and seeing a portal open, started to stir. The black swarm screeched with excitement as they took flight and headed towards Peter's house.

I n the darkness surrounding Peter's house, they hid themselves. Trying their best not to draw any attention, they slowly closed in on the small white cottage to where Peter sat in his couch, watching the night news.

"There are only six Guardians," the dry, raspy whisper of the scout announced. "We can take them."

"Yesss!" another softly hissed in the darkness and then gave the signal to the others.

Their red swords started to glow brighter and brighter as their hatred increased and the mob began to converge on the little white cottage.

Peter's watchful Guardians could feel the evil mass bearing down on the small building. "We need backup—there are too many," one Guardian said to the five others. "Jacob," he shouted as he focused in on one of the Guardians. "We will hold them—you must get word to Jophiel."

Jacob drew his sword, full of valor and ablaze with light, his countenance illuminated with brightness. Not wasting a second, he departed skyward through the roof with lightning speed, igniting a trail across the dark starless night.

The demons looked upward at Jacobs's rapid exit and took this as their cue and rushed forward, screaming as they dove in through the walls of the cottage.

THWACK! Screeches and screaming, green goo started flowing as wings were cut, battered, and torn. The Guardians defended their saint—they were armed, ready, and fought back hard, their blades alight with fire, swatting and chopping at every chance.

"Die Guardians!" the black hoards shrieked as one after another, the black slimy lizard like creatures rushed at them from above and from every side, trying to break through to Peter.

The Guardians' fiery blades arced and cracked at every blow

that the demons dealt, sending the black evil beings fluttering, spinning, and wheeling through the air.

The deafening sounds of screams and clanging of swords rang out throughout the night, unheard by any human ear. However, animals started to become restless, dogs started to howl mournfully, creating a chain reaction from one neighborhood to another. The night became darker as the battle raged.

What seemed like hours had only been 10 minutes. The Guardians' strength was waning, and it was harder and harder to stop the multitude that endlessly kept coming at them. With a mass of fluorescent white and red sparks, they continued to block each blow and protect Peter, but their wounds were becoming deeper and greater. "We must hold them till Jophiel arrives." They all nodded in agreement and fought harder to defend their saint, drawing strength from each other's determination.

Whilst the Guardians were distracted with the battle, a small demon with large spike like claws tried to lurch forward and grasp Peter. A Guardian caught him out of the corner of his eye, grabbed him, threw him back into the rest of the pack, and resumed his defending assault on the attackers.

Slashing, cutting, chopping, swatting, and pushing the immense evil back, they continued relentlessly in an attempt to keep their charge from any harm, and just when the angels started to falter—they saw them coming. At first, it was just a small radiant glow in the distance, rapidly growing larger and larger. The brightness of their imminent glory and power was getting stronger as they approached the cottage.

In blind panic and fear for what they could feel was coming, the demons ramped up their attack, desperately cutting, swatting, and clawing at the Guardians to get a chance to grip Peter. A vile, large demon with crooked facial features and deformed limbs charged at one of the Guardians. With a deafening crack, their swords connected. Arcing white sparks flew as a Guardian tried to hold the large demon back. The grotesque creature grinned a row of yellow, vicious, needle-like teeth as he swung his sword above his head. With one blow, he cut into the Guardian's shoulder, bringing him down onto his knees in a pain stricken and slumping heap.

"NOW!" the large demon screamed, and a small spindly black figure flew at Peter and sunk his large barb like claws into his flesh.

Suddenly, Peter clutched at his chest. The pain radiating down his arm was staggering as he buckled over, gasping in agony. "God, what's happening," he wheezed as he fell forward off the couch to his knees. Writhing in pain, he grabbed for the phone on the coffee table and pressed the emergency button before collapsing and slipping into silence.

"Retreat, retreat!" the large demon yelled and waved his giant sword. The mass exited the cottage just as Jophiel and his celestial army converged from the skies.

A few got away, but not many. Those not killed by the sword were vanquished by the sheer glory that filled the atmosphere. With shrieks of pain, one after another, disappeared from this world permanently.

Peter lay still in silence as a faint siren was heard in the distance.

CHAPTER TWENTY-FOUR

"He is very lucky to be alive," the doctor stated as he walked down the clinically pristine hallway of the hospital.

"Will he be all right?" Jack asked.

"He is in a coma at present. The angiogram didn't pick up any blockage and, in fact, he has amazingly good arteries for his age. We still are not sure what caused the severe cardiac arrest, but there is extensive damage to the heart muscle." The doctor noticed the look of worry on Jenny's face. "I'm sure he will be fine. These things take time, and it will be hard to know for sure until he wakes up. His son and daughter are in with him right now, if you want to visit?"

"Do you think it would be okay?" Jenny asked.

"I don't think they will mind," he replied.

Jack and Jenny walked into the intensive care room where Peter lay with tubes stuck in him, and a myriad of beeping and whirring noises monitoring his every breath. They exchanged pleasantries with his family and tears started to well up in Jenny's eyes as she looked upon Peter's fragility and pale frame lying there.

"He will be fine," Jack whispered to her. "We will keep praying for him."

And they did. For the next week, the church congregation formed a prayer chain, so every hour, Peter was covered in prayer.

"Another Failure!" Lothar shook his head in frustration. "You were supposed to KILL him!" he said as he glared out towards his cringing charges, noticing that there were fewer before him. "Useless bunch of dim-witted, brainless fools," he exclaimed. "Why must I put up with you pathetic, no good idiots? You continue to mess up; now the saints are unified in prayer for the preacher. You're making me look like an absolute *fool* before the Master. IDIOTS!" he screamed as he flew out of the building in rage.

MEG SAT SOBBING on her bed. She hadn't been back to school since that morning a few weeks ago, and she was emotionally and physically in pain. The doctors had prescribed a myriad of medications for her rash, but it hadn't alleviated it.

"Hey sweetie." Her mum Patty peered her head around Meg's bedroom door. "How are you feeling today?"

Meg started to cry again, and Patty came to comfort her on her bed. "It will be okay, this will go away, and you'll have to go back to school someday," she crooned, hugging her tight.

"But it hurts so much, these blisters and the redness, it looks so ugly. I can't hide them. Also…"

"Also what?" Patty gently asked.

"Well, I've been thinking, maybe Lora had something to do with this. She's really creeping me out and I don't want to be in class with her anymore."

"Oh, sweetie, how can this have anything to do with Lora? She can't do this to you?"

"Mum, you don't know what she is into—I don't know anymore… what if she can?"

"Well, I never did anything like that, it is only make believe."

"Mum," she pleaded with her eyes, "she is way into this, deeper than you ever were. Other kids stay away from her now, as she is so, I don't know… dark. Something isn't right."

"Meg, she is a preacher's daughter. I don't think that she would be getting into stuff that is not right, do you?"

"Seriously, mum, she is and she may be the preacher's daughter, but she hates God and *hates* her dad. She told me that ages ago."

"Well, I feel sorry for her parents then. Do they know what's going on with her?"

Meg scoffed, "I doubt it. She just locks herself up in that room and talks to her imaginary friend."

"Do you want me to talk with her mum?"

"What good would that do? She wouldn't believe you, anyway. Lora won't listen to her mum, she just thinks she's the doormat of the household and does everything her dad tells her to do." Meg started to cry. "I miss my friend mum, but I also hate her too," she sobbed.

Patty held her close and kissed her forehead. "I know sweetie... I know."

"Lora, hurry or you'll be late for school," her mum called out.

"Coming!" Lora yelled back whilst rolling her eyes at Crystalyn. "I'm so tired of my family," she said.

"Well, we can do something about them as well." Crystalyn smiled mischievously.

"No Crystalyn, as much as I hate my father, we will not do anything to anyone here," she replied sternly.

"Oh? No fun!" Crystalyn said sheepishly.

"But I would like to do something to a few kids at school." She grinned. "Come on, we have to get going," Lora stated as she grabbed her schoolbag and headed downstairs.

Jack and Jenny peered in through the door of Peter's hospital room to find him sitting up, drinking tea, and casually flicking through the TV channels.

"Hey Peter, we heard you were awake. How are you feeling?" Jack said, smiling as he and Jenny entered the room.

Peter looked up and with a large beaming smile replied, "I'm fine... just fine, great to see you two."

"WOW! You really gave us a scare," Jenny said. "We didn't think you would look so well."

Peter chuckled, "Yeah, me too."

"So what do the doctors say?" Jack asked.

"Well, they're treating it as a heart attack. It's all the symptoms of one, but there is no cause. The doc said that my arteries are pristine, no clots or plaque. He actually said that I have the arteries of a thirty-year-old," he said, smiling proudly. "So they're a bit perplexed why I had the attack. Unfortunately, I have sustained a lot of damage to my heart, but praise God, it will heal over time."

"That's great news, we were so worried." Jenny smiled.

"What exactly happened, Peter?" Jack asked.

"Well, I was watching TV and then it became all strange," Peter explained as he recalled the event carefully. "It was as though I could feel or sense a real darkness entering the room— something just wasn't right. It was an extremely heavy feeling, so I started to pray, but then it hit before I could get any words out, like something grabbing my heart and squeezing it hard and sharp. It was so painful, I managed to call emergency, but then I'm not sure what happened after that. I'm so thankful to wake up in this place, although Heaven wouldn't be too bad either. Least I'd get to see my Jude," he said with a smile.

"When are you out of here?" Jack asked.

"They say I'll be here for another week to be assessed and then I have to take it easy. I can't drive for six weeks or do certain things. No jogging, only a very light walk. I'm not even allowed to preach, as they said that would get me worked up. I had my big sermon ready," Peter said disappointedly.

"Well, just do what the doctors said. Your message has waited nearly two hundred years—a few more weeks isn't going to make a difference. Look, anything that you need just let us know, I can drive you around, no problem," said Jack.

"Thanks," Peter replied. "My daughter is staying with me for the next two weeks, but I'm so lucky to have good friends like you." He smiled.

CHAPTER TWENTY - FIVE

THREE WEEKS LATER.

Meg sat despondently on the park bench at the edge of the street. Looking down at the state of her angry red, blistery skin and her brown powdery nails, she started to sob. Wondering how it had come to this, why her friend would do such a thing to harm her. She had been avoiding Lora over the past few weeks. However, when Lora cornered her in the locker room and told her about what she and Crystalyn had done, Meg was so upset she ran out of her class feeling betrayed, hurt, and confused.

She took a deep breath and sniffled; wiping her tears away, she let out a slight whisper, "God... I don't know if you are real... but if you are really there, then please show me, I need you."

Her soft, faint prayer didn't go unheard, and the mighty Chale was standing there beside her. He motioned to Jophiel to give the signal.

PETER WAS out walking on this sunny afternoon, taking in the fresh air and thanking God that he was alive and healthy. He was recovering well but keen to get back into his old exercise regime, so he decided to do a gentle walk to the corner shop to get some supplies. He was casually strolling along the sidewalk when he came to the cross street, a block before the shops. His six Guardians walking beside him saw Jophiel raise his arm and give the signal. Peter had stopped at the curb before crossing the road to turn left, when one of the Guardians whispered to him, "Go the other way."

Peter stood there thinking, mulling over the mental map of the streets, and decided that turning right and taking a new route was definitely a better walk.

. . .

MEG WAS STILL SITTING on the bench when she noticed an elderly man walking down the street. Not wanting him to see that she had been crying, she sat up stiffly, wiped her cheeks, and looked in the other direction so he could not see her face.

PETER WAS HAPPILY strolling along the path towards a bench where a girl was sitting when one guardian whispered to him again, "This girl needs help. Stop, and talk to her."

He was just about to walk past the girl when he glanced and saw how distraught she appeared. He stopped just in front of her, catching her eyes and he said gently, "Are you all right, young lady?"

Meg tried to respond to the question, but her words would not come out. She gulped and tried again to answer the stranger standing in front of her. Holding back her tears, trying not to let the floodgates open, with all words failing, her emotions unfolded, and she wept again. Hot tears flooded her red face, embarrassed and trying to hide her arms and cover up the emotional turmoil that she felt—she could not hold it all in. "No, I'm not!" she squeaked out through the bitter tears.

Peter gently sat down on the far end of the bench, giving her enough distance but quietly waiting in silence for the girl on the other end to compose herself.

"I'm sorry," Meg said as she turned her head towards Peter, wiping the tears off her face again.

"No need to be sorry."

"I mean… Well, you don't want to hear about my problems. You look like you're a busy person," she said, half managing a sheepish smile.

"Believe me, I'm not busy. I have plenty of time," he chuckled.

"I'm just upset at my old friend, that's all—she's been doing some nasty things towards me lately."

"Oh? In what way?"

"Oh, you don't want to hear about it I'm sure, it's really silly stuff."

"Actually, I do. I'm happy to listen," he responded earnestly.

"Well, you probably wouldn't believe it, anyway."

"Try me… you will be surprised what I do believe," he said with a gentle smile.

"Okay, well, it all started when my friend Lora started becoming interested in spirit guides." She looked up at him to catch his reaction, and when he didn't flinch, she could see that it was safe. She continued to tell Peter everything that had happened to her and Peter sat silently, listening intently to the story.

* * *

"You don't believe me, do you?" Meg said when she finished.

"I do! I believe every word that you have said."

"But it sounds so crazy," she said timidly.

"Yes," Peter chuckled, "it does sound crazy, but you see, you're talking to someone who deals with crazy *every day.*"

"What do you mean?"

"Meg, I'm a local pastor in the area. I come across this kind of stuff all the time. In fact, it seems to be more often than not these days." He smiled warmly.

"Really, so I'm not going mad," she said in surprise.

"No, you're not," he chuckled. "Far from it, I might say."

"Well, what can I do then? You know… about this physical stuff?" she held out her arms to show him. "How do I stop this?"

"Do you believe in Jesus, Meg?"

"Sort of." She paused and continued, "Lora's dad is also a pastor here." She looked up to see if Peter reacted, he didn't so she continued, "I guess what I mean is if he is what people are like who believe in Jesus then, my answer is *No*, because I see no kindness or love there at all. It's all religion and rules. That's why Lora went that way—she wanted to find the truth… and… and I don't know what truth is anymore." She started to cry again. "Is truth what Lora is into or is truth what Reverend March does?" She paused. "Because if it's either of these then I don't want any of it." She put her head in her hands and sobbed.

Peter waited for a while, letting her cry. After what seemed like an eternity, he spoke softly, "You're right, who would?"

Meg lifted her head, composed herself once again, and looked surprisingly at Peter. "What?" she responded, looking baffled.

"You're completely right! I wouldn't want any of those options either."

"What do you mean?" she asked, very confused. "You're a preacher, that's what you believe, just like Reverend March."

"No, you're wrong… I don't."

"But-but I don't get it!" Meg said, tangled and frustrated. "That's what you preachers are all about, rules and religion."

"Religion is man made. I believe in a relationship with Jesus, Meg. Not in rules and regulations." He paused as she looked at him in total disbelief. "You see, Meg, it's *us humans* who ruin everything. When Jesus came and died upon the cross, He did it for you and me because He loves us. It's as simple as that. But man seems to complicate everything and create a big song and dance. Jesus said that the greatest commandment is to love God with all your heart, all your soul, and all your mind, and the second is to love your neighbour as you love yourself." He paused for a moment.

"Meg, I'll tell you what I believe. I believe in a God who is love, who gives life and freedom. A God, who sets people free from bondages, who heals, loves and cares for his children. A God, who gives free will, allows people to make mistakes, picks them up, and hugs them when they repent and return to Him. Who shows an abundance of forgiveness and grace towards us. That's what I believe." He paused, looking at Meg, waiting for her to respond.

Meg sat in silence, tears softly rolling down her red cheeks, processing what she had just heard and after what seemed like forever she spoke, "Yeah," she softly whispered, "I'd like to know *that* God," and looked over towards Peter.

Peter smiled. "You can!"

"How?"

"You need to repent of your sins… believe and trust in Him, and change the way you live… He will show you the way if you let Him."

They both sat quietly for a while. Meg was still thinking over the conversation when she broke the silence and spoke, "Okay... but I don't know how to start."

Peter gently smiled, "Would you like me to pray first and then you can follow... then we can talk about some scriptures?"

"Yes, that would be good." She faintly smiled at him.

THE ANGELS STOOD and watched in awe as they saw the streaming light come down from heaven and shine directly into Meg. Her heart glowing brighter and brighter as an incandescent whiteness illuminated from her whole being. A loud noise of songs, praise, and cheering broke forth in the Kingdom as every angel stopped and lifted their arms in joy. It was as if all of creation ceased and gave thanks for another lost soul redeemed.

CRYSTALYN LOOKED up upon hearing the angels praising their God and shivered with nervousness.

Lora looked questionably at her princess friend, but not wanting to cause another commotion with Mrs. Pempie again.

"It's nothing," Crystalyn said, but Crystalyn was clearly disturbed and uncomfortable with feeling the sudden shift in the realm.

ONCE AGAIN, Jophiel stood before Darius. "We now have Meg in the fold."

"Very good. Then it is all coming together, and the enemy isn't at all aware. What they used for evil... our Lord has turned for good." He smiled happily. "Give my commendation to the troops. Well done!"

CHAPTER TWENTY-SIX

"It's funny how quickly the weeks seem to roll around, one minute I'm in hospital and now I'm here in front of all of you ready to give my sermon," Peter said as he stood in front of his congregation on this beautiful Sunday morning. "I would like to thank all of you who helped me during this time. Let's worship!"

As the saints worshipped, once again, angelic hosts started dropping from the sky to join them in their praises.

"It's today!" Chale said to Jophiel, and the others gathered nearby. "So be on guard, as the enemy will not like what Peter has to say. Keep them away until he has delivered his message."

A number of demons in the distance were challenging the members of Jophiel and Chale's angelic armies, trying to get closer, to break through the circle of protection, and weasel their way into the church. The angelic warriors firmly stood their ground, not allowing even one to slip through their mighty fortress.

The worship ceased, and Peter took the microphone and began his message. "I've been waiting to give you this message for a little while now, but have had a few hiccups on the way." He smiled, then continued. "So I'm excited to share with you what God has shown me through Jack Daley over the last 18 months or so. Now, you all know me well enough to understand that I am a straight shooter, that I will only give you what I believe is truth and what I feel God has been speaking to me about, no matter the consequences. The message I bring to you is something that I haven't really spoken much about before. It's about the end times."

People started shifting in their seats, eager and excited to hear Peter's message.

"Now I know my previous messages on this topic have been

about Christ's followers being raptured or taken up before the tribulation starts, but this message is going to be much different." He paused and surveyed the crowd before him. "I have felt that God has been speaking to me and urging me to bring you all this message. You see… over the past year or so, Jack has been raising some valid questions regarding Christ's followers being taken before the great tribulation and the antichrist reign. He has spent countless hours in research and also debating me." He smiled over at Jack and continued on, "And try as I may, I argued we would go beforehand… but I now feel that God has been showing me otherwise." Peter paused, noticing some people shifting in their seats and eyeing him curiously, intrigued by what he was about to say.

"So, I will just say it." He paused again. "I now believe that we *may,*" he emphasized, "not be taken up before the tribulation."

Murmurs were heard amongst the congregation as Peter continued his message. "I believe God has been showing us we will have to endure until His return. I now don't believe that we will go beforehand." He paused and looked over his congregation, noticing that some were clearly uncomfortable with his message and knowing what was at stake for the history of this little town. Peter continued, even though he felt a sense of uneasiness come over him. He paused. "Jesus, please give me strength," he whispered quietly under his breath.

At that very moment, a being gracefully entered the building and stopped close beside Peter. With engulfing luminescence, His robe was pure light as he emanated warmth, peace, and love with His every essence. His gleaming brown silky hair gently cascaded to his shoulders, and upon His head sat a royal golden crown. At once the angels bowed low, some fell upon their knees for this was a Holy moment—their King had arrived in their presence.

Jesus gently spoke with the calmness of soft running water, "I am with you Peter!"

An almost visible wave ran outwards throughout the church and surrounds as he spoke. The angels fell face down at the power hitting them. The enemy in the outskirts scattered.

Peter slightly flinched as he could feel the strong, powerful voice resonate through his heart. He could feel the warmth flow over him, the thick sense of peace nearly suffocating him in a hallucinogenic way. He didn't want to speak or move as he stood there quietly, knowing in his heart that his King was standing right beside him. A heavy, permeating love came over him; he took a deep, lasting breath, and continued, now reassured.

"I haven't come bringing this message empty handed; there are many, *many* scriptures that seem to back up my argument today. So I would like to discuss the scriptures this morning and use these as the basis of my message." Peter again paused and took a deep breath before he continued.

"I will start in the book of Matthew, when Jesus is telling his disciples about His return. Matthew 24:29-31 says: 'Immediately after the distress of those days the sun will be darkened, and the moon will not give its light; the stars will fall from the sky, and the heavenly bodies will be shaken. Then will appear the sign of the Son of Man in heaven. And then all the peoples of the earth will mourn when they see the Son of Man coming on the clouds of heaven with power and great glory. And He will send his angels with a loud trumpet call, and they will gather his elect from the four winds, from one end of the heavens to the other.'

And Matthew 24:15-18 'So when you see standing in the holy place the abomination that causes desolation, spoken of through the prophet Daniel—let the reader understand—then let those who are in Judea flee to the mountains. Let no one on the housetop go down to take anything out of the house. Let no one in the field go back to get their cloak...'

Peter looked up to see the crowd sitting quietly. He continued, "I believe that these scriptures, and many others, clearly state the events that will happen before, and on Christ's return. It is evident that the events that will occur will be as follows.

"Number 1: We will see the so-called 'Horrible thing', being the statue of the Antichrist in God's holy temple.

"Number 2: We will be persecuted. It states in Matthew 24:9. 'Then you will be handed over to be persecuted and put to death, and you will be hated by all nations because of me'." Peter continued. "And Revelation 13:7 when talking about the beast, 'It was given power to wage war against God's holy people and to conquer them. And it was given authority over every tribe, people, language and nation.'

"Also, look at Mark 13:13. 'Everyone will hate you because of me, but the one who stands firm to the end will be saved.'

"Number 3: There will be turmoil on the earth. For example, the stars will fall from the sky, darkness will overshadow the earth, and there will be earthquakes.

"Number 4: Then the *whole* earth will see Christ return as depicted in Matthew 24:27; 'For as lightning that comes from the east is visible even in the west, so will be the coming of the Son of Man.'" Peter stopped and surveyed the congregation. He felt strengthened with a renewed excitement overcoming him.

"You know, there was a special day in this very town back in 1831 that put Evensmore in the religious history books. It was a day when a mere theory became what we now think of as truth, a day where our religious views of the end times would change forever, and Evensmore wasn't just a regular little town any longer. It all started here, in this town, and we have been proud of the history and of how it has affected the world. As this phenomenon spread around the globe, it became a fact in our eyes that we, the Christians, would be taken, saved, delivered out of the clutches of the evil one; that we would miss the time of the great tribulation." Peter took a breath before he continued.

"I stand before you now and challenge that theory. After much prayer, research, and disbelief that I could even question my mentors. I truly believe that we will have to go through the great tribulation. We will not be spared, but will have to endure! In fact, one of the men whom this theory originated, being Father Harvey, wrote a letter, begging his counterpart to not go ahead with the announcement all that time ago in 1831."

Peter saw people becoming visibly agitated, and murmuring uncomfortably with his statement. "Okay," he put his hand up to calm people. "I know that sounds preposterous, but I have evidence. A letter was found from the day that Father Harvey was killed."

People shifted and whispered amongst themselves.

"I have it here and I will read it to you now." Peter pulled out the letter from the canister and read it aloud. When he finished, he could see some people were astonished but accepting, with tears falling, but others were clearly angry.

He decided to continue. "I do not say this lightly, as I know how much it means to our faith to believe that our God will deliver us. It certainly has been testing mine." Peter smiled, trying to make light of the message, noticing that some faces staring back at him did not respond positively. He continued, "But I challenge you to find where it states in the Bible that we will be delivered and not have to endure, as I have tried and have failed. I went back to my mentors who taught me and questioned them, and even their statements could not bring about solid evidence. I had some state that we do not understand the history of the Bible, that many scriptures have further meanings because of the translation of the Jewish and Greek language. But in careful prayer, I truly believe that we haven't misinterpreted the word of God. It is what it is, and it states clearly for all to understand. God does not intend for His word to be confusing or a mystery. It is clear, and we can take it literally. As always, when He speaks in parables or in visions He clearly states this first, so there are no misinterpretations." Peter felt like his heart was on fire as he continued his message.

"Others stated that some of these events have already taken place with the invasion of Jerusalem. Again, I question this as well. For example, Matthew 24:21 says, 'For then there will be great distress, unequalled from the beginning of the world until now—and never to be equalled again.' These events haven't already taken place because of this statement made by Jesus that never again will anything happen like this. But we know it does in the great tribulation, therefore, Jesus *is* talking about the end times and it renders this thinking incorrect.

"The question was raised regarding the restrainer that Paul mentions who is holding back the Antichrist in 2 Thessalonians

2:7-8 'For the secret power of lawlessness is already at work; but the one who now holds it back will continue to do so till he is taken out of the way. And then the lawless one will be revealed, whom the Lord Jesus will overthrow with the breath of his mouth and destroy by the splendour of His coming.'

"I have always been taught that the one holding back the Antichrist is the Holy Spirit, and when the church is taken, the Holy Spirit is also removed from the earth. However, for salvation to occur, it takes the work of the Holy Spirit in the unbeliever's heart. This means that if the Holy Spirit is removed, then no one else will be saved and this is clearly untrue as Jesus states in Revelation 13:8-10… I'll read the next two passages being, Revelation 13:8-10, Revelation 14:12 from the Good News Bible as it seems clearer." Peter opened the Bible to where he had placed the tabs and continued to read.

"'All people living on earth will worship it, except those whose names were written before the creation of the world in the book of the living which belongs to the Lamb who was killed. Whoever is meant to be captured will surely be captured; whoever is meant to be killed by the sword will surely be killed by the sword. This calls for endurance and faith on the part of God's people.' (GNB), and Revelation 14:12, 'This calls for endurance on the part of God's people, those who obey God's commandments and are faithful to Jesus'. (GNB).

"In this passage, Jesus is still talking about His own people in the Book of Revelation as if they are still on the earth… long after the beast has been revealed and the Antichrist is reigning on the earth. Also, Revelation 7:14 says, and I'll go back to the NIV, 'These are they who have come out of the great tribulation; they have washed their robes and made them white in the blood of the Lamb.' It's very clear in this passage that there are saints who have had to endure the tribulation." Peter looked over his congregation to see if they were still engaged before he continued.

"Also, Revelation 11: 6 talks about the two witnesses proclaiming God's message. Therefore, it can't be Holy Spirit holding back the Antichrist as there are still people saved, even at this late hour.

"Another question I pose is the fact that Jesus states that ALL will see Him when He returns; therefore, it's not a secret rapture just for us. I believe that we have been falsely lured into thinking that Jesus will secretly return just for us, that there will be clothes laying empty where we once stood and we will just disappear into thin air to be with Him. That suddenly car drivers, pilots or loved ones will disappear and people will not know what is going on. There have been many books and movies that have been made based upon this happening and that the world will blame some other phenomenon, like a UFO or aliens for stealing us away. Where once I was a firm believer in the pre-tribulation rapture, I am now not. I believe Jesus will return at an hour that we do not know of, and it will be quick and sudden. However, I don't believe it will be a secret rapture—there are too many scriptures stating that the *whole* world will see Him return.

"In Revelation 1:7, there is an obvious example. 'Look, He is coming with the clouds,' and 'every eye will see Him, even those who pierced Him; and all peoples on earth will mourn because of him. So shall it be! Amen.'

"And Matthew 24:27, 'For as lightning that comes from the east is visible even in the west, so will be the coming of the Son of Man'." Peter took a deep breath.

"So, I then started to question why a theory like this was so widespread and that we, as Christians, clasped a hold of it in such a strong way. Is it because we want to think that we have the easy way out? That we think God will not put us through these testing times? And I started to reason." He paused with a smile. "Well, actually… Jack got me thinking, what happens to us when we believe this theory as truth. Do we become lazy and think that we are going up anyway, so we only have to sit back and enjoy the ride? If we miss it the first time, we can get the second train to Heaven?

"I believe that these times ahead are the age of refinement, the separation of the sheep from the goats. This is the time where

God will really see who loves Him and who doesn't. Who will endure and who will yield? These are the times that we need our faith more than any other age in history. We need to have a close relationship with our Lord, for if we don't," he paused and looked around at the crowd seated before him and said, "then we will be deceived... we will fall.

"Jesus clearly states that even His *elect* will be deceived so to be on guard. If He has stated this ahead of time, then we know that we need to be *absolutely fervent* in building our faith so we can endure and are not deceived or coerced into worshipping the beast. Jesus says that the beast will perform signs and wonders, therefore we need to be discerning and we cannot be discerning if we don't have a strong connection with our Lord.

"This is not to be taken lightly. This is an eternal decision—if we yield, then there are dire consequences. A portion of Revelation 2: 11 claims, '... those who win the victory will not be hurt by the second death.' The second death is the lake of fire and anyone who worships the beast or accepts the mark will spend eternity there. Eternity is a *very* long time—our brains cannot even fathom it. I would rather be put through pain for three years to be with my Lord than eternity in the lake of fire, which never goes out.

"Look, I hope you are all still with me on this." Peter paused and looked around. "However, I now fear that those who do not grow and strengthen their relationship with our Lord will struggle and fall under the pressure of what is coming. It will not be easy, it will be a time of extreme hardship and suffering, something that we have never seen before. I beg you all to read the word of God, pray and seek His guidance. Those who do this will endure and enter the kingdom of Heaven, those who don't will suffer eternity in Hell. Do not take this lightly... we have to endure.

"I realize my message has been a lot to take in, so I will leave you with one more thing. With much prayer, I asked God straight out what He had to say regarding the secret rapture of the church... and this is what I believe He said to me."

Peter got out his notepad and read the words that he had written down.

"Do not be deceived. It is a lie to numb my people, to make them sleep. The time is coming—it hastens, but my people are slumbering! Many people are being deceived into thinking that they will not have to endure, so they sleep and wait for my return. Laziness has overcome them—they lack the zeal and the passion for the gospel, to preach it and go forth and save my people. They are lax and are lacking fervor for my word—they are disobedient and do not wish to save others, but only themselves.

"Seek me first in all that you do. Be passionate about spreading the gospel and my salvation to those who are in need of hearing. The unsaved desperately need redemption, yet most of my people are too lazy to share my good news.

Be prepared for things to come. Time is drawing nearer to my redemption, but do not forsake those who are in need of hearing of my salvation.

"Endure! I cannot tell you when. Do not be deceived, for endurance is needed for the times ahead."

Peter looked up and addressed the congregation. "Look, I admit I am not a doctor of theology—there are many scholars who would disagree with my findings. But I just cannot shake the fact that God is speaking to me, and also Jack, about this misconception. I realize now that we are misled. That it has been a cunning plan by the enemy to keep us slack in our relationship with God, to weaken us and make us fall. To have a *'we are going out before it gets tough'* attitude and I'm afraid that we have been very wrong indeed. We have been deceived into believing a lie.

"So I ask you now... take my message on board, but please go and do your own research. Read other passages in the Bible, as there are many that I haven't covered with you today, pray, and ask God to reveal to you for yourself the truth. Please do not seek man's opinions on this, go to God. Even if all you get out of this exercise is a closer relationship with Him, then you will not be disappointed. I encourage you to go and research this yourselves. That's all I ask." Peter paused and surveyed the crowd before him. "Thank you, and God Bless You."

With that, Peter closed his Bible and gathered his notes, and stepped down from his pulpit.

The congregation rose to leave in silence; it was evident that some were unhappy with what they had just heard.

As the crowd dispersed outside the church, the angels broke ranks, stood by and watched as the enemy cunningly meandered and wound its way to each one of Peter's church goers, speaking lies and doubt into their minds.

A few angels stepped forward to intervene, but Chale raised his sword, signaling to leave them alone. "It is the Will of God," he said, "but it doesn't seem fair, does it?" looking at the strife and division the demons were causing. "Sometimes I wish this fight would end and the enemy would just disappear."

"It will all end someday… and I can't wait to go into our final battle alongside our King," said Jophiel.

"What a day that will be." Chale smiled in delight.

"WOW! THAT WAS AWESOME," Jack said as he embraced Peter in the back room of the church. "I could hear God just speaking through you."

"I was so nervous at first, then this wave of doubt came over me, but then, you're not going to believe this, but I just *know* Jesus was standing right beside me."

"Seriously!" Jack said with excitement.

"Jack… I instantly felt strengthened. It was unreal, *He* spoke right into me." Peter smiled excitedly.

"Well, I want you to tell us all about it over lunch. Let's go out and celebrate, hey—our treat," Jack stated.

"Gladly, I think my knees are still shaking," Peter responded with an enormous smile as they both walked out of the church to where Jack's family waited for them.

It was 10.30 pm Sunday night, and the phone rang at Jack's house.

"Hello?" Jack answered.

"Jack, it's Simon. Sorry to ring you so late on a weekend. I hope I didn't wake you, but I've got some fantastic news."

"Yes?" Jack replied hesitantly.

"We just got word that the I-Chip is going to be released nationally, meaning that they are asking people to accept this technology right now."

"How do you mean, in what capacity?"

"Well, there will be a campaign program stating that it is the *preferred* method and people should start getting the implant. It's voluntary, of course, but it's the way of the future. Can you believe this? This is huge for us, Jack!"

"Yes, Simon, it's very surprising," Jack said with an element of disappointment that Simon did not pick up on.

"Anyway, sorry for the short notice, but we need you down here tomorrow, so Tina has booked you on the first flight out of Stevenson at 7am. I figured it only takes you about forty-five minutes to drive there, doesn't it?"

"Yes. Thanks, Simon, I'll see you tomorrow."

"Great, see you then," he replied excitedly and hung up.

Jack heard the click of the dial tone and slowly put the phone back on the receiver. He stood for a minute staring into space and then made his way over to the couch. His brain was processing what he had just heard as he sat in silence, lost for words.

At that point, Jenny walked in from the kitchen. "Who was that on the phone?" she asked curiously as she surveyed Jack's expression.

"It was Simon; I have to go to head office tomorrow. They are releasing the I-Chip nationally." He looked up at Jenny and they both stared at each other in a knowing, solemn silence.

"How was it received?" Darius asked Chale and Jophiel, standing before him.

"Extremely well, sir. Peter delivered his message with success. However, the enemy were quick to speak into the saints' minds." Jophiel responded.

"Yes… of course. However, this will only strengthen Peter for the time to come… he will be fine. What of the girl?"

"We have peaked Megs' curiosity. Her guardians will start guiding her to the truth," Chale answered.

"Good," said Darius.

Meg was sitting in her bedroom, reading the new Bible that Peter had given her when her mother walked in.

"Hey Meggie, how are you feeling today?"

"Much better now that my skin and nails are back to normal."

"Yeah, that was amazing. It was like that new cream just worked overnight—what a relief, hey?"

"Well, I don't think it was just the cream." Meg smiled.

Patty didn't understand what she was getting at and continued, "You seem different, happier or something."

"Yeah mum, I am. Well I'll just come straight out with it. I asked Jesus to come into my life several weeks ago," she replied excitedly.

"Oh, well, good for you, honey, that's great news," Patty said, thinking that this was another teen fad that her daughter was going through.

Meg picked up on her mother's tone and said, "No mum, you don't understand, this is real. I'm not kidding. He has really changed my life, I'm happier. This rash has disappeared and I have a real peace that I've never had before—I really feel different." She paused, continuing to explain, "Mum, what do you believe?" she asked.

"Ah," she took a deep breath. "Umm… I believe that there is a God… of some sort… probably that there are *many* gods, really. I mean, my family always taught me about spirituality, guides, and a universal conscience. I guess I believe in a creation, like Mother Nature, a higher form of being. Ultimately, I believe that there isn't one way, you know!"

Meg shivered at the thought and how much she sounded like Lora. "No mum! There is only one true living God. The Bible says that Jesus is the *only* way. There is no other religion, no other gods, and no universal conscience. Look here." Meg grabbed her Bible with vigor and started reading passages from it. They both sat on her bed for hours talking about it, Meg reading the word to her mother while she sat listening and asking questions.

"Salvation will come by hearing the word," Chale said as he smiled at Meg's newly assigned Guardians. They gathered around to watch Meg and her mother openly talk about Jesus and how He came to bring salvation to the world.

After hours of conversation, Meg allowed her mother to sit and think for a while. She thought best not to push too much.

"So how has Lora been Meg? You haven't spoken about her much for quite some time," Patty asked.

"No, I haven't really seen much of her."

"You really think that she is into something dark?"

"Yes, she is… and I feel guilty because I encouraged her originally. It was me who wanted to go to that stupid fortune-teller. She didn't want to go—now look at her. Peter said that it opened a door. I really feel bad mum."

"Oh Meg, it was her choice. She didn't have to keep pursuing it."

"Yeah, I guess, but it still doesn't make me feel any better. Anyway, she's got this spirit guide called Crystalyn and they are really doing some strange stuff. She has all these witchcraft magazines too, with spells and rituals in them."

"Really? Crystalyn hey, that name sounds so familiar… where

have I heard that name before? Ah! Your nanna used to talk about her great aunt Emily, who had a friend like that called Crystal or —no… something like that, anyway. But they didn't like to say too much because of what happened to her. It was sort of the family shame, so to speak."

"What happened?"

"Well, she just committed suicide one day—it was quite horrific, actually. Apparently, she drank a concoction of arsenic and then pushed a knife through her own heart. Her sister, who is your great, great grandmother, found her a few hours later. It really traumatized her."

"I can't believe you haven't told me this before, mum? I never knew!" Meg said, taken aback and clearly horrified.

"Well, it's not something a family likes to talk about, one of those skeletons in the closet, so to speak… might be best to keep it that way too!" She patted Meg on the lap. "Anyway, that's why the whole family sort of cooled off on the whole spirituality side of things after that. Grandma only dabbled in a little tarot, but nothing too serious."

Meg raised her eyebrows. "I don't think there is such a thing as a non-serious dabble," Meg chided, thinking about Lora and her spells.

"Yes, well… I'm not sure Meggie, grandma certainly used to think it was harmless, but from what you've told me about Lora… maybe it's not."

"How do you know this Crystalyn guide had nothing to do with Emily's death?" Meg asked, concerned.

"Oh, Meg." She paused. "I don't know about that. I doubt it —how could he? They are *guides*, not murderers. They are just harmless spiritual beings that help us through our life imparting knowledge and wisdom."

"I don't think so mum—Lora was saying some pretty weird stuff about Crystalyn. I think they are capable of much more than what we think." Meg put her arms straight outward, which were now clear. *"Obviously!"* she said, looking at them.

"Yes, well… the one I had didn't seem so," Patty replied.

"You mean *you* had one?" Meg looked surprised. "So how serious about it did you get mum?"

"Well, I didn't get as far as Lora, if that's what you're asking. Your father came on the scene and my time and imagination were taken up by him," she said and laughed, reminiscing. "Ah, the good old days when your father's eyes didn't wander and look at other women." She caught herself and looked back at Meg. "Oh, I'm sorry Meggie, I won't talk badly about your father." She gently stroked a strand of hair off Meg's forehead and changed her tune. "Look, if you're really interested, go up into the attic and have a look through the old chest up there. You may find something regarding Emily. I know a lot of family books and other stuff were kept but I've never had the time to sit down and go through it all… and honestly, I really didn't want to delve into that situation because of how sinister it was, but if you feel you can handle it…"

"Good idea mum, I'll do that. Hey, thanks for listening to me, I really love you."

"I love you too," Patty replied as she put her arm around Meg and gave her a warm hug. "And I'll think more on what we talked about today," she said with a smile.

Meg sighed with relief.

"Good work." Chale winked at Megs Guardians before he launched into flight.

JACK SAT at the large polished oak table in the main conference room, with at least sixty others standing and seated within the room. Some were his colleagues and superiors seated around the massive table. He sat there in silence, drinking his coffee and taking in his surrounds that seemed so unfamiliar to him now. He knew quite a few people but not all, and felt very distant and disinterested, quite different to the others who were buzzing with excitement.

"Let's kick off this meeting, shall we?" Nick Jones, the CEO, announced. "As you are all aware, we are proud to announce that the I-Chip is to go national. But our wonderful customer has now since advised he would like to see this implemented throughout the world." With that news, the room filled with cheering and clapping. Nick raised his hands to calm the crowd and with a joyful smile continued, "So, on that note, I would like our remarkable customer to do the honor and take the floor."

Jack hadn't seen the man who Nick was referring to. His view had been obscured because of a colleague leaning forward slightly. Quite frankly, he hadn't cared, as he didn't want to be here, anyway. But when his colleague leaned back, Jack saw him. He felt a deep sickness rise in the pit of his stomach as it churned—he couldn't believe who he was looking at. He always thought that he had looked taller and younger on TV, a lot different to the person standing at the end of the conference table. Jack couldn't help but stare at the man who was apparently his very customer, the one who he had never even met or spoken to directly.

"Jason Crane, thanks for coming," Nick stated. "Let's hear it from you."

M eg reached up and pulled down on the rope, opening the roof hatch and releasing the ladder to the attic. It unfolded and came down slowly with a clatter and clunk. She looked up and saw some dust particles slowly floating and settling against the floor once again.

"It's been a while," she whispered as her memories started flooding back to the days she used to spend hours up there playing, pretending to be a princess or a damsel in distress, or sometimes just sitting and crying over her father leaving them. She slowly climbed the ladder and entered the attic space and turned on the old dusty light.

She stood looking around, wondering where to start. There were so many boxes, discarded toys and old clothes wrapped in plastic bags just collecting dust and cobwebs. She walked over to a pile of boxes stacked high. "Well, I guess, this is a good place to start," she said as she pulled the first box down to have a look through.

Meg sat there for what seemed like hours, finding things that took her back to her childhood. She laughed and reminisced about the many memories that these old boxes held.

Jophiel and Chale smiled as they watched Meg giggle and reminisce about her past, but they also knew that it was now time for the truth to be revealed. They motioned to Meg's Guardians to direct her view towards the rear of the room.

Meg heard a slight noise towards the back of the attic and looked over in that direction. She sat staring for a while until her eyes started focusing on an ancient rustic wooden chest that seemed tucked away, half under a worn dusty sheet. She was surprised that she had never laid eyes on this before. Covered in cobwebs and dust, she gently unclipped the front clasp and opened the lid.

She gasped at the sight of the vintage, eighteenth century clothes and pulled each one out carefully, looking them over in amazement and wondered why such treasures were hidden away. She couldn't believe her find and was eager to go downstairs and show her mum, but when she pulled the last garment out, there was a *clunk*. An old tattered leather-bound book fell onto the floor. She quickly picked it up, just knowing that this was the answer that she was looking for. Meg then sat down on the attic floor and started to read the diary of Emily Tucker.

"So, Jack, do you have anything to say?"

"Uh, umm… Sorry Nick?" Jack looked at Nick in a confused manner. He had been mesmerized by the man speaking, but had not actually heard a word that he had said.

Nick chuckled nervously and looked over at Jason Crane and then back to Jack. "Jack, do you wish to add anything to what Jason has just stated? You know… the fact that he would like this technology to be used in the New World Order." Nick motioned with his eyebrows, repeating what was just stated so Jack wouldn't look like a fool.

"Umm, yes," Jack stumbled. "It's truly amazing that something that started as just a concept has grown to this enormity. This is a big honor for our company and we are all excited to be a part of this new future." The words rolled out of his mouth impassively.

"Thanks Jack." Nick winked at him, happy and relieved with his response as he sat back down.

The meeting adjourned with a lunch spread brought in for everyone to enjoy. Nick came up to Jack at the first chance he could get.

"Wow, Jack, you must be just blown away—you seem awed by this whole thing. You've done a great job, and you should be proud of yourself. Well done!" he said and patted him on the shoulder as he walked away to talk to someone else.

Jack stood near the food and drinks, trying some sandwiches

in an attempt to calm his stomach and racing mind. People kept coming up to him, making small talk and congratulating him on his work.

"So *you're* the brains behind this technology?" Jack heard the voice and turned around to see Jason Crane extend his hand for him to shake.

Jack's stomach lurched, and he put his sandwich down. "Well, I wouldn't go that far, Mr Crane. It has been a team effort."

"Ah modesty, I like it. Well, it's good to finally meet you, Jack. But please, call me Jason or JC." He smiled, then continued. "I've heard so much about you. Thank you for all your hard work on this project. I know we pushed pretty hard to get it out sooner than you would have liked, but it's worked out nicely, I think. We'll talk again, I'll make sure of it." He smiled, revealing a row of perfectly gleaming white teeth, and walked away.

Jack stood there watching him move around the room, shaking people's hands and congratulating others on their work, impressing people with his intellect and overwhelming warmth. But something inside Jack stirred uncomfortably and he couldn't shake the ominous feeling that he may have just met the devil himself.

THERE WERE APPROXIMATELY 70 people gathered at the church on this Monday night. Shaun Barnard had been busily organizing people to come and confront Peter about his rapture message. He had wasted no time and spent the whole day not doing any of his work but running around spreading the word about the meeting.

Two particular demons, Gossip and Deception, had clung tightly to Shaun, their hooked fingers entwining him and their whispers vigorously egging him on.

Peter had accepted the invite, knowing that he was like the lamb to the slaughter. He had spent all afternoon in prayer asking for God's guidance, wisdom, and knowledge.

Many demons had spent their day muttering falsehoods into the saints' minds and doing their best to cause division. They were fervently attempting to quash Peter's message, for Lothar was angry that it had succeeded.

"This show will be good," one demon said to another.

"Yes, I can't wait to see the trouble that this stirs up. It should stop him in his tracks." The other snickered.

Peter's guardians scanned the crowd, noting the mix of both angels and demons gathered in the building. Their captains, Chale and Jophiel, were amongst them.

"This won't be a very nice meeting." Chale stated, shifting uneasily with the amount of demon eyes that lay upon them, as if sizing them both up as a valuable prize to conquer.

"No, unfortunately… it will be crushing for him. However, he will be stronger for it." Jophiel responded whilst cautiously looking around the building.

Shaun stepped up onto the platform. He didn't waste any time and came straight out. "You're totally wrong Peter!" Shaun said sternly, waving his finger angrily towards Peter, "What sort of message was that yesterday. You are wrong! Our God will save us. You can't say that was from God and THAT letter, well it's a fake that you wrote yourself," he said with venom. "You need to explain yourself, Peter; I think you need to repent before God because you are clearly in error. All throughout the Bible our God has saved His people, so I'm not sure why you have come up with this conclusion."

"Yes Peter," another of the congregation stood up, "this is clearly not from God; you are clearly in error."

"A false prophet," another exclaimed.

The barrage continued.

Peter stood astonished at what he was hearing, as people one by one stood up and told him that he was wrong and that they were disgusted that he would say that their God will not rescue them. When he tried to explain, they would not listen, but were even more enticed into a frenzy of anger, shouting abusive, hurtful words at him, tearing him apart.

Anger, Hate, Gossip, Murder, Pride, Deception, Lies and many other demons were gathered amongst the crowd, having a field day going from one person to another, spewing out their hatred and lies into each individual.

"He's a false prophet trying to make you think that your God will not save you," Deception said into one victim's mind. "He is from the Devil, trying to spread lies and deceive the body of Christ," he continued, grinning excitedly.

"Who does he think he is? How dare he go against the Word," Gossip spoke into another.

"He doesn't know what he's talking about, this vision of the rapture was given to people who were much more intellectual and godly than he is. It's Evensmore's history and credibility on the line too. He shouldn't even be a pastor here," Lies spat violently in someone's ear.

And so the barrage continued throughout the night. Peter just stood there, no longer trying to defend himself or quote scriptures to prove his statements. People who he thought he trusted, who were his friends, turned against him and said some very cruel things.

The angels also stood by and watched the enemy at work with strict, direct instructions not to intervene.

After nearly an hour, Shaun once again stood up onto the stage. "Well, we have received no solid answers—Peter is clearly in error and has been listening to the enemy. Evensmore is proud to have its name as the place where the truth of the rapture was founded and we will not have its history tarnished by Peter's lies." Shaun then spoke with utmost venom in his voice, "You are not fit to be the pastor of this church—you are a liar and a false prophet and should be removed from your position. But it's clear that you have the elders and church board eating out of your hand, so Peter, I will leave you to your church and I will have no part of it." With this statement, he walked out.

Peter could hear others murmur as they turned and followed Shaun out the door, not looking or uttering a word to Peter.

"But you haven't listened to what I was saying—you-you don't understand..." Peter's voice trailed off as he realized people didn't want to listen and were turning away and leaving.

Peter was left sitting alone in the deserted church building. He sat, deflated, crying and praying for what seemed like hours. He found the strength to get up, turn off the lights, and lock the church doors. His heart was utterly breaking as he went home to his small white cottage.

JACK SAT in his allocated aircraft seat, relieved to be away from the office and heading back home. He was one of the last people to board the aircraft and it looked like, much to his relief, that the window seat beside him was left vacant. He put his face into his hands and just softly whispered, "God, give me strength. This has been such a terrible day, what am I doing here, I can't do this anymore, I don't want to be a part of this, please help me get out of this position, I really want to leave, it's such a mistake."

"Excuse me, sorry to bother you, sir, but I'm sitting just there." The elderly man pointed to the empty window seat next to Jack.

"Oh, sorry!" Jack quickly unclipped his lap belt, stood and moved out of his seat into the aisle so the elderly man could squeeze past him and sit down. When the man had settled in, Jack sat back down and re-fastened his lap belt ready for take-off, feeling rather disappointed that he had company beside him.

Jack watched the aircraft safety briefing as they began to taxi down the runway and then take-off. He leaned back and closed his eyes as the aircraft climbed and banked towards home; he was hoping to get some sleep and try to escape this terrible day.

"You look like you've had a rough day," the elderly man stated.

Jack opened his eyes, not feeling like engaging in any conversation, but so not to be rude, responded. "Yes, it's been quite a challenging day, actually." Jack shifted his head sideways and softly smiled at the old man, hoping that was enough not to continue the conversation.

"Sometimes life can get a bit complicated, but I've always found that it only ever lasts for a season." He smiled at Jack warmly.

Jack suddenly caught his eyes—they were so peaceful, it was as though they were like deep pools of still water and he felt a sense of tranquility just by looking into them. He felt drawn in and started to deeply relax, but then, realizing that he was staring, he quickly looked forward again.

"I know everything is temporary, but sometimes I feel like I'm on the wrong path or..." Jack paused. "I don't know... that I'm not doing what I'm supposed to be doing, I guess. I feel like I've created something sinister, and it's now out of control. I just don't think I can continue where I'm at," Jack said and then felt a bit stunned at how he had opened up to this complete stranger.

"What makes you think you're not on the right path?"

"I guess because it *looks* bad." Jack softly chuckled to himself. "I mean, it's not what I would have envisaged. I had this plan around my success, that what I created was to be used for good, but it seems to have taken a different track. I feel like I'm helping the wrong people, if you know what I mean," Jack responded.

"Sometimes you cannot look at the surrounding circumstances. What we think we know, feel, and see is only one piece of the jigsaw puzzle. We hold one tiny piece in our hand and yet we cannot see the complete finished picture, the big plan for our lives. Only God can." He paused. "How do you know you won't be dead tomorrow?"

Jack was taken aback by the question. "Well... I don't I guess!" he smiled softly.

"Then you actually have absolutely no control over your life, do you? So, isn't it best to just trust and let God direct your path?" The old man paused, and Jack was again drawn into his eyes. The very presence of him made Jack feel so peaceful. He felt like he could sit next to him forever.

The man continued to speak. "You know, all God's children have a purpose, and God is ultimately in control. He knows the beginning from the end. Yes, you may wander off the path now and then through bad choices or ignoring, or missing His prompting, but God will always guide you back to where He wants you if you keep your heart willing and open. He knows what your decisions will be and where your life will lead you and the precise time He can step in and guide you back to where He wants you. So, really, there is no need to worry, as He will clearly show you what He wants you to do. You just have to continue to seek Him and listen to His voice." He smiled.

"Yes." Jack smiled. "Listen... I'm learning all about that."

"Well, actually, it's listen and trust." The old man smiled.

"Yes, you're right!" Jack sighed. "I need to trust Him more and know that He has my life in His hands. It's just hard sometimes, especially when things don't look so good."

"Jack, let me tell you something. You *are* doing what God has purposed for you and He wants you to stay the course and continue working where you are. Don't falter or doubt, remain in Him and remember this Jack, if God gives us a difficult assignment, then He will provide us with the strength and courage that we need to fulfill it." The elderly man stated, "He will never leave you nor forsake you. You just need to *trust* in Him. Stay the course, Jack... just stay the course," he repeated.

"Would you like a drink, sir?" Jack jumped slightly at the air hostess's interruption, snapping him out of his captivated state.

He turned towards her, "Ah, no, I'm okay, but my friend here may want one." Jack motioned to the seat beside him.

The air hostess looked at him strangely. "I'm sorry, sir?" she smiled curiously at what he had just said.

Jack turned slightly to speak to the old man and, to his amazement, there was no one sitting there, nothing but an empty gray vinyl seat. He jumped slightly with a fright. "Umm-I-umm. Sorry," he said, embarrassed. "No!" he swiftly responded. "I'm just tired, thanks for the offer," he said quickly and then turned back and just stared at the empty seat beside him—tingles started flowing through his spine.

The hostess moved on and rolled her eyes at her colleague as if to say, "*Another loony.*"

Jack just sat there staring at the empty seat, thinking about the conversation he'd just had with apparently no-one. Then he remembered. "He knew my name," he whispered in awe. "I never told him my name, but he knew it," and tears started to well in his eyes and fall softly down his cheeks.

PETER SAT in his cottage in silence, crushed. The cruel, harsh words were playing over and over in his mind. He couldn't believe that his so-called friends could treat him like this. *How could this message create such enemies?* he thought. He was lost for words, unable to utter the tiniest prayer, so he just sat, remaining in silence in the dullness of the night.

"It's times like these when faith and endurance are strengthened," Jophiel said. "He will be all right, but do not let the enemy near him," he said to Peter's Guardians.

They all nodded in agreement.

CHAPTER TWENTY-NINE

TUESDAY

Jack listened to Peter pour out his broken heart as they sat alone in the old church building.

"It really didn't go quite like I had expected. I mean, I knew there would be some of the congregation question my message but not abusiveness, lies and hatred towards me. All over such stupid things like the history and heritage. It was just crazy, Jack."

"I know. Their behavior has surprised me too," Jack said, comforting his friend.

"I think nearly over half of the congregation came up to me to give me their two cents... I really thought that they would take it on board and that it would provoke them to study it for themselves and seek God on it. You know, an opportunity to get closer to Him. I thought they would embrace it. Not think it was a slur on their ancestry or belief system."

Jack sat in silence, just listening.

"I knew it would be hard, but not *this* hard. I really didn't expect this, Jack."

"I know you didn't... no-one did."

"I couldn't believe Shaun, he was so full of animosity towards me... it was just shocking."

"I know. From what you've told me, it did sound pretty bad." Jack paused for a minute before he continued saying, "But I guess you have challenged his belief system. You remember what he was like at the men's group when he first told me about the rapture. He kept telling me we would be saved and wouldn't have to go through this—he was excited. So, I guess you have to understand that he is feeling extremely attacked and challenged by all of this. His whole ideal has been thrown out the window. Not to mention the pride that he has for this little town. Father Daniel was his ancestor, remember that."

"Yeah, you're right," Peter replied solemnly. "Maybe I should have expected this—I mean, we do live in a town that is known for the rapture theory being founded here. I'm not sure why I thought it would have been received so well here. Maybe I should have started my message somewhere else."

"Well, at least it provoked something for them to think about." Jack smiled, trying to uplift his friend's spirits.

"It sure did!" replied Peter softly.

Seth and Gabe stood beside Jack, softly speaking words of wisdom into his spirit to help him encourage Peter.

"People will come around, Peter, you'll see. We always knew that not everyone will agree with this, but at least some will go home and research it for themselves." Jack stated, "It really doesn't matter if we agree about *when* Christ is returning. What actually matters is that we are ready, and if we have to endure, then we will have the strength for it. It's silly that people are willing to leave the church and be divided over this, but you cannot control their decisions. You have done what God has asked of you, and that was to deliver the truth. What they do with it is up to them—there was nothing you said that was offensive or incorrect teaching."

"I thought I made that clear. I tried to state that at the meeting but no-one would listen."

"People are people, and they will only hear what they *want* to. Look, don't worry about it. You delivered the message with convincing arguments and evidence from the Bible. If some people do not want to accept it, then let them—it's not your concern, just pray that they read the Bible for themselves, and get closer to God through it."

"It matters to me, Jack." He paused for a while and took a breath. "I feel so disheartened."

"Don't be. You did well!" Jack replied. "You have done exactly what God asked you to do. What more *can* you do? Remember, you told me that this is God's plan, so don't you think He knew that this would happen?"

"Gees Jack, you sound like me," he chuckled.

"Well, what do you expect? We hang around each other enough to rub off." He laughed, happy to see his friend lighten up.

"Thanks Jack, I really appreciate your friendship."

"Oh yeah, you will never guess what happened to me on the way home last night," Jack said with excitement, and relayed his supernatural encounter on the aircraft.

Seth and Gabe just smiled.

LOTHAR WAS ANGRY, *very* angry, as his minions continued to fail him.

"You have **NO IDEA**, do you?" he said as he slammed down his fist. "I told you to stop that message. I also told you to squash that preacher like a gnat so he couldn't spread the word. But again… you all stand before me and deliver *more* bad news." He bellowed, foaming and spitting, as his foul breath emanated from his nostrils.

The multitude of demons before him cringed and nervously shuffled and twitched.

"*That* preacher is our biggest threat. Jophiel and his sickening army," he spat with detest, "have made it their mission that *he* spreads the truth. Now **GET OUT THERE** and do something about it."

"WHAT NEWS DO YOU BRING, JOPHIEL?" Darius asked.

"The enemy has taken the bait. They believe that Jack's mission has been fulfilled, and he is no longer a threat." Jophiel responded.

"Good… very good. Then stage one of the plan is a complete success." Darius smiled.

"Indeed, sir." Jophiel beamed.

CHAPTER THIRTY

I t had been quite a few weeks since Peter shared his first message on the end times, but he continued to talk on the subject, backing everything with scripture each Sunday. He had noticed that the numbers in the congregation had decreased significantly and many of his regular churchgoers, like Shaun, had not returned since that day. He knew that there was discourse amongst the people because of the differing in opinions, and he continued to pray for those who had been offended by his message.

"I see that you have made quite a stir in your church, Peter!" Reverend Jim March stated.

Peter shifted uncomfortably, wishing that he hadn't bumped into Jim on the main street today. "Well, sometimes you just have to say what God is calling you to say and not worry about the consequences."

"Well, I don't know Peter, I like to make my congregation feel like they are on the right path," he said condescendingly, "it then becomes a win-win situation… you know, they feel happy and continue to attend church and receive forgiveness." He smiled.

"You mean continue to give their money to the church," Peter said, then paused and watched Jim shift his weight and look at him sternly without an answer. "So that's what it's all about is it? Keeping the numbers up?" Peter said, annoyed. "I'd like to think that I had spoken the truth no matter what it cost!"

"Truth! What truth? I mean, come on, this rapture thing, it's really nothing to get all upset about."

"Isn't it Jim? What have you actually heard? The message directly from me or from some obscured Chinese whispers?"

"What does it matter what I've heard? All I can see is that I've gained a lot of your congregation. I knew it wouldn't last. You seemed to have the upper hand initially, but I think now the truth has come out, Peter," he said harshly.

"This was never a competition, Jim. I don't care how many people are in my congregation as long as I am doing what God has called me to do and as long as I don't compromise the truth. I want my congregation to be spiritually alive and on fire for our Lord, and I love my congregation, but if they choose not to listen, then that is not on my head. I'm really sorry, Jim, but it saddens me you think it is a competition. That you feel you need to have the biggest congregation in the town and that people mean money." Peter sharply turned and walked off down the street. "Please God, show him the truth," he desperately whispered, with tears in his eyes.

"I have!" came the response instantly, "but he chooses not to listen."

Several weeks later.

It was a rainy afternoon and Jack and Jenny were sitting on their veranda watching the clear drops gently fall, whilst waiting for the school bus to arrive.

"Jack, I know you feel terrible about the project, but you have to know that it's God's Will, and He is still in control," Jenny stated.

"Yeah, I know, but my faith seems solid and then I have these waves of doubt come over me. You and Peter are so much stronger than me. I feel every time I go back to the head office for a meeting, or link up for a conference call, this doubt comes over me again. I feel guilty about what I started and what it has become. You know… with Peter now going to different towns, preaching and spreading the message, it seems he's doing the right thing, what he was called to do. But I feel that I am not."

"You are! It just doesn't seem like it right now. God has got you in a place where He wants you and sometimes it's waiting for the next move that's the hardest. If you quit now, what have you achieved? You will never know why God has you in this position. You just have to be patient, wait it out and trust. We both do."

The dull humdrum of the kitchen radio in the background caught both their attention as it pierced through their conversation with important breaking news.

"The United Nations has announced that the head of the New World Order, or UNITED as it shall be known as, will be the peacemaker, Jason Crane," The radio announcer stated.

"What?" Jack said as he looked over at Jenny.

"We are pleased to announce that Jason Crane will be at the helm of UNITED," spoke the Secretary-General of the United Nations in the interview. "Jason has witnessed the suffering of some of the most defenseless people on earth, in war zones and in refugee camps. He has made it his advocacy to bring human dignity to the less fortunate, to serve as a peacemaker, and ultimately unite all countries together to make this world a safer place. We feel that his credentials and his headway into world peace make him the prime candidate for this newly created position. We at the UN have voted unanimously to submit to his leadership and guidance. We are so strongly dedicated to this cause that we will no longer be called the UN, but we will form a major part of UNITED. I'll now hand you over to our new Secretary General of UNITED." Cheers were heard in the background.

"Thank you, thank you, you are too kind." Jason Crane's soothing voice rang over the radio waves.

"I am deeply honored by this appointment. It has been my lifelong ambition to see peace come to our world, but I could never have imagined that I would have the honor of bringing it in." The crowd once again cheered.

Excitement was in Jason Crane's voice. "Please, please, do not cheer for me—it is a collaborative effort. The ones you should cheer for are the members of the UN and other national leaders, for they have allowed this historical event to come to fruition." The crowd clapped and cheered even louder. "So you may be thinking, what does this mean for our world? Only one word… change! Change for the better. A safer, secure world, where there will be no more wars but only reigning peace and I will put an end to this economic disaster once and for all." Jack and Jenny could hear the crowd go wild with excitement as Jason Crane was trying to continue, but clearly loving the accolades.

"In several meetings over the past week," he continued, "all heads of nations have pledged their allegiance to UNITED. Each presidential leader of each nation has stepped down from their position and has allowed me the honor to be the Secretary General of the World." Again, the crowd went wild, as they could hear people chanting Jason's name in the background. "We have signed a peace treaty with all nations, thus giving us the opportunity to unite and become as one. One order… a New World Order… that is UNITED!"

"What are they thinking?" Jack said in disbelief as he raced inside and switched on the TV so he would not miss anything. Both he and Jenny sat on the edge of the couch, leaning forward in anticipation of what was about to appear in front of them.

Jason continued to speak. "What we ask from everyone is cooperation as we transition this new order into effect. It will only take a short time, as preparations are already under way. To become one, we must all cooperate—we must transition all monetary funds into a single recognized currency. This will be a very simple change, as all currencies are electronic, anyway. Another change required is how to manage our new currency. To gain a secure world, a world without fraud or theft, a world where everyone is recognized as equal, we must incorporate a new unique way towards our monetary handling. We have the answer to this as well. We will usher in a new empire where there will be no need to have bankcards or identification cards. Watch and see our new realm before you." With that, Jason Crane motioned towards a large screen, and an advertisement appeared upon it.

"One World, One Currency… UNITED!" the smooth female voice over stated as the advertisement portrayed a happy family shopping and enjoying life whilst utilizing the I-Chip in their wrists to purchase the goods, open doors to their house and cars and generally loving life. "A world where there is no fear of theft or fraud, where everyone is safe and secure, a world of peace, the perfect world, UNITED!" The advertisement finished and, once again, the crowd went wild with cheers.

Jason stood and raised his hands, grinning and allowing the multitude to continue to cheer for a while longer before he motioned for them to stop and allow him to speak once more.

"This is a revolutionary breakthrough!" he exclaimed. "The UNITED Chip will allow all peoples of the world freedom and safety—it will bring peace. This is the first of many advertisements showing what the UNITED Chip can bring to our world. I would encourage all to consider this new form of liberation quickly, as it is only then that we can fully live in freedom and peace. Thank you all." Once again, the crowd went wild.

Jack hit the remote and turned off the TV. Both of them remained seated in the couch, in silence, dumbfounded at what they had just witnessed and the implications of what it meant.

"UNITED Chip? I need to call Peter," said Jack.

"GOOD, IT WAS RECEIVED WELL," Lothar said with a grin. The hordes of followers waited in silence for him to continue. "I want all of you to convince people that this is the way forward. Continue your vigilant attacks on those Christians and the preacher... and stop their sickening prayers. Do what you can to convince them they must take that chip. Get to work!" Many demons left, but one remained.

"Sir?" it meekly said.

"Crechus, what do you want!" Lothar snapped with loathe at the creature before him.

"I would like to redeem myself, Master."

"You are a failing, miserable embarrassment to me. You can never make up for this blunder." He hissed with absolute hatred. "I should have squeezed the life out of you when I first laid eyes on you. You're nothing but a thorn in my side—how can YOU ever redeem yourself?" he spat.

"Let me work on the preacher."

"NO! He is our greatest threat at present. I will not let a bumbling idiot near him—he is for Conca to deal with. Now leave me!"

CHAPTER THIRTY-ONE

"Are you getting that UNITED Chip?" Ned Tucker said to Ben Jackson as he was placing his goods on the counter.

"The what?" he replied with sheer confusion written all over his face.

"The UNITED Chip, you know... weren't you listening to the news yesterday?"

"Ned... I've no idea what you're on about and besides... I don't really like potato chips—they're bad for you!" he responded, confused.

"Ha-ha, good one Ben. Well, you better get one, because things are going to change around here. I'll expect folks to start using it to buy their goods here, it's more secure," Ned exclaimed.

"Okay, I'll... err... look into it then," Ben said as he turned and walked out of the store, unsure of what to make of that exchange. He looked up to see Jack getting out of his car. "Hey Jack!" he called.

"Hi Ben, how are you today?" Jack said as he walked over to greet him.

"I'm good. What brings you into town?"

"Oh, Jen asked me to pick up some bread and milk from Tuckers, so I'm just following orders." He smiled.

"Well, you better start paying with the UNITED Chip or something, cause Ned's raving on about it and how it's going to change the way he does business. Good luck!" he smiled and laughed as he walked off towards his old blue F250.

"Thanks," Jack replied as he let out a long dismayed sigh and started walking towards Tucker's store.

"I CANNOT BELIEVE how quickly this is taking off, Jen," Jack exclaimed when he returned home. "I mean, Ned is going on and on about it, how it's going to stop theft and it will be this awesome, wonderful, peaceful world," he said sarcastically. "It's crazy!"

"I know, the girls at tennis today were going on about it too, a few of them have already registered on-line to get it."

"Where are they doing *that*?" Jack asked.

"Apparently there will be a center set up in each town. They will probably start off using the town hall until they find some-thing more permanent."

"Oh, great, it has really gotten out of hand now, hasn't it?"

"No, it hasn't. It's God's story, so stop feeling guilty and sad and everything that you've been feeling lately… as it is pointless," Jenny scolded. "God has been telling you, and also *showing* you, that you are supposed to be in this Jack, so will you please stop doubting. You heard God clearly; you know this is right." She paused and softened. "Have you talked to Peter yet?"

"No, I've left a message on his mobile but he hasn't returned my call."

"Talk to him and I'm sure he will help you put things into perspective."

"YOU'D BETTER GET on board with this, or you will be left with nothing," a black, slimy demon whispered into Reverend March's mind. "You wouldn't want that, would you? Your congregation will leave, and you will have no money coming in. What will you do? You must survive," it continued. "Be one of the first… lead the way. Convince your congregation to follow."

Reverend March's mind was spinning with thoughts. "Yes," he said aloud, "this is the way of the future." He convinced himself.

The dark, devious demon stood back, grinning and very pleased. His work accomplished.

TWO WEEKS LATER.

"Hey Jack, it's Peter," the voice came through on Jack's tele-phone. "My mobile was playing up, and I didn't get any messages until I arrived back in Evensmore this morning. I couldn't believe my eyes when I walked past the town hall and they had set up a makeshift chipping center there."

"I know! I saw it too today. What amazed me was the amount of people lined up to get in."

"Yes, that was surprising. I even saw Reverend March in the line-up."

"Well, I'd heard that he has been telling his congregation to get on board with the change, that it is a part of God's great plan."

"Oh well Jack, we can only do what we can—everyone has a choice."

"Yeah I know, but it's happening so quickly and I can't believe that I started it," Jack said, still feeling remorseful.

"How *is* your work, Jack?" Peter enquired.

"We are wrapping up the finalities of the project. It's pretty much done now that UNITED have accepted it and is already using it.

They have asked me to stay on board and oversee the engineering side of it as a subject matter expert for UNITED. But…" Jack paused, then said, "I don't know… to be honest, I don't want to. I just want out!"

"What's God telling you?"

"My head tells me to run… but my heart says that I should stay. I'm *really* torn, Pete."

"Keep praying and get God's guidance on it, don't move until He tells you to okay, remember His last words were for you to stay. In the meantime, I'll be praying for you too."

"Okay, thanks. Hey, how are your speaking engagements going?"

"Really well, I'm so pleased not everyone's reaction is the same as my congregation's."

"Thank goodness."

"Yes, it is a relief. Most people listen and then go away and make their own judgements. Which was what I always intended. I want *them* to investigate and come to their own conclusions. I've been getting some really great feedback too, although there are still a few who are not accepting of my message at all… but I'm learning not to take the criticism to heart."

"That's great news."

"I'm actually thinking of holding a one-day conference here in Evensmore and invite all the preachers and teachers from around the country. I feel it will get the word out quicker."

"That's a brilliant idea, just like what Father Harvey and Father Daniel did, but in reverse." Jack smiled.

"Yeah," Peter chuckled, "I guess you're right."

"When are you thinking of conducting it?"

"Well, I'm arranging it over the next few weeks, but I need some help though to organize and send the invites out. Do you think Jenny could help me?"

"For sure, I'll ask her, but I know she would love to."

"Great!" Peter sounded excited. "Anyway Jack, I have to go. I've got to unpack my suitcase, and do the menial tasks like washing," Peter chuckled.

"No problem, thanks for the call… it's great to talk to you."

"Likewise, I'll see you soon."

Jack waited as the phone clicked to silence.

"It's time." Darius stated. "Tell Seth and Gabe to start the next stage of the plan."

Jophiel nodded… saluted and then took flight back to earth.

Later that afternoon, Jack sat in his armchair alone. Everyone had gone out, and he was thankful for some quiet time to spend with God. He prayed, "God, you know what the future holds, but I need the answer to how we can avoid this. You say that you will protect your children. I need you to guide me in the direction that you have for me." He sighed, enjoying the quiet, when the phone rang.

"Hey Jack!" it was Simon. "They need you down here tomorrow. We are ramping up the production, and we need your expertise."

"What do you mean, ramping it up? I thought it was already pretty ramped from what I see."

Simon laughed. "No, JC's going to make some big announcement and we got a directive to create more Chips. We need you down here to help figure out a more streamlined way. So, I hope you don't mind, but I've booked the 7 am for you."

"Yes, that's fine. I'll see you tomorrow," Jack said as he hung up the phone and sighed.

That night Jack got little sleep—he tossed and turned, worrying about what this announcement would be. The alarm came around all too quickly and next thing he knew, he was on the plane headed for the UNITED office.

CHAPTER THIRTY-TWO

Peter was up early also, busily working out details for the one-day conference he was planning. He was so excited. "Lord, thank you for this idea. Please make them come so I can spread the truth quickly."

JACK SCANNED his UNITED security card and walked into his office.

"Jack," Simon called out, "how was your flight?"

"Good." Jack smiled. "Traffic was the only thing that held me up."

"Yeah, it's a shocker this time of day, isn't it? The city doesn't stop growing! Well, I'll let you get your coffee, and then could we meet in my office?"

"Sure, I'll be there in 10 minutes."

Jack unpacked his briefcase, removed his laptop, and placed it on his desk. He grabbed his coffee mug and headed for the kitchen.

"Jack!" Without having to turn, he knew the all-familiar voice calling his name, and it sent shivers up his spine.

"Hi Jason," he said as he turned with a forced smile.

"I didn't know you were in the office today."

"I'm meeting with Simon regarding production."

"Ah!" his too perfect white teeth shone as he smiled back. "I'm so excited about the next phase—it's going to change the world as we know it. My dream of peace will finally come to fruition. I know you feel the same way too, Jack. I remember that's what you said when you presented this concept to our board all those years ago."

Jack stood listening to Jason talk. He couldn't put a finger on it, but just standing in the presence of this man made his skin prickle. He didn't trust him, and he hated to admit, he didn't like him either. There was just something disturbing about him. He looked perfect with his thick blonde hair, fit physique, handsome chiseled features, and olive complexion. However, the feeling Jack had every time he saw him—he just couldn't explain it. It was unnatural, like a malevolent presence was surrounding Jason… and Jack couldn't wait to get away from him every time.

Seth and Gabe shifted uneasily, facing the gigantic demon standing beside Jason. Neither of them wanted to start anything with this massive beast. It stood bearing its enormous yellowing wolf fangs, grinning maliciously, delighted to see their apprehension.

"Well, I won't hold you up any longer. Good to see you again," Jason said as he walked off down the hallway.

Relieved, Jack walked via his office, grabbed his laptop, and headed for the meeting.

As Jason walked down the hall, he addressed the dark being beside him. "Do I need to be concerned about Jack?"

"No Master," it responded, "he is not a threat!"

"JC is announcing that the Chip is now mandatory," Simon stated.

"Mandatory?" Jack exclaimed.

"Yes, it's the only way to enforce peace throughout this world," he stated passionately.

"But surely people should be given a choice, Simon—this was never my intent with this concept."

"Why should they? It's for their *own* good… and it's the only way it can be done as it will only work if everyone has one."

"I'm not sure it's such a good idea."

"Well, you don't have a choice… none of us do. We just have to make it happen, don't we?" Simon said with a sly grin, making Jack feel like he shouldn't say any more. "So," he sighed, "getting back to the job at hand, we need to increase production from 1 million to 25 million chips per day."

Jack's jaw dropped in shock at the vast number.

Simon continued to explain what needed to be completed. All morning Jack tried hard to keep his focus and put forward new ideas, but he found it difficult to concentrate. His mind kept wandering off to his family and friends, and how he was going to keep them from harm. He couldn't help but think what was ahead for all the innocent people.

"Jack," Simon said, "are you with me man... are you listening?" he said in a half-joking but half-serious tone.

"Ah, sorry Simon, I drifted off there for a minute." He paused before continuing. "Say, what will happen to those who refuse to take the chip?"

Simon looked around, slowly leaned over closer, and lowered his voice to a whisper. "Word is... if someone refuses, then they will be removed."

"What do you mean, *removed?*" Jack whispered back.

"Removed from society, they do not belong if they do not want to conform to the new world."

"How?"

"I don't know that much, but JC has implied that they do not belong in *this* world," he said as he tapped his finger on the desk, "if they don't want to follow."

Jack sat back, taking in a deep breath. Suddenly, his stomach lurched and his heart pounded and ached.

"You okay, Jack? You look pale, man!"

"I'm... I'm okay," Jack said as he got up out of his chair and stumbled. "Excuse me; I just have to go back to my office for a bit."

"Jack, you don't look so good... you want me to call someone?"

"No, I'm all right... I just need a minute. Excuse me," he mumbled as he left the room.

Jack ran down the corridor to his office and locked the door; his heart pounding as he dived for the waste bin and started throwing up the contents of his stomach. He crawled over to his desk and continued to hold the waste bin in case there was more to come. He sat with his back against the desk leg. "OH NO!" he cried, crushing tears streamed down his pale face as he continued to heave and gag until his stomach was empty. "What have I done?" he cried, overwhelmed by the weight of shame and guilt.

Gabe stood over him and placed his hand upon Jack's shoulder, and spoke comforting words into his spirit. "*The steps of a man are established by the Lord, when he delights in His way.*"

Swiftly Jack felt an overpowering peace settle over him... then God spoke, "*Do not despair my son, for I am with you, I have your future set before you, my plans are not your plans, I have you in the palm of my right hand. Trust in me, I love you.*"

Jack sat perfectly still, drinking in the message given directly to his heart. He was sitting peacefully in silence when unexpectedly Simon burst through the door, breaking the lock, splintering the wood across the carpet.

"Jack, Buddy!" he panicked, running towards him. "Are you okay?" he knelt down next to him.

"I-I'm fine. Just. Well, I think I might just have a stomach bug, no need to be alarmed."

"Are you sure? *Man*, you had me worried, especially when the door was locked—what was that about?" He looked confused. "I thought you might have been having a heart attack! You want me to call Jen?"

"No, no, please, trust me... I'll be fine. I'm just feeling a little nauseous. It must be from the flight this morning, we hit some bad turbulence."

"Well, if you're sure," Simon looked at Jack intently and cautiously for any more signs of illness. "I'm here if you need me, but I think you probably should go back to your hotel and take it easy—we've pretty much discussed all we need. I think we have a way forward now. Do you want me to take you?"

"No, I'll be fine. I can get a cab anyway if I need to. Thanks, Simon," Jack said, appreciating his concern. "I'll be all right."

"Okay, well, just holler if you need me," Simon said as he stood and slowly backed out the door, still watching cautiously for any signs of Jack's condition worsening.

Gabe waited for the door to close, then leant over and whispered gently to Jack. "Find a way Jack... you can do this."

Jack sat and waited a few minutes after Simon left. He packed up his briefcase and headed for the hotel, even if it was only for a few hours.

He needed some God time.

CHAPTER THIRTY-THREE

A thin, pimply teenage boy dressed in black jeans and a T-shirt, with a single silver piercing through his lip, sat directly opposite Peter in the church office.

"So, Jeremy, what brings you here? How can I help you today?" Peter asked.

"Ah, well, I'm just... I dunno!" he paused and looked down, showing a lack of confidence, fiddling with his hands. "I'm... you know, feeling down I guess."

"Right..." Peter nodded, encouraging Jeremy to speak.

"Well... mum and dad, they don't get it and... I dunno, my friends are just... well. No one gets *me*, you know?"

Peter nodded again, ready to listen, just letting Jeremy talk and trying to understand what he was saying.

After another 20 minutes, Jeremy left. Peter was thankful that it was time for him to lock up the church and go home. *That was an intense counseling session*, he thought. He eagerly walked across the lawn and heard the phone ringing as he unlocked his door to his cottage. It was Jack—he told him about the enforcement.

"So what are your thoughts, then?" Peter said.

"I'm not sure," Jack gripped the hotel phone tightly, still feeling very emotional. "I've been praying and I think I have an idea... but I don't know how it will fly."

"Shoot!"

"Well, each chip is given a unique identification number that is programmed into it upon production. I'm thinking... if I can take some and input them into the UNITED Chip register, we could use them."

"How?"

"Well, that's the tricky bit—I don't know. I'm not sure how we could use them and fit in normally. I'm really at a loss there."

"God will show you just keep praying."

"I need help, I don't know... another insider or something, someone who is knowledgeable and is there all the time. But it's just too risky."

"Be careful Jack, don't go talking to people. Let God bring them to you. It's His plan and He will provide, remember this."

"You're right... don't worry, I will wait—I don't know who to trust here. I'm going back to the office this afternoon so I'd better go now. I need to talk to Jen first."

"I'm praying for you."

"Thanks... I need it."

Seth looked over at Gabe. "Good," he said.

At 8.59 pm, Seth quietly unlocked the door to the UNITED storeroom.

At 9pm, Jack quietly slipped into the dimly lit storeroom and approached the shelves where the storage boxes were stacked. He looked around to ensure no one else was around in the room whilst he opened a box and took a few handfuls of the UNITED Chips, which equated to a few thousand, and placed them into an antistatic bag. If he could quickly enter these into the system tonight, then they would not be missed, he thought. "Dear God," he said, "I need someone to help me—I need another insider. Please bring one to me God, I can't do this on my own," he whispered the desperate prayer.

Seth turned to Gabe. "Okay, we're clear... but we must go *right now!*"

Gabe gently nudged Jack, urging him to leave the room. Jack sensed the urgency and obeyed. No sooner had Jack turned the corner of the corridor, the security guards came in at the opposite end.

"Bob! Maaan... you can't be so careless. This door was left open," one of them said, annoyed but not sensing anything wrong.

"Gees, yeah, I'm sorry, I'm not sure now, I thought I'd locked it," Bob replied confused as he locked the door and continued along with the security check.

PETER COULDN'T SLEEP. He tossed and turned until, finally frustrated—he got up. "Is it you, God?" he asked. Learning a long time ago that often when he couldn't sleep, it was God prompting him to do something. He made himself a hot chocolate and sat on the couch before asking again.

"Father, what do you want to say to me?" he asked.

The reply came rapidly, "Pray for Jack!"

"Pray for what specifically?" he asked.

"Just pray!" came the reply.

Peter sat on the couch and obeyed. He prayed, not knowing what to pray for. Sometimes he prayed in tongues, sometimes he just worshipped and lifted Jack up in prayer... but he obeyed and he prayed.

JACK SAT in his office upstairs and methodically entered each chip number into the UNITED chip register. It was late and no-one, he thought, was in the office at this hour.

"Burning the midnight oil?" the voice said.

Jack jumped in his chair and looked up to see that it was Jason. He quickly shut down the software with a keystroke that he had programmed in for occasions such as this. "Well, I just like to get everything completed before my flight home tomorrow morning," Jack replied with a smile.

"Ah, I love your dedication, Jack. I didn't mean to startle you, but I'm so glad you're a part of this team. We have the same vision, to see this world come together as one. I mean, you were the one who started this, so I actually have you to thank." Jason smiled.

"I wouldn't go that far. After all it was a team effort."

"Yes, yes, I know, you always say that—you're so modest.

Anyway, I'll leave you to it. Have a safe trip back." Jason smiled as he left the door and headed down the corridor.

"Thanks, I will," Jack called out in reply and soon thereafter let out a massive sigh of relief. "God, I need someone here," he said.

Seth and Gabe also breathed a sigh of relief at seeing the large demon walk off.

AKIO WAS a young Japanese software engineering graduate who had started with UNITED 12 months ago. He worked in a pool of nearly two hundred engineers, fine-tuning and upgrading the software that controlled the UNITED Chip. He was just a small fry in this big team. As Akio slept in the early hours, the Holy Spirit hovered over him, giving him a dream.

He saw himself meeting a man he had never seen before, but somehow knew him as a brother in Christ. He walked up to this man and said straight out, "The stars are so bright tonight, I wish I had brought my telescope." At that point, his dream stopped, and then, as if it was a film, it rewound and repeated. This occurred three times.

Akio woke in a daze, confused at what he had dreamed. He knew it was from God as his dreams were never as clear as this, nor did they repeat as this one had. "What does this mean?" he questioned God. "I don't even own a telescope," he queried, confused.

JACK HAD FINISHED ENTERING the last of the serial numbers for the chips. It was 4.30 am— he was tired, his eyes hurt, and his wrist ached profusely from RSI, a resultant of his night's work. *He had to get a hold of a scanner, he* thought, *but that was way too obvious,* he reasoned. *At least, this way he could keep it relatively inconspicuous… but it was so slow… and painful.* The chatter continued in his head until he finally shut down his computer, locked up, and left his office.

His flight was in three hours, and he was glad to be heading off to the airport.

Barely being able to keep his eyes open, he got into the cab. "Can you take me to the airport please?" he said to the cab driver politely.

The driver pulled out and headed in the airports direction. It was still dark, and the rocking of the cab quickly lulled Jack to sleep—he dreamed deeply. Clearly in his dream the words came to him, "the stars are so bright tonight, I wish I had brought my telescope." Jack looked at the young man in his dream and God spoke directly to Jack, "*This is the one I have sent you. He will be your helper.*" These were the words that Jack clearly heard.

"Excuse me sir, but we are here," the cab driver said softly, trying not to startle Jack too much out of his sleep.

"Ah... sorry, thank you so much," he said as he clambered out of the vehicle, giving the cabby a decent tip.

"I BRING NEWS GREAT MASTER." The small, black spindly messenger spirit bowed low before Lothar. "The announcement is today." He smiled a row of spike like teeth, knowing his master would be very pleased at the news.

"Good... very good," Lothar paused, "I have waited for this day for a very... long... time." He paused as he tapped his chin with his long talon. "Nothing can stop us now." He grinned. "We will enforce this and *all* of humanity will bow down to *our* Lord." He let out a small chuckle, very pleased with himself.

He stood and took a deep breath, his hulking chest expanding as he pulled his shoulders back while his wings gradually unfurled. The leathery vascular membranes rustled as they extended. A large bony spike curved like a hook protruded from the top of each wing as he stretched them outward, portraying authority over his kingdom. Lothar felt an abundance of confidence in his part of the grand plan. "Do your best to convince all to go forth and accept the chip," he said before he launched skyward, spiraling around looking downward for the Angelic hosts.

"Mark this day hosts," he bellowed out at the top of his lungs, "for today is the day that you fail." He laughed as he suddenly snapped his wings flat back, and sped off at rocket speed towards his Master, leaving a long black afterburner streak against the blue sky.

Jophiel, Chale, and their armies heard their enemy gloat. They looked skyward and watched… for they knew what was coming.

"I've got them," Jack said as he sat opposite Peter, sipping his coffee in Betty's diner.

"So… what next?"

"Well, that's what I'm not sure about. I've secured them in the system so they won't be missed but… I don't know what to do with them."

"You will, God will show you. He's been guiding you all this time and he will continue."

"I think he already did this morning when I fell asleep in the cab." Jack told Peter about the dream.

"Wow, I love how God speaks so clearly to you. It's refreshing." Peter smiled. "Also, did Jenny tell you we've already sent the invites out for the conference?" he said excitedly. "It will be in four weeks' time."

"Yes, and she told me she has already had 60 acceptances too."

At that moment, Jason Crane appeared on the TV mounted in the diner. Both Peter and Jack turned upon hearing his voice.

"I want to thank all who have accepted our new way forward. It is a momentous occasion, as I am very proud to announce there are nearly one *billion* people who have accepted the UNITED Chip. This will provide a safer, secure and a most peaceful environment for us all—however, to achieve this *fully*, we must ALL embrace it. Therefore, in moving forward in ushering in our new world, it is imperative that all peoples of the earth now comply and accept the UNITED Chip."

Jack heard some people murmur and shift uncomfortably. "I don't want no chip in me," he heard them say.

"I know this may come as a surprise," Jason continued, "but to live in a world of peace and freedom of fear, we must all comply so that we become one… UNITED together!" He paused and smiled. "One world without terrorism, war, theft, or murders. One world in which we can embrace peace and live in harmony—one world where everyone is UNITED."

The screen suddenly faded out and the female voice over was heard. "For us to become UNITED, please make your way to the nearest chipping center and register for your UNITED Chip implant." The picture panned out to reveal a happy community smiling and all in unison they chimed, "So we can become one!"

Jack looked around at the others in the diner. Some looked nonchalant and accepting and went back to their meals. Others looked concerned and started talking amongst themselves, clearly not comfortable about the enforcement.

"Okay… so what NOW?" Peter grimaced.

"Pray!" Jack responded, "Pray hard!"

Seth and Gabe stood waiting for direction from their Lord, but received nothing.

"We wait!" Gabe said… Seth nodded in agreement.

As Jack and Peter left the diner, they saw people congregating around the chip center. They walked in the opposite direction.

4 DAYS LATER.

"Good, all is going to plan," said Lothar, grinning widely, drool cascading down his jowls. The other demons chattered and jostled amongst themselves, all pleased with their efforts in this grand scheme.

At that moment, a small messenger demon came fluttering in the side window with a card. He bowed low as he excused himself and walked towards Lothar, carefully handing it to him.

"What's this?"

"Read, Master," he said as he slowly backed away and then quickly flew back out the window.

Lothar read the card in silence; his previous pleasure had now become sheer anger. He clenched his jaw. "Crechus, that imbecile started this," he whispered with utter detest. He looked up and addressed the crowd."The preacher is holding a conference to spread the word. Where is Conca? Get me Conca." He slammed his fist down and shouted furiously, "Tell him he needs to accelerate his attack."

I t was 11.30 pm when Seth and Gabe felt the prompting as they stood guarding Jack while he slept.

"We need to wake him," Seth said.

Gently, they placed their hands upon him, and he stirred slowly to consciousness. He laid there for a little while, then got up, went to the kitchen and made a hot chocolate.

"What is it, Lord?" he asked.

The response came instantly, *Go to the office tomorrow, I am making a way.*

"How? It's late and I can't just turn up to the airport—I need to book a flight. I also need a valid reason."

Trust!

"Okay Lord, I trust you!" Jack said as he finished his hot chocolate and went back to bed.

"You all right?" Jenny asked.

"Yes, but I have to go into the office tomorrow."

"Oh?"

"Don't worry, everything's fine—go back to sleep," he said as he lovingly kissed her on the cheek and peacefully went back to sleep.

CRYSTALYN HATED VISITS FROM CONCA. It always made him anxious, as his past encounters with this huge demon were never good. "What do you want?" he asked, glaring at the gigantic beast before him, hoping this was a quick meeting.

"Get the girl to hurry things up. Master commands you do it today. Right now!"

"Who are *you* to tell me what Master wants? I am in his favor, he should beckon me and tell me himself." He remarked arrogantly.

Conca leapt forward and grasped Crystalyn around the throat, clutching him tight. "Look idiot, I outrank you, so don't become insolent with me. I hate you and have no problem ripping you apart limb by puny limb. Unfortunately, Master needs you right now… but don't get used to it. It won't last." He spat with disgust, "… and I'll be waiting."

AT 5 AM, the alarm sounded. Jack awoke from one of the best sleeps he'd had in a very long time and strangely, he felt rested and rejuvenated. He carefully got up so as not to disturb Jenny and made his way downstairs to the kitchen. Suddenly, his mobile phone vibrated on the kitchen table.

"Hello?" Jack said curiously, not expecting a call at this hour.

"Jack, thank goodness! I know it's early, but I just had to call you," Simon stated.

"Why what's up?"

"I need you to come into the office today, sorry it's short notice. I didn't want to call your home phone, as I didn't want to wake your family, so I'm glad you answered your mobile."

"That's fine, I'm up anyway."

"I've booked the 7 am for you. Can you make it?"

"Sure, I'll see you in the office."

"Great! Thanks for this. See you soon," Simon said as he hung up.

Jack stood smiling. *Ah God, you are so perfect*, he thought as he finished his breakfast.

PETER ALSO GOT UP EARLY and was looking online at the UNITED website, checking the tally of people accepting the UNITED Chip. The website stated three billion. "God, they don't know what they are doing," he sighed.

· · ·

LORA STIRRED as Crystalyn slowly drew her out of her dreamy slumber. "Lorraaa... Lorrraa, wake up my darling friend."

"Crystalyn, it's too early." She looked over at her alarm, which wasn't to sound for another two hours.

"I know, but we need to do something now."

"What? Right now?" she said, sitting up, rubbing her eyes and yawning.

"Yes, can you set things up quickly?"

"Really... can't it wait? I'm so tired."

"Lora, come on... please." Crystalyn smiled sweetly.

"Okay," Lora tiredly obeyed, put on a sweater, and started to light the candles as she grabbed the chalk to draw.

IT SURPRISED Jack when he saw Simon waiting at the airport terminal, waving him over.

"Hi Jack, how was your flight?"

"Wow, Simon, I think this is the first time you have ever chaperoned me," Jack chuckled.

"I know, I know, I just thought I'd use this opportunity to talk with you privately in the car to fill you in on some challenges we have at the moment."

"Oh?" Jack said as he and Simon walked towards the cab Simon had waiting.

"Yes, I needed to discuss a few things *out* of the office; it's something that I didn't want upper management being concerned about just yet if you know what I mean."

"Sure... is it bad?"

"Potentially... well, if we cannot work out a way forward today. I really want to fix it before it escalates any higher. We may be able to manage it at this level so not to cause any concern. We just need your expertise."

"So, what's the big issue?" Jack said as he climbed into the backseat of the car.

"Well, as you're aware, we've always had a small failure rate with the chips, like one in 1000, but in the last few days we have had a higher rate than usual go awry."

"Mm, go on."

"So I've organized a meeting with some of our best engineers this morning to have a think tank and try to find out the cause and correct the problem before it affects our stats. We just need to find out what's changed and we should be back on track."

"What do you mean, what's changed?"

"We tweaked the design a few days ago and well… I think it's causing the problem."

"Why don't you just switch back?"

"It would take too long, as we have changed all the calibrations. If we can just find what's causing it, then we can get on with delivering the quantity required. Just here." Simon said to the cab driver. "Thank you!" he said as he waved his wrist in front of the scanner to pay, then climbed out of the car. "Okay, go get your coffee and I'll meet you in my office in 20 minutes."

"Sure." Jack smiled as they walked through the massive security doors of UNITED's headquarters.

PETER HEARD a soft knock on his door. He looked out, and it was Jeremy standing on his porch. He opened the door and smiled as he greeted him. "Hi Jeremy, what brings you around?"

"Ah… Hi preacher, I mean Pastor McKinnely." He corrected himself, looking down again. "I just um… well, I fixed your laptop… I fixed it real good… it works well now."

"Already?"

"Yeah, it was nothing," he continued to look down, scuffing his shoes and shifting around anxiously.

"Well, come in and… well, do you want a drink, a coke, or something?"

"Yeah, I guess." He looked around cautiously and walked into the house.

· · ·

IN A ROOM of about twenty other engineers, Jack and the team were busily running the new chips through a series of scanners, capturing metrics and carefully looking at the various design changes and potential faults. He was so focused that he didn't notice the young engineer from the other side of the room occasionally staring at him.

They broke for lunch, came back and further continued into the evening darkness. After hours of testing, stepping through code and analyzing, Jack saw the problem in one of the metrics' paths. "I think we have it," he said. The other engineers started breaking off from their groups milling around, closely staring at Jack's laptop.

"Yes, yes, *that's IT*," one of them said ecstatically.

"Yep, that is definitely the problem," another responded.

They all cheered and patted each other's backs in relief.

"Great work, guys," Simon said, smiling, overjoyed at the result. "Okay, let's move and get this fix down to the factory and reload the software." He paused and looked at Jack. "Thanks Jack, I knew you'd find it!" He smiled, then hurriedly turned and strode out the door along with the rest of the team... except for one.

Jack was packing up his laptop and briefcase, not realizing that there was still someone left in the room.

"Mmm-hmm."

Startled, he looked over to the person clearing their throat.

"The stars are so bright tonight, I wish I had brought my telescope."

Jack looked at the young Asian man standing at the other end of the room. "I'm sorry?"

Akio shifted awkwardly, clearly nervous about this encounter. "The stars are so bright tonight, I wish I had brought my telescope," He repeated louder this time.

Jack sat staring at the man silently for a moment, recapping events in his brain until he remembered what God had previously told him. The day had been so long and eventful that he nearly had forgotten all about it. A smile slowly appearing on his face as he stood up. He walked over and wholeheartedly embraced the young man. "Thank God," he said, "You are the one!"

Akio embraced Jack back, relieved that he was right and hadn't confused him with the wrong person. "I am relieved, so relieved, that you responded this way. I was so nervous I'd get it wrong." He smiled.

"God told me, He told me the exact phrase and said that you would be the one to help me," Jack said excitedly.

"He showed me your face," Akio said and smiled, amazed that it had worked out. They both were so excited about how God had orchestrated their meeting.

"We must talk... but not here," Jack exclaimed.

Akio nodded. "There is a diner about two blocks from here—we could go there?"

"Sounds good!"

In the heavenly realms, Jophiel stood before Darius. "They have met," he said.

"That's excellent news... our plans are coming together nicely." Darius smiled, extremely satisfied with the brave warrior standing before him. "Now you must constantly cover them, as the enemy cannot discover their intent. We *must* provide more time for the saints."

Jophiel nodded his head in agreement. "I will make sure of it, sir."

CHAPTER THIRTY-FIVE

J ason Crane was talking in his office at UNITED, but not to anything human.

"I think like this!" Jason said as he stiffened his arms downward. "Then you lift me, let's show them I have all the power." He grinned.

The gargantuan demon just looked at him, nodding his head in agreement. He was simply placating this arrogant little man whom he absolutely detested, simply another pawn in the grand scheme that he had fooled. Besides... he was only following *his* Master's orders, the highest Master in his army... Satan.

"Let's try it, shall we?" Jason said and the colossal demon stepped forward obligingly, grinning.

JACK AND AKIO talked into the night, getting to know one another and sharing stories of how they came to know God.

"I'm so blessed to know you Jack, you are an amazing man, and I am astounded at what you have accomplished."

"Really?" Jack was stunned, "because I don't see it that way."

"No Jack, you are remarkable. You have been doing what God has ordained you to do. It is such an honor to achieve our calling."

"Well, I'm relieved God sent you Akio. I really need someone inside UNITED who can help me. I've got some chips and entered them into the system but," Jack paused, "I'm at a loss for what to do next!"

"I too have been planning on how to help people avoid this chip."

"Go on."

"Every spare moment I have, when I'm not at UNITED I've been experimenting, I have a lab set up at home. I not only have a degree in software engineering but also Biomedical as well...

anyway, I've come up with a new concept, where the actual chip is extremely thin and flexible. I've experimented with it and have bonded it with a porous silicone substance so it becomes similar to skin tissue," Akio said as he unzipped the inside of his jacket and pulled out his sample.

"WOW!" Jack said as Akio handed it over to him carefully so no one could see. "It's amazing! It's no thicker than a millimeter, if that and so... well so... ductile," Jack said with excitement whilst feeling the softness and flexibility of the new thin film.

"The chips that you already have, I can encode those IDs into each one of these." He paused.

"... And we can wear them!" Jack finished his sentence with a smile of understanding, "Absolutely Brilliant!"

"Yes," Akio beamed.

"You're amazing; this is exactly what we need."

"No... *GOD is amazing!*"

"Yeah! He sure is." Jack smiled.

Gabe and Seth grinned with delight.

CRECHUS HAD BEEN SKULKING around undetected outside of Jack's house, trying to piece together a plan to bring this man down. Revenge for exposing the letter and getting him into trouble. He was cautious not to be detected, so he lay low, creeping undercover, spying and eavesdropping. Even though he hated Crystalyn, he wanted to achieve this on his own. Crystalyn had been getting all the Master's attention. He looked around, but he couldn't see Jack anywhere. Disappointed, he went into town and see what mischief he could stir up.

THE TRIP HOME for Jack was much different from the flight there. He felt a renewed vigor, that there was a possibility to avoid being detected without actually having the chip implanted, to live normally for a little while longer.

He and Akio had worked tirelessly into the night, switching

the chip IDs over to the new I-Skins as they decided to call them. They had gone back to Akio's apartment, where he had set up a scanning device and undetected software that he had written to connect into the mainframe of UNITED.

It amazed Jack at what this kid could do. He couldn't wait to get home and tell Jenny and Peter what they had done.

When the aircraft touched down, he decided he would call into Peter's place on the way home to tell him all about it. He grabbed his briefcase, disembarked, waited for his luggage, and then quickly headed to his car.

As he rounded the corner to Peter's cottage, his jaw nearly hit the ground, flabbergasted to see two police vehicles parked out the front and Peter being escorted in handcuffs into one of them.

Jack hit his horn as he pulled over and jumped out of his car. "Hey, what's going on? What are you doing?"

"Stand back!" One officer held up his hand in warning.

"You've made a mistake. Peter's a pastor... what has he done?"

The police officers simply ignored Jack, pushed through, and went about their business. Jack saw them going in and out of Peter's cottage, taking things out and placing them in the vehicles.

A crowd was drawing and people were staring and whispering amongst themselves.

"I demand to know what's going on." Jack barged in front of one officer.

"Out of my way, or I'll arrest you for obstructing justice. If you want to know you can come down to the station and talk to him yourself, *AFTER* we process him. Is that clear?" the officer responded abruptly in Jack's face. "Now get outta my way!"

Jack ran over to the police car window to see Peter sitting in the back. His face streaked with tears and pain, looking back at him.

"What's going on?" Jack said through the closed glass window.

Peter simply looked away, shaking his head, visibly upset.

"I'm coming down to the station!" he shouted as the police car sped away with his friend cuffed inside.

. . .

Meg was walking home along one of the back streets of town when she heard hushed voices down the alley. She stopped just behind a dumpster and listened in on the conversation.

"So, did you do it?" a girl's voice asked.

"Yeah, but I don't know if I should of, I don't feel right." a boy's voice replied.

"It's what was asked of us… so we must obey," the girl stated.

"I guess."

"Crystalyn said that this is for the good of the *entire* community, that it's best."

"Okay, well, I gotta go. They want me back at 3 pm," said the boy nervously.

Meg could hear them walk off in different directions. *Crystalyn*, she thought as she peered around the corner of the dumpster to see the back of Lora walking off down the alleyway. *I wonder what she is up to,* she thought as she continued on her journey home.

Peter was beside himself behind the bars of the cold cell, explaining to Jack what had happened and why he was here.

"He's accused you of WHAT?" Jack exclaimed.

"Sexual abuse! That's what he's claiming." Peter replied, distraught.

"How? Why? Who is this kid anyway?"

"I've been counseling him over the last month—he's a confused, lost, depressed teenager. I don't know, I thought I was helping him—making progress." He paused and continued explaining, "I never laid a hand on him Jack, you have to believe me."

"I believe you, Peter, you don't even have to tell me that," Jack said, distressed, thinking of how this could happen.

"Even worse too, is that the police took my laptop and have found child pornography on it." Peter choked out those last words as he covered his red, tear-streaked face.

"Oh Gees…" Jack sighed, "but how… how could *that* be on there?"

"I don't know how the heck it got there," Peter blurted, confused. "How can that just appear? I hardly use that laptop. It's been sitting in my office unused for months collecting dust until…" He stopped and looked at Jack with realization.

"Until what?"

"Until Jeremy took it home to fix it," Peter stared blankly back at Jack.

"You're saying you gave it to *that* kid?"

"Yeah, he told me he could clean it up and make it run faster."

"Gees Peter," Jack said frustrated, "there's your answer. Have you told the police this?"

"No, I've just realized it then. I haven't been thinking straight. Can you get someone here? I don't know an attorney, but could you help me?"

"I'll do everything I can. You are innocent Peter and I do not know why you're being framed."

"The preacher is now out of the way. His reputation has been shattered," Conca said confidently as he brought Lothar the good news.

"Good… Good." Lothar grinned. "You and Crystalyn have again excelled yourselves."

"I don't know how long the charges will stick though, sir," Conca respectfully responded.

"That doesn't matter. His reputation is now in tatters—we will ensure this ends up in the papers and no one will take him seriously anymore. He is forever stamped with this slur. We are winning, and with him out of the way, it makes it all much easier. We will stop the spreading of his message." He roared with laughter, happy with what his demonic minions had achieved.

CHAPTER THIRTY-SIX

Lora sat on the floor of her bedroom. It was very early in the morning—the moon was full, and the shadows danced and skipped across her bedroom walls like puppets. The single candle sitting in the middle of a pentagram drawn on the floor was gently fluttering and flickering in the small breeze entering via the open window.

"Go deeper... deeper, Lora. Come with me into a deeper place. You must reach another level," Crystalyn spoke, wooing the girl into her innermost being.

Lora's trance seemed bottomless, the deepest that she had ever experienced. She felt herself dissolving and floating into an altered state as she descended further and further down with Crystalyn beside her. They held hands as Crystalyn showed Lora another place in her subconscious, revealing the wonders of the universe deep within herself and answers to profound yearning questions.

"Is God real?" Lora asked.

"We are all gods made of the one substance—we control our own destiny. There is not one God, but many, Lora," Crystalyn replied soothingly.

Crystalyn sat alongside Lora on the floor, weaving more magic. She was so deceived and completely believed everything the black, sinewy demon told her. Lora had come as far as the many other subjects that had come before her. Crystalyn could ask Lora anything and she would now obey.

Master will be so pleased, Crystalyn thought.

At 7.30 AM, Jack arrived at the police station with an attorney.

"You have no right to hold my client. Release him as there is no proof," the attorney stated.

"You want proof? We have a boy saying he was sexually

abused AND we have his laptop with child pornography. I think that's proof enough," responded the detective.

"Until it is proven it is *his* doing, you cannot hold my client."

"Fine, I'll release him, but he will not be leaving his house, not even to put his garbage can outside if I can help it."

Thirty minutes later, Peter, Jack, and the attorney stepped into Jack's car and headed home. However, the newspaper photographers had already snapped photos of Peter leaving the police station... they had their story.

It was midnight, and Crystalyn decided to teach Lora to visit the astral planes. "Go deep, much deeper than before," Crystalyn beckoned. "Get into the vibration state that I taught you."

Lora was deeply relaxed lying on the bed with Crystalyn coaching her.

"When you're ready... reach for my hand and we will go."

Lora took a few breaths and then reached out, and Crystalyn took her hand.

Lora suddenly felt a tingling, then rushing sensation as she came out of her body. She opened her eyes to see herself moving and elevated above her form—Crystalyn was beside her. They exchanged smiles.

"Are you ready?" Crystalyn asked.

"Yes," she said excitedly.

"Let's go!"

They ascended effortlessly through the roof and Lora gasped at the exhilarating feel and awe of going through solid mass. They rose higher above the rooftop, out into the cool night air, and hovered for a few seconds. Then Crystalyn motioned for her to look ahead. As she did, she moved forward, flying, gliding ever so lightly. It was thrilling, and she couldn't contain her excitement.

"Whoopee!" Lora shouted.

Crystalyn laughed as they moved faster.

They glided over the streets until they got to Selwyn Street, where the school and hospital were located. "I want you to do something now, Lora," Crystalyn said as they hovered above. "Say a curse over this street."

"Why?"

"Just do it, it's for a good purpose, there are very bad people here and we need to punish them."

"Okay."

Crystalyn told Lora what to say, and she repeated it. They went from street to street repeating the same statements... but some streets they avoided, as Crystalyn knew there were Christians gathered there.

Crystalyn stopped mid-air and pulled Lora back as he watched the demons rushing into the streets where Lora had cursed. Dropping from the sky, more and more arrived.

"Why have we stopped?" Lora asked.

"Oh, I just wanted to enjoy the view," Crystalyn said and beamed. "Let's get you back home before you get too tired—you will need your rest after this."

Demons crawled through the streets, attaching themselves to people, causing havoc. There was disruption, fights breaking out, and pure chaos exploding. Drunks and drug addicts roamed the streets yelling and screaming at one another. Someone threw a bottle through a shop window and the alarm went off whilst a scuffle broke out across the street.

The demons were in party mode.

"WELL DONE," Lothar complimented Crystalyn in front of his peers.

He responded by bowing low in respect to his callous Master.

Crechus just stood in the crowd and watched, seething.

"I am pleased with your efforts. I will promote you in due time once we have accomplished our plans." Lothar stated.

"Thank you, Master." Crystalyn grinned.

"You have the girl completely now?"

"Yes master, she does what I say, we can use her fully now."

"Excellent! We can use her to bring down more and more of the enemy. This is perfect."

A WEEK LATER, Jack and Peter sat at a booth and ate breakfast together at Betty's Diner.

"I can't thank you enough," Peter looked squarely at Jack.

"I'm just relieved that they have dropped all charges—it was a joke, Peter," Jack declared with disgust. "I can't believe they didn't question the kid more thoroughly before they came and got you."

Peter sighed, played with his food a little before he spoke again. "I guess my reputation has taken a pretty big hit, hey," he said sadly, before he continued. "I've had 37 pastors since cancel out of the 149 who accepted the invitation for the conference. What's that telling you, Jack?"

"People will think what they want to think no matter what the truth is. I am spreading the word. I've asked the newspaper to print the truth, so I'm sure it won't be too long until the people hear Jeremy made it up. Don't worry about it, just continue what you were doing. You're the one who is always telling me that the enemy is trying to stop God's work. This is just another example, don't you think?"

"I guess," Peter nodded despondently.

"Listen Pete, why don't you just take a few days of rest... spend the time immersing yourself in God's Word. It will help you. Besides, you need to refocus and get ready for the conference in a few weeks."

"Maybe I will. Thanks Jack, you're a good friend," he half smiled as they continued to finish their breakfast.

"Did you see the news the other night, the fights that broke out in Selwyn and Brown streets?" Jack asked with surprise.

"Yes, I did. I've never seen anything like it here. I know I'm not a fan of having so many bars in the town, but I couldn't believe what I was seeing on TV. How many people were hospitalized?"

"Three apparently. I thought I'd left all that behind when I moved here."

Unseen by Peter and Jack, a brilliant light suddenly flashed before them. Jophiel had arrived, and Gabe and Seth stood immediately to attention before their captain.

"Good morning, sir," Gabe greeted.

"How are you, my friends?" Jophiel replied warmly.

"Very well," Seth returned with a smile. "What orders do you have for us?" Seth said, eager to find out the next stage.

"It is time… we must bring in the girl."

Seth and Gabe both nodded.

"We will give the command and have the guardians prepare the way." Gabe replied.

It was Tuesday night, and Lora was deep in meditation. She and Crystalyn were chanting in unison.

Meg stood in front of Lora's front door, took a nervous deep breath, and softly knocked. She waited, listening, and then heard footsteps coming downstairs.

"Who is it?" Lora asked.

"It's Meg," she replied, not knowing if Lora would open the door and let her in.

"What do you want?" Lora snapped as she opened the door.

"I just want to talk, that's all."

Lora contemplated for a few seconds, suspiciously eyeing her up and down.

"Well… can I come in?" Meg asked boldly.

Lora stepped back and let Meg walk through. "My parents are out at a church meeting," Lora said as she walked back upstairs towards her room. Meg followed Lora, feeling that she really wasn't welcome here.

Lora plonked herself on her bed as Meg stood uncomfortably and looked around the room. She noticed how much it had changed. There was a darkness about it. The colors had changed, and it was no longer a sweet little girl's room but painted in dark shades with heavy metal rock band posters scattered around the walls. She shuddered as she looked around to see a witch poster in full view.

Lora sat waiting patiently, just staring at Meg while she surveyed her room.

"Wow, it's changed since I've been here last," Meg muttered softly. "What do your parents say about this?" She gazed around, amazed at the transformation.

"They're not allowed in here! Anyway, this is more *my* style," Lora replied sarcastically as she viciously squinted heavy dark-lined eyes. "And you haven't been here for a *very* long time," she grinned nastily.

"No, well if you remember you told me you didn't want my friendship."

"Yes, and I think it's worked out well, don't you?" Lora bragged cynically. "Why are you here anyway… what do you want?"

"Umm… well, I want to ask what you were doing in the alleyway the other day talking to Jeremy."

"What's it to you? You spying on me, are you?" she said, agitated.

"Well… no, I was walking home when I overheard your conversation."

"What of it?"

"I want to know if it is to do with Jeremy accusing Pastor McKinley of abuse, that's what?"

"It's none of your business," she hissed.

"It is actually, he is a friend of mine and I think he's been unjustly accused."

"Since when are you befriending pastors, anyway? I didn't think you liked them or even believed in a God."

"Well, I've changed, and besides, Peter is a good man who loves God and people."

This is a concern… Meg shouldn't be here. Crystalyn thought.

"You know nothing!" Lora spat with absolute venom and hate. "I've seen how so-called Godly preachers treat people." She paused. "You of all people know that I experience the loving kindness of a preacher first hand," she fumed with sarcasm mixed with utter bitterness. "I think you should go… get out of my house." She started towards Meg angrily, her dark eyes staring her down.

Meg shifted backwards; she suddenly could feel the rage and torment stemming from Lora. It was as if an unseen whirlwind had started within the room. The feeling of something dark and invisible rushing around her became evident, pressing into her, intimidating and willing her to leave. She wanted to run, to get out of the room. She felt the panic rising inside.

Lora stepped closer, happily feeding on Meg's fear. Her facial features started to change; Meg could see a flicker of someone else, or *something* else.

"I can become whomever I want," Lora's guttural voice resounded. She grinned with someone else's smile.

Meg's skin prickled like gooseflesh—she felt like it was going to dance right off her body, her hair stood like wire on its ends. It was as if she could feel each individual strand wanting to make a quick exit. The fear inside her started to soar—she wanted to run, she wanted to escape, to get away from this evilness, but she knew she had to see this through, for the sake of Lora. She prayed under her breath.

Chale stood in the corner waiting and watching as Crystalyn hovered all over Lora, changing Lora's features, hair color and egging her onward, whilst thinking that he was in *total* control.

CHAPTER THIRTY-EIGHT

J ack's phone rang. It was Akio.

"I've entered 15,000 more into the system," Akio said. "They won't know as they are chipping so many per day."

"Great work," Jack paused. "So, when and how are we going to do this?"

"I guess I can be the first guinea pig, and test it. At least they will only come after me if it fails. No one else will get hurt."

"Gees Akio, are you sure?" Jack sighed nervously. "We have to be so careful."

"If we don't do this, then many of our brothers and sisters will be in danger. We have to take this chance and trust God that this is what our purpose is."

Jack took a moment and thought of his family and what Simon said about the enforcement. "Yes, you're right, let's start it."

Akio hung up the phone and placed the I-Skin that he had just programmed for himself onto his hand. It looked perfect—the special silicon organism he had specifically created magically morphed before his eyes and conformed to his skin tone, matching faultlessly. Nothing looked out of place. He proceeded to the main entry door and waved his hand near the scanner. The door opened.

"Thank you for visiting UNITED, Akio Yoshida," a female computerized voice said. "Enjoy your evening"

"Oh, I will," Akio muttered as he walked out of the building into the cool evening air.

MEG REMAINED SILENT AND STUNNED, looking at the dark, ever changing features of Lora glowering before her.

Without thinking, she blurted out quickly, "Is Crystalyn here?" she asked in a slightly panicked voice.

Crystalyn looked up with serious concern.

"Of course, she's here," Lora said smartly. "Crystalyn is always with me. Why do you ask?" she said curiously, but not appreciating the change of tact.

Meg took a deep breath and, in her mind, said a quick prayer before she spoke her next sentence. "Okay, Lora, I'll just come out with it then. Ask Crystalyn about Emily Tucker," Meg said, getting straight to the point.

At this, Crystalyn whipped around, looking straight at Chale, eyes scowling with hatred.

"What?" Lora stated, "Who?" She screwed up her face in bewilderment, her features returning to normal.

"Go on, ask," she insisted.

Lora looked over at Crystalyn to see her friend shifting from side to side uncomfortably.

"Do you know what she's talking about?" she asked Crystalyn.

"No!" Crystalyn said, but clearly disturbed by the question.

"She said no," Lora told Meg in a mocking tone, frowning at her.

"Ask again, Lora, ask IT what happened to Emily Tucker?" Meg replied.

"What? *IT?* Whom are you talking about?" Lora exclaimed, "Crystalyn's a *girl*," she leant forward with venom.

"Ask IT," Meg said sternly back, her bravado returning.

Lora turned to Crystalyn, who by now was very upset at what was unfolding. "Well, do you know an Emily Tucker?"

"No," Crystalyn replied again.

Chale stepped toward Crystalyn in a threatening stance with his sword. "Tell Lora the truth!" Chale said forcefully.

Crystalyn jumped backwards in fear and cowered.

Lora looked at her, trying to make out what was going on with her friend and why she was acting so strange.

"Crystalyn, what's wrong with you? Why are you acting like that?"

"Tell her," Chale repeated and started toward Crystalyn, his sword now ablaze and intimidating.

Lora watched as Crystalyn started fumbling, stuttering for words, cringing in the room's corner. She could not see the angelic hosts intimidating her friend. "Yes, yes, all right" Crystalyn cried, whimpering, and cowering, "I know her... okay, I do."

Lora looked over at Meg in puzzlement. "Well, she knows Emily... so what? And why do you keep saying IT?" she started getting angry again. "Crystalyn is a princess... a GIRL."

"Just ask what happened to Emily. Ask Crystalyn about Emily's friend, who was also called Crystalyn," Meg said.

Lora shook her head, "Meg, what's this all about?" she put her hands on her hips in a hostile stance.

"Lora, Emily Tucker was my great, great aunt. She lived in Evensmore and had a friend just like you do, and that friend's name was Crystalyn, too. Don't you think that's too coincidental?" she asked.

"No, not really. I'm sure that there are plenty of spirit guides that have the same names."

Meg ignored her and just continued saying, "Emily Tucker killed herself at 18 years old by drinking poison and then pushing a knife into her heart Lora," she paused, "She left a note saying that Crystalyn had convinced her to do it, that they would be happy for eternity in the universal conscience—together forever."

"No, I don't believe that. Spirit guides are our helpers—they do not harm, they are here to show us the way to a better life and empowerment."

"I don't think they are our helpers Lora, I think they pretend to be, but only to lure us in," Meg stated.

"LIAR!" Lora screamed at Meg. "Crystalyn is my friend and would never do anything to harm me. What happened to your aunt was her own stupid doing. That's why they call it suicide!"

"That's what Emily thought too," Meg shouted back. "She thought that Crystalyn was her BEST friend."

Lora paused and composed herself, rethinking her response.

"Well, maybe... maybe she is with this other Crystalyn... who knows."

"Well, why don't you ask *your* Crystalyn then where she is, I bet IT knows. After all, IT is a spirit guide too and they must know each other, especially if they have the same name," she said sarcastically.

Lora slowly turned, eyeing Crystalyn, who was looking back and forth between her and the many angels in sheer panic.

"Well, answer her," she said to Crystalyn, "I want to know now too."

Crystalyn, clearly troubled, replied, "Well... of course," with words gushing, "now I remember, that's where I know Emily—she is in the universal conscience."

"Liar!" Chale moved forward towards Crystalyn.

"I-I mean... well, I do know her yes, and well... I'm not sure where she is right now, but I... I-I'm sure she's there somewhere."

"What do you mean, Crystalyn? Is Emily there or not?" Lora said, frustrated at her friend's avoidance of giving straight answers.

Meg interjected, "I think Crystalyn knows where Emily is Lora, and I think Crystalyn really *was* Emily Tucker's guide!" She looked toward where Lora's eyes were gazing.

"NO, no that's not me, I am not *that* guide, I am not. No!" Crystalyn replied desperately.

Lora gazed at Meg questioningly, with an element of concern on her face. She turned back towards Crystalyn. "Well, are you who she says you are? Are you the Crystalyn that was Emily Tucker's guide?"

Crystalyn squirmed unhappily, looking over at the angels standing in the room.

"What do you keep looking at?" Lora probed suspiciously.

"Me?—well, no one, there is no one else here," Crystalyn replied sheepishly.

"Liar!" Jophiel stepped forward.

"They are angels, Lora," Meg claimed and then smiled at her

lovingly. "There are angels in this room and we all want to show you the truth about Crystalyn and what IT *really* is."

Lora abruptly exploded into a rage. "What truth, that Crystalyn has been a better friend than you ever have! That Crystalyn has shown me the truth about this life and the afterlife. That is truth. Not this God and His angels crap," she retorted, with tears welling in her eyes, "Go on Crystalyn, tell them that there is NO GOD, that it's all a religious farce to control people and take their money." Lora looked over at Crystalyn, who was edgy and rattled by the question. "Go on," Lora said, "tell her—tell Meg the truth, and tell her that Jesus was just a prophet and that there is NO one God, everything that you've told me... TELL HER CRYSTALYN, TELL HER!" she screamed.

"Um, well, ah." Crystalyn looked up at the angelic hosts in fear. Chale took a step closer and Crystalyn whimpered, struggling to keep the beautiful princess façade. Crystalyn's countenance started to flicker and fade intermittently.

Lora could see that her friend was clearly troubled, so she softened her voice. "Come on Crystalyn, tell her what you've told me all along... tell her *everything*."

Then slowly, before Lora's very eyes, Crystalyn's appearance started to change. The beautiful princess girl Lora came to know and love as her best friend gradually was transformed, revealing an ugly, sinuous, grotesque, and distorted being. Crystalyn's gorgeous green eyes turned a dead hallowed red, bulging in fear. The once long slender fingers with exquisitely manicured nails turned into spindly black talons, clenching into fists. The princess girl with the attractive body was now exposed, revealing black leathery wings cowering flat against the demon's bony spine. The changed facial features unveiled a distorted head, scarred with scabs and tufts of wiry fur.

Crystalyn was now unmasked, cowering and recoiling with intimidation from the Lord's Hosts.

CHAPTER THIRTY-NINE

Lora let out a panicked scream, her hands quickly covering her mouth as she stared in fear and horror. Crystalyn looked and realized what had just happened... that he had inadvertently transformed back into his true self.

Lora stared, unable to speak—she shook and convulse into panicked sobs. She then stopped and followed his gaze toward the angels standing in the room. She recoiled backwards, not knowing where to turn, not wanting to go near that monster, but afraid of the glorious beings that stood in front of her very eyes.

"Meg!" she screamed and looked over to her, "what's going on?"

"It's okay Lora, it's okay!" Meg said as she started slowly walking towards her.

At that moment, like a flash, Crystalyn seized his chance. He dove at Lora and entered her body. Her physique immediately changed, her human features took on elements of the demon inside her.

She hunched over and hissed. "You will not have this one." Crystalyn's dark, raspy voice spoke as he screamed through Lora's vocals. "She gave herself willingly to me and she is mine—she does not belong to you. She is not one of yours, but one of ours. She follows our Master, not *yours!*"

JACK ANSWERED HIS MOBILE AGAIN.

"It's working!" Akio said excitedly. "I've just bought take out and caught a cab back to my apartment. It's been perfect. I'll check the logs later tonight to ensure there's nothing out of place."

"Fantastic! Let me know as soon as you view the logs, I want to ensure that this is safe and it can't be identified as being any different to the real thing."

"Will do!"

MEG STEPPED BACK and took a few breaths so as not to completely freak out. "Calm down," she said to Lora. Her hands were raised and motioning to Lora to settle down. Meg suddenly felt like she was way over her head.

"Shut up, you—you spoiler—you trouble maker. Everything was going fine until you came along," Lora screamed at her uncontrollably. "You are my enemy, I will *kill* you."

Meg jumped, startled at the verbal attack—she quickly prayed under her breath. This was not how she had planned it. This was bigger than her, and she panicked at the enormity of what was happening. She wasn't sure of what was going on and didn't know that this sort of thing could happen. Her mind was racing in sheer terror of what was unfolding before her.

Chale saw Meg's confidence drop and the fear and terror rise in her eyes. He stepped over toward her and put his hand on her shoulder and whispered gently, "Remember that you have authority, Meg, the spirit that raised Christ from the dead lives within you. Christ defeated Satan at the cross—you have authority. Use it!"

"Get away from her," Lora screamed, frantically looking at Chale. "You stay away, don't you talk to her." Then, suddenly, Lora grabbed her own throat, squeezing and tightening her grip. "I'm taking her, I'm taking her, she's mine," Crystalyn screeched through Lora's voice. "She's not yours… she's ours. She belongs with us."

Meg jumped forward and grabbed Lora's arms and tried desperately to pull her hands away from her throat. Lora grappled with Meg on the floor, scratching and scraping at her face. She reached out and grabbed Meg by the neck and threw her with such inhuman force against the wall that it knocked the wind out of her.

"Use your authority, Meg," Jophiel shouted.

Like a penetrating wave of peace, those words broke through Meg's fear ridden mind and she stood straight up as though nothing had happened and said, "By the authority of Jesus Christ in me, I command you Crystalyn to come out of Lora."

Crystalyn strained hard against the power of those words and dug in his claws deeper to keep hold of Lora. "NO," Lora's voice screamed at Meg. "Leave us alone, leave us be," Lora whined.

Lora writhed on the floor, drooling, hissing and growling, staring hatefully at Meg and the angels.

Use your authority! A clear voice resonated through Meg completely. She stopped and took a deep breath, straightened and regained her confidence, then glared at Lora thrashing on the floor before she spoke. "In Jesus' name Crystalyn, I command you to leave Lora."

With a crack of brilliant fiery light, Crystalyn was violently thrown out of Lora's body, landing against the wall, stunned and shaking. The angels quickly stepped in and had their swords drawn towards him so he could not try again. They pinned him against the wall.

Lora recoiled, rubbing her neck, gasping for breath and shaking uncontrollably. She cried, looking over at the scene that was before her, of many angels standing over one ugly black demon. She couldn't believe what she saw.

"Lora," Meg said, "Lora listen, you *must* accept Christ as your Savior."

At that, Crystalyn hissed. "She's mine—I will have her. Just like I took Emily and all the others before, she too will go to Hell and join them." Crystalyn cackled and drooled uncontrollably, foaming and spitting everywhere.

"Shut up in Jesus' name," Meg shouted, clearly surprised that she had even heard the demon speak. "You must Lora, this is not a game—it's *really* serious. If you do not accept Christ then he," she pointed towards the demon, "will return, but not alone, with many, many more of them," she said, staring into Lora's teary eyes, "They *will* kill you." She implored, "Jesus is the only one who can save you, Lora... nothing or no-one else."

"Oh Meg, what do I do. I don't want to be religious like my father—I hate him for that," she cried, sobbing against Meg's shoulder. Her black mascara mixed with the tears started running down her red face.

"Lora, your dad is not a true representative of Christ. I'm sorry to say that, but he isn't," she replied tenderly. "Following Christ is not like that. You cannot look at your dad or any other person for that matter and judge Jesus to be like that, because He is not. He is love and freedom and everything that your father *isn't*. You don't need to do certain works like your mum, say specific things to be forgiven, or perform any rituals. That is not God, it's man-made religion," she said. "Look at me, Lora. I didn't believe in God *at all*, but now I do. I've changed so much now that I know Jesus."

Lora looked into Meg's eyes and then glanced over towards where Crystalyn sat with his mouth shut tight, and said, "Yes, Meg... I do. I accept Jesus as my Savior." She shook and burst out with desperate words. "Oh Jesus, please forgive me. I want to be free—help me, God. Jesus, please come into my life and help me," she said as she sobbed uncontrollably on the floor.

The angels stood in both reverence and awe, always amazed at seeing a new Christian being born. They watched as they could see the thick black darkness encasing Lora's heart crack and break apart as the light pierced through it. The inky dark shards around it crumbled, and her heart burned with an incandescent light.

At seeing this, Crystalyn became agitated and fearful, pushing himself back against the wall, cowering.

"Be still," Chale said, and glared at the squirming creature at his feet. "Now to deal with you."

Lora could hear his muffled cries as the mighty Chale plunged the sword into Crystalyn. She watched as the demon disappeared into thin air, leaving just a trail of gray furling smoke behind.

She looked up at Chale. "Thank you," she whispered gratefully to him.

"You must not thank me, but thank our Lord Jesus." He smiled back at her.

THE NEWS of Crystalyn's demise moved swiftly through the ranks. A fluttering messenger delivered the gruesome news to his master.

"Your majesty," he said as he bowed low, "I bring terrible news, sire."

Lothar glared at him, waiting intently. "Go on!"

"I bring news of Crystalyn's fall, sire. The hosts have banished him." He paused and then stammered. "A-a-and... we have lost the girl... she is now one of them." He stepped back quickly to ensure he was not within arm's reach.

Lothar stood up, angered, but stayed in silence for a few moments before he spoke. "They will pay for this. Get me Crechus!"

"WELL DONE, my comrades. The King is pleased," Darius commended Jophiel and Chale. "You have hurt the enemy greatly."

"Thank you sir, but unfortunately in time she will be replaced by another." Jophiel said, feeling a little battle weary.

"Yes, and we will be there again to free another." Darius encouraged.

Chale put his hand on Jophiel's shoulder. "We will."

"Peter, that was a great message—I will study it for myself. Thank you for stepping out and delivering something so controversial," one pastor said after the conference had finished.

"Great view point Peter," another said. "Although I'm not entirely convinced of the timeline, but like you said, it doesn't matter whether we go before or after, just as long as we are ready and we don't fall. I like that, and I will teach my congregation that we have to prepare and strengthen our faith. Thank you again for taking the time to share with us."

"Thanks Peter, this has always been a contentious issue in the body of Christ. I've seen arguments start and division created over this very subject. I am definitely going to further research this for myself as I too listened to others to form an opinion. I've already thought of some sermons I can do, and I can't wait to get the message out into my church."

Peter was ecstatic. The day had been a total success, and Jack and Jenny were waiting patiently in the throngs to congratulate him and take him out for a celebration dinner.

Chale and Jophiel's ranks had spent the last week before the conference extremely focused. They had visited each invitee on Peter's list to prompt them to seek God and find out the truth about the false propaganda about Peter. They had also encouraged other teachers who hadn't received an invitation to request to attend. Everything had gone perfectly.

LOTHAR WAS FUMING. "If we hadn't lost Crystalyn, we could have sabotaged this pathetic conference… AND you idiots, more preachers turned up than were originally invited, anyway. You fools can't disrupt anything."

"But-but sire," the messenger demon responded cautiously, "the enemy was far too numerous—we didn't stand a chance, anyway."

"FOOL!" he bellowed. "NEVER say that they are stronger, there is ALWAYS a way." He paused. "If it wasn't for Crechus and his stupid mistakes, we wouldn't be in this predicament. Now this is undoing what we worked so hard for... he has set us back. I now have to report this to *my* Master." He slammed his fist down, leaped up, and flew out of the building into the sky, screaming. "YOU WILL PAY HOSTS."

CHALE AND JOPHIEL heard the bellow and looked up to see Lothar fast heading westward. They looked straight at each other and just smiled.

A WEEK LATER, Peter, Meg, and Lora sat in the church building.

"Lora, are you okay?" Peter enquired. "Meg told me what happened."

"No... not really. I'm so confused—I just don't understand. I can't believe that I was so blinded."

"You're not the only one and you won't be the last," Peter claimed. "Many people are fooled by Satan into thinking that this is just harmless fun. There are TV shows, movies, magazines and books that say it's not bad at all, but good and harmless. Some even believe that they have been given a gift from God."

"So, was it really a demon? I mean, will it come back?"

"Yes, it was a demon, but no, it won't return now that you have accepted Jesus into your life. You may have other demons try to harass or hinder you, but they have no power if you continue to build your relationship with Christ and use your authority." He paused. "Let me tell you something. I converted a Satanist to Christ 15 years ago. He told me he could put a curse on someone and have them dead within 21 days, but he couldn't touch the Christians—he was powerless against them. It made him so angry that he made it his mission to find out why—he is now a pastor of his own church. So you see Lora, there is nothing to worry about now you have God in your life."

"But what about all the stuff about the universal conscience, I mean... is that true?"

"What's the best way for your opponent to divert you from knowing the truth?"

Lora shrugged her shoulders.

Peter continued, "To provide so many other choices other than the truth itself. Islam, Buddhism, Hinduism, Kabbalah, Scientology, Eastern Philosophies, Psychic healing, Universalism, Witchcraft, the list goes on and on, so pick one... how does one find the truth in all of this mess? Satan has set this up so people can continue searching and do whatever they choose, other than choose the truth. I've seen it countless times when someone tries to come out of a false religion or doctrine to seek after Jesus. Satan will come in with another tact or lie to steer them away into something else other than Christianity. There is no other God but our Jehovah. None hold any power but Him. So, do not believe in anything other than Jesus, read the Bible and live by it daily."

"But what about the fortune teller? She knew everything about me? My cat, my aunt dying... everything?" Lora said, her head still reeling with confusion.

"That's not a mystery either, Lora. There are demonic, familiar spirits that know everything about a person. They're assigned to a person and spend their existence studying them and knowing how to get at them. When a medium, psychic, fortune teller, tarot reader, whoever, seeks information for their client, those familiar spirits pose themselves as some kind of energy or disguise themselves as the actual deceased. So Lora, when she told you about your cat and your aunt, it was the demon speaking into her mind to fool you... and her into thinking she has a wonderful gift. You see, it's all a deception to lure people away from the truth... which is and always will be Jesus Christ. No other!"

"So Crystalyn was a demon... and was pretending to be a

guide?" She slowly spoke, looking straight at Peter, letting her words sink in.

"Exactly, there are no friendly spirit guides—they are merely demons posing as such. Lora, this Crystalyn would have eventually killed you when you had served your purpose—you know that, don't you? That demon would have convinced you to do something to yourself or even have done something to you. It was never a friend. It was always a demon who was set upon using you to destroy others and yourself."

Lora's eyes welled with tears as she looked over at Meg. "Thank you for coming to my house and saving me from that monster."

Megs' eyes instantly watered. "Your welcome! I'm just so thankful that you didn't get as far into it as Emily did," Meg put her arm around Lora's shoulders. "I've read her diary—she did some terrible stuff Lora, totally convinced that it was right."

"I did some really bad stuff, too!" Lora said meekly, her heart bursting with guilt. She turned towards Meg, "I'm so sorry Meg, about what I did to you. I feel so ashamed. I really hurt you and you have been my loyal friend all along. I understand if you never want to speak to me again."

"Oh Lora, I forgive you and I love you." Meg smiled at her friend as they both hugged and cried together.

After several minutes passed, Lora composed herself and then a thought came to her about Peter. "Your last name is McKinley?" she asked, half knowing what the answer would be.

"Yes," Peter replied.

Lora hung her head and after a few seconds said, "I have to apologies to you too." She paused. "Crystalyn had me do something towards you as well."

"I know," Peter said gently.

"You do?" Lora looked up, surprised.

"Yes, God told me what was going on. Both Meg and I have been praying for you to see the truth, and God used Meg to show you."

"I'm really sorry," Lora said as she wept, tears streaming down her cheeks.

"I forgive you Lora and so does God." Peter replied. "Now it's time to move forward into your new life. Don't dwell on the things of the past. What you have done is now washed away, so do not feel guilty anymore. God states that He removes our sins as far as the East is from the West. That's a long way." He smiled and continued. "But you also need healing so you can be free from what has happened. I know a lady who does prayer counseling. She prays and asks God what you need to help you get free from your past and He reveals to her ways to help you. Would you like to see her?"

"Yes, I would like that," Lora replied. "I want to forget about Crystalyn and everything that has happened."

"You won't ever forget," Peter added, "but you'll be able to forgive and move forward, and the pain and guilt that you feel now in your heart will no longer be there."

Meg happily smiled and embraced Lora once again. "I've got my best friend back," she said excitedly.

JEREMY SAT ALONE IS his room, plagued by what he had done to Peter. He spiraled deeper and deeper into dark thoughts. Two demons, Depression and Suicide, hovered over him like a dark ominous, stalker, beguiling and pressing him into a deep, vast despair.

"You are nothing—no one likes you! You're an outcast anyway!" the demons screamed at him. "Everyone knows what you did. You are a freak... a failure. Everyone HATES you!" The demons' long needled talons drove into Jeremy's mind, working together, projecting wretched thoughts into him like an injected toxin throbbing through his veins.

"No one cares—you'll be doing *everyone* a favor," the demons continued in their malicious way. The painful thoughts pulsated throughout his core, his heart burning and aching at each thought, and the savage, ruthless pain throbbed with every beat.

He could hear his blood pulsing—the ache grew more intense, and the tears began to fall. His body ebbed with defeat—he could see no future.

The demons did not stop; they were ruthless, continuously planting despondent thoughts into the night hours until Jeremy began to give in.

Suicide quickly engulfed him like flames licking at dry cinders; faster and faster, Jeremy was intoxicated in the feelings until he succumbed to the pit from where the demons called to him.

The soft yachting rope was in his cupboard... it only took a few minutes...

CHAPTER FORTY-ONE

14 MONTHS LATER

The tally on the UNITED website showed that over four billion people had accepted the UNITED Chip. Jason Crane slammed his fist down hard onto his desk, shaking and knocking over the stationery holder, scattering paper clips and pens across the floor. "Why have only *half* the people accepted?" The anger rose.

Simon stood fearfully, unsure of what to say or do. He didn't like it when this man became angry.

"It's been 14 months since the enforcement, Simon. Yes, we have global peace, but..." Jason stared at him, waiting for an answer. "Why haven't they *all* accepted?"

Simon cleared his throat and tried his best not to show his nervousness. "I've done some research into it and people are not accepting for many reasons. They don't like force, they feel that they have the right to freedom. Some people just haven't made it a priority and have simply been too lazy." He inwardly cringed at the last statement, wishing he hadn't said that.

"A priority? Are you serious?" Jason raised his voice angrily. "I'll make it a priority for them." He wandered the room with his hand, anxiously tapping his chin, deliberating. "I think now is the time—we have given them long enough. I want a powerful message that if they do not want to become one with us, then they cannot buy anything or even sell their goods. Their businesses will suffer. That's it! We will force them to join us."

"But are you sure that's a good idea? People may starve." Simon said in shock.

"I can do whatever I please. Now make it happen," he snapped back, eerily grinning.

The large demon stood beside Jason, smirking, expressing his support and approval for the decision.

. . .

JENNY SAT in the couch with the TV on when an important announcement appeared. "Jack," she called, "quick come here they are announcing something."

On the TV, Jason Crane was standing at a lectern. He spoke, "From this day forward, all systems of trade will require the UNITED Chip. You cannot purchase any goods or sell any product unless it is through the UNITED Chip. This is for the sake of our world and the peace that we will bring through this process. I will make it very simple and clear. If you do not want to become one, then we do not want you with us. Join us to be safe, secure, and live in peace. It's your choice." A female voice then spoke, "If you do not have the UNITED Chip, you must make your way to your nearest chipping center ASAP. Join us for our future of peace."

"Just like the Bible said," Jack sighed. "Well, I guess we will now have to activate our I-Skins, I'll call Akio in the morning and get us on the grid."

CRECHUS HAD to get something on Jack to please Lothar. Now that Crystalyn was gone, he didn't have anyone to help him do the dirty work. He had to come up with some ideas himself.

LORA WAS FRIGHTENED; she didn't like what she saw on TV, so she rang Meg. "Meg, I can't stay at home, I know dad is just going to drag me down to the chipping center."

"Come stay here," Meg replied.

She packed a few things in a duffle bag, left a note for her mum, and ran over to Meg's house.

LOTHAR SAT OMINOUSLY on his throne. "The command has been given, and it is now time to ensure that as many mortals receive this chip. Go out and convince them that it is fine to accept it. Do whatever it takes to persuade them, as it will simply make it easier for us in the end. Go now," he commanded.

THE NEXT DAY, Peter, Ben, May, Meg, Lora, Patty, Jack and Jenny sat in Jack's living room. Jack was going around meticulously placing the I-Skin on each one of them. It was miraculously conforming to their skin tones.

"What if it gets wet?" asked Ben.

"It's fine, don't worry about it," Jack replied.

"Will it really work?" queried Meg.

"Yes, you will be fine." Jack smiled as he placed it on her right hand, reassuring her. "Akio and I have tested the heck out of this thing—our lives depend on it."

"For how long, though, I mean… how long do you think we can go undetected?" May inquired with a concerned look on her face.

"That, I can't say… we just have to be *really* careful. We mustn't tell just anyone and if we do… we have to ensure that they are genuine."

"But how will we know?" Meg asked.

"Let God be your guide," Peter said comfortingly. "There will be many people who do not want to accept this chip. Some will be followers of Christ, some not, but let the Holy Spirit guide you in whom to tell. We must help others—we can't just keep this to ourselves. Jack and Akio have many to give out."

"This is so risky," Jenny declared, looking at her children with uncertainty.

"And *not* having this is even more risky, Jen. Come on… don't lose it on me now. What choice do we have?" Jack consoled. "This is only temporary but it may bide us just enough time." He pulled her close. "We have to remain strong, for now this is the only way I can think of."

"But you said that this may not be the mark of the beast," Ben stated, "so we could potentially get the real chip?"

"I'm still not sure, Ben—I'm just not taking any risks. I think we will find out soon enough, but for now let's just try to play it as safe as we possibly can and act like we are happy and continue on our daily activities. If you get the real deal, then you can't get rid of it—they can track you. At least this way we can flush them. Anyway, this will give us more time, but… we do need to have a backup plan."

"Yeah, I've already thought of that and I have just the place too," Ben advised.

"Good… you may want to start preparing it then, because there may come a day when we have to use it," Jack exclaimed as he looked around at the others. "But for now, we go with this plan… agree?"

"Agree!" they all responded in unison.

A WEEK LATER, Jack walked into Tucker's Grocery store.

"Gee's Jack, about time you got yourself one of those IDs, I didn't want to say it, but I was nearly going to refuse you service when I saw you walking in." Ned Tucker paused. "Thank goodness you came to your senses!" He smiled and started scanning the groceries Jack had put on the counter. "It's a great thing you know," Ned continued to chatter.

"What's that?"

"Well, this here scheme of the IDs and all," He paused. "I mean, I've noticed that it's safer around here, not that it was a bad place, don't get me wrong. But, I can't recall any thefts of my produce since this has been enforced, and I've seen no violence on the news either, only a peaceful existence. It's surely been a great invention to bring into this world, don't ya think?"

"Yeah… well, I guess if that's what you're seeing."

"Well, aren't you? Haven't you noticed a big difference in the community?" Ned looked at him surprised and questionably.

"Well, sure Ned, I've noticed a *difference!*" Jack responded.

"Yeah, that's what I thought. Everyone thinks the same too. They're happy and everything just seems so much easier. That's $58.40."

Jack held out his hand and Ned passed the scanner over it until it made a beeping sound.

"All done! See, it's so much easier! Ya should have done it ages ago." Ned beamed.

"See you Ned." Jack waved as he walked out the door. Just in time for his mobile phone to start ringing. It was Peter.

"Hey Pete," Jack answered.

"Hello, hope you're having a great day!"

"I am what about you?—hey, where are you?"

"I'm over in Belmont, but I'm ringing to see if I could send some *relatives* over tomorrow for a visit as they need some *IT* advice."

Jack smiled. "No problem, how many are coming?"

"There will be eight arriving at 10 am if that suits?"

"Sure, that will be fine. Also, did you check if they are willing to take the *advice* and share it with others?"

"Yes, they definitely will, Jack."

"Take care, Pete," he said as he hung up the phone.

CRECHUS HAD BEEN WATCHING Jack intently and noted there were new players on the scene. They weren't small, in fact, they were huge warriors, and it made him very nervous. He observed carefully at a distance. He wasn't convinced that Jack's mission was over with simply finding the letter and persuading the preacher. *There had to be more to this mortal*, he thought.

TWO DAYS LATER, Jack was back at UNITED headquarters. It was late and Jack was cautiously walking down the hallway towards the UNITED chip storage room. Gabe suddenly sensed an evil presence lurking in front, around the corner to the left from the storeroom. "Wait." He whispered urgently to Jack. He quickly gave a signal to the others with a flick of his sword.

Jack heeded the word, stopped and waited.

Two tall muscular men were walking down the hallway, one

blond, the other dark-haired. They saw Jack waiting as they came around the corner behind him.

"Hey Jack," the blond-haired man said as he casually walked over. "How are you doing? Are you working back, buddy?"

"Yes, doing what I can for the cause," he smiled at the two men that he had never met before.

"Well, you certainly do it well. Hey, can I help you with anything? Is the quality of the chips still causing you problems... are you still investigating the issue?"

"Ahh..." Jack looked a little confused at the question, as he hadn't heard there was a problem.

The dark-haired man suddenly interrupted him before he could finish his answer. "Yeah, I've heard that you're making a breakthrough with the improvements so we can get *many* more out there and increase the numbers—hey do you need a hand?" The dark-haired man offered. "How many chips do you need to do your research tonight?"

"Umm..." Jack said, perplexed at the conversation that was unfolding between them.

"Give him twenty thousand, that way he can get a good sample to check." The other man stated. "We don't want any more mishaps to the assembly line—it's been causing a lot of problems lately."

"Okay, thanks... that would be really helpful," said Jack, surprised.

"Great, I'll go get them for you... hopefully you will find the problem." The dark-haired man said as he walked off towards the storeroom.

The man soon returned with a bag full of UNITED chips. The two men then walked back with Jack to his office, casually talking with him whilst attentively scanning the perimeter before leaving him alone.

Crechus came out from his hiding place around the corner from the storeroom. He had overheard everything. *Maybe Master is right... Jack's not a threat*, he thought, as he slowly moved his black hulking frame down the UNITED hallway in the opposite direction. His concerns now alleviated.

Gabe later addressed the blond and dark-haired men who had now transformed back into angelic warriors. "That was close, well done my friends," he commended. "Keep this up and stay vigilant."

CHAPTER FORTY-TWO

26 MONTHS LATER

J ack's mobile rang.

"Hey Jack," Simon said, "I've booked the morning flight for you. But I'd need you to stay for three days as we have some major meetings and I must have your expertise."

Jack's initial response was to get out of it. The thought of being anywhere near that place made him shudder. Then, he pondered… *this is the perfect opportunity to see Akio and get some more Chips.* "Sure Simon, I'll be there."

CRECHUS STOOD in the distance and watched as Jack boarded the aircraft. He had been occasionally watching Jack and still sensed that there was more to this man. He had been so heavily guarded the past 26 months. *Something was off,* he thought. Even though Lothar was convinced that the preacher was the real threat, Crechus remained doubtful. He had recently overheard Simon stating to JC how wonderful production of the new chips had been and that there hadn't been any major problems for ages. This again reignited Crechus's interest.

"I'll find out, just you wait and see." His evil eyes leered at the plane taxiing down the runway.

CHALE AND JOPHIEL stood before Darius in the heavenly realms.

"I've heard that you have done well," said Darius.

"Yes, sir, thus far, we have thwarted any attempts from the enemy. Any suspicions that have been aroused, we have had the enemy detained and vanquished." Chale answered.

"Good… very good." Darius nodded with approval.

"However, sir, without sounding doubtful," Jophiel interjected, "I fear we may not hold them for much longer. UNITED swarms with the enemy and their numbers are increasing daily. They tolerate us because we are only few, and this doesn't arouse suspicions, but if they find out the real mission… then I'm afraid that it may be over."

"Then we will discreetly increase our numbers." He paused for a moment, sensing that the two mighty warriors before him needed encouragement. "I too have felt a shift in the Spirit… the time may be drawing nigh. You have done what you can, you have given the Lord's people more time… *much* more than what they would have without this intervention. The King is pleased with your achievements. Let's just continue to do what we can to hold them off."

PETER HAD SPENT the months covertly but aggressively spreading the word about the secret rapture lie and the necessity in enduring the end times. Chale and Jophiel's angelic warriors had covered him constantly, and the enemy could not get near him or know his plans. He had held many secret conferences, encouraging other ministers to spread the word, and he had travelled many miles across the country to ensure that the truth was heard… and Lothar was very displeased.

"I can't believe you haven't stopped the preacher, he has hurt us greatly and you bunch of dimwits can't even get near him or find out where he is speaking… we now have more threats because of him encouraging other preachers to do the same."

"Sir, there are way too many warriors protecting him."

"You'll have to find a way then, won't you?" He sneered at the spindly dark messenger spirit before him.

AKIO AND JACK EMBRACED, but only when Jack was back at his hotel for the evening.

Jack and Akio had spent countless hours together, secretly scanning, organizing and distributing the I-Skins to the wider Christian community globally, helping people integrate into society undetected. They had been extremely careful, and so were all the other distributors who were helping. It had been a successful team effort. They had succeeded and remained undetected.

"You are like a long-lost brother. I'm so thankful that God included me in this plan with you," Akio exclaimed.

"I feel the same way Akio!" However, Jack was taken aback, overwhelmed that someone would be so thankful to be here now. "You're quite serious, aren't you?"

"Of course, I look upon this as a privilege that God chose me to be in a time such as this. I am fulfilling God's plan for my life, and I am honored. I was born for this destiny, for this time and age, and am so proud that I could contribute the way God ordained me. There is no greater honor than to serve my Lord in the way He had planned."

And all I have been doing is complaining and worrying, Jack thought to himself. "You're amazing," he said, shaking his head in wonderment.

"Our I-Skin community has now grown to over 11.3 million," Akio stated happily.

"WOW! I can't believe we have done this," Jack exclaimed, becoming emotional. "I mean… well Akio, we've beaten the system." He grinned triumphantly.

"For now!" Akio smiled. "We cannot become too confident. We still have to work hard to remain unnoticed, and this peaceful existence will not continue much longer. Also, this week I completed a device that will render the UNITED chip useless— you just wave it over the person's hand. I will give it to you when we get back."

"When would we need to use this?"

"I'm just taking precautions. I thought if someone already has a UNITED Chip but then becomes a Christian, we can't remove it, but at least this way it will be unusable and can't be tracked."

"Good idea, I never thought of that." He paused, and then with a smile, Jack said, "Let's go get some dinner. I'm starving!"

"Yeah, let's do this on a full stomach this time." Akio chuckled.

. . .

A FEW HOURS LATER, Gabe and Seth were busily protecting Jack back at UNITED headquarters. They worked alongside Akio's two Guardians, Zeke, who stood a massive 17 feet tall and was built for combat, and Delmar, a seasoned warrior ready for any battle.

As Jack and Akio neared the corner to the UNITED Chip storehouse, Seth placed his hand on Jack's chest to stop him.

"Wait!" Jack whispered to Akio.

Footsteps were heard from the guards who had just checked the lock and were walking in the opposite direction, casually talking about their day.

Gabe gave the all-clear signal to Seth.

Seth spoke softly to Jack, "It's clear!"

Upon feeling this word spoken, Jack moved forward around the corner. He had now become very familiar with listening and obeying the promptings.

Jack gently unlocked the storehouse and Akio and Jack busily took handfuls of chips and placed them into the anti-static bags. They had done this countless times, sometimes with help from the blond and dark-haired men they saw here occasionally. However, they knew from experience that they only had a 35-minute window before the guards came back around to check this section of the building again.

Gabe and Seth stood with Jack and Akio whilst Zeke and Delmar stood watch at the corridor. Other warriors were scattered about, hiding in their usual stations.

Zeke saw him first and quickly signaled to Delmar. They both jumped backwards into the storehouse undetected.

Gabe saw the signal from Zeke and shouted to Jack, "Quick, hide NOW!"

Jack, suddenly startled, swiftly grabbed Akio. He literally dragged him as they both dove under a desk in the darkest corner of the room. Gabe and Seth covered them and dimmed themselves to a completely invisible state.

It skulked and slithered in slowly like a serpent, prowling and probing for anything deemed suspicious. The murky blackness ebbed before it; stopping short at the entrance of the storehouse door. The angels could feel it before they had even laid eyes upon it— its rich hatred oozed from its forceful being.

Zeke looked over at Delmar and sensed his trepidation. "Don't let it enter," he silently mouthed. Both Zeke and Delmar stood waiting nervously, for it wasn't in fear for them, but for Jack and Akio. They had to protect their charges and the greater cause.

They could sense the dark being intensely examining the situation, hesitating and considering whether to enter. It paused, then started to press through the door, absorbing and encompassing the wooden fibers throughout its being.

BAM! It was knocked backwards with a powerful thud. Out into the corridor it tumbled over and over. Its claws screeching, scraping and scratching at the glossy white floor, its wings spread to stop its forceful momentum. The dark being became enraged as it saw Zeke standing sternly in the corridor, challenging him.

"RAAAAAAAAHHHHHHH!" It rushed at Zeke like an unstoppable freight train. Zeke ran down the hallway in the other direction, just keeping ahead, taunting and fluttering, inciting more anger in the chase. They both ducked and weaved, the being was closing in. It was powerful and determined to gain a kill.

WHOOOSH! SMACK! Zeke felt the sting of the demon's blade as it opened up his heel. He tumbled forward into the elevator shaft and fell, spiraling downward, 23, 22, 21. He could see the floor numbers rushing by and heard the rasping breath of the being following close behind.

"WWWRAAAAAAAGGGHHHH, I'LL KILL YOU ANGEL SCUM!" it screamed as it pressed its wings hard against its back, streamlining its black body like a base jumper to gain momentum… 20, 19, 18, further and further downward they went.

The dark being grabbed Zeke by his injured foot. Excruciating pain shot into his leg, incensed, Zeke swung his mighty blade, and they connected. *SWING! CHANG! CLANK!* The blades sparked as

247

they fought and tumbled downward farther and farther... 17, 16, 15, 14, *CHINK! CLANG! ZING!* As they smashed their swords, red and white arcs of explosions flew off each blow. Sparks were flashing past as farther and farther they fell... 13, 12, 11... Zeke was fighting for his very life, for this being was no easy game. He felt his strength ebbing with every forceful blow. So, with all his strength, Zeke swung his majestic sword. *"FOR MY KING!"* he yelled as he felt the connection of flesh and bone slash through and tear against his regal sword.

"AAAAAAAAGGGGHHHHH!" it screamed in sheer agony as three quarters of its wing was detached.

Zeke watched as the severed leathery wing floated and danced freely, like a parachute down the elevator shaft.

The demon fell violently, unable to regain any control as it spiraled downward, twisting and churning into the darkness below.

Zeke snapped his brilliant wings wide open and immediately pulled up from his rapid descent; he waited and listened to the creature's tormented screams getting farther and farther away.

GABE, Seth and Delmar had managed to get Jack and Akio away safely, unharmed and undetected. They were back at Jack's hotel and were eagerly waiting for Zeke's return. They had a sigh of relief and all embraced when Zeke entered through the door, limping but very thankful.

"Did he see them?" Gabe asked worriedly.

"I don't think so; I think I got to him in time," Zeke exclaimed.

"Well done, my friend." Gabe, Seth and Delmar all congratulated and patted Zeke on his back. "You are a great warrior; our King will be proud."

THE INJURED DEMON with a missing wing stood before Lothar. "What's wrong with you, you miserable fool. It's a mere flesh wound!" He paused, then slowly smirked. "Did the little angel hurt you, did he?" He leered. "The new look becomes you!" He laughed and taunted before his anger turned again. "You failed! Why I even put up with you. Go find out what was going on... else I will do more than just cut off your wing." He grinned with sheer evil and malice.

Crechus respectfully bowed and took a few steps backwards before he felt safe to turn and walk away from his Master. He was humiliated and in sheer agony, his wound fresh—the bone was jagged, seeping, and still very raw. "I will get you for this, Jack," he vowed.

CHAPTER FORTY-THREE

I t was in the early hours of the morning and Meg was staying over at Lora's house. They had been talking most of the night.

"I feel like something bad is about to happen," Lora whispered softly so not to wake her parents.

"Like what?"

"I'm unsure, I feel a shift, it's weird I can't explain it."

"Maybe you're just worried because things are going so well?"

"No, I don't think so," Lora whispered. "There is definitely something up."

"I wish I could see what you see Lora, it must be so cool," Meg said with excitement.

"Sometimes it is. I mean, I like watching the angels—they are amazing. But I really don't like the dark beings. Especially when they know I can see them. It really creeps me out."

"Yeah, I suppose. That's the thing I wouldn't like either. Scary!" Meg paused. "Tell me what the angels look like."

"Each one of them is magnificent in their own right." Lora paused, as if in wonderment. "They sometimes radiate and are majestic with their swords, then other times they blend in and look like regular people. They are always on the lookout and are constantly protecting us... and their wings, well... they're simply amazing."

"Wow!" was all Meg could say in awe.

"We better get some sleep, hey." Lora giggled.

"Yeah, I suppose," Meg responded cheerily as she pulled up the blanket and snuggled into its softness.

It was 4 am. Crechus was back at UNITED... thinking, retracing his steps from the other night, desperate to redeem his credibility with Lothar. *I know they were up to something,* he thought. He went up to the storeroom and slowly entered, carefully scanning the room for signs. Looking around, he saw something glistening on the floor. He bent down and grinned as he picked up the small Chip between his fingers... he chuckled. "I know what you're up to now."

JACK WAS on the 6.00 am flight home, snoozing in seat 14C of the Boeing 737, when the breakfast cart bumped into his elbow.

Ouch, Jack thought, rubbing it. *Well, got to wake up anyway, I guess.* He was relieved that Simon booked the early flight home for him after those intense meetings; he couldn't wait to get out of there. *It had been a very strange few days,* he thought to himself.

CRECHUS STOOD before the overwhelmingly large demon, eagerly spewing out the news that he had discovered about Jack. He was secretly overjoyed that he could give this news directly to Jason Crane's keeper and leave Lothar out of the loop completely. *He shall get a reward for this for sure,* he thought. *Maybe even a rise in the ranks.* He grinned.

ONE HOUR LATER, Jack was on the tarmac and walking toward the carpark. His mobile rang.

"Jack," Akio said in a whispering and panicked voice.

"What's wrong?"

"I can't talk long. We've been found out. I have to leave now, and you better leave too."

"What do you mean, found out? How? I just left... what's going on there?"

"I don't know how, but they've traced all the IDs we used. Everyone who has an I-Skin is exposed. Listen to me carefully, Jack, you *must* get away, take your family and the others and leave. They are coming after you—they know!"

"How do you know this? I mean, how did you find out?"

"God… he told me this morning in a dream. He said for me to call you and tell you to leave now."

"Okay!" Jack responded with dread, it was as if the conversation was in slow motion "Are… well, are you going to be all right? Can you make it to me like we planned?"

"No… there's no time. I'll have to go now. I must leave straight away."

"Where will you go?"

"I don't know. I will contact you using the secure radios I made for us. Just do as I say and leave today—right now if you can." He paused briefly and with a deep knowing, he spoke, "Thank you for your friendship. If I don't see you again on this earth, I will embrace you in eternity. Goodbye Jack." Akio paused, struggling to get the next words out. "I love you my brother, may God keep you and your family safe for when Christ returns."

"Goodbye Akio, until we meet again be safe and stay strong… I love you too, you are a good and brave friend, thank you for everything," Jack's voice broke as he said the last few words, tears streaming down his cheeks. He wept as the phone went silent.

He spent a few seconds composing himself before he took action and broke into a sprint towards his car, frantically punching out the number to his house.

"Jen, it's happened. Do what we have planned." He hung up and dialed the next number.

"Ben, they know! We have to move now!" He hung up and continued to the next number.

"Peter, we leave now!"

Jack hurriedly got into his car and drove straight to the safe deposit box to empty its contents.

As AKIO RAN down the stairwell of his unit, something stopped him. He listened carefully and heard the UNITED guards coming up a few flights below—he turned and ran back to his unit and locked the door, dragged a table to block the entrance and clambered out the window and down the fire escape.

JENNY and the children flew into action—they knew exactly what to do. They ripped their I-Skins from their hands, and while Jenny flushed them all down the toilet, Matthew and Sarah both ran and grabbed the five pre-packed duffle bags full of clothing and survival supplies from the basement.

Whilst Matthew loaded up the quad bike and its trailer, Sarah was hurriedly saddling Mustard.

Within 12 minutes of Jack's call, they were ready. Matthew and Jenny sped off on the quad and Sarah galloped alongside them for the two-mile leg to Ben's house.

MAY WAS ORGANIZING the last of the supplies while Ben was gathering the horses for their preparation. He quickly saddled those needed for riding and put the pack saddles on the rest—he wasn't leaving any behind. He rushed back up to the house to help May.

JACK ARRIVED at Peter's place and found him very distraught.

"Jack, quickly come, look on the TV— it's Akio."

"Akio?" Jack exclaimed in sheer panic. "I was just speaking with him only forty-five minutes ago."

"I'm so sorry Jack... they've got him."

CHAPTER FORTY - FOUR

"This infidel is the first of the conspirators against UNITED," Jason Crane stated in anger, the expression to which he was not trying to hide. "Trying to usurp our peaceful society, he is a barb in the fabric of our ideology."

Akio stood a few feet away from Jason, along with two UNITED guards beside him, gripping him. Jack saw Akio's face and could see that he had been severely beaten. Fresh blood trickled down his forehead from an open wound above his eye. His face was swollen with redness and bruising. Jack also noticed his lips were moving ever so slightly. He was praying and Jack grieved for his friend.

LORA AND MEG were also in front of the TV, watching in awe. They too had received the call from Jack, but were stuck, mesmerized at what was unfolding before them. Lora's tears fell ever so slowly down her soft teenage cheeks; she didn't even notice the warm flow cascading.

"Tell me, what can you see, Lora?" Meg asked urgently.

Lora spoke, "I see many angels gathered around Akio. It's like they are standing guard but also strengthening him too." She sniffled. "I also see a very large demon beside Jason, along with many, many other dark beings," she confided despondently.

"What do you think is going to happen?" Meg asked, panicking. "I mean, they are not going to kill him, right? They... they wouldn't do that!" Meg kept glancing at Lora for an answer.

Lora looked at Meg with sad eyes. "I don't know," she said, whispering softly to her friend... but inwardly she did.

. . .

Ben, May, Jenny and the children stood in May's kitchen, hypnotized by what was unfolding before them on the TV screen.

Jason continued explaining, "We have no tolerance for anyone who is against UNITED, for if we do, then it sabotages the very purpose of our society. We strive for peace and wellbeing amongst our culture and, therefore, we cannot allow antagonists who will not conform. For if we simply allow one, they will spread like poison, killing what we, as a community, have worked so diligently for." He paused, looking straight into the camera. "This infidel beside me represents one of many. We have uncovered the deceit that lay within our very own that threatens our world and what we are striving for. There are many others out there, we know the Chip IDs of every one of them." He looked into the camera angrily and exclaimed, "And we will hunt them down. No one will escape."

Akio felt as though he was in a peaceful dream. He could visibly see the angels beside him. Some were comforting him and he was transfixed by their magnificence. He felt no pain but only strength and love for his Lord God. He knew his time had come.

Zeke and Delmar stood firm, guarding their charge amongst the hordes of bloodthirsty demons that surrounded them.

Jason turned toward Akio. "I will give you one last chance, dissident, to change your ways and save yourself. Bow down before me and show the UNITED community that you are repentant of your actions."

Akio remained unmoving… unfaltering.

Jason stepped closer toward him. "I said, bow down before me." He waited.

Akio remained silent. Jason stepped forward and whispered something to Akio that no one else could hear. Then said sternly, "BOW… DOWN!"

Suddenly, Akio's voice broke through. He spoke with a strong booming clarity, as if magnified 100 times over. It resonated louder than Jason's microphone voice through the TV and shocked Jack and Peter. "I shall not bow down before you. I worship the true and living God, my King and Savior the Lord Jesus Christ and I will not bow down to any other!"

Jason visibly became enraged that he had been humiliated on Global TV. "I *AM* HE," he angrily shouted. "You shall bow down before me—I am your true living God!"

Akio was silent, rigid, and firm in his stance. He did not waver. "Father, receive me today," he said boldly.

No one could believe the events that were unfolding or even fathom what they were about to witness live on global television. It became slow motion, like a time warp—the events could have been choreographed, the movements were so clear and rehearsed. A UNITED officer ceremonially handed Jason Crane a stainless-steel Smith & Wesson revolver. Jason stepped forward and pressed the barrel hard against Akio's forehead.

Point blank!

He paused and glared into Akio's eyes, waiting for him to change his mind or show any fear.

Akio stood firm… waiting!

Jack held his breath.

Peter was praying, watching.

Ben and May stood stunned, and Jenny was sitting in silence, staring at the screen but covering the eyes of her children.

Lora and Meg sat weeping.

UNITED did not try to hide, nor cover up the gruesomeness of the event—it was unfathomable to watch. A loud crack pierced through the TV, echoing throughout airwaves, Akio dropped to the floor like a solid heavy sack. A blanket of scarlet splattered across Jason's chest, his white shirt dancing with the spots of fresh blood.

The camera zoomed in on Akio's body, lying limp in a pool of his own crimson liquid. A part of his skull was jagged and exposed, a piece of white brain matter was hanging out, and thick fluid was starting to ooze onto the floor. The camera showed no compassion, zooming in to watch as his body started to instantly pale and become lifeless and limp.

He was gone!

JACK QUICKLY LOOKED AWAY and felt the bile rise in his throat. He started to dry reach. He looked again at the TV and noticed the plastic already pre-laid out on the floor to capture the mess. *Premeditated!* He thought as he gagged again, covered his mouth, and ran to Peter's bathroom.

Peter fell face down to the floor and started crying out to God, weeping in distress, overwhelmed and sickened at what they had just witnessed.

The camera panned back to Jason's face, stoic and cold. "Those who do not conform… take heed… we will not tolerate rebellion. We know who you are and UNITED are coming after you. Those who aid and abet will be terminated. Observe my words, if you know or suspect anyone who has these fake IDs, you must report them or you risk your own life." He paused, then spoke with such boldness.

"For I AM the true and living God, whoever worships me shall be saved. Those who are against me do not belong in this world. I declare today a new decree, those who are for me, who choose to worship me from this day forward, show allegiance to me… your almighty God."

As Jason said this, he moved his hand slowly over his chest and the TV camera caught the blood that was spattered, disappearing, leaving a clean, crisp white shirt.

Peter couldn't believe it, *was he? Hang on, he was, Oh Lord he was!*

Jack returned to the room, wiping his face with a cool, dampened cloth. He stopped and dropped it. Terror rose in his eyes as he fixated on the TV.

BEN AND MAY looked at each other in trepidation. "What's happening, Ben?" May touched his arm, whimpering and backing away from the screen. Jenny could feel the hairs prickle and stand up on her body.

LORA STARED at the TV in silence, and in knowing of what was happening. Meg covered her face and cried.

PETER AND JACK gazed intensely at the TV in silence, absorbed in what they were witnessing. They watched, captivated with astonishment, as Jason Crane ascended, unassisted, rising higher with every word he spoke. At around 100 feet off the ground, he spread his arms outward, like a cross, as if to show the utmost love to the world.

"Bow down before me and show me your faithfulness, those who believe in me shall be set free. Come to me like little children and I will protect you. I will reward you and give you everlasting life for I am eternal, I am the creator of all things, and I am indeed... the true living God whom you shall serve." As he levitated and spread his arms wide, Jason's expression showed nothing but pure love.

"Convincing isn't he!" Peter exclaimed in disgust.

The camera panned out to a female UNITED employee. "Please make a note of the following photographs, for these are enemies of UNITED. If you know these people, you MUST report them immediately." Jack's photograph was the first that appeared on the screen. She continued. "To pledge allegiance to our God, you must make your way to the centers to receive your new UNITED ID. You have one week to do so. Those who do not..." she paused, "will be terminated!"

"Pete, we better get moving," Jack stated, backing away from the TV.

"I can't."

"What do you mean can't?"

"I can't leave. Not yet."

"Why, but this has always been the plan."

"I know, but something is telling me I need to stay. I need to be among the people... to warn them."

"Pete," Jack became emotional, "you know what can happen... you just *SAW* what's going to happen if you stay." He held Peter by the shoulders. "You have to come with us. Please, Peter."

"No... Jack, I have to stay! I know it doesn't make sense to you. I just know this is what I need to do. I have to speak the truth amongst the people, as there are so many who will bow down to this creature and spend eternity in Hell. I can't let that happen without trying to persuade others into standing firm in Jesus Christ. What else was I put here for? To die is gain!" He recouped his thoughts. "Jack, you extended the timeframe so even more people could be saved—you have done what God has called you to do... it is fulfilled. Now you must go."

"But..."

"No Jack, you are my brother and very dear friend. You *must* go without me," he exclaimed as tears trickled gently down his aging face.

Jack resigned to the inevitable and stepped forward. They embraced for the last time and quietly wept together and said goodbye.

CHAPTER FORTY-FIVE

"You can't!" Bethany March screamed, "she's our daughter!"
"You just saw what happened," Jim March bellowed back. "If we do not show allegiance to our God, then we will die."

"No Jim, please, I beg you," she screamed, hanging onto his arm, fighting to hold him back.

Jim violently ripped his arm out of her grapple and shoved her aside.

A gray, scaly demon was enticing him, whispering, "You must rid yourself of her—she is not a believer in God, she is a believer in the devil. If you don't, then you will die. Turn her in and you will have favor in God's eyes," it laughed happily.

MEG AND LORA heard the yelling but couldn't make out what it was about.

"Meg, come on, let's go," Lora said nervously.

Unexpectedly, her locked bedroom door erupted open—fragments of sharp splintered wood hit Lora and Meg in the face as the lock was shattered.

"Lora, you're coming with me!" Jim yelled as he grabbed her brutally, reefing her by the arm.

"No, dad, let me go. Let me go." She struggled, kicked, and squealed, trying to pull away.

Meg launched herself onto Jim's back, punching at his head and shoulders. He whirled around frantically, fighting and flinging her off where she landed against the wall with the wind knocked out of her, and her head slamming into the bedside table.

Bethany burst through the doorway, jumping towards Jim, defending her daughter. "No Jim, NO, I will not let you do this." He threw her off like a rag doll.

"You don't believe me Bethany, but she is one, I know it. She is a traitor, she is against God."

"No, she's our *daughter*. Have mercy. You can't hand her in."

Jim held tight onto Lora's arm and started scraping at the back of her hand, digging and scratching at her soft pale skin. Lora started screaming in pain. Sharp, bloodied scratches appeared.

"It must be on her other hand," Jim yelled, and started fighting Lora to get to her other arm. Lora flailed and flapped her arm about, trying to pull away, but in a flash, he seized it.

"Let me go, let me go, *daddy please*, let me go," she bawled.

Jim again started scratching at her. This time the thin silicone skin gave way, revealing a visible edge. He kept scoring at it until the I-Skin came away, floating and fluttering to the floor.

"Traitor, traitor, against our true living God," Jim yelled.

Bethany screamed, "No, no, no Lora, what have you done?"

Lora screamed back, "You are both fools… can't you see. Jason Crane is not a God, you're being deceived. Don't believe him. He is false, and he will take you to Hell. I see demons all around him."

"BLASPHEMY," Jim bellowed and slapped her hard on the cheek. "How dare you defy God."

"Mum," she shouted, "don't accept the new ID you will spend eternity in Hell. Please, mum, please come with me," she begged, looking longingly at her mother.

"SILENCE TRAITOR! Your mother will do as I say. We are all going down to the center where you *WILL* repent and declare your allegiance to our God."

"NO!" Lora shrieked at the top of her lungs, "I believe in Jesus Christ, I will not follow Jason Crane, the false messiah."

With all the strength in her, she kicked her father in the groin, buckling him over with agony. Meg took her chance too, leapt up and lunged at him, hitting him with full force, knocking him to the floor.

Like a pair of gifted athletes, they both jumped over Jim's

writing body and snatched up their ready packed bags as they ran out of the room.

Lora yelled loudly back as she ran through the house, "Mum, remember what I said, don't accept it, come with me, you know my favorite spot, I'll wait for you there." She finished calling out as she ran down the front path out the gate.

ZEKE AND DELMAR had now joined Seth and Gabe, as their charge Akio was now standing in awe before the King. They had watched as Jesus commended Akio and honored him. However, it was now time for them to help guard Jack. They moved swiftly ahead, checking and watching at every point to ensure Jack's safe escape.

LOTHAR WAS FUMING, not just because Jack had fooled them, but also because Crechus went behind his back to Jason Crane's keeper. He was humiliated and enraged at the same time. "How dare you, Crechus," he seethed. "Find Jack... and FIND CRECHUS." He bellowed to the black swarming mass standing before him. They exited with a rush, scattering and fanning outward in search of their victims, leaving Lothar sitting alone in the old pump station.

"Jophiel..." Lothar exhaled furiously, "I can't believe you deceived me. You will pay for this... I vow it," he said as red vapor started to slowly emanate from his nostrils in rage. His demon eyes burned with sheer hatred. He looked heavenward as his giant black wings began to surge, pounding in rhythm with strength and power. He launched upward and soared at full speed towards the township... looking for his archrival.

CRECHUS WAS 14 minutes ahead of the evil pack—the UNITED guards had been dispatched and were closing in, speeding along the road towards Jack's house.

· · ·

Jack turned the vehicle into his driveway and practically skidded to a stop into the garage, nearly hitting the end wall—leapt out and raced upstairs and grabbed the last few things that he knew he would need.

With Seth and Gabe consistently urging him on, "Go, go, hurry!" Jack felt the urgency and panic rise—he quickly ran back down the stairs and out the back door to the shed.

"Where is she, Meg?" Lora exclaimed in frustration.

Meg didn't respond but just stood, silent.

"She knows to come here... she heard me, didn't she?"

"Yeah, I'm positive. You yelled it loud enough."

"Well, why isn't she here?" she said frantically, tears welling in her eyes. "I can't leave her, Meg, I just can't. She's my mum," she said desperately.

Bethany stood defiantly beside Jim in the extensive line up at the UNITED chipping center, turmoil stirring deep within her. She knew all these years that Jim was wrong.

Why did she just blindly follow? she chastised herself in silence and unyielding, profound regret. Jim glanced sideways at her with disdain. *Did I even love him?* she pondered, repulsed by his stoicism and harshness towards her. *Where is the love of God in this man?*

Jim nudged her, signaling that the line was moving forward. They shuffled a few steps, and the line again halted.

An unseen angel stood beside her, and once again roused her heart and thoughts. *What am I doing? I've given this man every-thing, I've followed... I've obeyed him. For what? I'll be the one account-able when I stand before God, accountable for my own actions. Standing before God... alone... standing before almighty God!* She sighed despairingly.

"What's wrong with you?" Jim spat as he grabbed her arm

and shoved her disapprovingly, but not obvious enough for anyone else to notice.

"Nothing Jim, I'm just waiting," she returned, saddened and hurt by his harshness towards her.

"Well," he paused and then continued, "you're muttering!"

C rechus had arrived at Jack's house. He slowly sauntered up to the front of the house, scanning the area for any sign of Jack, his hatred growing by the second, eager for revenge.

Zeke and Delmar spotted the cunning creature and tried to head him off before he discovered where Jack was.

But it was too late. Crechus heard the kick-start turn over on the motorcycle. He dashed into the shed and with all his full force, *BAM!* He smashed straight into Jack, knocking him backwards off the bike.

Jack flipped, tumbled, and crashed to the ground. The pain was searing as he held his stomach and gasped for air—the wind knocked from his lungs. He wiped the blood and dirt from his mouth as he lay there stunned, unsure of whom, or more so, *WHAT* had hit him.

Crechus didn't subside in his rage—he lurched forward and picked up the bike.

Jack looked up, totally confused and wide-eyed, gazing to see the motorcycle hovering in mid-air before him.

Crechus let out a scream, "AAAAHHHHHH!" and with all his full force, threw the bike towards him.

In full flight, Gabe and Seth dove with all their power at the motorcycle, pushing it off course as it came crashing down just inches away from Jack.

Jack quickly rolled his body away, fearfully, unbelieving what was unfolding before his eyes.

"Lora, we have to go, I'm sorry!"

"Please Meg, just five more minutes," she begged. "She'll be here, I know it."

"But they're expecting us—they're waiting Lora, my mum and everyone else. We have to move now, otherwise it will be too late," Meg said anxiously looking around.

"Please…" Lora pleaded, "please, trust me I know she'll come."

THE SUN WAS HOT, and every sound and thought seemed to intensify as Bethany was standing beside her husband.

This man who I hardly know now, she thought. *God, what am I doing?*

The line shuffled closer.

Which God? Who is God? This Jason Crane is surely not God, and I know that for certain. At that thought, she captured herself, taking in a quick breath of realization of what was happening around her. *I can't do this. Lora is right!*

The line shuffled closer.

Think, Bethany, think. I can't do this. It's true! It's a lie!
Jim looked at her again, making a stern face of disapproval.

The line shuffled closer.

"Next." She heard the call. They were now second in the line. She had to act, she had to get away, her life… *her eternity* depended on it. She felt panic rise from the pit of her stomach —her hair felt like it was on its end with the comprehension and enormity of what was about to happen. *This will cost her… her life.*

"Are you sure he is God, Jim?" she asked.

"What?"

"Are you sure that he, Jason, is the Messiah?"

"Of *course*, woman, are you blind?" he whispered with

contempt, "Have you not seen what he can do? Now shut up, and keep moving," he snapped.

Tears along with panic welled in Bethany's eyes. She was at a loss. *What will I do?* She thought with overwhelming despair and terror. Her face paled at the realization of what was about to happen.

The line moved forward.

LORA SHIFTED ANXIOUSLY, looking through the trees to see any sign of movement. She saw nothing. "Meg?" she said as tears streamed down her face.

JENNY WAS TRYING NOT to think about it, she was busily helping pack the horses. The scene of Akio kept repeating through her head. *That could be us if we don't leave now*, she thought, with a hint of panic arising. She looked at her children, who were frantically assisting May and Ben. "God help us!" she whispered.

BETHANY WAS SILENTLY DISTRAUGHT; *I have to leave, but how?* She let out a panicked prayer under her breath. "Oh, Father God, please help me, I need to get away."

Swiftly, the angel firmly poked her in the stomach, causing her to buckle over with extreme pain. "Aaah!" she cried out.

"What's wrong now?" Jim snapped.

"I don't know," she squirmed. "I have an excruciating pain in my stomach area. Ahhhh… it hurts!"

"Next," the guard called.

"What are you doing? We're up now, we have to go!" Jim snapped.

"I can't, look… you go ahead, I have to rush to the bathroom, and I don't want to embarrass you or make a scene."

"Can't you just wait till after we have the new ID?"

"Come on, you're holding up the line, move forward." The guard ushered to them both. "Hurry up you two," he said angrily.

"Sorry, but my wife is in pain and needs to visit the bathroom," Jim said meekly and clearly embarrassed.

"Well, step aside and wait over here until she returns. You!" he pointed to Bethany, "go sort yourself out and come back quickly," he said with an element of annoyance. "Okay next," he called, signaling to the next person in line.

ZEKE GRABBED A HOLD OF CRECHUS, he screamed, "AAAHHHHRRR GET OFF ME!" Gabe, Seth, and Delmar tried to hold the demon back and get a good angle on the blades to get rid of him. They fought and scuffled.

"They're coming. Hurry!" Zeke yelled as the angels continued to battle the demon.

"Hahahaha ha ha," Crechus laughed. "Time's running out for your little saint—isn't it hosts?" he leered, growled, and snarled as he continued to dodge their blows.

The UNITED guards had turned the corner into Jack's lane way, the dust was billowing from the gravel road as the cars sped over the rocks and corrugations.

BETHANY HURRIEDLY WALKED the 70 feet to the bathroom block— the pain was excruciating. She quickly opened the door, and the pain suddenly vanished. She immediately felt fine again. Confused, she stopped, turned back around, and gingerly glanced back out of the doorway. Carefully she looked to her left, back towards the line where Jim was standing and then to her right towards the covering of the bushes nearby.

"*RUN!*" She felt a rush, a voice so clear it could have been audible. The angel took hold of her with urgency, and she made a dash for the bushes. No one saw her. She peered back to watch

Jim still standing waiting for her. Overwhelming sadness for her husband began to engulf her, her emotions of compassion and sorrow for him started to rise.

"*MOVE NOW, RUN!*" Again, that voice.

She turned and ran for her life!

CHAPTER FORTY - SEVEN

Jack had managed to turn the bike upright, still dazed and unsure of what was unfolding around him. He could feel the battle waging around him like a tornado and felt the sheer urgency to get the bike going. *Brrrrr, brrrrr, brrr,* Jack cranked the kick start over and over, "Come on," he chastised the machine, his panic rising as he continued in his attempts.

Crechus saw Jack on the bike again and dove at him, breaking and smashing through the angelic barrier separating them. They blocked some of the force, but not enough. *OOOOF!* He fell with the bike on top of his legs—he kicked and pushed and pulled until his legs broke free of the machine. Crechus lurched forward and clasped his fowl talons around Jack's neck.

Jack gasped for air. He felt the terror inside of him rise as he could feel the life squeezed from him—his throat constricted, choking, and rasping for oxygen—he started to weaken. Then he saw it—it was horrible and in his fading state he could see it so very clearly.

Its black, scabby, gnarly hands were gripping his neck, the long sharp talons were savagely biting into his skin. He could feel its immense weight bearing down on his chest like an unstoppable, continuous, crushing force. Its bulging red eyes staring at him with the utmost hatred, its yellowing, needle-sharp teeth baring and loathing him. He could see it was willing him to give up and die. He could even smell the fowl stench of death emanating from it. In a surreal like panic Jack was praying, in his mind he was calling out to Jesus, but also mesmerized and dazed by what he could see, he was reaching a dreamlike state with the lack of oxygen and he felt himself slowly slipping from this realm.

DRIVEN BY ADRENALINE, Bethany kept running, her face and

hands getting whipped and scratched by branches as she ran amongst the bushes for cover. *I have to make it to Lora,* she thought.

Jenny was trying to hold back her tears and tried not to show the panic inside. She looked at both Ben and May and mouthed, "Where is he?"

Ben and May both shrugged, with apparent anxiety and unease written on both their faces.

Jack was struggling, and his attempts at gasping for air were futile. His fading vision was of the dark force bearing its fangs with delight at his demise.

Suddenly, with a bright flash, he saw a sword come down upon this evil being. In this airless, haze like state, he saw everything, the majestic brightness of the angels, their immense wings and their massive swords attacking, pounding and striking the evil force until... "*GASP! Aaah ah.*" He inhaled and sucked in the air—he was free.

Jack quickly grabbed his neck and was heavily breathing and gasping as he watched in amazement at what was unfolding before him. The bike miraculously righted itself and the motor suddenly started into life, just waiting for him to get on.

Gabe forcefully picked Jack up from the ground and literally threw him on board the bike. Jack felt the rush like never before as Gabe grabbed hold of the bike and pushed Jack on his way. He sped off down the road at full throttle, totally in awe of what had just happened. Zeke caught up with him and continued to push the bike from behind at a rocketing speed.

"NNOOOOOOOOOOOOOOO!" Crechus screamed at the angels, as he came at them swinging and raging, ripping and slashing through the air with his gigantic blade.

"We must finish him, lest he warn the others," Gabe yelled.

The UNITED guards had turned into Jack's driveway; a large dark being was just ahead leading the way. It was Lothar. He had arrived with his hoard of demons escorting the UNITED troops as they drove towards the house, eager to gain their prize.

Seth dodged a blade. Gabe made contact.

"AAAHHHHHH!" the demon screamed in pain, slime like substance oozed from his side, red foam started to slowly drip from his jaws in rage.

SUDDENLY, a snapping of twigs, along with soft breathlessness, was heard.

Lora peered through the bushes. "Mum!" Lora hastily cried, "I knew you'd come. I prayed you would." Lora said with excitement.

Meg hugged Bethany. She could see that she had been weeping; dusty tear stains had clung to her face, revealing the evidence.

"Let's go," Lora said as they all stealthily ran towards Ben's property.

They ducked, darted, and hid their way through the town. Lora and Meg saw several others they knew who had the I-Skin escorted away by UNITED guards. It made them more determined to survive.

A SMALL DEMON from outside Jack's house heard the ruckus coming from the shed and broke away from the others to investigate.

SLASH! WHOOSH! "You won't have me," Crechus screeched as his blade cut through the air. "You're finished! The others will come. WE will win."

SMASH! CLANK! The angelic blades connected and sparked with every powerful blow.

The small demon came closer, eager to see what the commotion was.

SMASH! RIP! CUT! SLICE!
"You WILL fail," Crechus laughed.

The small demon heard the laughter and ran towards the shed.

CLANG! SWOOSH! CHOP!
Suddenly, there was sheer silence as the angels watched their enemy fall to the ground. Seth had made contact, and they watched the severed head drop to the ground and slowly roll away. His yellow, menacing teeth were still bared and his bulging red eyes gazing blankly.

"Let's go," Seth said as they all dove straight down, 100 feet into the earth, their swords drawn ahead of them as they sped through the rock and the deep cool soil.

THE SMALL DEMON rapidly burst into the shed to see Crechus's body lying there limp.

The dust was just settling as Lothar came in behind and walked over to the detached head. "I knew you were nothing but a useless fool... absolutely useless," he said as his foot connected with the oozing mass, and like a football, was catapulted out of the shed.

They continued to look around the premises to find Jack, but to no avail... he was gone.

JACK ARRIVED to see everyone frantically grabbing gear and taking it over to Ben.

Sarah and Matthew were distraught and crying as they ran towards him. They all embraced. "I was so worried," Jenny said.

"You wouldn't believe what happened!" he said, "but I'll have plenty of time to share that with you later. We must hurry! UNITED guards are looking for me at our house right now."

"Do they know you're here?" Jenny said anxiously.

"I don't think so, not yet! But it won't take them long to figure it out."

"I'll put what I can in the packs—hopefully we can fit everything in," Ben called out anxiously. "May is finishing up in the house, getting what she can. She is very upset to have to leave her home," he said, with tears in his eyes, "So am I… I have a mind to stay and just accept what may come."

"They will come for you, Ben," Jack responded as he walked towards him.

"Where's Peter?" Ben asked.

"He's not coming!"

"What?" Ben screwed up his face in disbelief at what he was hearing.

Jack just looked back and shook his head, upset, unsure of how much more he could take today.

"Well, where are the girls, then?" Ben asked.

"You mean they're not here?" Jack exclaimed with worry.

Patty looked at Jack with concern. "Meg rang me from Lora's house, Jack—they should have been here already," she said as tears appeared.

"Well, we can't wait much longer," Ben stated. "We must make the start to the mountain range before nightfall, otherwise it's just too dangerous. How much longer should we wait?"

"I don't know… something must have happened," Jack said with concern. "Peter said that they were prepared and ready to run. We can't just leave them, Ben—they won't survive on their own."

"No, Ben!" Patty said, upset, "We can't leave them!"

"I just hope they come soon, for all our sakes," Ben said anxiously. "We are running out of time."

As Ben finished that sentence, they saw in the distance three figures sprinting up the dirt driveway, and everyone let out a sigh of relief.

Each waited beside their respective horses and watched as May stood before her house, taking one last long look. She picked a yellow rose and then hurried towards them, visibly heart-broken. "Let's go," she said with tears.

Everyone mounted.

"We head for those mountains," Ben explained as he pointed upwards. "It will take us two days to get across the range and reach them, then another day to reach our destination. There is a large cave that we can make our new home until this is all finished. There's no visible trail, it's rough, and it's only accessible on foot or horseback. That's the best chance I can give us." No one responded.

The angels stood guard, watching, looking outward toward the perimeter of the property for any signs of the enemy.

Gabe turned and gave the order, "Cover their tracks!"

As the horses moved out, angels gathered and brushed the dirt, covering all signs of animal or human trail.

Ben led the way. All except the children were towing one or two packhorses, and each was loaded with supplies that Jack thought he would never need. Even Mustard carried his fair share. They hurried the horses into a canter so to make ground in case UNITED were on their way to Ben's farm. They only slowed once they were under the cover of the forest.

THIS HAD BEEN a year of planning and storing, a preparation for such a day as this. Sadness overwhelmed Jack as the rocking, lulling movement of his horse moved onward. His thoughts went to Akio and the events that had just occurred that morning. *I can't believe it's come to this,* he thought, *a life on the run!* He couldn't fathom what the future would hold; all he could think of was how to protect his family.

They all moved in silence, each too shocked to speak, each reliving the day in their own emotional turmoil. Each apprehensive about what lay ahead.

After three hours of riding, they dismounted at the edge of a creek and let the horses rest for thirty minutes before they started the ascent.

Ben rallied them around. "Now listen up, it's tough going for the horses, so just let them have their head, but be diligent and guide them the best you can. If we can make it halfway up, it'll be safe enough to make camp for the night. No one will track us here."

"Well, what about staying just here?" Matthew asked earnestly, while discreetly rubbing his aching crotch.

Ben smiled. "We don't want to make it too easy for them, do we? Sorry Mattie, we have to keep going."

PETER WAS ON THE RUN; he'd heard a ruckus and had seen the UNITED guards up the end of his street arresting his neighbors, the Jessop family. He grabbed his laptop, pre-packed bag, and ran out the back of his cottage hoping for a head start. He found a hiding place on a hill in the park nearby and sat undetected under the brush. From his vantage point, he could peer down and watch the township.

This hadn't been his plan, he thought, *he was supposed to go with Jack —that's what they had prearranged for so long.* But something changed, and he knew in his heart God wanted him to stay. *For now,* he thought.

Tears quietly fell as he saw people dragged from their houses, beaten and humiliated. Some were made to strip and go to the chipping center naked and demeaned. The UNITED guards were merciless.

. . .

BEN WAS RIGHT. It was three days of grueling ascent. There was no easy track to rely on, slowly meandering around fallen trees, boulders, and through densely forested ravines, relying on a trusty guide to lead the way. Most of it done in silence, everyone too focused on guiding, leading, and pushing the horses onward and upward—it was physically and mentally draining.

Relief was evident when a large clearing in the trees, along with the small opening of the hole in the mountain, came into their view.

They stopped out the front, and all dismounted.

"So, this is now home." Jack smiled, trying to pick up everyone's spirits.

"This is it!" Ben exclaimed, looking around. "Now we just have to do some hard work and get it looking more like a home, but not obvious if you get my drift."

Jack nodded in agreement.

CHAPTER FORTY-NINE

TWO MONTHS LATER

Peter crouched under the dense green bush, watching as he saw some of his fellow believers taken away by UNITED guards. They grappled with them, ripped the fake I-Skin from their arms, and pushed them aggressively into a van. One man resisted violently, pushing back with his arms and feet straining hard against the open doors of the van.

Peter saw the guards look at each other and then one of them pulled out a revolver, placed it on the back of the man's head, and pulled the trigger. A loud shot rang out throughout the air and instantly the bright red blood, bone, and brain matter splattered over everyone and a frenzy of panicked high-pitched screams broke out. Peter closed his eyes as they slammed the van door and drove away, leaving the body in a heap, twitching and jerking whilst lying in its own pool of glistening cherry red fluid.

Peter heaved and gagged at the murderous sight left on the concrete. Weeping silently whilst he held his hand over his mouth to silence his emotional heart wrenched muffles. He waited for 10 minutes after the van had left before he slid out from his cover and started running cautiously again. Nausea and throbbing pumped through his body at a rapid rate; his heart ached with torment at the thought of what he just witnessed. He wanted out, out of this disgusting, evil, sin-ridden world.

"I WANT everyone who is not a follower to be gone; they are sinners and need to be punished. We need to be rid of them, otherwise they will poison the society," Jason Crane stated to his UNITED management team. "I want it to be known that anyone who isn't a part of UNITED is to be removed, let them know, also show them the consequence of their dissidence. Now make it clear, it's worship me or die."

The large demon beside Jason grinned at what he was hearing. Jason turned to him after the others had left. "You seem pleased."

"I am Master, very pleased," it responded. "Everything is going as we planned."

"Yes." Jason smiled, reflecting on his achievements, "We need to cull this world, bring about selective intelligence, and rid ourselves of the substandard intellect."

"And also the weak Master, do not forget them."

"Yes, you are correct; I think we need a culling program, for not only the disbelievers but the substandard as well. Let's make this society a super intelligent race," he said, smiling ruthlessly.

"Good idea!" the demon stated in agreement.

"Also…" Jason paused for a moment, thinking… tapping his finger on his chin, "guillotine, or gun?"

"Definitely guillotine Master… for it is much more effective, it strikes fear into any mortal." He responded with a sinister, malicious smirk.

PETER WAS in an overwhelmed state as he guardedly headed back to his hideout. Suddenly, he heard a commotion to his left, "OOOF! SMACK! OUCH!" he gasped and buckled over as the wind was knocked out of him by a punch to his stomach, "Stop, please, I'm not an enemy." He held up his hand in defense.

"What have you got in your backpack, old man?" Peter braced himself against the three youths who rushed at him and took turns in pushing him around. They had ragged, dirty, and torn clothes and were clearly in need of a meal.

"Just clothes and some water, nothing really," Peter responded cautiously.

"Gimme a look." The largest of the three snatched the bag from Peter's grasp and started pulling out everything and looking intently through each item.

"You got any food?" one youth piped up.

"I have nothing! Else I would share it with you," Peter

answered as he watched his drink bottle shared around between them.

"What do you need a laptop for?" another youth questioned. "You playing games on it?" They laughed.

"No, please, just give that back—you can take everything else, but please hand that over."

"Oh, this is precious to the old man." The large youth waved it about mockingly as the others laughed. "Why do you need this? I could do with one of these."

"Look please, just give that back," Peter asked politely but desperately.

"Nah, I think I'll keep it."

"Please, I need it. I need to spread the word."

"Yeah, I can spread the word whilst playing games too," the large youth mocked as they all laughed.

"Please don't!" Peter paused. "I really need it," he pleaded.

The large youth ignored Peter's plight and put the laptop into the backpack, slung it over his shoulder and started to walk off. The others followed, laughing.

"Hey! You guys… give that back." A tall, dark-haired man ran swiftly towards them from the nearby bushes, completely taking them by surprise.

"What? Who are you?" the large youth said in defiance. "We can do what we want—leave us alone," he responded as he walked off.

"Give me the laptop else you *will* suffer," the man stated sternly, not backing down.

The youth hesitated for a moment before continuing walking towards the bushes.

The man leapt forward and grabbed the backpack, ripping it from the youth's shoulders, twisting him sideways and driving him down hard to the ground. "Leave this man alone," the dark-haired man stated forcefully, holding the boy down firmly before letting him get up.

They faced each other; the youth glowering at the man before realizing that he was defeated.

"Like I said, leave this man alone," the dark-haired man demanded.

The large youth thought for a quick moment. "We're cool," he said, holding up his hands as he backed away slowly and returned to the cover of the bushes.

The dark-haired man walked over to Peter and handed him the backpack.

"Thank you so much," Peter responded gratefully.

"Peter, your work is not finished here. There are still many that need to hear the message of Christ. The false messiah is fooling so many and those who do believe in Christ are being forced to relinquish their faith, they have not prepared for this time. Continue to encourage the existing believers, to strengthen their faith so they do not fall… and continue to bring the message to those who do not believe. Fear not Peter, for your time is not yet come."

Peter stood in silence, stunned by this complete stranger who knew him so intimately by name.

"Peter, do you have enough water?" the man hurriedly asked.

Peter snapped out of his transfixed daze and glanced down and rummaged through his backpack. "Ah… um yes, I have three full bottles that strangely weren't there before," he exclaimed, confused before looking up to see no one standing before him.

The man had vanished.

CHAPTER FIFTY

The old pump station reeked of putrid hate; the hordes of demons had grown and were crowding into the old building. Tussling and fighting amongst themselves, awaiting notification.

The tiny messenger flitted into the building, bowed before Lothar and whispered the message into his ear.

"Shut UP, SHUT UP," yelled Lothar. "We have the word." They all cheered in response. "SHUT UP, QUIET," he raged. "Now that Crechus is gone… the stupid fool," he muttered, "there is no room for any more mistakes. I want all of you to wreak havoc on all who roam the earth. I don't care who it is. This is OUR time, OUR time to RULE, deceive everyone, we need SOULS!" he screamed excitedly.

Cheering and yelling came from each one, grins of excitement as they realized what this meant. This was freedom, freedom to do whatever they wanted. To create anarchy, to harm, to kill, to destroy.

"Go NOW and FINISH THIS," Lothar yelled, holding up his sword in victory.

Like a loud rushing vortex, the air sucked out of the building as the mass of fowl demons exited. The clear blue sky became dark as they spread out across the firmament.

THE ANGELS LOOKED up and saw the mass converging and dropping into the towns. They knew that this was going to be one of the toughest battles to keep their saints covered and safe.

PETER SHIVERED as he felt an overwhelming darkness creeping

over the land. He looked and saw that visibly the sky had darkened and he knew in his spirit that there had been a shift in the realm and it wasn't for the good. He hastened to his hiding spot above the township and readied himself for the night to come.

"YES, YES, that's it. Come now and fill the lands. I am King, I am the ruler, rid us of the sinners," exclaimed Jason, exalting himself.

"You are a great Lord!" the large demon encouraged, filling Jason with more pride but hating every moment he spent with this pathetic mortal.

PETER WAS safe in the gap between two large boulders resting against the cliff. It wasn't a large crevice, but it protected him from the elements. He also had a vantage point to see if danger was approaching and was elevated enough that he could watch the goings on below in Evensmore. It was the perfect hideout for one and it was where he spent his nights, wrapping himself in blankets for warmth.

During the early mornings, he would sneak down to the library and crawl underneath the building. He had created an electrical outlet under the flooring, and this was where he sat, hidden for two hours each day to recharge the laptop batteries.

His days were going between the library, searching for food and water, then making it back to his safe haven before the darkness fell. He dare not stay out beyond daylight, as everything was worse at night, people were malicious in the nightfall, and no house was safe.

However, tonight felt very different. The air was thick, and the atmosphere was intense. Peter could hear an unnatural distress of howling of dogs echoing throughout the night. There was something else going on as the increase in evil permeated throughout the atmosphere. He could hear frantic screams in the distance... there was terror encroaching upon the land. He prayed.

His guardians stood out front of the boulders, dimming themselves to invisibility and hiding the safe haven so the enemy could not see it. They had increased their numbers, for Peter's purpose was not yet fulfilled. He pulled out his laptop and covered himself under his black blanket so the light would not shine and give him away. He blogged;

"Dear followers,
Tonight, there is a presence, an increase in the enemy's ranks. I do not know what this means or what our future holds, but I assure you that Jesus Christ, God's only begotten son is the only true and living God. Not Jason Crane, who proclaims himself as Lord.
He is a false prophet, a mere human puppet for the enemy, Satan. He holds no power and is only driven by the power that Satan has bestowed upon him. Do not be fooled. Do not bow to him. Do not take the mark, for if you do, then you are doomed to an eternity in Hell. It is written in the scriptures Revelation 13:16-17:

It also forced all people, great and small, rich and poor, free and slave, to receive a mark on their right hands or on their foreheads, so that they could not buy or sell unless they had the mark, which is the name of the beast or the number of its name.

This is happening NOW! I must stress to you, do not take the mark, which is this new ID, endure the tribulation for it is nothing compared to eternity.

Jason Crane is false, he is a thief, and he is a liar from the pit of Hell. Do not listen to him, choose Jesus Christ as your Savior and do not follow Jason Crane, for if you do, then you will burn for eternity.

If you do not know Jesus, then simply ask Him to come

into your life, ask Him to forgive your sins, and help you change your ways. It's as simple as that.

There is no time left people—we are running out of it. This is the end times, Jesus Christ is returning soon, very soon and when He does, if you do not know Him, then it will be too late. Those who do not know Him will perish and spend eternity in the lake of fire. There are **NO** second chances. I repeat, once Jesus comes, that is it! You cannot repent then… there is NO second chance.
Pray the prayer and become a child of God. Then… to die is gain!

Bless you all! Until we meet in Heaven, may you all stay safe and come to know JESUS.
Love
P."

Peter encrypted the message, then hit the submit button and waited.

"It's up!" a UNITED team member yelled.

"AARRGGH… Who is this P? Come on, can't you trace it?" Jason was infuriated. "Why can't we find him? Are you all stupid? I thought you were the smartest hackers? Useless bunch of idiots, get it off now before they see it," he ranted.

"He's using VPN software, so it's very difficult to pin down," one employee stated.

"REALLY?" Jason yelled sarcastically. "This is why I'm paying you people. You're supposed to be good at what you do," he said, frustrated. "What's he saying now, anyway?" Jason said as he sat in front of the computer screen and read.

"NOOOO! get it off now, I am the one, I am the true and living God, get it off now. If you don't, I swear I will kill you all." Jason became enraged. "You need to find this rebel—he is spreading lies. YOU!" he pointed to one of the team, "write up a counter blog quickly, and let me proof read it."

The team of software engineers and hackers were frantically trying to bring the site down, perspiration dripping from their brow from the intense stress. It was like this every time a post went up.

PETER SAT and watched as the reply messages poured into the webpage in response to his blog; he knew there was only a brief window before they worked out a way to take it down.

```
"Dear P, thank you, I was going to go to
UNITED in the morning to accept the mark
out of pure desperation for my family.
We've had no food for four days. My chil-
dren are starving, but I saw your message
and we have all accepted Jesus as our Lord
and Savior. Thank you and keep up the
fight. Please pray for us. Jasmin."

"Hi P, thanks for your encouragement. I
know it's hard, but please keep the
messages coming. We need to know that there
are other believers still out there… alive.
God Bless you! John."

"Thanks P, I read your message, and I've
now asked Jesus into my life. I'll see you
in Heaven when we get there! Jesse."

"P, where can we get food? We need to eat
and UNITED is the only one providing it.
Help us… we are starving. Joel."
```

Peter quickly typed in a response:

"Joel, I barely can find food myself, so I understand. I pray for you all daily. Keep the faith and do not give in and go to UNITED. Stay true to the Living God Jesus and He will make a way. God bless! P."

"Dear P, when will this end? When will Jesus return? I'm tired of running; I'm hungry and thirsty and frightened every second. From Desperate."

"Desperate, Jesus is coming soon. Just hang in there. I'm praying for you. P."

"Dear P, Yes I believe in Jesus, but this is HARD! I spend my days constantly hiding and protecting my family, along with searching for food. I am so tempted to march down to the chipping center just so I can feed my family. I am willing to sacrifice myself for the sake of my children. I can't do this much longer. Please pray for me. Tom."

"Tom, please do not give in. I know it's hard, and I cannot imagine how much harder it is seeing your children and family suffer. Please stay strong, for it is not worth sacrificing your soul for eternity. It will only be a short time before Christ returns in comparison. You MUST have an eternal perspective. If you die now, you go to Heaven. If your children or wife dies now, they go to Heaven. However, if you accept the mark, you will **NEVER** see your family again... you will be separated forever. It's not worth it. Stay strong brother, I am praying for you."

"Dear P, it has been one week since I

watched my husband be brutally killed. I
managed to get away, but I now wish I had
stayed and died alongside him. How can you
say your God is a loving God when He allows
this to happen to us? I am lost, sickened,
and deeply distressed. I do not know *who*
God is. Is it Jason Crane or *your* God… for
it seems that none is full of the love or
grace that you continue to speak of. I will
remain undecided and follow neither.
Sarah."

"Oh Sarah, I am so sorry that you have had to endure this
pain and loss, and I know my words will not come close to
comforting you. Unfortunately, we live in a fallen world
that the enemy can walk freely. God does not condone this
behavior, nor will He allow it to go on for too much longer.
It pains Him to see this suffering happening, but the
human race has pushed Him out of their lives long ago
and has chosen to follow Satan. God loves everyone
enough to allow freedom of choice, no matter the consequences. If He forced us to love Him, as Jason Crane is
doing, then it is not love at all.
Know that this time will end soon, Jesus will return and
when He does, those who do not know Him will perish.
I hope you choose Jesus, Sarah… I truly do!
Psalm 147:3 says, 'He heals the brokenhearted and binds
up their wounds.'
God loves you, Sarah, and He is waiting for you to make
the decision!
I hope to meet you in Heaven. P."

Dad, keep up the message. It's making a
difference. We all love and miss you so
much. Love your Son.

Son, oh how I miss you and your sister, keep the faith and endure always. If I don't see you again on earth… then I will see you in Heaven. Give my love to your family. I pray for you daily.

I love you always, Dad.

Peter sat in silence and kept reading the replies. His heart was breaking for the many people suffering, along with his very own family. "God, please come quickly."

Then suddenly, he saw the black text of - *The page cannot be found* appear on the blank white webpage. "Well, at least it took them 45 minutes this time," he said. He was pleased with his efforts tonight. Sometimes it would only be up for 10 minutes before UNITED took it down. *However, tonight was a good night,* he thought. He had his message out there and had touched some souls.

"USELESS!" Jason stated as he stormed back to his office, the large demon close beside him.

"Who is this P?" he asked the demon angrily.

"We cannot locate nor confirm his identity, Master," it responded.

"Why not, you know everything… can't you do something?"

"I've sent scouts out to the realms, but they have returned with nothing—he is being protected."

"Protected by whom?" Jason snapped angrily.

"By the enemy, my Lord… your enemy."

P eter powered down for the night after he had surfed the internet and read other believers' blogs and messages. He wasn't the only one sending out a forceful message about Crane.

He'd become quite learned in the ways of avoiding detection over the Internet. *UNITED must be so busy tearing all these down every night,* he thought. He was exhausted from the events of the day, so he tucked himself into the thick blanket and got comfortable and quickly slipped into sleep.

* * *

"EEEWWWWW! AAAAARG!" it screamed. "Give me food!"

Screeching, scratching and clawing, it pulled the blanket from Peter, ripping him from his sleep. Frightened, he recoiled, pressing his back firmly into the crevice as it grasped for him, lurching forward, trying to grab his legs. It was ugly, but it was human.

The grotesque woman, who was covered in dirt, scratches, scabs and matted hair, seemed utterly possessed. Her eyes were not normal, nor were her features fully human. Her face was pale gray, like a zombie, her voice was guttural. She lurched forward, trying to grab a hold of Peter. Too frightened to speak, his heart was racing and nearly leaping out of his chest with fear—he kicked out and hit her hard in the face.

"Aarrggh!" she fell backward, recoiled, touching her cheek in pain, then went to lunge forward again, but something caught her attention and she backed away in fear. Her eyes became wide, and she was in distress at what she saw.

"Don't harm me!" she shrieked. "I have no fight with you!"

Peter sat, coiled tightly in a ball, and watched her.

The Guardians slowly edged forward towards her, swords drawn ready.

"Leave me alone," she screamed, backing up towards the rocks. "LEAVE ME ALONE!" she yelled, echoing throughout the darkness.

The Guardians pinned her against the rock and waited. She stood with eyes wide in fear, with her back pressed firmly against the cold solid granite stone. There was no escape.

"Peter, come speak to her. She needs freedom," one Guardian whispered into Peter's ear.

Startled at how audible the voice was, Peter was fear stricken and couldn't move.

"Peter, help her!" the response came again.

Peter crawled out terrified, moving slowly and not taking his eyes away from the insane woman. He was too afraid to go near her, but whispered a small prayer.

"SHUT UP YOU!" she snapped at him, hissing and glaring. "SHUT UP!"

Peter tried again, his whispers became audible as he prayed for her release.

"NOOOO! You have no right. She is ours, she belongs to us," she screamed.

Peter kept praying. The Guardians stood steadfast, wielding their swords.

"Have her then, she's not worth it, there are plenty of others," she screamed and then slumped into a heap on the ground. Her face instantly changed, her eyes became clear and her features returned to humanlike. She laid there for several seconds before she came to, then delicately said, "Thank you!" her voice soft and feminine.

Peter stepped forward and offered to help her off the ground. She accepted and stood up, facing him. "Are you all right?" he asked.

"I am now; I've been in torment for months. Thank you!"

"It wasn't me, but Jesus, do you know Him because I suggest you do, otherwise they will return... but with dozens more."

"Please tell me more," she asked.

Peter told her about Christ and she accepted Jesus into her heart there and then.

They both sat on the ground, breathing in the night air, but still heard the howls and screams in the distance.

"Where have you come from?" Peter asked.

The woman responded. "My name is Amy and only two months ago I was living with Jason Crane as his girlfriend."

"What? Really?" Peter looked astonished. "What's happened and why are you here?"

"We were together for three years but he got bored with me and simply told me he wanted a newer model, someone who had more presence in society," she said with tears in her eyes, "He just threw me out like I meant nothing to him, I had nowhere to go, nothing to take with me… it was all his."

"Do you have the UNITED Chip?"

"Yes, but I never got it changed with the new ID. Jason thought I had, but I never had to buy anything because everything was provided for me being his girlfriend, so I never needed to… and also I just simply forgot." She paused, realization hitting her. "Now I have nothing… I have absolutely nothing," she cried.

"So what happened… where have you been?"

"I don't know. It's all a blur, these voices in my head, pushing me, taunting me, making me do things. It's been terrible. I felt like my soul was suffocating, drowning… I honestly can't recall where or what I've been doing. Where am I now?" She looked around in wonder.

"You're in Evensmore."

"Evens WHERE???"

"You obviously don't remember how you got here?"

"No, I don't know what I've done or where I've been. Voices… only voices." She broke down and cried.

"Do you remember anything?"

"I remember getting ready to go out to dinner, and then Jason's henchmen came in and told me to leave and then they said some really weird stuff to me. That's it. It's like I blanked out and have been wandering."

"Can you remember what they said?" Peter enquired.

Amy sat in silence for a while. Peter could tell she was trying to remember. After about one minute, she spoke. "Umm... I remember them telling me I had to leave." She paused. "Then... they said that I would forget everything and then said something in a language I don't understand... I had heard it before, but I've never understood it. That's it! The rest is blank."

"Okay, well, I guess you can stay here the night—there is not much room though."

"That's fine, thank you so much. I just need to sleep as I'm so tired," Amy said as her eyes started to close. She crawled into the crevasse, curled up, and went into a deep sleep. Peter put some blankets over her to keep her warm, then sat very uncomfortably and dozed restlessly throughout the night.

* * *

AMY DID NOT WAKE until late the next morning. She had been exhausted. She stirred, then eventually asked, "What time is it?"

"It's 11."

"Wow, what a sleep, I feel great!"

"Amy, I have to go... if you want you can stay here, but I need to go charge my laptop batteries."

"I can come with you."

"No, it's better that I just go. It's too risky with two people at this hour and it's up to you if you want to stay here or go your own way," Peter said as he got up to leave. "I will be about three hours. If you're still here, I will see you then."

Peter said goodbye and expected never to see her again. He walked off cautiously. It was much later in the morning than he had preferred.

Three hours later, he returned and was surprised to see Amy still in the hiding spot. She had prepared something to eat for them both. "Wow, where did you get that?" he asked, surprised.

"I went exploring and found a stash of cans," she smiled. "Cold baked beans all right with you?"

"Perfect!" He smiled, relieved to have some company.

They conversed over their meal. "So, this is all you do all day?"

"I blog at night, but yes, that's all I do, really."

"Blog what?"

"About how Jesus Christ is Lord, not Jason Crane."

Amy eyed Peter for a while, "Ah hang on," she paused in deep thought, "are you… P?"

"Yes."

"Oh wow! That's so funny. Jason would get so upset at what you wrote. I used to watch him rant about how he couldn't find you and the others that were blogging against him." She paused. "And I found you," she giggled. "How ironic!" she said with a smile and a hint of revenge.

"I always hope that it takes time for them to bring the blog down."

"Yes, I would too, as I loved to see him panic when it was up… it was so funny," she said with malice.

"So, there wasn't much love between you two?"

"No… I guess it was time I left—I saw through him. He is just a controlling, arrogant individual, not worthy of the accolades that he gets. I was tired of him. He's gotten worse over the past year though and I became scared of him and his anger, but also, I found it funny to watch him and his imaginary friends' converse."

"Imaginary friends?"

"Yes, he used to talk to someone… or something, I don't know, but they would talk for hours, planning and scheming. I would sometimes crack the office door open and listen. Some things he would do and say were really off—I mean, I'm talking weird. I simply thought it was a childhood thing."

Peter thought for a while before he spoke. "I don't think it's a childhood thing, Amy. I think he was conversing with demons or the devil himself."

Amy chided, "Na, are you serious? Really… is that what you think?"

"Yes."

"Okay then." She paused. "Um well, I'm not sure what to say then as that is just freaky."

Peter smiled. "You don't know the half of it."

They both grabbed a blanket each and leant against a crevasse wall opposite each other.

"We need to find a bigger hideout if you're sticking around," Peter stated.

"If you don't mind, I was hoping I could stay with you. I feel safe—you remind me of my grandfather and... well, you seem normal." Amy smiled.

Peter smiled. "Gee thanks!" he laughed, "Good night Amy."

* * *

PETER AND AMY set off in the early morning to the library to charge the batteries. They then carefully investigated potential hideouts that could house a greater number than just two people.

"I think we should prepare for the future to help others," Amy commented as they moved off cautiously through the trees.

Peter was amazed at Amy's tenacity. She had taken charge, thinking ahead, and was already sourcing places to house more people to hide.

"If we can get a big enough place, we can create a safe house and live together and help one another," she whispered as they continued to covertly scour the township. "But I think we should get out of town and go further out. Do you know the area very well?"

"I do, but not for hideouts. Many people had bunkers, maybe we could look for something like that."

"Perfect!" Amy exclaimed. "Let's go!"

Amy and Peter walked for hours, ducking in and out of hiding spots, when a vehicle approached. They scoured the countryside until they came across an inconspicuous door in amongst the bushes. They cautiously opened it and looked in. There were stairs leading downward.

"Are you game?" Amy said with a mischievous smile.

"Only if you are," Peter responded with more of a grandfatherly concern.

"Let's do it!" Amy said as she headed down the stairs into the darkness. "This is perfect," she said as she looked around at the vast opening in front of her.

"How can you see?"

"Oh, I can see… and it's perfect!"

"WE CONTINUE TO COVER PETER, so he remains safe," Jophiel said to Darius.

Darius nodded his approval, very pleased with his charge's progress. "I hear many people are coming to our Lord daily because of the messages of truth that Peter is conveying."

"Yes sir, many are being encouraged by his words and choosing not to bow to the enemy."

"Good… he is doing exactly what our Lord asked of him," Darius smiled back. "Help gather the other believers to him for their own safety… however, remain vigilant." He cautioned.

CHAPTER FIFTY - TWO

Only three months later, Peter and Amy had 27 other believers living in the shelter with them.

Amy had perfectly managed and coordinated food scouts to go out every day. It had become a well organized band of believers, hoping to survive until the coming of Christ.

Peter concentrated on his blog every day, sometimes blogging up to five times a day just to get his message out there. He had managed to put hidden messages for food drops in his communication for those who were starving.

John 3:16 says, "For God so loved the world that he gave his one and only Son, that whoever believes in him shall not perish but have eternal life."

He would then tell Amy before he posted it, the address of where to place the food parcels. John Street, unit 3/16. Alternatively, if it were an address in another local town, his other contacts would do the food drop. There were many believers scattered across the globe, secretly communicating daily and so far, the plan was working, UNITED was none the wiser.

Each night, they would pray and conduct a Bible study to build their faith and encourage one another for the times ahead. However, it was tough! Tougher than anyone would have imagined. Every night there were stories of loved ones being tortured, family members turning from their faith in fear and accepting the mark. People would break down in heart wrenched grief while reliving the events. Many nights' people were in tears, consoling and helping one another to forgive and look to Jesus for restoration.

Peter tried to end the nights on a note of lightness and not dwell on the sadness, even though it was extremely hard. For no one knew their own future, nor how it was going to end. The hope of surviving until Christ's return was the only thing driving them.

The hideout was not paradise. The living conditions were cramped, and only having one bathroom between 27 people was proving difficult and unhygienic, even though some endeavored to constantly clean. Bickering and terseness would break out daily due to the frustrations of all. Peter and Amy were constantly pacifying and praying for people, sometimes even chastising and reminding them of where they were and why they were here. It was tough!

Amy arose at first light, quietly stepped over her slumbering roommates, and slipped out into the still dewy, cool morning air. She sat and relished the silence and time alone. A rarity!

JASON CRANE WAS ALSO AWAKE, slipping out quietly from under the bedcovers so as not to disturb his new lover. He put on his silk robe and walked along the long hallway to his office.

"Good Morning Master," the large demon spoke.

"Good morning, I trust that your work was fruitful while I slept."

"Of course!"

"Where are we at?" Jason asked blankly.

"We made progress last night, Master. We found some more Christians and will have them executed publicly today."

Jason scanned the room, looking at the twenty-six other demons filling the area, waiting for direction.

"Good! But hurry up and find that 'P' fellow, he is a thorn in my side... get to work," he said as he waved his hand.

The demons quickly rushed out of the room.

Jason slowly meandered back to the bedroom.

AMY HEADED off towards the library with the several laptop batteries that they now had gained. She cautiously made her way through the winding path she had become accustomed to so well. Her two Guardians walked along with her.

. . .

PETER AWOKE, disturbed. He had a bad dream—it was about Amy being captured. He got up and went to look for her, to tell her about it and discuss precautions for the day, but he'd discovered that she had already left. "Lord, please protect her!" he prayed as he gathered others to do the same.

AMY WAS QUIETLY MAKING her way towards the town; her thoughts were elsewhere; she didn't hear someone sneak up behind her. *WHACK!* She slumped to the ground and slipped into blackness.

Her guardians did not stand a chance from the onslaught of the enemy. Wounded and left lying alone, injured. The enemy had gotten what they wanted.

PETER INSTANTLY KNEW something was wrong. He and the others kept praying, but his spirit was telling him that Amy was in trouble.

JOPHIEL AND CHALE looked up as they noticed two lone figures in the distance flying slowly towards them. Amy's guardians, who were severely injured, both landed awkwardly, falling hard in the dirt in front of their captain.

Jophiel and Chale both rushed to them and helped them to their feet.

"They have got Amy," one guardian said, wincing in pain.

Jophiel quickly motioned to a large white crystal shimmering angel. His prismed light was emanating outward, radiating shards of piercing sparks. He touched the two guardians' and watched as their wounds healed and their torn and tattered wings instantly mended.

"Thank you." They both said.

"We could not protect her." One guardian said sadly.

"I know you would have done your best," Jophiel said as he

put his hand upon his shoulder to comfort him. "We can only hope that she does not fall."

Amy slowly awoke to the rocking sensation of the vehicle, and in her daze, she started rubbing the back of her head. She felt the gooey moisture and glanced at her hand to see the clotted blood smeared on her fingers from her wounded skull. Seated across from her in the back of the van were two UNITED guards, expressionless, hostile, and glaring at her.

"Where are you taking me?" she demanded, now fully aware of her situation.

"Back to headquarters," one of them responded bluntly.

"Why?"

"Because our orders are *not* to kill you. We've been following you. You must be stupid to think that your UNITED Chip didn't give us your location."

She suddenly felt a weighty coldness creep over her body of the realization that the others may be in danger. She didn't speak but sat quietly, secretly praying for the rest of the five-hour journey.

Peter and the others sat in silence; they all knew something was not right.

The van stopped, and they shoved Amy out the door into the grasp of another two guards. She was standing in front of UNITED headquarters; they started pushing her towards the door and directing her into the elevator. She felt panic rise as she watched the floor numbers—she knew where they were taking her.

The elevator doors opened, and they directed her down the hallway to Jason's office. They opened the door and Jason was waiting, leaning back on his oak desk with a wry grin.

"Amy darling," he sarcastically spoke, "my, you look well. It's been a long time. Leave us," he said and waved the guards away. "How have you been?"

Amy didn't respond, but stood petrified.

Jason sauntered towards her and gently ran his hand across her cheek, downwards and slowly across her shoulder. She stiffened at his touch. "I have missed you," he crooned and whispered lustfully in her ear. "Have you missed me?"

"No," she snapped and backed away.

He seemed taken aback that his advances were rejected. "Come on Amy, surely you want to be with me again."

"No," she said emphatically.

"My, you have changed, haven't you, a different Amy before me I see." He paused and looked her up and down. "Actually, I think if we did a little pampering and spoiling," he continued as he gently touched her face again, "you would look even better than before. The raw environment has made you toned." He smiled.

She recoiled at his touch in disgust.

SLAP! He smacked her hard on the cheek. "HOW DARE YOU LOOK AT ME THAT WAY! What is *wrong* with you? You *do not* treat me with CONTEMPT!" he yelled.

She backed away in fear—her back was pressing hard into the wall, and her cheek was red and throbbing from the blow.

"I could offer you all this and more," he said as he swept his hand outward.

"I had all this, Jason, don't you remember. You kicked me out without a thought."

"Ah, so this is what it's about. You're still upset with me… maybe I was a little callous, but I think I could accommodate you again." He smiled.

Amy felt her stomach churn with sickness—she wanted to vomit. "No Jason, I'm fine. I don't want to come back."

"Oh, that's a shame, I was warming to the idea of having you by my side again… along with Rosemary, that is."

Amy looked at him with detest. "You're sick!"

"No, just industrious at getting what I want."

Amy didn't react.

"Well, if that's your choice, then I guess you can just give me the information that I'm after."

Amy swallowed nervously. "What information?" she whispered timidly.

"The information on the Christians you've been hanging out with." He waited and watched her expression change—he knew her too well. He could read her like a book. "You see, I think you know where I can find them and you may even know where I can find this P fellow."

Amy gulped. She knew he had her!

CHAPTER FIFTY-THREE

P eter and the others sat in the shelter nervously. No one dare go outside.

DARIUS STOOD SILENT, saddened by the news of Amy.

"We cannot get in there." Jophiel reported with disappointment.

"Then... she is on her own, she knows the truth... and that is our only hope."

JASON CONTINUED HARASSING AMY. "It will not take long for my guards to find them. They are scouring the area where they picked you up from as we speak. You are not protecting them by not telling me, so stop wasting time and just say it."

"I know nothing, Jason," she responded meekly, looking at the floor.

"Ah pretty Amy, I know you better than that. I believe you know a lot more than what you are letting on. You best tell me or..." He stopped short.

She looked up, "Or what?" Her bottom lip quivered.

"Well, I don't want to say. I still love you and would hate for anything terrible to happen to you. It's best that you just let me know what I need."

"I can't," she whispered.

"It's best that you do or else..."

Amy cried in panic—her nerves had gotten the better of her. She slid down the wall and sat on the carpet, her chest pounding as the fear was tightening her throat.

"Come, come Amy, it's not that bad. Just tell me."

"I can't, they are my friends."

"I'm your friend."

"No, you're not," she snapped. "You kicked me out—I had nothing, and my mind was crazed. I don't know what you did, but you didn't love me then and you sure as hell don't love me now!" she yelled angrily, quickly standing back up and pointing at him.

"Ha ha haha." Jason laughed. "Oh Amy, I love it when you get mad." He walked towards her.

"I hate you Jason, I don't love you and never will again. You are a cheat and a liar."

"Don't you dare call me that, I am god."

"Ha, you're no god, you are nothing Jason, absolutely nothing!"

Enraged, he rushed forward and grabbed her around the throat. "Don't you dare say that!"

Amy couldn't breathe. She felt herself choking.

"I'd like to kill you right now, Amy, but I want to know more," he said as he let go.

She gasped for air and slid down the wall onto the floor again, catching her breath, holding her neck, her eyes wide with fear and grief.

"Guards!" Jason yelled, "take her away."

Two UNITED guards came into the office and dragged her out and down the hallway. They came to a room and threw her in; the lights were off, and she was in utter pitch-black darkness.

"Taunt her!" Jason said to the large demon.

"PETER NEEDS PROTECTION," said Darius, "for it won't be long until they find the hideout."

With that, Jophiel saluted, and with a flash exited the heavenly realm at missiles speed back to earth.

TEN DEMONS FLEW AHEAD into the pitch-black room and instantly started shoving Amy. She fell back against the wall and screamed, hitting her head again. The fresh blood started to gently trickle through her hair. She was blind in the darkness, unable to see who was attacking her. The fear rose even higher as she slowly stood again.

SMACK! SHOVE! THUMP! "OOOF!" the wind was knocked out of her repeatedly from unseen assailants. She fell backward, and then she started fighting back, striking outward, and kicking hard.

The large demon grabbed her by the leg and swung her around, letting her go. She hit the wall hard and landed on her stomach. She panicked and got back up to her feet, punching the air in what seemed like nothing but pitch-black darkness.

She could feel the evil in the room and knew that these were not men, but spirit entities. "Go away, go away, leave me alone," she cried out, but they kept attacking her. They pushed her against the wall. She screamed. They held her down and tried to choke her. She screamed and fought back.

Finally, she yelled, "I believe in Jesus, you can't touch me."

"Yes, we can. We own you. You never forgave, therefore we have a right," one evil entity responded.

Shocked that she heard it talk back, Amy defiantly said, "No, that's not true!"

"Oh, it's true," another small evil being responded. "I don't blame you though, Jason was terrible to you wasn't he, throwing you out like that."

"Shut up!" She screamed.

"It's true, he was so mean, and he didn't care."

"Stop it, stop it—Stop it."

Another demon with needle-like spines all the way down his back pushed into her chest, squeezing out her breath. "Really?" it whispered, close to her face. She flinched in fear. "Didn't he just discard you... throw you out as if you meant nothing to him? You were with him for three years, Amy! Three years!" he said as he released the pressure on her chest.

"Yes, I was," she responded, exhausted and hopeless.

"You didn't deserve that, did you?"

"No, I didn't deserve it."

The large demon smiled and nodded for the other to continue his work, liking the change of tact.

"Well, why should he get away with it? You deserve better, Amy," the spiny demon continued.

Amy was tired and traumatized. "Yes, I do, don't I." She felt anger and hate rise inside her.

"Then why should you forgive him? He doesn't deserve your love nor your compassion, does he?"

"No, he doesn't." She groaned. "I hate him. He hurt me and deserted me—I had nothing. I hate him, hate him, hate him and I will never forgive him," she screamed, pounding her fists against the wall in anger.

"That's right Amy, let it all out." They grinned with malice. "Jason was mean to you... but he still loves you."

Amy slid down the wall in silence onto the floor, exhausted, defeated, and confused at the mixed feelings she was encountering.

"Ha ha-ha." The large demon laughed. "Where are your friends now, Amy? Where is your God?"

Amy broke down, taunted for over two hours and captured 14 hours ago. She felt drained. "I don't know," she barely whispered.

"They have deserted you—your God is not real. Jason is the real God, can't you see?" the spiny demon stated.

"NO! My God is real, Jason is not God!"

"Yes, he is... he is the *REAL* God. What have you seen *your* God do?"

Amy closed her eyes, tears rolling down her cheeks, her mind fuzzy. "I don't know, I can't remember."

"He has done *nothing* for you. Tell me, Amy, what have you seen your God do?"

She couldn't think, she was too tired.

"Tell us Amy, what has your God done?"

"I don't know, leave me alone, I can't think."

"Doesn't a true God bring peace and unity? Jason has already done this."

Amy said nothing. She was busy thinking, trying to gather her muddled thoughts.

"Jason has done many miracles. You have seen him, Amy. Don't you remember?"

"Yes, yes, I remember," she responded meekly and in a state of confusion.

"That is another sign, wouldn't you say?"

"Maybe... I don't know... I can't remember anymore," Amy spoke weakly, drained of all willpower.

"What miracles have you seen your God do?"

"Shut up! I don't know... please just leave me alone." She whimpered.

"We won't until you see the truth Amy—we want you to see it. That is... Jason is the true and living God."

"No... he can't be... I mean, he is a man and Peter said he is false."

"Peter, hey?" The spiny demon looked at the others, grinning. "Is that P?"

"Um, I guess so, yes. I mean, I think it is." Amy didn't know what she was saying anymore. Her head ached, her body was in pain from the beatings, her face was swollen, and her lip was split, bloodied, and bruised.

"Jason is God, Amy. These people are traitors and are against the *real* God."

"No, I don't think so," she responded. "They are good to me."

"Are they really? What have they done for you?"

"I... I... well I don't know." She put her hands to her face and cried again, the tears stinging her swollen and scratched skin.

"There, there Amy, it will be fine if you follow the true God, Jason. Just say it, just say that Jason is the true and living God and all will be fine. We will let you leave and you will be free."

"Free?" she questioned hopefully.

"Yes, just say it, say that Jason is the Lord, it's easy, and then we will let you go."

"I, I don't know, I'm not sure, I don't think it's right." She shook her head, trying to gather her thoughts.

"It's simple, Amy." The demon's voice softened as he transformed himself into her dead mother.

"Momma!" Amy gasped with relief.

"Yes Amy, all you have to do is say it, renounce your God and follow the true God... Jason. Then you will be free, for all eternity. You will have such peace."

"Peace?"

"Yes, peace... you will be filled with peace, say it."

"Maybe."

"Say it, and you will be free."

PETER SAT with the others and prayed. They all knew Amy was in trouble. "God, please help her," Peter whispered.

ALL AMY COULD THINK about was being free. She was shattered and confused seeing the image of her mother before her. "I can't think."

"Just say it and you will have peace—think of the miracles Jason has performed. You were there, you saw them too. How can you deny he is God?"

"Yes, I was there, wasn't I? I saw them," she said. "Maybe you're right, but I'm not sure anymore, maybe..."

"You know I'm right, it's the truth... it's simple." The spiny demon disguised as her mother pushed. "Just accept Jason as your Lord and savior and you will have freedom. You've seen the good he has done—your God has done nothing! Jason has brought the peace, your God doesn't care, he has abandoned His people... can't you see?"

"Yes, I... well, I think you could be right... I don't know anymore."

"Then just say it Amy, the sooner you say it, the sooner you will have your freedom. Just say that you renounce your God and accept Jason as the true and living God and you will receive such peace and freedom."

"I-I don't know."

"They deceived you Amy, they've brainwashed you. Jason took care of you and loved you. He still does, and he is our Lord. Your Lord... surely you can see this now?" The image of her mother implored.

Amy sat in silence and said nothing as they continued to push.

Another demon interjected, "Oh, he has performed such miracles, hasn't he? You've seen them yourself. Isn't that a true sign of the Messiah?"

"I guess!" Amy responded feebly... she was ready to crumble.

"Then all you need to do is renounce your God and say Jason is the true and living God and then you will experience such peace."

"I-I don't think I can... I'm not sure."

"Come on Amy, you *know* Jason is God." The demon pushed even further. "Don't be deceived—just say it and you will finally have the freedom that you have always dreamed of."

Amy was silent for a long while. She breathed out a vast defeated sigh and then spoke softly, "I... I renounce my God." She broke down in defeat and forcibly pushed the words out. "And I accept Jason Crane as the true and living God."

Immediately, something changed. Amy felt the spirit of God swiftly leave her. Coldness crept over her body and deadness stealthily filled her soul. She immediately panicked and then curled into a ball of anguish on the floor and cried sorrowfully from the depths within. Her soul ached, as she knew then that she had done the wrong thing. "I'm sorry God... I didn't mean it," she said emptily.

"It's too late, Amy—your God won't accept you now. You have made the right choice anyway, haven't you?"

She sat up, wiped her eyes, and slowly nodded in acceptance.

"Then come and worship Jason, your Lord," the large demon stated with a grin.

The guards came back in and led her back to Jason.

CHAPTER FIFTY-FOUR

P eter and the others gathered around and watched a live stream that UNITED was airing. What he saw broke his heart. Amy was dressed smartly, her makeup perfect, and she was happily standing by Jason's side. A woman from the media asked a question, and Jason nodded towards Amy to answer.

"Yes, Jason, my Lord has graciously accepted my repentance and allowed me back into his fold. I am thankful that he is so forgiving and is happy to love me again. He even miraculously healed my face from the terrible accident that I incurred on my way back to worship him," she said as she smiled warmly at Jason.

"Leave now!" An angel prompted Peter.

Peter quickly shut his laptop down, unable to watch anymore. "We must leave now. Gather your things."

A woman approached Peter, distraught and shocked. "How could she do this, Peter?"

"Rosa!" Peter stated calmly but firmly, "you do not know what she has been through, do not judge her. Just don't follow in her footsteps as she has sealed her fate." He turned away before she could see the pain in his eyes and agony in his heart. His spirit grieved for his friend and her loss, knowing that he will never see her again. He paused and took charge. "Everyone, hurry, they will find us now—pack lightly and gather back here. We must get away quickly."

The many angels rushed around, preparing their saints to leave, urging them on to hurry.

However... it was too late—the door crashed open and gunshots rang out. Two lay dead—the rest were dragged outside into the daylight.

"All of you get on your knees," a UNITED guard yelled.

Everyone immediately obeyed and dropped to the ground in fear.

"Which one of you is Peter, the one who calls himself P?" one guard yelled.

"I am," Peter spoke loudly; he wanted this to be quick, so no others were harmed.

"Right." The guard grinned and exclaimed, "our Lord will be pleased to see you at the end of this train ride." he paused briefly, "I want everyone to stand up and walk in a line back down to the train station. There will be no talking. If anyone disobeys, they will die—if anyone tries to escape, they will die. Are we clear?"

Everyone nodded.

"Start walking," he shouted.

The angels were unmistakably outnumbered, the loathsome demons surrounded them, waiting for just one to start the fight.

"We must get word to Jophiel." One angel secretly whispered. "We will comply and not start anything here."

Peter and the others followed in a line behind seven guards, followed up the rear by another six; they all had weapons and were keen for bloodshed. They walked an hour to the Evensmore train station, where a train was waiting.

"Get on the train," one guard instructed as another pulled opened the heavy wooden sliding door.

Some started to weep in fear as they boarded the stock car carriage.

Rosa whispered to another and asked fearfully, "Where are we going?"

The guard instantly turned and grabbed Rosa by the throat, put the barrel of his revolver to her forehead, and pulled the trigger. Everyone shrieked as the blood sprayed over the rest of the captives nearby. They all screamed in panic.

In the commotion, a single angel slipped out unnoticed from the carriage. He stealthily crept away, ducking and hiding in the shadows until he was out of sight. He then flew at breakneck speed to find his captain.

"Shut up! If you don't, I will shoot you all. Now SIT DOWN AND DO NOT TALK!" the guard yelled harshly, waving his gun angrily.

Everyone instantly quietened, choking back tears and pain as the guards threw Rosa's body off the carriage onto the concrete platform.

Peter couldn't believe what he was seeing—he sat and silently prayed. His heart was in agony, and he could feel fear encroaching upon him.

The train slowly pulled out of the station. The carriages were full of people he didn't recognize, families with children sitting on the hard wooden floor in fearful silence.

The carriages rocked and creaked in the darkness for eight hours. No one could look out or see what direction they were headed. Everyone sat in silence. Some had been weeping since they had boarded. No one knew what fate lay ahead.

"IT'S NOT HIS TIME," Jophiel addressed the regimented troops that stood valiantly before him. "We must defend and protect Peter."

"We are prepared," Chale responded courageously, raising his sword high, encouraging the enormous army of warriors gathered, eager to go to battle.

"WE WILL FIGHT!" They all shouted in unison, their voices carrying throughout the frosty night air.

LOTHAR WAS VERY pleased at the news the tiny black messenger spirit had just delivered. "It is time." He smirked, "we have the preacher... Let's go." He commanded.

Like a cloud of bats, hundreds of demons rapidly exited, swarming and blackening the sky above.

Lothar was at their helm.

THE EARLY DAWN light just started to peek over the earth's surface when the train slowed and descended. The guards yelled out, "STAND UP!" and everyone stood. Some shrieked in terror at what they saw. Peter looked out between the boards of the carriage and was repelled by the sight. His hands gripped tight on the panel as his face paled and his legs started to tremble and give way.

CHALE WALKED over to Jophiel and placed his hand on his shoulder. "This is your chance, my friend."

"I'm ready!" Jophiel stated confidently.

AS THE TRAIN descended the mountain, Peter had a clear view, looking outward over a vast fenced area with masses of guillotines. There were lines of people, screaming and begging for mercy, and he could see some taken away as they repented on their knees. The guards were beating people as they pushed them forward in lines. They showed no mercy as they quickly locked them in, and the massive guillotine blades came down. It was a vile sight and Peter stood overwhelmed, his knuckles turning white as he gripped the side of the carriage whilst surveying the horrific slaughtering camp that awaited him.

IT'S amazing what can be done when people are determined to survive, Jack thought. He awoke and rose in the dawning light of the clear, fresh morning and walked outside to gaze at what they had created. The plans Ben had drawn up in his own living room nearly two years ago had come to fruition. Jack was astounded at Ben's tenacity to set this place up as their hideout. Ben had made over a dozen trips by himself with his packhorses to bring well-needed supplies and hide them securely in the cave for when they finally arrived. *He certainly is an exceptional planner,* Jack thought.

The horses lazily grazed in the clearing. They had fenced off the perimeter but ensured that the fence line remained hidden within the dense forest surrounding it, so as not to be visible from the air. They had sectioned off a large area under the trees for when they heard aircraft in the far distance, they quickly gathered the horses and hid them under cover so not to draw attention to the open area.

Their lookout was on top of the jagged boulders hanging directly above the entrance of the cave. The view was breathtaking. It was the highest point on the range, but it remained camouflaged by the scattered trees and bushes. The cave was perfectly hidden from every aspect.

Spring water gently trickled and flowed down the rocks around the corner to the right of the cave, pooling and ebbing into a deep-worn hollow in the rock base itself, as if God had shaped it into a bath for this very occasion. It was the perfect hideout.

The entrance of the cave was relatively small, but once inside, it opened wide with smooth, cool gray limestone. From the main entrance, it wound back, branching off into little nooks, which created natural private rooms. It was an enormous cavern, which twisted back deep into the mountain. They had wandered and traversed the cavern as much as possible, but still hadn't explored all of it, as it was so vast.

It was a simple existence. Every day, they would set traps, hunt, and tend to their vegetable patch. Every night they would sit inside the cave around the fire talking about God, reading the Bible and reminiscing about old times. Ben had his harmonica and Matthew his guitar, so they could also joyously sing praises and songs when they felt like it.

When it got late, Jack would wind up the radio Akio had made and just repeat the words, "Pete, are you there?" and patiently wait, listening intently. Only silence returned. He hadn't heard from Peter since the day he left... and he deeply missed him.

The angels continued guarding their charges day and night, keeping watch for any enemy. None had been detected, nevertheless, they were diligent and never faltered in their protection.

Jack sensed today could be unusual—he felt a little uneasy. The sky looked slightly different, too. Jack couldn't pinpoint it, *a different hue than normal*, he thought.

The angels gathered around in discussion.

CHAPTER FIFTY-FIVE

A vortex of evil had started to descend over the death camp. The blackness spun and swirled like a viscous twister as the demonic beings slowly coasted downward. A dark shadow grew across the land beneath as Lothar was leading his troops into the settlement below.

"The preacher will arrive here soon. We will finally find out where Jack has been hiding. That's one mortal that I want revenge upon, for he has cost us greatly… also," he snickered, "I will enjoy the preacher's demise, to finally shut him up." Lothar said with malice to one of his majors as they both gradually descended from the sky.

JOPHIEL STOOD WITH HIS REGIMENT; hiding and waiting to receive the Lord's signal to attack. Chale stood ready, unseen in the distance with his squadron.

PETER SNAPPED out of his fear-ridden trance when he heard the shots ring out. People were panicking at the sight of the death camp and the guards had taken to simply shooting them instead. The more they shot, the more they panicked. It was crazy… people were clambering over each other, trying to get out of the carriages, but they couldn't—the doors were locked.

SIGNAL RECEIVED… it was on! Jophiel raged forward, his brilliant sword drawn. He wanted to take his rival down.

· · ·

THEY'D TAKEN him off guard... at the last-minute Lothar saw the Hosts appear. He called for retreat as he knew this was not the time to stand and fight... he did not have the numbers. Confusion set in the ranks as demons tried to backtrack at Lothar's command. Instead of banding together, they were scattering.

JOPHIEL DUCKED and weaved through the falling demons, cutting black torsos and slashing necks as he maneuvered his sword from side to side. He pushed through the evil darkness, disposing of the black screaming mass and leaving a trail of swirling murky vapor from his wrath. He had his eye on the prize!

LOTHAR SAW Jophiel coming at him like a fiery missile. His hatred rose for this Lord of Hosts Captain; he angrily spun around to face the threat, deciding he would finish this once and for all.

JACK MEANDERED AROUND THE HORSES, checking each of them for any injuries and their general wellbeing. They hadn't ridden them much since arriving here, only when they needed to venture out further and forage for wild food.

Jack had his favorites and enjoyed scratching, patting, and talking to them. He appreciated the contact of an animal and occasionally relished the downtime away from the others. Sarah was always fussing over Mustard though, and would ride him around the paddock daily.

Jack leaned against a tree whilst scratching a bay gelding on his neck as he wondered how Pete was doing.

THEIR HUGE WINGS roared in the airstream as they dove straight at each other. Their swords connected and locked with a *CLANG* in midair as they spun around at the force of their collision. Red and white sparks arced off their blades. They matched each other in both strength and their desire for victory. Lothar swung around trying to off balance his opponent, but Jophiel's large glorious wings stabilized him as they battled on.

They descended and ascended in the mid-air combat, both opponents waxing and waning, but each matched by their yearning for triumph.

"So, how long will this battle last... hours or days?" Lothar sneered, "You can't defeat me, *Captain!*" he mocked. "I beat you before, so why do you think you can beat me now?"

Jophiel said nothing, just kept his eye on the grotesque dark being. He flew forward fast and hard—they connected again as Jophiel smashed into Lothar's chest, sending him tumbling backwards with the force of the hit. Jophiel didn't waste any time and followed like a bullet after him, chasing Lothar as he plummeted uncontrollably downward, and hitting the hard earth, leaving a deep crevice in the ground from his powerful landing.

Lothar quickly jumped to his feet, ready for his assailant as Jophiel again smashed into him with his full force, driving him backwards once again.

Jophiel could see that Lothar was losing confidence. He knew he was stronger this time and that he had the upper hand. It was his time, and he was prepared.

Their swords clashed repeatedly, flashing and sparking with exploding flares. They pushed, they shoved, they dodged, they cut and slashed, both trying to vanquish each other permanently.

BANG! BANG! BANG! Peter screamed and ducked, as three people beside him fell from the piercing hits and dropped dead on the floor. The guards had resorted to randomly firing at those now trying to escape out the gap at the very top of the carriage. Peter leapt to the floor in panic. He could feel the sheer terror taking a hold of him, and he recoiled into a corner, sitting in a pool of someone else's fresh crimson blood, looking straight into the dead person's listless eyes.

. . .

317

ZIIING! CLASH! CHINK! Lothar sidestepped a blow and rammed his torso straight back into Jophiel. Their swords locked against their mighty chests, they stood with their stance unyielding, face to face, their noses nearly touching.

"I WILL TAKE YOU DOWN!" Lothar shouted, his putrid deathly gray breath coiling up in the air between them.

Jophiel remained silent and then spun around, tearing loose from the stalemate stance. He backed up slightly and then rushed toward Lothar with a *ROAR!*

Jack was still relaxing against the tree with his horse company when he thought he'd better continue doing the rounds. He made his way up through the vegetable patch towards the chicken coup. He was happy when he found they had laid 14 eggs. "Good girls," he commended them.

Lothar responded to the attack and lurched forward in fury. He would not let this archenemy take him out, no matter what.

They collided!

Again, Jophiel was the stronger and smashed Lothar's torso back into a large granite bolder, knocking the rancid air right out of him. Jophiel braced him firmly, this time with his sword to his throat, slowly slitting into his dark skin and revealing the flesh within.

"You think you've won!" Lothar rasped. "Well, you're wrong, you will NEVER win. WE are in control of this world, WE will win, and NOTHING can stop us," he said as he felt a renewed strength and started pushing back with all his brute muscle.

He swiped at Jophiel with his long taloned hand and caught his face, smashing him sideways and backwards. He continued his relentless frenzy and grappled to seize the Captain around the throat. Jophiel could feel the deathly vice like grip tighten. Lothar started to grin—the thick black gelatin saliva began cascading down his jowls in the imminent event of victory.

"I have you now... *Captain*." He leered.

S uddenly, the sky lit up like pyrotechnics. Streams of glorious light beam ribbons streaked across the firmament along with a thundering sonic explosion.

Everyone, including the UNITED guards, dove to the floor of the train carriage in fear—instantly, the train jolted, shuttered, and shook.

The large locomotive engine shut off and the emergency brakes triggered—the sound of the brakes was deafening as the rail wheels locked. Sparks, flashes and metal shards were sheering off from the iron. The grating of steel against steel was so piercing that Peter had to cover his ears from the penetrating noise biting his eardrums. The carriages started to buckle and derail as they were ramming and crunching against each other. Peter could feel his carriage beginning to tip.

LOTHAR LOOKED UPWARD in shock at the kaleidoscopic beams flashing across the heavens, momentarily taking his mind off his prey.

SHOVE! SHIIIING! SWASH! SLICE! Bleed! The sound of metal cutting through flesh and bone rang out. Lothar backed away, buckled over in sheer agony and disbelief at the power of his attacker. He looked in horror at his black leathery membranous wing lying half-folded and immobile on the ground; the bone severed cleanly through as if from a bandsaw blade. His wound was gushing profusely.

JACK JERKED with fright when he heard the explosive noise—a loud whip crack echoed across the land. He ducked as he looked up and saw bright aurora lights, like arcing ribbons lashing and radiating across the sky. Bright yellow and orange mixed with white flashes struck crossways over the blue firmament, and at every flare there was a massive booming sound that followed.

PETER GRIPPED TIGHTLY as the carriage went over, smashing onto its side and pulling the other freight carriages downward with it one by one.

The big locomotive at the front was the last to fall as it smashed onto its flank and slid down the embankment. The grating of metal and rock was deafening as the train and its carriages continued to slide down the large mountainside, ripping, cutting, and crushing through the earth and vegetation that lay before it.

JACK STOOD MIXED with both fear and awe, mesmerized and frozen by the visions before him.

Ben and the others came running outside to watch. They all scrambled to the lookout to gain a better perspective of the surrounding spectacle.

"What is it daddy?" Sarah huddled into him, scared.

"I'm not sure, sweetheart." He held her close to his side as he and the others watched in wonderment.

Unexpectedly, they saw an aircraft in the far distance falling from the sky.

"Oh no," Jenny cried. She held her hands to her face, gasping with disbelief.

They watched in absolute horror as they saw several planes dropping, plummeting, rotating uncontrollably to the earth, and then bursting into detonating firestorms upon the impact.

Another arc flashed across at least 50,000 feet directly above them; they screamed in panic as they could feel the intense heat and the jarring boom that shook the solid stone beneath them. They all ducked and started running, scrambling and clambering down the rocks to reach the protection of their cave.

It seemed to intensify, the cracking arcing, the heat and vibration. The cave shook with every rumble. The occasional loose debris and dirt rained down into their hidden sanctuary.

They huddled together under the thick granite protection and sat listening to the echoing cracks across the land, feeling the vibrations and praying for their safety.

The angels stood firm and provided a covering, protecting each one from any harm.

THE ADVERSARIES FACED each other as the eruption of flashing red and orange arcs continued above them.

Lothar was rattled at the events unfolding.

"You think you're still in control now Lothar?" Jophiel said sarcastically whilst he pointed skyward. "*My Lord* is the one in control... not yours," he said as he set his battle stance and readied his sword once again, his strength renewed.

Lothar grimaced in pain as he took on the challenge. He slowly positioned his sword and prepared for the conflict to begin again.

Jophiel could feel his aggressors' self-assurance diminishing.

BRIEFLY KNOCKED out from the impact, Peter regained his breath with the taste of dirt, grit, and blood in his mouth.

A fresh, earthy smell mixed with smoke and dust lingered in the air. He went to move and then buckled in sheer agony, then looked and saw a piece of jagged metal sticking out of his thigh. He lay there assessing the situation and looked around at the carnage before him. There were so many dead lying nearby, some who were still alive were crying out, groaning in agony.

The sky continued to light up, flash, and thunder all at once— it was a frightening sight.

LOTHAR LURCHED in full force towards his antagonist, but Jophiel was ready and bolted upward, somersaulting over him, knowing that Lothar could no longer fly. He now had the advantage.

As Jophiel landed, he drew his sword and struck Lothar just under his other wing, tearing through the muscle and rib cage, creating a cavernous wound in his back.

"AAAAHHHR... DAMN YOU!" he shrieked and wheeled around; his only wing rendered useless. Lothar was fuming, ignoring the biting pain he grimaced and lurched forward again in attack. "AAAARRGH!"

Jophiel met his blow and pushed back hard, but Lothar was weak from the battle, his wounds had drained him mentally and physically. They held their stance; swords locked as Jophiel slowly but sturdily pushed down on Lothar, forcing him to the ground onto his hefty black knees.

Jophiel's sword ignited with power—he could feel that victory was imminent.

PETER DRAGGED himself away from the wreckage and then sat up, propping himself up against a large rock. He took a few breaths, bracing himself for what he had to do, then firmly grabbed a hold of the metal shard that was in his leg with both hands and pulled hard. He screamed in agony, never experiencing such pain before. Blood gushed out of his wound as he quickly tried to suppress it. He passed out.

THEIR SWORDS LOCKED AND ALIGHT, Lothar was on the ground, incensed with rage as he struggled against the force of Jophiel's glory and strength. He quickly twisted sideways to put Jophiel off balance, but he couldn't outmaneuver his opponent. He stared up at Jophiel as his bright burnishing blade came down upon him, cutting deeply through his enormous chest.

"No—You can't! Damn... you... Jophiel." The air from Lothar's final breath left his bloodied jaws, hissing as the last of the red vapors furled out from his nostrils.

In an instant, Lothar was gone.

It was night when Peter came to. His leg wound had clotted nicely whilst he had lain unconscious. The sky continued lighting up—the sonic booming sound was deafening. In between the roars of the heavens, he could hear people groaning in agony all around him.

It was Hell!

Chale and Jophiel stood once again before Darius in the heavenly realms.

"Well done, my friends. You have fought well," he commended. "Our King is well pleased with you. Tell the ranks that they will be rewarded." He paused before continuing, "What of Peter?"

"He survives," Chale replied.

"Good!" he smiled satisfactorily.

F or three days it continued, the lightning, the loud booming noises cracking throughout the sky.

Jack stood watching, as the horses were frantic; one had staked itself on the fence, severely injuring its leg. Jack and Ben diligently tended to its wounds in trepidation of the arcs, not knowing if they could save the animal. The other people constantly remained inside the cave, afraid to come out unless it was necessary.

Then silence!

Stillness, never felt before, crept across the land. Not even a breeze fluttered the leaves, or a bird or insect heard. It was eerily quiet for two days, and then, once again, the arcing and booming returned.

For weeks, it came and went and in the time between, they hurriedly tended to the horses and chickens, collected food and ensured that they had enough supplies for the days that the sky lit up like a firecracker.

After two months, normality seemed to have returned. There was silence again.

Jack never understood the events that had occurred or if it would start again. It was a mystery.

"You ready to check the traps?" Ben asked Jack.

"Yep, I'll be with you in five minutes."

They walked the familiar long winding path towards their favored hunting grounds, hoping to catch some game. Suddenly Ben stopped. "Shhhh!" he whispered and held up his arm in a signal to wait. He cocked his rifle and moved out of sight behind some bushes. Jack followed his lead. They waited and listened, watching intently.

Jack could see movement in the distance through the trees. He couldn't quite make it out, but it looked like someone on horseback.

Ben signaled to stay low and wait to see if the intruder came closer. They both hoped the stranger would keep their distance and ride away from their base. Desperate to keep their family safe, they waited, silently breathing… frozen, as the dark bay horse and rider gingerly picked their way through the dense forest brush.

The rider edged closer, then abruptly stopped. Surveying the area as though they sensed someone was near.

Jack could just make out that it was a male rider. He could feel his heart banging wildly in his chest. He could hear the rush of blood pumping through his head; his senses were on high alert. *This is it!* He thought, *this could be the end of us.*

The rider gently encouraged his horse slowly onward and turned directly towards where Ben and Jack were hiding in the dense bushes. Jack's stomach nervously lurched as he calculated that the horse would step right on top of him in about three minute's time.

Suddenly Ben jumped up, gun poised. The horse startled, shying away, snorting, and nearly unseating its rider. He pointed the barrel straight at the stranger, "Hold it right there, Mister," he shouted.

"Ben, Ben, don't shoot! It's me, Peter," the voice yelled back with his hands held high in surrender.

"Peter… what the heck?" Ben dropped his weapon and both he and Jack ran towards him as he jumped off his horse and embraced them both.

"I'm so glad I found you." Peter smiled.

"I'm so glad I didn't shoot you," Ben replied, and they all laughed.

"ANARCHY IS the only way to explain it, pure lawlessness," Peter said as they sat around the night fire sharing roasted rabbits, potatoes, and carrots. "Well, when you all left, I spent most of my time running to different hideouts with my laptop, broadcasting the truth about Jason Crane over the Internet. A band of us stayed together and looked out for each other, spreading the word, conducting food drops for others out there and simply helping everyone to stay undercover. I tried my hardest to get the message out about faith and endurance to the end."

Jenny, sensing that Peter's stories were going to get worse, quickly ushered Sarah and Matthew to their rooms and put them to bed. She returned a few minutes later.

Peter continued explaining, "You wouldn't believe what I've seen." He paused. "I thought seeing Akio being killed was terrible, unfathomable… but now I've seen even worse." He stopped and pondered his next sentence. "I've never encountered a man filled with such hatred towards our God and His people. In the time you have been gone, there have been hundreds put to death ceremoniously and publicly, all seemingly more horrifying than the next to make his point clear. They beat and torture them first to see if they will relent, repent, and worship the 'New Christ' as he now likes to be called."

"How many give in?" Jack asked.

Peter sighed, tears welling in his eyes; he shook his head. "Sadly, I'd have to say roughly… 70% maybe even 80%."

They all gasped, knowing what that meant for eternity.

"I'd do what I could to save as many as possible, but once captured, then you really need all the strength you can get." He waited as everyone pondered what he said.

"I saw some of my old congregation stand firm. It made me so proud to see that God had used me to make a difference." He paused, then said, "Remember Bill Johnson and Ted Brown?" They all nodded. "Well, I actually saw them confronted by some UNITED guards, but they didn't back down—they did not succumb to taking the mark," he said with a knowing smile. "I know where they are right now."

The others sat silently. Peter continued. "It's truly what we always talked about Jack, it's a test of faith. It's worship the beast or be put to death." Peter's tears flowed freely as he spoke, nearly choking on his next words. "He doesn't even care if it's little children, and in fact he uses them to force their parents." He wiped his face, distraught and exhausted.

They all sat in silence as Peter regained and gathered himself.

He looked so worn, Jack thought. *While we have been hiding in our shelter, he has seen and been at the brunt of it.*

Peter persisted through his emotions, though remained delicate. "The thing is," he said, stopping as if chastising himself, "I can't help but think that we should have been prepared earlier, I mean if I hadn't believed the secret rapture theory, I could have spent my entire years teaching about strength and endurance, preparing for *this* time... and not telling people that we would escape this."

"Everyone was deceived, Pete," Jack stated.

"You weren't." Peter looked straight at Jack. "You were bold enough to research for yourself, to not listen to the teachings of men." He paused and sighed a breath of defeat. "I guess what I have to take away is that I am thankful for the little time we spent spreading the truth, I just wish it had been much sooner. We could have saved more people if we had the extra time to prepare them, they would have been able to endure it and not give in so readily."

"Have you seen Jim?" Bethany interjected with hope in her eyes.

"Yes, I have." He paused, gravely. "I'm sorry to say that he is one of Jason's biggest advocates and one of our worst enemies in spreading the lie about Crane."

Bethany rose slowly, visibly upset, and silently walked to her room.

Lora followed to comfort her.

"What about those flashes?" Ben asked.

"Yes, they were amazing!" Peter exclaimed. "I didn't know what the heck was going on, I thought the Lord was coming," he chuckled. "But they turned out to be solar flares from the sun. Everyone was so frightened."

"We all were!" Jack stated.

"Yes, I could imagine!" Peter continued. "Well, that's when it got even worse. You see, it took out all power and communications globally."

"So… no communication whatsoever…" Jack stated, getting a handle on the information. "That's why we saw aircraft going down." He shook his head in understanding.

"Yes, that was terrible. Anything electrical simply stopped. That's why people are in more of a panicked state because all the UNITED Chips are useless, people can't access their money, there's no electricity. All cars, motorcycles, trains, aircraft, fuel pumps, etcetera are useless. Anything that requires a power system will not work. So, people are breaking in and raiding stores, stealing food and any transport that doesn't rely on power, that is push bikes, skateboards, horses… even cows. I'm sorry, Ben, but you would hate to see your property now."

Ben looked across at May with sadness.

Peter continued. "They have frantically been trying to mend the cables, satellite communications and power grids, but then a flare just takes it out, so they've pretty much given up. You can't beat God!" he chuckled, then became solemn before he continued. "It's nothing for someone to point blank shoot another person over a can of beans. There is no love, compassion, or mercy. It's all for themselves. They will trade their own mother for a loaf of bread." He paused with sadness written in his eyes. "Water is scarce as the pumps don't work, and for some reason the creeks have dried up and people are fighting over what they can get a hold of. I even witnessed someone hack another to death to steal the food they were carrying." He shook his head in dismay. "I had to leave—it was too dangerous, and I wasn't really helping anyone. Without communication, it's very hard to spread the word."

"So, what is UNITED doing then? Does that mean that Jason has lost control?"

"Well, you would think that wouldn't you," Peter said with disdain. "No, he hasn't. He has his UNITED Troops now on horseback, and they've confiscated just about every decent horse in the land." He smiled incredulously.

"So how in the heck did you get yours?" Ben asked.

"That you wouldn't believe. She was just there waiting for me, saddled up and ready to go. I don't know how, but I'm extremely thankful."

Gabe looked over at Peter's Guardians and winked at them with a smile.

"So how is UNITED bringing order?" Jenny asked.

"They do it by shooting, maiming, bribing, capturing, torturing and fear mongering those who have deserted. There is a splinter group that they are trying to control as well, those who don't believe in God or UNITED. So now, UNITED are burning the ID numbers on those who are in alliance with Crane."

"You're kidding!" Jack said in shock.

"I'm serious. The mark has now become a tattoo of allegiance, and anyone who does not have one is shot, no questions asked. They are still controlling, probably even more so now, because if you don't have a visible mark, then you do not receive your food rations. People beg and plead, but if you don't have it, then they will simply kill you. There is no regard for life."

Again, a wave of sadness shadowed across Peter's face. He panned the group, looking seriously before him, then he again spoke. "There are beheadings," he choked, forcing the words out like lumps catching in his throat. "I-I witnessed one." He paused as tears streamed down his face.

He sighed as he continued. "I saw six UNITED guards in the street, so I ran and hid under a dense hedge along the sidewalk. They didn't see me, but I couldn't move to make an escape, so I had to wait it out. They were scanning the area when they heard a noise. There was a dumpster no more than 60 feet away from me. They went up to investigate and found two males and a female hiding there. They dragged them out onto the sidewalk and asked them to show their mark. I recognized two of them from the splinter group, so I knew they wouldn't have one. The guards started beating them, and it was as if they were in a crazed frenzy —they would drag them onto their feet again and continuously beat them. They then told them all to kneel on the concrete."

Peter stopped for a moment and held his head in his hands, then wiped his eyes before he continued. "They asked each one if they would accept the mark and follow the New Christ. The first one refused and spat at the guard, swearing, and another guard stepped forward and with one stroke of a machete took his head clean off."

Jenny gasped and put her hands to her face, and cried. The others were extremely distressed and upset at what they were hearing.

Peter continued. "The other two were so frightened and traumatized that they simply accepted the mark. I was so sick to the pit of my stomach at what I had seen—they just dragged the other two off and left the body lying in the street. I waited for 20 minutes after they had left before I was brave enough to move. I didn't realize my clothes were soaked through from the sweat of fear."

Peter took a breath before continuing. "Also... I narrowly escaped a mass killing camp, where thousands were being beheaded by guillotines." Gasps of shock came from the others and tears again started spilling down Peter's face as he relived that terrible time. Peter broke down and sobbed. "I've never felt so frightened and trapped and I've never seen so much evil."

They all sat solemnly for a few minutes whilst Peter silently regathered himself.

"So what do we do now?" Jack asked.

"I'd like to go back and get the few other believers who are still in hiding and bring them here if you would agree to it?" Peter said. "However, I needed to find you first. I remembered the instructions, but I couldn't risk bringing the others in case I got lost. They are hiding in a small bunker a long way outside of town."

Jack looked around at the others, and they nodded unanimously. "Of Course!" Jack said. "Ben and I will help you bring them here."

It was late; everyone was tired and retired to their respective bedrooms. Peter sensed that Jack wanted to talk alone with him.

They walked out into the brisk night air, climbed up to the lookout and sat on the solid cool rock beneath them.

The sheer clearness and darkness of the night sky made the stars look like they were dancing off their black velvety blanket. It was silent apart from the odd chirping of a cricket or rustling of a small animal; the smell was fresh, earthy, and cool to their senses. They sat in silence, taking it all in for some time, until Jack spoke.

"How are you… really?"

He knew! Peter thought, the despair of what he had endured was etched into his face. "I've seen better days," he responded and paused before starting the conversation again. He told him about Amy and broke down crying when he finally realized the pain of losing another friend, but this time it was forever.

"How many will do what Amy did, I mean, to know the truth but give in under the pressure?" Jack asked.

"Many, I'm certain. I've seen countless already, and that's the sad part. I've come to the realization many more believers will submit and accept the mark. It's just so hard out there Jack, I knew it would be, but nothing prepares you for it. I'm so glad I'm strong in my faith—that's the only thing that keeps me going… but so many aren't strong and sadly will not make it to Heaven. I pray for them daily, for them to hold out and not let fear overtake them and succumb to the enemy."

Jack sighed with bleakness. "How long do you think we have to live like this… how long until Christ returns?"

"He put the idol in the temple," Peter responded, "so I'm estimating about another three years." He looked over at Jack, whose face showed absolute hopelessness at the answer, and noticed Jack's eyes starting to glisten with moisture in the dim moonlight.

Jack felt an overwhelming despondency come over him at the thought of surviving this.

"Jack," Pete said encouragingly, placing his hand on his shoulder to comfort him, "this *is* what we talked about… this *is* endurance. To be faithfully waiting for our King's return. Helping who we can, encouraging one another in Christ, but never giving in." Peter felt himself heartened, even though every fiber in his aging body ached and longed to go home, to be with his Lord and his precious Judy. "This is a tough time to go through and to be honest there have been countless nights where I've laid awake wishing someone would end my life so I could leave this body and just go home." He paused. "But by God's will, I'm here and I'm alive and with every fragment of my existence, I will fight for God and His people. We *will* win Jack, the end is already written, and those who endure earn the right to wear a crown. Think upon that, Jack... *ETERNITY!* These few years are absolutely nothing compared to *eternity!*" He waited silently and then, to lighten the moment, he let out a small chuckle.

"What's funny?" Jack looked at him quizzically.

"You know, I've always wondered about the passage in the book of Revelation, where it talks about the great battle. It states that kings of the earth and their armies will be on horseback and the birds will eat the slain horses and riders' flesh—I thought it strange, as it just didn't seem to fit our generation. So, I always took it metaphorically because we have such advanced technology and weaponry systems that... I just didn't take it as being literal!" He looked over at Jack. "How things have turned!"

They sat in silence, not a word spoken, as they looked outward across the shadowy moonlight-covered land, not knowing what the future held.

Jophiel, Chale, Seth and Gabe stood alongside and watched, for they knew that the real battle was about to begin.

333

PLEASE REVIEW

I hope you enjoyed reading *The Lie* as much as I enjoyed writing it. If you liked it, please take a moment to post a review and tell a few friends to help other readers discover it. Reviews are vital for any author... especially new ones. Even just a line or two can make a big difference.

Also... it's very exciting when I get notified that a new review has arrived—I love reading them and each review has encouraged me greatly. So thank you to those who have taken the time already, as it has spurred me on to keep writing.

Also, there are more books coming... Follow Me at Amazon and be notified when they are released.

ABOUT THE AUTHOR

Kym Streat discovered her passion for writing only a few years ago, and with encouragement from her husband, she decided to take a leap of faith and complete her first novel. Her vision is to create a positive influence through her writing and deliver strong messages of hope and endurance, along with providing stories that are interesting and sometimes challenging.

Kym works in the engineering field during the day, and during the night she escapes all the bureaucracy and formalities and creates her own tranquil world through her writing. *The Lie* is her debut novel.

ALSO BY KYM STREAT

SECOND CHANCE

What if your death could bring you life?

Dr. Jason Miller was at the peak of his career. He had everything! Fast cars, luxury lifestyle and an owner of a multi-million dollar company that spanned across the nation.

A life that most envied!

But in an instant, Jason's life is turned upside down. In one night, the world as he knows it is about to change...

Forever!

Thrust into a realm of unimaginable terror, Jason comes to the realization of his eternal fate.

A place void of life... a place far from God.

But in an extraordinary gift, Jason is given a second chance, a choice to change his past... a chance to rewrite his future!

With a transformed life, Jason will stop at nothing to demolish what he previously built, to end his own sinister medical empire and change the world's belief systems and paradigms.

Caught in a struggle to reverse his mistakes, can he fulfill the promise and end the wickedness that breaks God's heart?

And has something Evil followed him home?

A riveting journey jam-packed with twists and turns that keep you immersed to the very last page! Nat B. Editor

AVAILABLE ONLINE NOW!